Clements R. Markham

The War between Peru and Chile

1879-1882

Clements R. Markham

The War between Peru and Chile
1879-1882

ISBN/EAN: 9783337383060

Printed in Europe, USA, Canada, Australia, Japan

Cover: Foto ©Andreas Hilbeck / pixelio.de

More available books at **www.hansebooks.com**

THE WAR

BETWEEN

PERU AND CHILE,

1879---1882.

BY

CLEMENTS R. MARKHAM, C.B., F.R.S.

London:

SAMPSON LOW, MARSTON, SEARLE, & RIVINGTON,

CROWN BUILDINGS, 188, FLEET STREET.

1882.

LONDON:
PRINTED BY GILBERT AND RIVINGTON, LIMITED,
ST. JOHN'S SQUARE.

TO

𝕿𝖍𝖊 𝕽𝖊𝖛𝖊𝖗𝖊𝖉 𝕸𝖊𝖒𝖔𝖗𝖞

OF

Dr. DON FRANCISCO DE PAULA GONZALEZ VIGIL,

The great Peruvian Scholar and Philanthropist, and Author of "Paz Perpetua," is dedicated this narrative of the undeserved misfortunes of that land of the Yncas which he served so long and faithfully, and loved so well.

He who laboured earnestly and nobly to secure the blessings of perpetual peace for South America, and who denounced all wars of aggression and of conquest ; he who exclaimed, with feelings of deepest pity and sorrow, *"Heu miseri qui bella gerunt !"* would still have approved the heroic struggles of his countrymen in defence of their native land.

A 2

PREFACE.

THE war on the west coast of South America between
Peru and Bolivia on one side and Chile on the other
has continued for nearly four years   There have been
naval operations of considerable interest, and there
were three distinct and successive campaigns in
different and widely separated regions, but all three
on the Pacific coast.

The naval campaign is deserving of attention,
because in it the armoured-ships of recent construction encountered each other for the first time,
and because guns of extraordinary range, torpedo-
boats and torpedoes, and other late inventions have,
also for the first time, been used in actual warfare.

A study of the operations on shore, during the
course of the three campaigns, brings the English
reader once more into communion with the descendants of those Spaniards and Indians of whom he
has read, surely with more than passing interest, in
the pages of Prescott and Helps.   The battle-fields
are in the land of the Yncas.   The combatants belong
to two races, to that race which was ruled over by

Atahualpa and attained to the highest civilization of which aboriginal Americans were capable, and to that race which followed Pizarro in his career of conquest. The results of the war will permanently affect the welfare of those races. For this reason the campaigns on the Pacific coast should have an interest for readers in this country.

The authentic materials for a narrative of the war are now sufficiently extensive, although they are almost exclusively supplied from the Chilian side. The ground has been carefully described in a series of publications issued by the Chilian Hydrographic Department, entitled "Noticias sobre las provincias litorales." The official despatches, diplomatic notes, and reports of correspondents, are contained in the "Boletin de la guerra del Pacifico," published at Santiago periodically from April, 1879, to March, 1881.

The history of the three campaigns, has been written, in copious detail, by one of the most distinguished literary men in Chile, Don Benjamin Vicuña Mackenna.[1] The author's powers of description, of delineating character, of critical analysis are of a very high order. His industry in collecting materials is extraordinary, and it is equalled by his ability in arranging them. Vicuña Mackenna is above all things an historical biographer. He could not, if he would, omit a trait or an incident, however much

[1] "Guerra del Pacifico;" "Historia de la Campaña de Tarapaca" (2 vols. pp. 865 and 1189); "Historia de la Campaña de Tacna y Arica" (1 vol. pp. 1172); "Historia de la Campaña de Lima" (1 vol. pp. 1216). Santiago de Chile, 1880, 1881, 1882.

their mention might tell against the view he advocates. His love of historical truth amounts to a passion. From no writer, since the days of Ercilla, are we more certain to get the good, equally with the bad points of an enemy. His work is, therefore, invaluable.

Don Diego Barros Arana, in his "Historia de la guerra del Pacifico," gives us the history of the three campaigns, as well as of the naval warfare. His narrative is less interesting and not nearly in such full detail as that of Vicuña Mackenna. We also have the Memoir of the Chilian Minister of War for 1881,[2] which gave rise to an acrimonious paper war between the minister and the general commanding the army, and thus many things were made public. The general replied in a volume containing all the official despatches.[3] There are also a few monographs of special actions, such as "El Combate Homerico" and "Estudios sobre la vida del Capitan Arturo Prat," which are useful.

Chile, assuredly, has been fully heard. But Peru and Bolivia, apart from official reports, are silent so far as we are aware. If books have been published they have not become accessible here. The whole story, with the exception of private letters regarding the proceedings or the fate of individuals, and mere official utterances, is told by Chilians. Impartiality and common fairness, therefore, demand the utmost

---

[2] "Memoria del Ministerio de la Guerra correspondiente al año de 1881" (pp. 193). Santiago, 1881.

[3] "Partes oficiales de las batallas de Chorrillos y Miraflores" (pp. 420). Santiago, 1881.

care in judging of the acts and motives of their opponents. If an unbiassed stranger does not adopt the Chilian view with regard to the causes of the war, the justice of its continuance, and the character of some of the events, he at least argues from the same premises. The facts have been supplied almost exclusively by one side; and if the historian feels obliged to condemn the proceedings of Chilian statesmen and soldiers, he must, at the same time, commend the fairness of Chilian writers.

CONTENTS.

Part I.

INTRODUCTORY CHAPTERS.

Part II.

THE WAR.

x CONTENTS.

WORKS ON PERU BY THE SAME AUTHOR.

1. CUZCO AND LIMA. 8vo, 419 pp. 1856.
2. TRAVELS IN PERU AND INDIA. 8vo, 572 pp. 1862.
3. PERU. *Sampson Low and Co's. "Foreign Countries Series,"* 192 pp. 1880.
4. TRIBES WHICH FORMED THE EMPIRE OF THE YNCAS. *Royal Geographical Society's Journal.* 1871.
5. PERUVIAN BARK: *with accounts of the cultivation of Coca, Peruvian Cotton, Cuzco Maize, and Quinua.* 8vo, 550 pp. 1880.
6. QUICHUA GRAMMAR AND DICTIONARY. 8vo, 223 pp. 1864.

TRANSLATIONS.

7. OLLANTA. An ancient Ynca drama. 8vo, 128 pp. 1871.
8. CHRONICLE OF PERU, by Cieza de Leon. *Translation, with introduction and notes.* First Part, 1864. Second Part, 1883.
9. ROYAL COMMENTARIES OF THE YNCA (Garcilasso de la Vega). 2 vols. *Translation, with introduction and notes.* 1869.
10. SEARCH FOR EL DORADO. *Translation, with introduction and notes.* 1861.
11. NARRATIVE OF THE ADELANTADO ANDAGOYA. *Introduction and notes.* 1865.
12. LIFE OF ALONZO DE GUZMAN. *Translation, with introduction and notes.* 1862.
13. EXPEDITIONS INTO THE VALLEY OF THE AMAZON. *Translation, with introduction and notes.* 1861.
14. REPORTS ON THE DISCOVERY OF PERU (Xeres and Astete). *Translation, with introduction and notes.* 1872.
15. RITES AND LAWS OF THE YNCAS. *Translation, with introduction and notes.* 1872.
16. ACOSTA'S HISTORY OF THE INDIES. 2 vols. *Translation, with introduction and notes.* 1879.

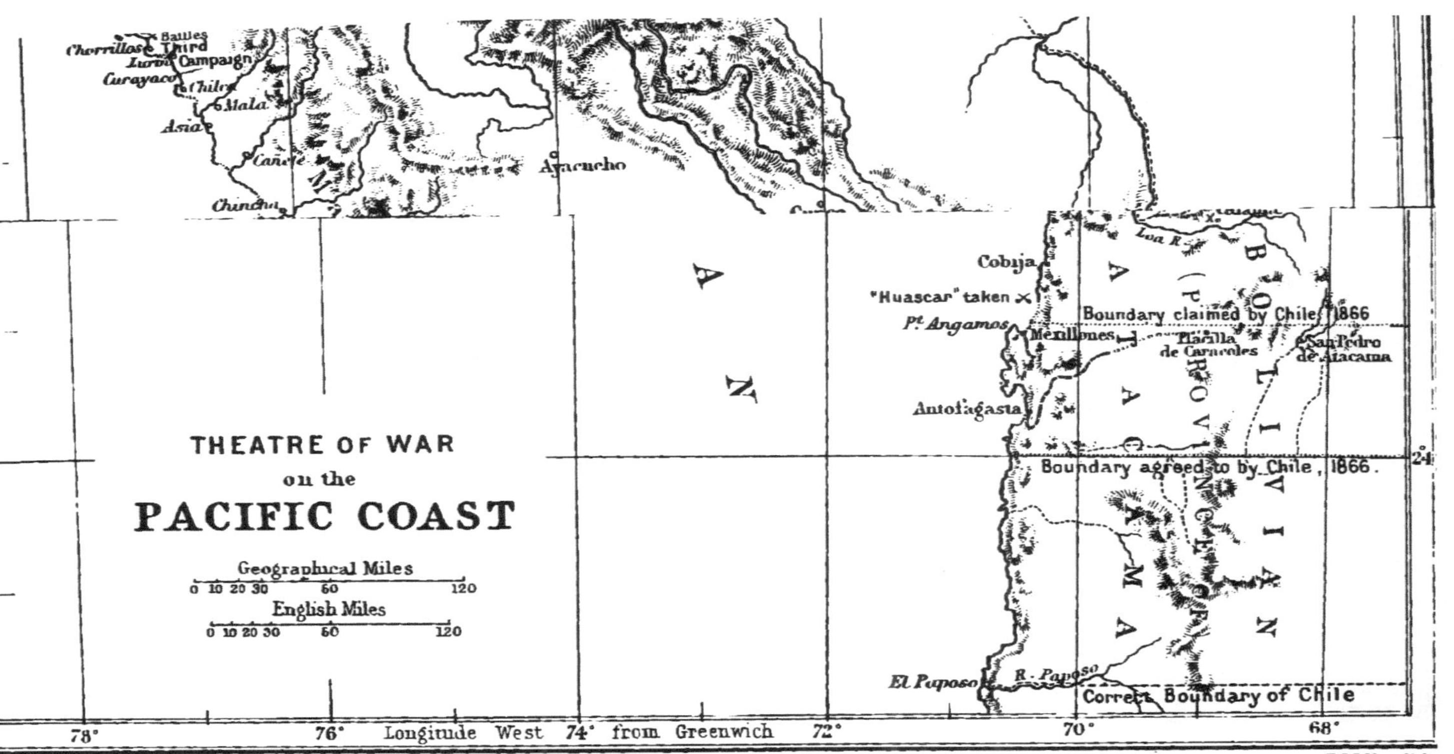
THEATRE OF WAR
on the
PACIFIC COAST
Geographical Miles
0 10 20 30   60   120
English Miles
0 10 20 30   60   120
Chorrillos
Barnes
Third
Lurin Campaign
Curayaco
Chilca
Mala
Asia
Cañete
Chincha
Ayacucho
Cobija
"Huascar" taken ×
Pt. Angamos
Mejillones
Antofagasta
Loa R.
BOLIVIAN
PROVINCE OF
ATACAMA
Boundary claimed by Chile, 1866
Placilla de Caracoles
San Pedro de Atacama
Boundary agreed to by Chile, 1866.
El Paposo
R. Paposo
Correct Boundary of Chile
A N
78°   76°   Longitude West 74° from Greenwich   72°   70°   68°
24°
F. Weller, lith.
London; Sampson Low, Marston, Searle, & Rivington.

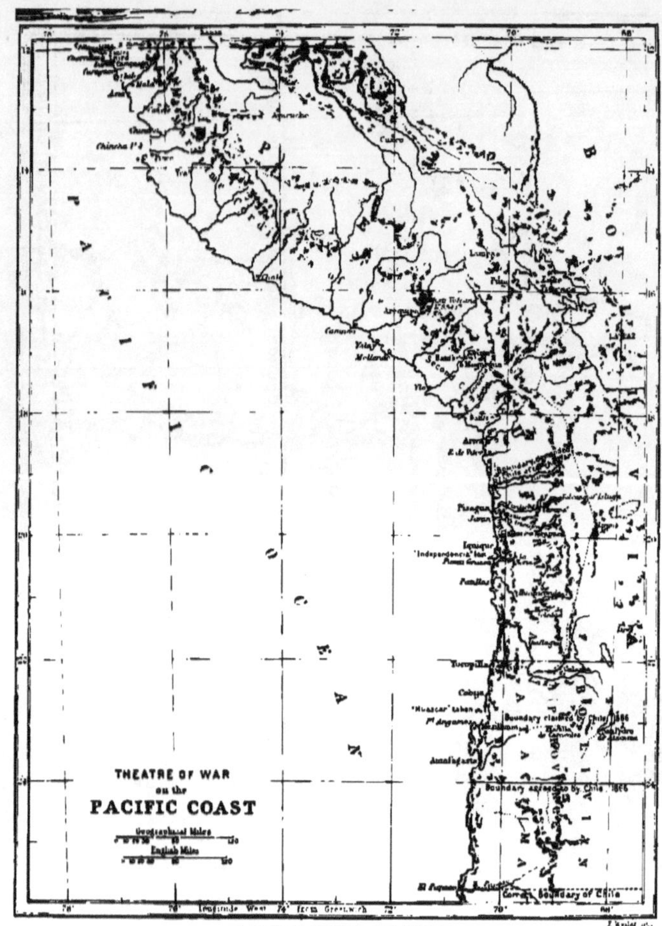

THEATRE OF WAR
on the
PACIFIC COAST
Geographical Miles
English Miles
PACIFIC OCEAN
BOLIVIA
LA PAZ
Chincha I.s
Arequipa
Camana
Islay
Mollendo
Pisagua
Junin
Iquique
"Independencia" lost
Punta Gruesa
Pabellon
Tocopilla
Cobija
"Huascar" taken
Pt Angamos
Amalgarita
El Paquen
Boundary claimed by Chile 1866
Boundary assigned to Chile 1866
Correct Boundary of Chile
Longitude West from Greenwich

THE WAR BETWEEN PERU AND CHILE.

Part I.

INTRODUCTORY CHAPTERS.

CHAPTER I.

PERU UNDER THE YNCAS, AND UNDER SPANISH VICEROYS.

THE war between the Republics of the Pacific coast has been an unmixed evil. Peru has been thrown back into a worse state of anarchy and confusion than she has known since the independence ; while the advantages secured by conquest may bring more evil than good to the successful belligerent. It is not a policy of aggression and foreign conquest which has hitherto secured prosperity to Chile. But there are useful lessons to be derived from this contest, from more than one point of view ; and the reader who has a general knowledge of the former history of the countries engaged in it, will find that the story of the war is not without interest.

B

It will be well, therefore, to preface the narrative of military events of the last two years, with a brief review of the history of Peru and of her former dependencies.

The regions which were comprised in the Empire of the Yncas embraced every climate, and teemed with the products of every zone. Traversed by the cordilleras of the Andes from north to south, from beyond the equator on the north to far south of the tropic of capricorn, the great altitudes, with an arctic climate, supplied products of the frigid zone, while the lower slopes displayed in succession the richest pastures, crops of hardy cereals and roots, harvests of Indian corn, cotton and fruits, down to the dense vegetation of tropical forests. The extent of the empire as regards latitude increased the variety of its wealth ; and the action of the trade winds was alike the cause of teeming forests to the east of the Andes, and of the arid deserts and rainless tracts of the Pacific coast.

This region, so marvellously favoured by nature, was the home of a civilized race whose rulers knew how to use all these varied sources of wealth and comfort, and to adapt the forces of nature for the well-being of their people. The Yncas of Peru, commencing their system of administrative rule at Cuzco and in the lovely vale of the Vilcamayu, gradually extended it over the whole Andean region of Quito, Peru, and Chile, far into the eastern tropical forests, and along the Pacific coast. Roads were constructed along the dizzy precipices of the cordillera, and over the sandy deserts ; terraced cultivation converted the ravines into hanging gardens; well-conceived systems of irrigation works, both in the mountains and on the coast, turned barren wastes into smiling valleys and rich pastures. The system of *mitimaes* or colonists provided for the supply of tropical products to the dwellers in the mountains, and of meat and corn to the settlers in the forests and on the coast. Carefully-considered rules secured the industrial prosperity of the agricultural labourers, the absence of poverty, the distribution of handicraftsmen, and the due supply of servants of the State for duties either in peace or war. Nor were the amusements of the people neglected, and the institution of periodical festivals provided for their pleasure and relaxation. At the same time the gradations of rank and of duties in the civil administration fitted perfectly into the warlike needs of the empire; and, without disturbing the economy of the agricultural and manufacturing or mining interests, large disciplined armies periodically extended the limits of the empire. Conquest converted distant tribes from a savage state to a condition of order and well-being. The religions of the conquered people were neither persecuted nor uprooted; their prejudices and traditions, which were not opposed to an orderly and well-regulated life, were neither discouraged nor ignored.

The accuracy of this description is shown by a consensus of testimony. The Ynca civilization excited the enthusiastic admiration of the best of the Spanish conquerors, and afterwards endured the test of a more critical examination by trained lawyers and administrators. So far as it was possible, the most gifted of the Spanish rulers of Peru preserved or endeavoured to imitate the Ynca system. The empire whose people enjoyed this beneficent rule extended from the equator to the river Maulé in the south of Chile, and from the shores of the Pacific far into the tropical forests to the east of the Andes.

Peru, Bolivia, and Chile (except the extreme south) were parts of the empire of the Yncas. The imperial race which created it, in spite of all the terrible wrongs and sufferings that followed the Spanish conquest, still forms the bulk of the people; and the main point of interest, as regards the recent war, is the way in which its operations will affect the Ynca Indians. In so far as the Chilian conquerors have injured or slaughtered those long-suffering and once happy people, they and their works deserve the curse which must for ever rest on the deeds of Francisco Pizarro and his worst followers. If the Chilians have sought for wealth and territorial aggrandizement, regardless of the sufferings which the attainment of those ends may entail upon an innocent people, they have been doing the accursed work for which history condemns Pizarro. It is from this point of view that the belligerents must be judged; and it is on the results of their work, as it affects the people whom their ancestors so foully wronged, that the republican Spanish-Americans must be acquitted or condemned.

It is 350 years since the empire of the Yncas was overthrown by the Spanish conquest. The once happy people, with their lands and possessions, were then parcelled out among the ancestors of those Peruvians and Chilians who have so recently shown their appreciation of Ynca civilization by re-enacting the horrors of the conquest. The republicans who threw off the yoke of Spain some sixty years ago, are never tired of upbraiding the mother country for her colonial policy. But it is upon the settlers and their descendants that the real responsibility rests. They took the place of the original inhabitants, and from them the account of their stewardship must be required.

Let us then, with all impartiality, examine how the account stands. It is difficult to throw the whole blame on the actual conquerors, those gallant adventurers who performed deeds of such heroic daring that the whole civilized world was amazed ; some urged on by the excitement of discovery and the love of knightly achievement, others by baser motives. There is nothing in history more romantic than the story of Pizarro's famous appeal on the Isle of Gallo. " Gentlemen," he said, as he drew a line on the sand with his sword-point, " on this side are labour, hunger, thirst, fatigue, wounds, sickness, and every other kind of danger that must be encountered in this enterprise until life is ended. Let those who have the courage to meet and overcome such obstacles cross the line, as a testimony that they will be my faithful companions. Let those who feel unworthy, return to Panama, for I do not wish to put force upon any man. I trust in God that, for His greater honour and glory, His eternal Majesty will help those who remain with me." The sixteen men who crossed that line were heroes, if ever men deserved that name. And there were still nobler spirits among the first conquerors of Peru. When the worst among them, led on by Pizarro and

Almagro, resolved upon the judicial murder of the Ynca Atahualpa, there were not wanting men of honour and courage who raised their voices against it. Their names are even more worthy of remembrance than those of the sixteen who crossed the line drawn on the sea-shore at Gallo. Foremost among them was Hernando de Soto, the future discoverer of the Mississippi. Next came the brothers Francisco and Diego de Chaves. The former, as true a knight as ever lived, fell in defending Pizarro from his assassins at Lima. Another was Blas de Atienza, who had reached the South Sea with Vasco Nuñez, and had crossed Pizarro's line at Gallo. There were eight others. The body of conquerors was leavened with such spirits as these, and with this fact before us, we may assume that the true story of the overrunning of the Ynca empire is not quite so black as the picture which modern writers have painted. If further proof were needed, it is afforded by the sympathy shown in the writings of some of the earliest Spanish authors ; and by the conscience-smitten cry of such a man as Mancio Sierra de Lejescma. " We have destroyed the government of this people by our bad example," he exclaimed on his deathbed ; and this cry of remorse is a witness on the side of more lenient judgment for the conquerors.

Yet the story is black enough. Adventurers, inferior to the Yncas in civilization, but with an immeasurable superiority in material force, poured into the country, some with lofty aims, but the majority in the hope of fulfilling their dreams of wealth and power. Historical evidence proves, however, that the settlers were the oppressors, while the Spanish rulers strove constantly to restrain them. Mr. Helps bears testimony that "those humane and benevolent laws, which emanated from time to time from the Home Government, rendered the sway of the Spanish monarchs over the conquered nations as remarkable for mildness as any perhaps that has ever been recorded in history." Mr. Herman Merivale has stated his opinion "that, had the legislation of Spain in other respects been as well conceived as that respecting the Indians, the loss of her western empire would have been an unmerited visitation." It is due to Spanish interference that the extermination of the Indians was not completed, while their decimation was the evil work of the settlers.

Pizarro was empowered to grant *encomiendas* or estates to his followers, and the exactions of these colonists were so intolerable that the Spanish Government enacted the code known as the " New Laws" in 1542, by which these *encomiendas* were to pass immediately to the Crown after the death of the actual holders, all forced labour was forbidden, and a fixed sum was ordered to be settled as tribute to be paid by the Indians. The promulgation of these just laws excited a howl of furious execration from the colonists. Gonzalo Pizarro rose in rebellion in Peru ; and the opposition was so strong that it was considered unsafe to persist in the attempt to enforce the " New Laws." They were revoked in 1545. The *encomiendas* were redistributed by the President Gasca, and they were granted for three lives in 1629. But the law prohibiting the forced personal service of the Indians was boldly promulgated by the royal judges at Lima in 1552. This was immediately followed by another formidable rebellion under Giron. It was not until 1554 that the Viceroy Marquis of Cañete trod out the last sparks of revolt, by a mixture of severity and prudent conciliation. In this long struggle the Spanish Government was always on the side of justice and humanity; while the settlers strove to maintain their evil power to oppress and enslave the natives.

Don Francisco de Toledo, who became Viceroy of Peru in 1568, was a ruthless politician, and his administration is stained by the judicial murder of the young Ynca—Tupac Amaru. But he was a great legislator, a statesman of considerable ability and untiring industry. Future viceroys referred to his enactments as to a received and authoritative text-book. The Indians admitted that the country had not been so well governed since the days of the Ynca Yupanqui. He fixed the tribute to be paid by the Indians, exempting all men under the age of eighteen and over that of fifty, thus putting a stop to arbitrary demands. He arranged that the natives should be governed by chiefs of their own race, who alone were empowered to collect the tribute and taxes, and who also exercised magisterial functions under the Spanish *corregidors* or governors. But, in deference to the demands of the colonists, Toledo enacted that a seventh part of the adult male population of every village should be liable to what was called the *mita* or forced labour. He made rules to limit the distance they might be taken from their homes, and to secure payment for their services. It was the abuse of the *mita* system, and the evasion of the rules which were intended to mitigate its horrors, which led to all the misery of the Indians under Spanish rule, and to the rapid depopulation of the country.

Anxiety for the welfare of the native population appears in the reports of successive viceroys. In 1615 the Marquis of Montes Claros impressed on his successor the importance of obliging all classes of Spaniards to treat the Indians well, and of chastising oppression with rigour. The Count of Castellar, in 1681, stated that one of the points most dwelt upon in the instructions given to the viceroys, in repeated royal enactments, was the humane treatment of the Indians ; and he declared that he always sought to enforce these orders from the day he landed in Peru.

In 1660 the Count of Alba de Liste, in obedience to orders from Spain, assembled a Junta to consult respecting the instruction and good treatment of the Indians. As regards religion the native population enjoyed immunity from trial by the Inquisition, for it was decreed that all natives were catechumens and, consequently, incapable of heresy.

While these continuous efforts were made by the Spanish viceroys to protect the Indians from oppression, their ancient chiefs, descendants of the Yncas, were treated with respect and consideration. In addition to the official position they were allowed to occupy, they were exempted from personal service and the payment of tribute, and the Viceroy Prince of Esquilache reported, in 1618, that many of them were rich and powerful.

But side by side with this evidence of the good intentions of the Spanish Government, lies the testimony of the same viceroys that their efforts to enforce humane laws were fruitless, and rendered of no effect by the opposition of local governors, and almost all complain of the rapid depopulation of the country. In 1620 the Prince of Esquilache reported that the arm of the viceroy was powerless against the negligence and mal-administration of the corregidors. In 1681 the Count of Castellar said that he had to correct and punish the excesses both of the governors and the clergy. The Duke of La Palata, in 1697, speaks of the depopulation of the villages caused by the forcible detention of the Indians at mines and in the farms and factories of Spanish colonists. In the reports to viceroys one reads of the women and children of a village assisting each other in tilling the fields, and returning from their labours hand in hand, singing a melancholy song, and lamenting the cruel fate of husbands and brothers who were toiling in the mines and factories.

The tribute, the *mita*, the exactions of the clergy, and the excise duties called *alcabala* were all patiently borne. But another method of extortion at length exhausted the patience of the long-suffering Peruvian Indians. This system, called *repartimiento*, was ostensibly for distributing European goods to the natives, but it was converted into a means of wholesale robbery. The tribute fixed for villages when they contained a thousand men was continued the same when the population had decreased to a hundred. The *mita* was enforced so mercilessly that whole districts were left without a single adult male inhabitant. The clergy extorted exorbitant fees, and towards the end of the last century the oppression became unbearable.

There were several good men who steadily protested against this misgovernment. Don Ventura Santalices, the Governor of La Paz, devoted his time and fortune to the cause of the oppressed Indians. Don Juan de Padilla represented the state of things with forcible eloquence. Don Agustin de Gurruchategui, Bishop of Cuzco, Don Ignacio Castro, Don Manuel Arroyo, names which ought not to be forgotten, lifted up their voices, but in vain. Their vigorous remonstrances bore no fruit.

The Home Government manifested a desire that the Indians should be justly and humanely treated to the end : but the rapacity of local authorities and settlers, many of whom were Spaniards, but quite as many Creoles born in the country, could not even be checked. At last, in 1780, the beginning of the end came.

Before referring to the uprisings against Spanish rule, some of the other results of the conquest and the colonization of the Chilian dependency must be touched upon. The Spaniards, while receiving maize, potatoes, tobacco, chilis, other valuable crops, and quinine-yielding bark, as well as precious metals from Peru, gave more in return. Llamas were the only beasts of burden of the Yncas. Their conquerors introduced horses and mules. Cows and bullocks, sheep, goats, and pigs rapidly followed. In 1550 the first bullocks were yoked to a plough in the valley of Cuzco. The wife of the good knight Diego de Chaves, already mentioned as having protested against the murder of the Ynca Atahualpa, raised the first crop of wheat in Peru. Barley came with the wheat. As early as 1560 there were vineyards in the warm valleys near Cuzco ; and the olive, the sugar-cane, and European fruits and vegetables were introduced soon afterwards.

Something also was done for the mental development of the Peruvians. The University of San Marcos at Lima is the oldest in the new world. The Prince of Esquilache founded a college at Cuzco for the education of Indians of noble birth. The schools of Peru produced a fair proportion of scholars and men of letters. The learned Dr. Peralta y Barnuevo of Lima has earned a place in Ticknor's " History of Spanish Literature." A list of Peruvian authors in viceregal times occupies a long chapter in Montalvo's " Life of St. Toribio," the Lima archbishop. Nor was Peru wanting in men of high scientific attainments. The expedition to measure an arc of the meridian in 1740, and the subsequent botanical expeditions stimulated such studies. Francisco Davila, a native of Lima, was a naturalist who had charge of the museum at Madrid in the reign of Charles III. Dr. Cosme Bueno was a cosmographer and statistician whose geographical writings, 1769-70, were republished in 1872, and are still valuable. Dr. Gabriel Moreno, a native of Huamantanga, a little village in the Andes famous for the excellence of its potatoes, was an eminent botanist, who studied under Jussieu, and died at Lima in 1809. The illustrious Don Hipolito Unanue, editor of the *Mercurio Peruano*, and author of an important work on the climate of Lima, was born at Arica in 1755. Much that he wrote was made known to English readers by the publication of " Skinner's Peru," and the learned Peruvian has since found an able biographer in Señor Vicuña Mackenna.

But the principal charges against the rule of Spain have been the commercial monopoly, and the deprivation of any outlet to ambition for the colonists, all high posts being given to Spaniards. As regards the short-sighted monopoly, it was more and more relaxed all through the eighteenth century, while the complaint that the colonists were shut out from all high appointments is opposed to facts. Among Peruvians alone, eighty-three families were ennobled ; one receiving a dukedom, forty-six being granted marquisates, thirty-five Peruvians were created counts, and one viscount. As many as 136 natives of Peru, during Spanish times, received the highest judicial appointments, not only in their own country, but also in Cuba, Manila, and other places. There were ninety-eight archbishops and bishops who were natives of Peru, and the sees over which they presided were not always in their own country. A native of Callao was Archbishop of Zaragoza, and a Limeño occupied the see of Aquila in Italy. Peruvians also attained to high rank in the army, and as statesmen and diplomatists. Several were generals, others were captains-general of provinces, ambassadors to European courts, and councillors of state, and one was appointed a viceroy. It is not true, therefore, that the colonists were cut off from these careers, and were not allowed an outlet for legitimate ambition. These complaints were not the real causes of the revolt of the Spanish colonies.

The great rising of the Ynca Indians was caused by the oppression of the conquerors, and both Spaniards and colonists were to blame. The subsequent rebellions were the inevitable consequence of the course of events in Europe, and the independence of the South American Republics must sooner or later have followed the increasing intercourse with Europe, and the abolition of monopolies under any circumstances. The republicans of the governing class in Peru and Chile, are in fact mainly Spaniards. Many, especially in Chile, are of Basque descent. Some are half-castes, and in Peru not a few pure Ynca Indians have attained to the highest posts in the State. It is, therefore, alike unjust and misleading to cast reproaches on the colonial policy of Spain for the evils which have been developed since the independence. It is nearer the truth to allow that the worst features of the colonial times were due more to the settlers, the ancestors of the present republicans in Peru and Chile, than to their Spanish rulers. The republics have improved upon the former rule in all respects, and have made great advances in spite of civil dissensions and disastrous wars ; but the improvements in the mother country have been equally marked, and her advances in material prosperity are quite as great.

CHAPTER II.

CHILE is a long strip of coast-land pent in between
the lofty chain of the Andes and the Pacific Ocean,
extending from the desert of Atacama which
separated it from Peru, to the island of Chiloe; its
width varying from 40 to 200 miles. The principal
part may be described as one broad valley running
north and south, with narrow lateral intersecting
valleys, each rising step-like above the other, to the
foot of the giant wall of the Andes. These mountains
have a mean height of 11,830, with peaks rising to
22,296 and 20,269 feet. In the north is the rocky
and sandy region rich in mineral wealth, central Chile
is agricultural, and contains the principal cities and
ports, while in the south are the forests and lakes of a
colder and more rainy zone.

Northern and central Chile formed part of the empire of the Yncas, and the tribes of Chile had enjoyed
the advantages of the enlightened Peruvian rule for
nearly a century before the appearance of the Spaniards.
Professor Philippi tells us that the Ynca road to Chile
still exists. The famous march of Almagro into Chile
with a large Peruvian contingent under the Ynca
Paullu, took place in 1536. Three vessels were pre-

pared to bring provisions by sea, but one only reached
the Chilian coast.   When the news of her arrival was
brought to Almagro he sent the commander of his
vanguard, a young soldier named Juan de Saavedra, to
communicate.   Saavedra found the little schooner in
a port to which he gave the name of his own native
village in Spain, a place called Valparaiso, near Cuenca,
which he was never destined to see again.   He was
hanged at Lima by the cruel Carbajal.   His leader,
Diego de Almagro, abandoned the Chilian enterprise
in 1538, returning to Peru to misfortune and death.

Pedro de Valdivia was destined to be the first permanent settler in Chile.   In 1540 he marched southward from Peru, and founded the city of Santiago on
the river Mapocho, on the 24th of February, 1541.
After receiving reinforcements under Francisco de
Villagran, he advanced south into the country of the
wild Araucanian Indians, building several fortified
posts.   He confirmed the name of Valparaiso given by
young Saavedra to the port of Santiago.   The rising
of the Araucanians, the treachery of Lautaro, and the
final capture and death of Valdivia, form the most
romantic episode in the well-known poem of Ercilla.

It seems probable that the inner valleys of Chile
were inhabited by a people allied to the Araucanians,
but with much mixture of Ynca blood, while a fishing
tribe called *Chancos* dwelt along the coast.   These
tribes had been civilized by the Yncas, and they submitted easily to Spanish rule, but the Araucanians in
the far south were indomitable.   When the news of
Valdivia's death reached Europe, Don Garcia Hurtado
de Mendoza, afterwards Marquis of Cañete and Vice-

roy of Peru, was sent out, and he was accompanied by the young Biscayan soldier and poet, Alonzo de Ercilla, who served in the war from 1554 to 1562. Never had a people fighting for independence such a poet to record their valour in the ranks of their enemies. He enlists the sympathy of his readers for the very foes who, in almost daily encounters, were seeking his life. His stirring cantos were written by the camp-fires, night after night, after the battles had been lost or won. No one who wishes to know anything of Chilian history should fail to read the "Araucana" of Don Alonzo de Ercilla.

In 1599 Martin Garcia de Loyola, the Governor of Chile, was slain by the Araucanians, who destroyed, at the same time, the Spanish towns of Concepcion, Valdivia, Angol, Imperial, and Chillan. These wars continued without intermission until 1640, when at last the Marquis of Baides, Captain-General of Chile, through the intervention of Jesuit missionaries, made a treaty with the Araucanian Indians.

Meanwhile central and northern Chile were settled, towns rose up, and a trade was established with Peru. In the reign of Philip V., at the commencement of the last century, there was a large immigration from the Basque provinces and Aragon, the settlers finding a temperate climate and fertile soil in the country of their adoption. The appointment of Captain-General of Chile was sought after, because it was often a stepping-stone to promotion. Several of the ablest Viceroys of Peru received their training in administration at Santiago de Chile ; including the Marquis of Cañete, the Count of Superunda, Amat, Jauregui, and O'Higgins. The latter official was one of the best rulers that Chile has known. He ameliorated the condition of the labourers by suppressing the *encomiendas* or fiefs in 1791, made the excellent road from Valparaiso to Santiago, and his son Bernardo was the founder of Chilian independence.

The university of San Felipe was founded at Santiago in 1747, and the monopoly of education hitherto enjoyed by the monks and Jesuits was thus destroyed. The last of the good and laborious Spanish rulers of Chile was Don Luis Muñoz de Guzman, who built several of the more important public edifices in Santiago, including the mint. (But Chile was the poorest of the colonies, and the industrious Basque settlers had to strive for competency through hard and steady work as merchants and farmers. It is to these habits that the later success of the Chilian republic is mainly due. Chile was, in Spanish times, unable to meet the expenses of its government, and received an annual grant in aid from the Viceroy of Peru. The rich mines of Copiapo were not then worked, and agriculture was the principal industry, Peru being the market for the dried meat, hides, grease, and wheat of Chile. The original inhabitants have intermarried with Spanish settlers so constantly that there is now but one race which, when the War for Independence began, numbered about 500,000 souls.

CHAPTER III.

THE oppression of the imperial race of the Yncas
caused an insurrection which shook the colonial power
of Spain to its foundation, and prepared the way for
its complete overthrow. The condition of the people
excited the indignation of a young chief, a direct
descendant of the Yncas, named José Gabriel Con-
doncanqui, the fifth in lineal descent from the Ynca
Tupac Amaru, who was judicially murdered by the
Viceroy Toledo in 1571. Adopting the name of Tupac
Amaru, this champion of his people began by sending
in petitions for a redress of grievances. At length
his patience was exhausted, and he resolved to make
an appeal to arms, not to throw off the yoke of Spain,
but to obtain some guarantee for the just administration of the laws. His views were certainly confined
to these ends when he first drew his sword, although
afterwards, when his moderate demands were only
answered by taunts and menaces, he saw that independence or death were the only alternatives. In
November, 1780, he entered the town of Tinta, near
Cuzco, and addressed the people as to his present
conduct and ulterior views. Mounted on a fiery
charger, attired in the princely costume of his ances-

tors, he exhorted his countrymen to lend an attentive ear to the legitimate descendant of their ancient sovereigns, promising to abolish the *mita* and the *repartos*. Crowds flocked to his standard; and on the 13th he defeated the Spaniards at Sangarara. On the 27th he published a very ably written document, setting forth the causes of his revolt. Nothing was heard amongst the Indians but acclamations for their Ynca and redeemer.

Before attempting to force his way into Cuzco, Tupac Amaru addressed letters to the bishop and to the municipality. His proposals were met by defiance, and after a fight which lasted for two days he retreated to Tinta, where 60,000 undisciplined men had assembled. His chance was gone. In February, 1781, a large Spanish force reached Cuzco; the Ynca was defeated near Checacupe, and he and his family were taken prisoners.

The hideous cruelties which were perpetrated on the illustrious captives, by order of the Spanish judge, before death relieved them from their sufferings, is a proof that the tyrants were thoroughly alarmed, and with good reason. Never was a just and well-planned revolt so nearly successful. In the cruelty of the judges may be traced the terror of dastardly and craven minds.

Thus fell the last of the Yncas. He was a man of whom his nation might well be proud. Having enjoyed an excellent education at the college of San Borja in Cuzco, he brought a cultivated mind, a clear understanding, and untiring industry to his important duties. He displayed patient perseverance in representing the wrongs of his people; and finally, in his appeal to arms, he combined promptitude in action with great moderation in his demands. His edicts were remarkable for their good sense and humanity; and he died for his country. Tupac Amaru deserves the first place in history among the heroes of South American independence.

But the revolt did not end with the Ynca's death. All the Indians of Upper Peru were in arms, and gained several advantages over Spanish troops near Puno. It was not until the winter of 1783 that the rebellion was suppressed. The brave Ynca and his followers did not die in vain, for in their fall they shook the colonial power of Spain to its foundations. Reforms were at once instituted. The *repartos* were abolished, and the rules respecting forced labour were much modified. In 1784 the hated office of *corregidors* was abolished. From the cruel death of the last of the Yncas may be dated the rise of that feeling which ended in the expulsion of the Spaniards from Peru.

The people bided their time, and in 1809 an independent government was formed in Upper Peru (the modern Bolivia) called an " Institucion de Gobierno." But the patriots, ill-provided with arms, were defeated by the Spanish General Goyencche at Huaqui, near Lake Titicaca; though another royal force, under Pezuela, was kept fully employed by a patriot army from Buenos Ayres, led by General Belgrano.

Then it was that the opportunity was seized of commencing a rebellion at Cuzco, under the auspices of the Ynca Indian chief Mateo Pumacagua. So

unanimous had the feeling against Spanish rule become
that the colonists of European descent joined heart
and soul with the Ynca Indians in the insurrection.
The cacique Pumacagua was united with men of good
family, such as Astete, Prado, and the ardent young
poet Melgar. Cuzco, Guamanga, Arequipa, and Puno
were successively occupied. But the Spanish Government was fortunate in having an able and very active
general, with a well-disciplined though small force.
This commander—General Ramirez—easily dispersed
the brave but half-armed and wholly undrilled followers of Pumacagua. On March 25th, 1815, the
patriots were defeated in the battle of Umachiri ; the
aged chief was executed ; and thus ended the second
great rising of the Ynca Indians under one of their
own chiefs, after a campaign which lasted ten
months.

There was a similar rising in Chile, which was then
a remote dependency of the viceroyalty of Peru. A
national government was formed on the 18th of September, 1810 ; and in 1812 a constitution was promulgated by José Miguel Carrera, according to which
the Spaniards were declared to be brothers, Ferdinand VII. was recognized as king, while at the same
time the sovereignty of the people was maintained.
It was in Carrera's time that the first revolutionary
newspaper appeared in Santiago, edited by a friar
named Camilo Henriquez, who had enthusiastically
embraced the cause of independence. But this rising
was easily suppressed by the Viceroy of Peru. He
sent a force by sea under General Pareja, who landed
at Talcahuano. A convention was signed, by which

the rebels agreed to recognize Ferdinand VII. and
the Regency at Cadiz, and the royalist army was to
evacuate Chile. The Viceroy, however, refused to
ratify the convention, demanding unconditional surrender. He sent another army under General Osorio,
who entirely defeated the insurgents at Rancagua, in
October, 1814; Carrera, O'Higgins, and the other
leading patriots fled across the Andes to Mendoza ;
and the whole of Chile submitted to Spanish rule once
more. During the following three years, from 1814
to 1817, the sway of the Spaniards in Chile was un-
disputed.

The Viceroy of Peru who secured these results was
Don José Fernando de Abascal, a native of Oviedo
in the Asturias. He was a man of great ability.
He was resolute, and had collected the sinews of war ;
while he had the support of competent generals.
Lima, the capital of Peru, was his headquarters. From
this central point he crushed the rising in Upper Peru,
the insurrection of Pumacagua at Cuzco, and the
rebellion in Chile. He had concentrated the still formidable resources of Spain; and it was evident that
Peru and Chile must wait for help from more distant
colonies, where, owing mainly to their distance from
the central power, the efforts at emancipation had
been more successful. Peru had taken the lead, and
had made two gallant and desperate attempts to
throw off the hated yoke. Chile had followed. Both
had failed.

Don José de San Martin, with his Argentines, was
the destined liberator of both Chile and Peru ; a veteran
who had been trained in the war with France, and

had fought in the battle of Baylen. He was circum-
spect, cautious, and with a remarkable talent for
organization. As General of the Argentine Republic,
he established a camp at Mendoza, in 1814, where he
was joined by O'Higgins and other Chilian fugitives.
After much careful preparation, San Martin resolved
to cross the Andes with a force of 3000 men, and
invade Chile. This march, during February, 1817, is
one of the most remarkable in military history. The
men carried their own provisions; the field-pieces
were conveyed on the backs of mules. The small
liberating force, descending from the snowy pass, took
the Spaniards entirely by surprise. They were defeated at Chacabuco; the capital was occupied by
the invaders; and the Chilians offered the government
to San Martin. But the liberator said that his work
was incomplete until he had also freed the capital of
Peru. He declined, and Don Bernardo O'Higgins
was declared Supreme Director of Chile. On February 12th, 1818, the independence of Chile was proclaimed; and in the following April San Martin
gained a decisive victory over the Spaniards on the
plain of Maypu. Chile thus became free, and General
San Martin began to collect a fleet for the deliverance
of Peru, the command of which was given to Lord
Cochrane. With the aid of the Chilian Government
eight ships of war and sixteen transports were assembled at Valparaiso, commanded and mainly officered
by Englishmen; and San Martin embarked with
4100 men, and arms for 15,000.

The Viceroy Abascal had returned to Spain, and
General Laserna, the last of the viceroys, had to make

the final struggle to retain her rich colony for the
mother country. San Martin landed, and by his
skilful manœuvres obliged Laserna to retreat into the
interior of Peru. The liberator occupied Lima without resistance, and on June 28th, 1821, the independence of Peru was proclaimed. It was for this aid
that the people had eagerly waited. They now flew
to arms in all directions, although the viceroy still had
a formidable army under his command at Cuzco.

The Peruvians promptly showed that they were
actuated by the same spirit which had brought San
Martin to their help. The Colombians were still
fighting for liberty against the enterprising Spanish
General Ramirez. An auxiliary Peruvian division,
led by Andres Santa Cruz, an Ynca Indian of high
lineage, was assembled at Truxillo, joined the
Colombians in Quito, and bore the brunt of the
action which secured the independence of Colombia.
The battle of Pichincha was fought on the 24th of May,
1822. The Colombian General Bolivar then resolved,
in return for this succour, to bring his forces into
Peru, and joining with the native patriots, to complete the deliverance of the land of the Yncas. San
Martin, feeling that he had performed his share of the
great work, resigned his powers to a Peruvian Congress, and retired into private life. On the 1st of
September, 1823, General Bolivar, with his Colombian
auxiliaries, entered Lima, and reinforced the patriotic
soldiers of Peru. The English General Miller became
chief of the staff, and soon afterwards received the
command of the cavalry. In August, 1824, General
Bolivar was present at a cavalry action with the

Spanish commander Canterac at Junin, in the lofty plateau of the Andes north of Lima; and this victory, due to the gallantry of the Peruvian Colonel Suarez, placed the whole country as far as Guamanga in his power.

Bolivar then returned to Lima to hasten up reinforcements, leaving his friend and companion in arms, General Sucre, in command of the army. The viceroy was still at Cuzco with a large and well-supplied force. He advanced to the neighbourhood of Guamanga, by wild paths in the very heart of the Andes. The two armies faced each other at a place called Ayacucho, amidst glorious scenery, and 11,000 feet above the sea. On December 9th, 1824, General Sucre marshalled ·his force of 5780 men. Three Colombian battalions formed the centre, under Sucre and Lara, and four under Cordova were on the right. The left wing of infantry was entirely Peruvian, under General Lamar, while the whole of the united Peruvian and Colombian cavalry was led by General Miller. The Spaniards, occupying higher ground, were 9310 strong, under the Viceroy Laserna. The provisions of the patriots were nearly exhausted, and they were short of ammunition. So hungry were they that the sign and countersign of the night was " Pan y queso " (bread and cheese)—to fight was a necessity for them. Early in the morning of the 9th the two forces beat to arms. One Spanish division under Valdez attempted to outflank, and was resisted by the Peruvians under Lamar. This was the turning-point of the battle. A battalion, led on by Lara, reinforced the Peruvians, who were also aided by a brilliant cavalry charge delivered by Miller. The rout of Valdez was preceded by the complete success of Cordova against the viceroy on the right. The victory of the patriots was decisive. The viceroy and all his generals were taken prisoners, and the royalist army dispersed. By a curious coincidence Laserna was created "Conde de los Andes" by Ferdinand VII. on the same day.

Thus terminated the Spanish power in South America. The battle of Ayacucho was conclusive. Peru and Chile became independent republics. Upper Peru, although inhabited by Aymara Indians, who speak a language akin to Quichua, and a part of the empire of the Yncas, as well as of the Peruvian viceroyalty during 200 years, had been transferred to the new viceroyalty of Buenos Ayres in 1778. But the Argentine Republic generously relinquished any claim she might be supposed to have on this territory. An assembly of notables was called together to decide whether Upper Peru should be incorporated with Peru or declare itself an independent state. In August, 1825, this assembly decided in favour of a separate existence, and decreed that the new republic should be called Bolivia, in honour of the liberator. A small strip of sea-coast was secured to it between Chile and Peru, comprising the Atacama desert, the other boundaries were settled, and General Sucre, the hero of Ayacucho, was elected the first President of Bolivia.

General Bolivar finally left Lima on the 3rd of September, 1826, to return to Colombia ; and was followed by the Colombian troops in March, 1827.

General Lamar, who led the Peruvians at Ayacucho, was elected the first constitutional President of Peru in June, 1827, and the Count of Vista Florida, an enlightened and upright statesman, became Vice-President.

CHAPTER IV.

THE REPUBLIC OF PERU.

ABOUT thirty years before the independence, in 1793,
a rough census was taken under the superintendence
of the learned Dr. Unanue, and the population of
Peru was reported to be 1,076,977. The majority
(617,700) were pure Ynca Indians, there were 241,255
mestizos or half-castes, 136,311 Spaniards and Creoles,
40,000 negro slaves, and about the same number of
free mulattos. The negro element was confined to
the coast valleys, where there were slaves on the
sugar, cotton, and vine estates.

Unfortunately the result of success over the
Spaniards was that the military party obtained, and
long kept the supreme power, while the official posts
were filled for the most part by men without experience or training. Yet the gain to the country
was immediate. All monopolies disappeared, trade was
thrown open to the world, foreign merchants and settlers
arrived, and there was free and unrestrained contact
with outside civilization. The Ynca Indians obtained
equality and citizenship. The *mita* was entirely
abolished, while the tribute was continued until 1856.
It was levied, as arranged by the Viceroy Toledo, on
every male between the ages of eighteen and fifty ;

and as nearly every individual between those ages cultivated his own piece of land, or shared the produce of a larger piece with others, the tribute was really a land tax, and not objectionable on principle. Three loans had been contracted for in London, to carry on the war of independence between 1822 and 1825, amounting to 1,816,000*l.*, with interest at six per cent.

There were evils caused by the seditious conduct of military men which kept the country in an unsettled state, while the system of forced recruiting gradually became almost as oppressive as the old *mita*. Still the independence brought with it, to all ranks of the people, solid advantages which outweighed the evils of civil war and dishonest or incapable administration.

The first president, General Lamar, unwisely attempted to settle a boundary dispute with Colombia by the sword, instead of by arbitration, and his failure led to his downfall. The second president was a native of Cuzco, named Agustin Gamarra, born in 1785. He had seen much service as an officer in vice-regal times, and had risen to the rank of colonel in the royal army. Changing sides, he was chief of the staff at Ayacucho. He was elected President in 1829, and continued in office during the constitutional period of four years. His successor was Don Luis José Orbegozo, a tall and handsome, but weak and incapable man. He had no sooner been elected than Gamarra seditiously attempted to depose him, and dissolved the Congress by force. On this occasion there are two circumstances which are worthy of record. The first is that a sentry, named Juan Rios, defended the door of the Congress at Lima against two companies of mutineers until he was mortally wounded. The second is that the sense of the country was so entirely against the unprincipled ambition of Gamarra and his supporters, that their attempt failed.

General Andres Santa Cruz, the hero of Pichincha, had succeeded General Sucre as President of Bolivia, and had continued to hold that post since 1829. He was an Indian of noble descent on his mother's side, and had attained high rank in the Spanish service. He had displayed considerable ability, but rather as an administrator than as a soldier. He had for some time conceived the idea of uniting Peru and Bolivia under one head, and the anarchy caused by ambitious military chiefs seemed to make this arrangement still more desirable. A treaty was ratified with President Orbegozo in June, 1835. Gamarra and other military adventurers, who were in arms, were defeated and banished. The fatal mistake of shooting General Salaverry and several other prisoners was committed by Santa Cruz, on the ground that they had themselves declared war to the knife. Peace was then established. The Peru-Bolivian Confederation was organized, consisting of three States—North Peru, South Peru, and Bolivia—each with a President and Congress, and General Santa Cruz as Protector of the Confederation. The country enjoyed peace for nearly three years. The new régime gave the benefits of order in the administration, purity in the management of the public funds, internal quiet, and active promotion of useful engineering and other works.

It was at this juncture that the Republic of Chile began to wage her first war with her neighbour. The Chilian Government acted as if it believed that for Chile to be prosperous, it was necessary for Peru to be in a state of anarchy. Arica had been declared a free port, and several fiscal regulations had been introduced which were considered to be detrimental to Chilian commercial interests. The prosperity of the Confederation was viewed with jealousy. The Chilian ex-President Freyre had obtained two vessels in Peru when he commenced one of the frequent revolutionary movements which have taken place in Chile. These were the causes of the war. The Protector Santa Cruz only thought of the development of the resources of his country, and of remaining at peace with his neighbours. Callao Castle had been dismantled, and the Peruvian fleet of twelve sailing-vessels was disarmed and laid up in ordinary. Then, as now, the command of the sea was the main thing necessary for a successful invasion of Peru, and this the Chilian Government well knew. But their method of securing it was not creditable.

The fleet of Chile then consisted of two small sailing-vessels, the *Aquiles* and *Colocolo*. They were sent to the Peruvian ports of Callao and Arica, in time of profound peace. They were hospitably received and entertained, when suddenly they seized upon the unmanned and unarmed Peruvian ships and carried them off. Having gained this immense advantage, war was declared on the Confederation. An army of

3000 men, commanded by General Blanco Encalada, was landed at Quilca on the Peruvian coast, and advanced towards Arequipa. The Chilians were out-manœuvred by Santa Cruz, their supplies were cut off, and eventually they agreed to capitulate rather than risk a battle. But the Protector only longed for peace. There was a Plenipotentiary, Don Antonio J. de Irizarri, with the Chilian army, and the Treaty of Paucarpata was negotiated with him on November 17th, 1837. The invaders were allowed to embark again on condition that the war ceased.

As soon as Blanco's force was safe, the Chilian Government broke the treaty, and despatched another army of 6000 men to invade Peru, accompanied by all the military anarchists and malcontents who had been banished. The Protector was still in the south, and Lima was therefore occupied without difficulty, after a brush with part of the garrison just outside the gates, at a place called Guia. Santa Cruz advanced from the south, the Chilians fled before him, and on the 9th of November, 1837, he reoccupied Lima and Callao. If he had followed up his advantage he would easily have secured another Paucarpata, but a fatal delay of six weeks at Lima gave time for the invaders to get safe off to the northern provinces of Peru, where the native malcontents busily collected recruits, until the original force of 6000 Chilians was increased by 2000 Peruvians.

Santa Cruz still sought to appease Chilian animosity, and to secure peace without further bloodshed. He proposed to retire with his army to Bolivia if the Chilian invaders would also return to their country; that a National Assembly should be convoked as soon as Peru was free of all foreign troops, and that the people should again be allowed to decide whether or not they would adhere to the Confederation. The proposal was made to the Chilians by Colonel Wilson, her Britannic Majesty's Minister, the British mediation being a guarantee for an exact compliance with the terms. But these peaceful overtures were brusquely rejected; and Santa Cruz was obliged to march against the invaders. In his anxiety for peace he had neglected the needful military precautions; he had no reserve, and he committed several extraordinary blunders in the field; so that an easy victory was won by the combined invaders and malcontents at Yungay, on the 20th of January, 1839.

The Confederation was dissolved. Chile sought for indirect domination over an anarchical Peru through her own nominees. Gamarra, therefore, was allowed to return to power with the aid of Chilian bayonets, and the unhappy land of the Yncas was once more plunged into anarchy and strife, which continued from 1839 to 1844. For this state of things the Chilian Government was responsible. The motives of the war were bad, the incidents of the seizure of Peruvian ships and the breach of the Treaty of Paucarpata were discreditable, and the results were ruinous strife and misery entailed upon a neighbour. Forty years of peace and progress had redeemed Chile from the discredit of this aggressive war. But now that she has entered upon a similar career, the interests of historical truth require that her policy connected with the attack upon the Confederation should be remembered.

At length a man arose in Peru who restored peace to the distracted country. Ramon Castilla was an Indian of Tarapaca. His father worked the refuse silver ores of the mines of El Carmen, and was the discoverer of the class of ores called *lechcador*, chlorobromide of silver. Young Ramon acted as his father's *leñatero*, or woodcutter. He afterwards entered the Spanish army, rose to the rank of sergeant, and on the arrival of San Martin he joined the patriots. He was a colonel at the battle of Ayacucho—a small man of the true Indian type, with an iron constitution and great powers of endurance. He was an excellent soldier, brave as a lion, prompt in action, beloved by his men. Uneducated and ignorant, he was shrewd and intelligent, while his firm grasp of power secured a long period of peace. For this inestimable blessing Castilla deserves to be held in grateful remembrance by his countrymen.

Ten years of peace followed the election of Castilla as constitutional President in 1844. He has the great credit of having commenced the payment of interest on the foreign debt. None had been paid since 1825, but in 1849 an agreement was made with the bondholders to issue new bonds at 4 per cent. per annum, the rate to increase annually $\frac{1}{2}$ per cent. up to 6 per cent. Arrears of interest were to be capitalized, amounting to 2,615,000*l.* The Constitution of Peru was promulgated in 1856, and received modification after the report of a commission in 1860. The legislative power is vested in a Congress consisting of two chambers. Every 30,000 citizens, or fraction exceeding 15,000, elects a representative for the lower chamber, and every citizen has a vote. With each representative another to supply his place is also elected. The Senate represents the departments or territorial divisions, each department returning senators according to the number of its provinces or subdivisions ; and there is a property qualification. The executive power is vested in a President and two Vice-Presidents, elected by the people, the qualification, scrutiny, and time of election being arranged by Congress. The President holds office for four years, and cannot be re-elected until an equal period has intervened. The exercise of the presidential office is vacated when the President commands an army in the field or is disabled by illness. The first Vice-President then takes his place. The Cabinet, or council of ministers is nominated by the president, but ministers are responsible to Congress, with the privilege of speech in either chamber. The departments and provinces are governed by Prefects and Sub-Prefects, nominated by the executive. The municipalities of towns are elected by the people. The principal change in the Constitution of 1856 was the abolition of slavery. The negroes on the coast were emancipated, and a grant was voted as compensation to slave-owners. The tribute hitherto paid by the Indians as a capitation tax was also abolished.

Peru found a strange source of wealth, which was as fatal to her as the great influx of gold and silver was to the mother country. The trade-winds are loaded with moisture from the Atlantic, which produces the rich vegetation of the Amazon valley; but when they reach the snowy ridges of the Andes the last drop of this moisture is wrung from them, and they come down to the Pacific coast without a particle. Guano can only accumulate, as a valuable manure, where there is no rain. The great deposits of nitrate of soda have also been formed in deserts where there is no rain. The exhausted lands of the old world needed these manures, the farmers were willing to pay high prices for them, and there were vast deposits on the islands and headlands, and in the deserts of Peru. A wise Government would have treated this source of revenue as temporary and extraordinary. The Peruvians looked upon it as if it was permanent, abolishing other taxes, and recklessly increasing expenditure. The guano demoralized public men, and is the chief cause of the country's ruin. The exportation of guano commenced in 1846, and from 1851 to 1860 the amount of shipping that loaded at the Chincha Islands represented 2,860,000 tons. Between 1853 and 1872 there were 8,000,000 tons shipped; and in the latter year the Chincha Island deposits were practically exhausted. But other deposits were discovered. From 1869 to 1871 over 800,000 tons were shipped from the Guanape Islands; and since 1874 large deposits have been discovered on headlands of the coast of Tarapaca. In 1875 the guano exports amounted to 378,683 tons, valued at 4,000,000*l*. The deposits of nitrate of soda have been worked since 1830 in the province of Tarapaca, the chief ports of export being Iquique and Pisagua. From 1830 to 1850 the export amounted to 239,860 tons. It reached its maximum in 1875, when 326,869 tons left the country in one year. In 1877 the number of ships that cleared from the port of Iquique was 253. In 1878 the number of tons of nitrate exported from the ports of Tarapaca was 269,327.

(Other industries rapidly rose into importance during the long period of peace which Castilla secured for Peru.) The sugar estates on the coast were worked by negro slave labour until the emancipation in 1855. Chinese labourers then began to arrive, and over 58,000 landed between 1860 and 1872. In 1859 the sugar exported from Peru was valued at 90,000*l.* ; in 1876 it had increased to 71,700 tons, valued at 1,219,000*l.*, of which quantity 63,370 tons went to Great Britain. A very excellent kind of cotton is grown in the coast valleys, the value of the crops in 1877 being estimated at 160,000*l.* ; and there are extensive vineyards. Rice is also cultivated in the north, besides olives, mulberries, and cochineal. From the Andes the staple exports are silver and wool.

When General Castilla finally retired from office in 1862 he was succeeded by General San Roman, an old Ynca Indian of Puno, who, as a boy, had fought with his father under Pumacagua. The Republic had existed for forty years, during which time it had suffered from civil and external wars for nine years, and had enjoyed thirty-one years of peace. Very great advances had been made in prosperity during that time ; trade had increased, education had been extended, and the condition of the people had been improved, while, since 1849, the interest on the foreign debt had been regularly paid.

The venerable President, Miguel San Roman, died in 1863, less than six months after he had taken office. He was a man of large experience, who had acted a part in every political event since the rising of Pumacagua in 1814. After that insurrection was suppressed, the elder San Roman was shot at Puno, in his son's presence, and the boy of fourteen became a sworn enemy of Spain. The moment Lord Cochrane's fleet arrived at Callao he made his way down from the Andes to join the patriot army, and so his long military career began. He was gifted with a wonderful memory and great conversational powers, and many an interesting tradition and good anecdote passed away with the old chief.

The Vice-President, General Pezet, a handsome and accomplished officer, son of a French physician who was settled at Lima in Spanish times, succeeded San Roman. But he became unpopular owing to an arrangement of claims made by Spain, which was considered derogatory to the national honour. He was replaced by Colonel Mariano Ignacio Prado on November 26th, 1865, who successfully defended the port of Callao against the attack of the Spanish fleet on May 2nd, 1866; a day which has ever since been honoured in the Peruvian calendar. A province, a regiment, a college, a fort were named " 2° DE MAYO." The war upon which Spain unwisely entered with her old colony was caused by the ill-treatment of some Basque immigrants, a question which ought to have been settled by arbitration.

Colonel Prado's position during fourteen months was that of a military chief who had lawlessly seized the supreme power ; but early in 1866 a Congress was convoked, and he was declared to be constitutional President. His rule was not, however, approved by the country. The aged Grand Marshal Don Ramon Castilla rose in arms in Tarapaca with a handful of men in 1868. But he died very suddenly while on the march. The old warrior breathed his last, wrapped in a cloak by the roadside, in the ravine of Tilividie. Prado's downfall was, however, at hand. On the 22nd of September, 1867, the second Vice-President of the government of San Roman, Don Pedro Diez Canseco, put himself at the head of a rising at Arequipa, while Colonel Don José Balta declared for him at Chiclayo in the north. Prado attempted to take Arequipa by assault on the 7th of January, 1868, but was repulsed, and retired to Chile. Canseco then assumed his constitutional position as Vice-President in charge, assembled a Congress, and on the 2nd of August, 1868, Balta was elected President of Peru.

Colonel Balta, led on by speculators and contractors, was unfortunately induced to enter upon a career of extravagant expenditure with the help of foreign loans. He pushed forward the construction of railroads and other public works with feverish haste. In 1870 he raised a loan of 11,920,000*l.* at six per cent. ; and in 1872 another of 36,800,000*l.* to include the old debt, and for the construction of public works. Colonel Balta also guaranteed a loan of 290,000*l.* for a railroad ; so that the whole liabilities of his government became 49,010,000*l.*, besides an internal debt of

4,000,000*l.* It seems almost incredible that these loans could have been raised, when the revenue of Peru was notoriously small and precarious. The speculators who undertook to advance such sums, only a portion of which ever reached Peru, must have known perfectly well that the continuous payment of the interest on them was simply impossible. These matters are not intelligible to an outsider; but the historian will consider the unhappy people of Peru, not the exceedingly clever financiers who arranged the loans, and were well able to take care of themselves, as the victims. The railroads are largely in the hands of English capitalists.

From Payta, the most northern port of Peru, there is a railroad sixty-three miles long to the city of Piura, facilitating the shipment of cotton crops. Further south a line, forty-five miles long, connects the port of Pimentel with Chiclayo and Lambayeque. The rice crops of the Ferreñape valley are brought to the port of Eten by a line fifty miles in length, which is said to be entirely the property of an English House. The railroad from Magdalena to the port of Pacasmayu, ninety-three miles long, taps the fertile valley of Jequetepeque, and is a State enterprise. The sugar and rice estates of Chicama reach the coast by a line of twenty-five miles from Ascope to Malabrigo. The city of Truxillo is connected with its port of Salaverry by a line eighty-five miles long. The city of Huaraz, between two ranges of the Andes, is to have a railroad to the coast at Chimbote, 172 miles long, but only fifty-two are as yet finished. The capital was connected with its port of Callao by a railroad, in 1851, and with the fashionable watering-place of Chorrillos in 1858. Another line, forty-five miles long, goes from Lima to Chancay. South of Lima the vineyards and cotton estates of Yca are joined to the port of Pisco by a line of forty-eight miles. The railroad from Mollendo to Arequipa was completed in 1870, and runs over 170 miles of desert. In order to supply Mollendo with water a pipe was laid alongside the line for eighty-five miles, starting near Arequipa, 8000 feet above the sea, and discharging 433,000 gallons in twenty-four hours. This is the largest iron aqueduct in the world. The line from the port of Ylo to Moquegua is sixty-three, and from Arica to Tacna thirty-nine miles long. There is also a system of railroads in Tarapaca, from the nitrate of soda works to the ports, comprising, when finished, 180 miles. All these lines were planned to meet existing needs, and they tap rich and valuable districts.

But the great lines across the Andes were undertaken prematurely. One passes from Callao and Lima, across the western and central cordilleras, to Oroya in the lofty valley of Xauxa, and is to be 136 miles long. It was commenced in 1870, and rises 5000 feet in the first forty-six miles. It then threads intricate gorges of the Andes, along the edges of precipices, and over bridges that seem suspended in the air. It tunnels the Andes at an altitude of 15,645 miles, the most elevated spot in the world where a piston-rod is moved by steam, and will terminate at Oroya, 12,178 feet above the sea. There are sixty-three tunnels. The bridge of Verrugas, spanning a chasm 580 feet wide, rests on three piers, the centre

one of hollow wrought-iron, being 252 feet high. Of
this Oroya railroad eighty-seven miles were completed
when the war broke out, and it had cost 4,625,887*l.*
Another line crosses the Andes from Arequipa to
Puno on the shore of Lake Titicaca, which was opened
in 1874, and is 232 miles long. Steamers have been
launched on the lake.

The whole scheme of Peruvian railroads, if ever
completed, would have a length of 1281 miles, private
lines 496, and two projects partly private 253, altogether 2030 miles, to cost 37,500,000*l.* In 1867 a
telegraph company laid down a number of lines.

The rule of Colonel Balta, though ruinous to Peru
from a financial point of view, was throughout a period
of peace and internal prosperity, ending in the opening
of an international exhibition at Lima. A wretched
military outbreak, in which the President was killed, on
July 26th, 1872, gave it a tragic termination ; but the
sedition itself was at once put down by the spontaneous
uprising of the people on the side of law and order.

Don Manuel Pardo became Constitutional President
of Peru on August 2nd, 1872, and was the first civilian who had been elected. It was hoped that he
would inaugurate a new era of retrenchment and
reform. The son of a distinguished patriot of the
revolution, he was born at Lima in 1834, and received
a good education partly in the universities of Lima
and Santiago, and partly in Europe. He founded the
first bank in Lima, had been minister of finance, and
was a man of considerable literary attainments, of
moderate and enlightened views, and of high principle. He came to the helm at a period of great

financial difficulty, and he undertook a thankless but patriotic task.

He found his country loaded with a debt amounting to 60,000,000*l.*, and that a sum of 4,000,000*l.* was needed to pay the annual interest. A contract had been made with Messrs. Dreyfus, of Paris, in 1869, in order to pay off another debt of 4,000,000*l.* by the sale of 2,000,000 tons of guano, delivery of which was to commence in 1872. But the whole of the proceeds of the guano was more than absorbed in meeting the liabilities created by the foreign loans. Both demands could not possibly be met, and the payments of interest on the loans ceased in 1876. They had been regularly met since 1849, and the failure was a great national misfortune.

All the new President could do was to curtail expenditure in every branch, and he hoped to bring it down to 3,000,000*l.* The customs' receipts only amounted to 1,500,000*l.* in 1875, and there were no direct taxes. He reduced the army, regulated the Chinese immigration, promoted the exploration of navigable streams leading to the Amazon, organized an efficient scheme for the collection of statistics and for a census, and supported the interests of literature. He was the best President that Peru has ever known, and when his term of office came to an end, he was peacefully succeeded by General Prado, on the 2nd of August, 1876. Don Manuel Pardo afterwards became President of the Senate, and his assassination by an obscure wretch, when entering the hall of the Senate, on November 16th, 1878, was a great national calamity.

General Prado is the same officer who defended Callao against the Spaniards on the famous 2nd of May, and who had already been in power for two years, 1865-67. He made several attempts to come to some arrangement with the bondholders of the foreign debt in which Peru had unhappily become involved, but the problem was not capable of solution, and before long the country was confronted with the overwhelming misery of the Chilian invasion.

As a customer of Great Britain the Peruvian Republic held an important position. In 1878 Peru received woollen and cotton goods and other manufactures from us to the value of 1,369,836*l.* In return her exports to Great Britain in the same year were worth 5,232,305*l.* The number of British vessels that entered Callao in 1877 was 720, of which 198 (tonnage 194,973) were sailing-vessels, and 522 steamers Englishmen, therefore, have material as well as moral reasons for regretting the ruinous disasters of so good a customer.

Peru had, during the fifty-four years of her independence, made progress in education as well as in material prosperity. It is true that the country labours under many disadvantages, and that progress is slow and difficult. But there is progress. The country can already point to the honoured careers of several illustrious sons. In Dr. Vigil Peru has produced an eloquent and fearless orator, an enlightened statesman, and a bold and sagacious scholar of profound learning and keen intellect. To Colonel Espinosa the country also owes much for his remarkable writings. Regardless of the prejudices of his countrymen, he yet loved his country, and he fearlessly and eloquently told the truth. Republican Peru can also boast of some eminent men of science. Nicolas de Pierola was a native of Camana, on the coast of Peru. He studied under Dr. Luna Pizarro, at Lima, went to Spain in 1814, and became a deputy of Cortes in 1820. He was a professor in the university of Madrid until 1826, when he returned to his native country. Devoted to the natural sciences, he was director of the Lima museum, member of the committee on public instruction, and editor of two scientific periodicals. He died at Lima in 1857, leaving several children, one of whom was destined to take a prominent place in his country's annals. Dr. Pierola's learning was equalled by his modesty, but Professor Raimondi has immortalized his name in that of a new species of violet found in the Amazon Valley, the *Viola Pierolana*. The friend and colleague of Pierola was Don Mariano Eduardo Rivero of Arequipa, who, in conjunction with Dr. Von Tschudi, published that magnificent work the "Antiguedades Peruanas," which has been translated into English. Rivero studied in England under Sir Humphrey Davy during five years, and afterwards in France under Berthier, completing his education as a mineralogist in Germany. In 1822 he explored Colombia, returning home in 1825. In Peru he was director-general of mines for many years, and his scientific eminence shed a lustre on his native country. He died in 1858. Among Peruvian lovers of science Dr. Cayetano Heredia must not be forgotten, who was born in the humble little village of Catacaos, near Piura, in 1797. He not only studied medicine with enthusiastic devotion, but sent Peruvian

youths to acquire a knowledge of that science in
Europe at his own expense, and was himself rector of
the College of Medicine at Lima from 1845 to his
death in 1861. His able successor, Dr. Miguel de los
Rios, who founded the botanical gardens at Lima, and
established professorships of botany and chemistry,
justly claims a place among illustrious Peruvians.

Don Antonio Raimondi may also be looked upon
as a Peruvian, for this accomplished naturalist and
geographer has devoted thirty years of his life to the
service of his adopted country. Having systematically
explored every part of Peru, the Congress resolved
that his great scientific work should be published at
the expense of the Government. President Pardo, in
June, 1873, arranged the details with enlighted libe-
rality, and the first three volumes have since appeared.
Raimondi has given up the labour of a lifetime to his
adopted country, and Peru has known how to value
so precious a gift. The great savant trembled lest
he should not be spared to finish the work; and it
will be one of the results of this hateful war that its
completion will be indefinitely postponed—an injury
not to Peru only, but to the whole civilized world.

General Mendiburu, whose biographical dictionary
is a monument of research and learning; Sebastian
Lorente, the historian of Peru; Manuel A. Fuentes, the
antiquary and statistician; Ricardo Palma, the writer
of historical tales and fictions; Paz Soldan, the intro-
ducer of the most improved penitentiary system and
the eminent geographer; the professor of literature and
charming writer of sonnets, Numa Llona; the poets
Althaus and Marquez; these may be mentioned among

living Peruvian writers of eminence. Nor are the paintings of Laso and Monteros, or the sculpture of Luis
Medina unworthy of a cultivated nation. The spread
of education has made steady progress among the
mass of the people, additional colleges have recently
been established in the large towns, and many schools
in the villages. The Constitution guarantees gra·
tuitous primary education.

The latest census, that of 1876, gave Peru a total
population of 2,704,998 souls, of whom fifty-seven per
cent., more than half, are pure Ynca Indians, and
twenty-three per cent. are *Mestizos* or half-castes.
For this population there is one university of the first
rank at Lima, there are five lesser universities, thirty-
three colleges for boys and eighteen for girls, 1578
schools for boys and 729 for girls, all supported by the
State, besides private schools. (The people of Peru have
advanced since the Independence in spite of unsettled
government and all other drawbacks ; and the condition of the imperial race, the Ynca Indians, notwith-
standing the forced recruiting, has vastly improved.)

The unsettled state of the country is always grossly
exaggerated. Between the battle of Ayacucho and
the present war with Chile a period of fifty-four years
has elapsed. In that time there have been foreign
wars lasting three years, and civil dissensions continuing for six years and six months—in all nine
years and a half of disturbance in Peru. On the
other hand there have been forty-four and a half years
of peace. In the same period of fifty-four years there
have been eighteen changes of government in Peru,
and twenty-one in England.

CHAPTER V.

SOCIAL CONDITION OF THE PEOPLE OF PERU.

THE unsettled state of the government in Peru has been much exaggerated. It has had but slight influence on the moral and material condition of the country. The social relations of the people are only temporarily and indirectly disarranged by disturbances and struggles for power among political leaders. Those relations have gradually been developed since the Spanish conquest under varying circumstances, which are practically unconnected with party politics. The causes affecting the condition of the people lie much deeper, and it would require more space than could be devoted to the subject, in accordance with the plan of the present work, to explain them. But it is necessary to convey to the reader some idea of the social state of a people whose sufferings and misfortunes will form the main subject of this volume.

Without tracing down the history of the relations between the Spanish settlers and the former subjects of the Ynca Empire, from the days of the conquest, we may at least glance at the actual condition of both races at one particular time, and no period is better adapted for our purpose than that in which

E

the men, who have now reached mature age, passed their boyhood and received their education a quarter of a century ago.

The most important part of Peru is the region of the Andes, the home of the Ynca race, with its main centres of progress at Caxamarca, Huaraz, Xauxa, Ayacucho, Cuzco, Puno, and Arequipa. Throughout this region there are many families of pure Spanish descent, whose sons have always taken a prominent part in their country's annals. They have maintained the traditions and associations of their ancestors, several were ennobled in Spanish times, while some, such as the Elespurus and Ormasas,[1] take pride in the thought that their ancestral homes are still standing in the lovely valleys of Biscay and Guipuzcoa.

One such family may be selected as a type of the Peruvian upper class in the Andean region. Some thirty years ago the old family mansion of the Tellos, at the north-west corner of the great square of the city of Ayacucho, was occupied by Don Manuel Tello y Cabrera, his four sisters and their children. Possessing large estates, and representing the marquisate of Valdelirios, Don Manuel, then in the prime of life, was Prefect of Ayacucho, and one of its most influential citizens. The house is built round a

---

[1] *Elespuru* means at the head of, or above the church, in the Basque language. In that position the ancestral palace of the Elespurus still stands, with a lovely view over chestnut groves, and rich cultivation in the valley of Baquio, on the coast of the bay of Biscay. A distinguished branch of the family was settled at Cuzco. *Ormasa* signifies a series of walls in Basque. The family also has its old home in the valley of Baquio, while the Peruvian branch is at Ayacucho.

courtyard, all the living-rooms being in the upper story, and a wide covered balcony overlooks the great square. There was a long dining-room, with some family pictures, opening on to the balcony, where there were chairs and sofas. This balcony was the usual resort of the family for conversation and social intercourse. At one end of it there was a small library, at the other a guest-chamber. A gallery, open to the courtyard, passed round the house, with doors leading from it to the *comedor* or dining-room, to the large *sala* or drawing-room, and to the various sitting-rooms and bedrooms of the different members of the family.

Don Manuel's eldest sister Josefa was a childless widow, who, in her youth, had rejected an offer from the Spanish Captain Narvaez, afterwards the famous Duke of Valencia in Spain. The next sister Mercedes was the widow of another Spanish officer named Huguet, and she had four promising sons named Blas, Joaquin, José Antonio, and Felipe. The elder was a graduate of the Ayacucho University, the second was in the army, and the two younger attended the classes at the college of San Ramon. Manuela, the third sister, was the wife of Colonel Ormasa, an officer of noble Basque descent, and had two young children, Gertrudis and Estanislao. The youngest was Micaela, who had married General Zubiaga,[2] a native of Cuzco, also of Basque descent, in 1841, and became a widow in the following year, with one child Agustin, then a boy attending the college with his cousins. There never was a more

[2] Zubiaga means a bridge in Basque.

affectionate and united family. Don Manuel, its head, was universally beloved and respected, owing to his constant solicitude for the welfare of all classes of the people and his tried capacity as an administrator. His sisters were accomplished and most agreeable in conversation, and all were good musicians. The house was the resort of the best society in Ayacucho. After breakfast dignitaries of the church, lawyers, and *hacendados* or country gentlemen dropped in to converse with Don Manuel and his sisters, on the balcony. The conversations were intellectual, and lively. Here, with full local knowledge, the Marquis of Moyobamba described the events of the battle of Chupas and the defeat of Diego de Almagro the lad. Here Doña Josefa related the story of the marvellous career of the Nun Ensign Catalina de Erauso, whose disguise was detected at Ayacucho in 1618. Here Dr. Taforo, now Archbishop of Santiago in Chile, displayed his great conversational talents ; while the questions and remarks of the younger people served to enliven and give zest to the narratives of their elders. In the evenings young ladies and gentlemen often assembled in the *sala*, and when a sufficient number came, there was music and dancing. Among them were the fair Concita Arias, the sprightly Asunta de Guzman, the lovely and most charming Jesucita Canseco, so soon to be borne to an early grave.

The young people, in the Tello family, the Huguets, the Ormasas, and Agustin Zubiaga, were intelligent and manly, diligent at their studies, fond of long rambles in the mountains, good riders and good shots. Surrounded by glorious scenery, the neighbourhood of Ayacucho is also rich in historical associations. Colonel Mosol, the prefect's aide-de-camp, had served in the famous battle which gave independence to Peru, and was able to describe the events of the great day on the spot, in minute detail, to attentive and enthusiastic young listeners. The ride to the battle-field was long, and it was necessary to pass the night in the neighbouring village of Quinua, while the day was spent in hearing the veteran's able exposition, and in scaling the craggy heights of Condor Kunka. Among the rising youth of Ayacucho, in those days, were Andres Avelino Caceres, and Victor Fajardo, whose father was a Chilian colonel long settled in the city. Juan Bautista Zubiaga, a nephew of Doña Micaela, was also a frequent visitor, though his home was at Cuzco. All these bright and promising lads, brought up under such happy auspices, and surrounded by many endearing ties of love and affection, were destined to fight and to die like heroes, in defence of their country.

Don Manuel Tello had a pleasant country house surrounded by fruit-gardens on the heights above Ayacucho, and large wheat estates at Cochabamba on the battle-field of Chupas, at Dean-pampa and La Tortura. The relations of the family with the Indians were most friendly and cordial. All its members spoke the Quichua language, and the ladies took a lively interest in the welfare of their poorer neighbours. Scarcely a day passed without an Indian woman or young girl coming to seek advice or help, generally from Doña Micaela Zubiaga, the youthful widow whose saintly life was so devoted to good works, that she and her young son Agustin were spoken of as *huaca* or almost sacred. As Don Manuel rode or walked along the roads, it was pleasant to see the people working in the fields, hurry to the hedges to exchange greetings. He had a few words of kindly inquiry for all of them, and they in return asked after his sisters and their children by name. The market-place of Ayacucho was covered with huge shades, consisting of circular bands of plaited straw with a pole in the centre stuck in the ground. The women sat under them, in their picturesque costumes, with their heaps of fruit, vegetables, and coca; their milk, eggs, and fowls. The ladies and children threaded their way amongst the labyrinth, making their purchases and exchanging news with their humbler friends; while frequently some young Indian girl would offer a prettily embroidered band for tying up the hair, or a quaintly carved little calabash for the toilet-table, to a passing lady from whom she had received kindness. In the mind of one who has watched all these things from day to day, and from week to week, there can be no doubt that the Peruvians deserve sympathy in their misfortunes. The Tello family is not exceptional, but is simply one example of the families of country gentlemen in the Peruvian Andes.

In Cuzco, the old city of the Yncas, the same humanizing and civilizing influences prevailed among the upper classes, and there was a higher degree of culture. Here the ground floors of the houses often

consist of the superb masonry of the imperial
people, on which the Spaniards have raised an upper
story. The rooms are long and often handsomely
furnished with old-fashioned chairs and tables, and
cabinets inlaid with mother of pearl and *haliotis*, for
the Indians of Cuzco are very skilful in carving and
carpentry, and beautiful cabinet woods are supplied
by the forests to the eastward, and the designs and
workmanship are very creditable. In Cuzco there is
a university, a college of science and art, an excellent
school for girls, a museum, and a public library.
Society is agreeable and intellectual, and warm
friendship and affection exist among the families of
the upper classes. In the days when those who are
now mature leaders in the defence of their country
were receiving their education at Cuzco, the old city
included among its residents a number of learned
men and accomplished women. Dr. Carazas, the
dean of the cathedral, and Don Julian Ochoa, the
rector of the university, were well-read scholars, very
learned in the history of their own country, and active
promoters of education. Dr. Miranda, the leading
barrister, had served for a short time as one of the Duke
of Wellington's Spanish aides-de-camp. He had translated " Hamlet " into Spanish, was an improvisatore,
had extraordinary conversational powers, and possessed a fund of anecdote. He organized theatrical
entertainments in the great cloister of the Jesuit
College, and was the leader in all social gatherings.
The country gentlemen and their families had houses
in the city, and the Astetes, Novoas, Artajonas, and
Nadals formed centres where agreeable evening

parties frequently assembled. The venerable Señora Astete de Bennet had a mind stored with all the traditions of the Yncas, and of the risings of Tupac Amaru and Pumacagua. Young Victoria Novoa, and other beautiful daughters of the Ynca city, were carefully educated, bright, amiable, and intelligent, and their presence increased the charm of Cuzco society; while all were good musicians, and every house contained a pianoforte. At Urubamba, in the lovely vale of Vilcamayu, and in the country houses of the *hacendados*, the numerous guests enjoyed the same agreeable society, enhanced by the lovely scenery and the pleasures of a country life. In these houses the *salons* opened on gardens with tall clipped hedges, little statues, and beds of roses, pinks, heliotropes, and salvias. Beyond were the fruit-orchards and rows of maize, fourteen feet high, rising up in terraced fields, and backed by the glorious eastern cordillera. The principal charm of Cuzco society consists in the frank cordiality of the heads of families, the unstinting hospitality, the evident affection which ties all the members of households together, and above all in the bright intelligence and curiosity of the younger people, combined as it is with simple and ingenuous manners. The girls are true-hearted and virtuous. Their brothers are courteous and most hospitable. They are brave, too, as the last two years have shown. Their bones have whitened the burning sands of Tarapaca and Tacna, where they have fallen with their faces to the foe in defence of their native land ; and a son of Cuzco fell foremost in the fight, with his feet under the Chilian gun, on the heights of San Francisco. It is sad to think of the anguish caused among the amiable and kind-hearted families at Cuzco and Ayacucho by this accursed war.

In Arequipa, the city under the volcanic peak of Misti, and surrounded by a green and fertile valley, there are many distinguished families which, generation after generation, have produced men who have attained distinction in their native land. The Riveros, among many others of equal note, may be mentioned. Of one of them, a poet and writer of sonnets, the great Cervantes said that his genius had created perennial spring in Arequipa,—

> " Su divino ingenio ha producido
> En Arequipa universa primavera."

Another, the eminent antiquary and mineralogist, has already been mentioned.[3] The family of Melgar has produced poets and statesmen, and the death of one of them shows the cool heroism of which a Peruvian Creole is capable. The enthusiastic young poet Melgar joined the rebellion of Pumacagua against Spanish tyranny. He was taken prisoner and condemned to be shot. Proud and erect the patriot was brought out for execution, and he faced the row of loaded muskets with a countenance calm and thoughtful. A priest was in attendance to give him the last consolations of religion ; but the father was commissioned to offer the dying man a pardon if he would betray his comrades, and confess what he knew of the designs of the insurgents. All this was whispered into his ear. The young poet's face became agitated

[3] See page 46.

and troubled. He exclaimed to the priest, "You have betrayed your trust. You pretended to prepare my mind for eternity, but you have brought it down to earth, by making a base and dishonouring proposal." Then, turning to his executioners, he said,— "Will any one give me a cigar, for the love of God." One was handed to him. He smoked about half, and then threw it away. His countenance had again become calm and unruffled. He gave the signal to fire, and in another moment he had breathed his last.[4] The ladies of Arequipa often sing the plaintive "*despedidas*" of the poet Melgar, which have been set to music. The same spirit which inspired him in his last moments has been shown, again and again, by the youth of Arequipa in the hour of their country's great need.

The upper classes, in the Peruvian Andes, are not all of pure Spanish or Basque descent. Many are *mestizos*, or half-castes, especially among the priests, and some are pure Indians. The Ynca Justo Pastor Sahuaraura was Archdeacon of Cuzco, and author of a work entitled "La Monarquia Peruana;" Don Luis Titu Atauchi, another descendant of the Yncas, was a lawyer of eminence; and Dr. Justiniani, the learned Cura of Laris and depository of ancient Quichuan folk-lore, was lineally descended from the Ynca Manco, who besieged the Pizarros in Cuzco. Don Agustin Aragon, one of the most enterprising of the planters and explorers in the Amazonian forests;

---

[4] This anecdote was related to the author by the poet's brother, an accomplished statesman who was a minister under President Castilla. The story is also told by Stevenson.

and Don Juan Bustamante, the author of an entertaining volume of travels through all the countries of Europe, are also of Indian descent.

The mass of the people is composed of the different tribes which, under the wise rule of the Yncas, were welded into one powerful nation. The Quichuas or Yncas inhabited the valleys and mountain sides of the department of Cuzco, the Chancas people that of Apurimac, the Pocras are the dwellers round Ayacucho and Guanta, and the valley of Xauxa is the country of the Huancas. In the mountains of Cangallo, west and south of Ayacucho, are the turbulent Morochucos, and to the east of Guanta dwell the brave and tenaciously faithful Yquichanos. In the basin of Lake Titicaca are the people of Colla or Aymara race, while Arequipa and Tacna were settled by *mitimaes* or colonists from the Andes. Some of these tribes had become one people with the Quichuas or Yncas; but others, which had only recently been subdued when the Spaniards arrived, have to a great extent retained their peculiar characteristics. Such is especially the case with the Morochucos and Yquichanos.

The Peruvian Indians average a height of from five feet five to five feet eight inches. They are of slender build, but with well-knit muscular frames, and are capable of enduring great fatigue. Their complexions are of a fresh olive colour, skin very smooth and soft, hair straight and black. The women are frequently very beautiful even now; but the pictures contemporaneous with the Spanish conquest must be seen to form a correct idea of the features and bearing of men and women of this imperial race in the height of their pre-eminence. The portraits of Ynca nobles and princesses in the churches of Santa Ana and the Compania in Cuzco, at Laris and Azangaro, can alone furnish evidence of what the noblest type of the American people was like after many centuries of culture. We see their descendants after three centuries of cruel oppression ; and of course the change is great.

The Peruvian Indians are good cultivators. They raise the finest maize crops in the world without any comparison, and this superiority is due partly to favourable soil and climate, but mainly to intelligent selection of seed and expert tillage. Their terrace cultivation, and ingenious irrigation systems are admirable ; and their method of raising and picking the coca crops is only successful because every stage is watched and provided for with patient skill and constant attention. Under their hands the lofty and inhospitable mountain sides, even up to the snow-level, are made to yield crops of *quinua* and edible roots ; while the fine crops of potatoes, the best in the world, furnish supplies of food to the people, in a preserved form, which enable them to carry provisions sufficient for many days into the Amazonian forests. The *chuñu*, or preserved potato of Peru, is prepared by a process of freezing and drying, and is highly nutritious.

But it is as shepherds that the Peruvian Indians excel by reason of their patience and invariable kindness to animals. It is probable that no other people could have successfully domesticated so stubborn an animal as the llama, so as to use it as a beast of burden ; and constant watchfulness and attention alone enable the Peruvians to rear their flocks of alpacas, and to produce the large annual out-turn of silky wool.

The Peruvian Indians live in stone huts, roofed with red tiles or thatched with the long grass called *ychu*, and they are well supplied with food and clothing. For the last century and more the dress of the men has been a coat of green or blue baize with long soft nap, having short skirts and no collar, a red waistcoat with ample pockets, and black breeches loose and open at the knees. The legs and feet are usually bare, but in cold weather they wear knitted woollen stockings without feet, and untanned llama hide *usutas* or sandals. The *montero* is a velvet cap with broad straw brim covered with the same material, and ornamented with coloured ribbons and gold or silver lace. At Cuzco it is worn both by men and women. But at Ayacucho the women use a graceful head-dress consisting of an embroidered cloth lying flat on the head, and hanging down behind. In the basin of Lake Titicaca the head-dress is again different. All the women wear a white or red embroidered bodice, a blue or green skirt reaching a little below the knees, and a *lliclla* or mantle of some bright colour secured across the chest by a large pin, usually with a spoon bowl at one end, of silver or copper. The men have an embroidered cloth bag, called *chuspa*, slung by a line over one shoulder, to contain their coca leaves.

The people are fond of singing, especially when at

work, and the little shepherd lads enliven their long
hours of solitude with plaintive tunes on the *pincullu*
or flute. Three centuries of oppression have naturally given a melancholy tinge to the Indian character,
and the people are, with good cause, reserved and
suspicious. They dread the conscription to which
they are still subjected. It is but another form of
the old Spanish *mita* or forced labour. One song,
which is often heard among them, is the despairing
farewell of a recruit to his mistress, the refrain
of each verse being,—

" Ya me llevan de soldado
A las pampas de Huancayo." [5]

In other respects the Indians are no longer oppressed. The Republic has brought them freedom
and citizenship, and in 1856 the tribute was abolished,
so that they no longer pay any direct taxation. Yet
the memory of former wrongs has tinged their most
popular songs with sadness. The young mother lulls
her infant to sleep with verses the burden of which is
sorrow and despair, and the " yaravis," or love-songs,
usually express the most hopeless grief. Still there
are many festivals when the people indulge in cheer-
ful intercourse, and they are fond of flowers, of sing-
ing-birds kept in cages, and of bright colours. Nor
is their artistic talent to be despised. The paintings
of Quito and the wooden images of Cuzco are re-
nowned, and in Ayacucho the Indian sculptors carve

[5] " Now they take me away for a soldier, to the plains of Huancayo."
It was at Huancayo that one of the chief places of rendezvous for recruits
was fixed in Spanish times.

figures and groups out of a soft white alabaster. These statues often possess real artistic merit, and the works of the Ayacucho sculptor Medina, at the Lima Exhibition, were universally admired.   News is brought to the people in all the secluded valleys of the Andes by the Collahuayas, or itinerant doctors, who extend their wanderings from Quito to Buenos Ayres, so that there is a knowledge of passing events in their own and neighbouring countries, while the memory of former times is preserved in songs and traditions.

The Ynca Indians, when experience has taught them to set aside their natural feeling of suspicion and caution, become faithful and trusty followers. They are most affectionate to their families, and have an intense love of home, are naturally gentle and humane, and are habitually kind to animals.   At the same time they are hardy, enduring, brave, and endowed with indomitable resolution when their hearts are in a cause.   One fact must suffice to illustrate their fearless determination.   In the rebellion of Pumacagua against the Spaniards, several insurgents were taken in arms at Asillo, and brought before General Ramirez at Azangaro.   He caused them to be mercilessly flogged and tortured, cut off their ears and one hand each, and then let them go as a warning to their companions of the treatment they had to expect if they continued in arms.   After the crushing defeat of Umachiri, all these mutilated but still undaunted patriots, were found bravely fighting in the insurgent ranks.[6]   The Spanish cruelty

[6] Information from General San Roman, confirmed by Don Luis Quiñones of Azangaro, and Dr. Cardenas of Asillo.

had simply had no effect in deterring them from the path of duty and of honour. These people are descendants of men who conceived and created a civilization and an administrative system which was unsurpassed in fitness and efficiency, and even now they retain many of the virtues and high qualities of their ancestors. The Ynca Indians are representatives of an imperial tribe, and their leaders are the countrymen of Melgar, the hero poet.

On the coast of Peru, between the Andes and the sea, the population is entirely distinct ; and this part of the Republic, owing to the changes wrought in the last three centuries, can no longer be considered as representing any part of the empire of the Yncas ; for the original coast people, the civilized Yuncas of the grand Chimu, have almost entirely disappeared. Only a few isolated communities of Indians survive at Catacaos, Eten, Chilca, and a few other villages. They have been replaced by African negroes, and many shades of half-castes, and more recently by Chinese labourers.) The African portion, debased by slavery, has not been improved by emancipation, and forms a dangerous element in the coast valleys and cities.

In the days when slavery was legal—before 1856— the sugar, cotton, and vine estates in the coast valleys were worked by negroes, who lived in villages surrounded by high walls, called *galpones*, with a gate, which was closed at night. Each estate had its *galpon* near the house and factory. The valley of Cañete may be selected as a type of these coast valleys. It was divided into eight sugar estates. Two were owned by the monastery of Buena Muerte at Lima, and rented by Englishmen. The rest had resident owners, country gentlemen of good family, who were upright, honourable, and kind to their slaves and dependents. The buildings on the estates were extensive and handsome. Round the courtyard were the *trapiche* or sugar-mill, the boiling-house, refining-house, store-rooms, the chapel, and handsomely furnished dwelling-house. The proprietors rose very early, and rode over the fields until a little before noon, when they had breakfast. Dinner was at four p.m., the company consisting of the proprietor and his family, the steward, chaplain, refiner, engineer, and any guests who happened to drop in. A frequent interchange of visits and dinner-parties kept up a feeling of neighbourly good-will throughout the valley. Flower and fruit gardens were attached to each house, with a running stream for irrigation. Here are groves of tall chirimoya-trees, paltas, orange and citron-trees, figs, and bananas. Passion flowers climb over the trellis-work, and supply refreshing granadillas.

Before 1856 the negroes appeared to be a happy and contented race, for, though their labour was forced, the sale and separation of families were unknown, and they received clothing, food, and lodging. Early every morning the voices of women and girls were heard at the door of the chapel, chanting a hymn of praise on their knees before going to work. This was repeated at sunset when the day's work was concluded. On the vine estate of Don Juan de Dios Quintana, at Chavalina, near Yca, all the married slaves and workmen were allowed a piece of ground rent free, on which they grew vegetables and raised poultry and pigs. Their children took the produce to market on donkeys, and sat before their little piles of merchandise in the market-place of Yca. They thus earned money, and lived in comparative comfort. The country gentlemen of the Peruvian coast, as a class, were remarkable for their attention to their estates, their charity and benevolence, and their cordial hospitality. The emancipation of the slaves, and consequent increase of the lawless element on the coast, and the immigration of Chinese in large numbers, has very much altered the condition of the population, and not, it is to be feared, for the better. Yet the fertility of the valleys, and their advantageous position now that so many railroads have been completed, make it certain that this part of Peru, when peace is restored, will recover from the effects of a devastating war, and again become rich and prosperous.

The Peruvian people, although composed of different races speaking distinct languages, undoubtedly contain, within themselves, the elements of progress and advancing civilization. The Spanish and Basque families, as well as the half-castes, possess many redeeming virtues, and, on the whole, their relations with the Indians are satisfactory. The domestic ties are strong and enduring, public spirit is not wanting, and the desire for improvement is apparent. The labouring classes are industrious, hardy, and intelligent. The war, from the horrors of which they are suffering, as regards the great mass of the people, is an undeserved calamity.

CHAPTER VI.

THE REPUBLIC OF BOLIVIA.

THE region of Upper Peru, which in 1825 became the
Republic of Bolivia, is in a peculiarly isolated position.
It comprises the lofty plateaux of the Andes, including
half the basin of Lake Titicaca, and the old province
of Charcas, besides a vast Amazonian region. Within
these limits are the famous silver-mines of Potosi, the
gold of Tipuani, the towns of La Paz, Oruro, and
Cochabamba, and the city of Chuquisaca, which was
fixed upon as the capital of the new republic. But
the largest and most important town is La Paz.
When the new State was formed, a strip of coast-line
was secured to it, extending from the river Loa and
ravine of Tocapilla, which are the southern limits of
the Peruvian province of Tarapaca, to the northern
limit of Chile, including the northern part of the
desert of Atacama. But there was only one wretched
port, called Cobija, and the vast wealth of the coast
region in silver and nitrate of soda was then scarcely
suspected.

The main outlet for Bolivian trade is through Peruvian territory to the port of Arica, which involves a long
and difficult land transit as well as heavy dues. There
is another still longer route to an outlet at Buenos

Ayres. The great difficulty in opening good roads, and the consequent isolation, have been the main causes of Bolivian backwardness. To the eastward vast tropical forests and navigable rivers are, it is true, within the bounds of the Republic ; and these virgin lands yield the best coffee and chocolate in the world, besides the chinchona bark which is richest in quinine. But Bolivia has not yet been able to convert her eastern rivers into efficient fluvial highways for her commerce. This important work, though ably projected by Colonel Church and others, is still unaccomplished.

The first Bolivian Congress was installed at Chuquisaca, on May 25th, 1826 ; a Constitution framed by Bolivar was adopted, and General Sucre was elected, in conformity with its principles, as President for life ; but he would only accept office for two years. The people he had undertaken to govern are the Colla or Aymara Indians, whose ancestors formed part of the Ynca empire. They still have to pay the *tribute*, from four to ten Bolivian dollars a year, and live in villages or *comunidades* under a governor or *alcalde*, who is one of themselves. The whole population in 1854 was 519,226, of whom 441,746 were pure Aymara Indians, and 77,480 white and half-castes, or only fifteen per cent. The build of the Aymara is massive without being large. He is short, thick-set, and beardless, broad shouldered, with long body and short legs. The features and profile are decidedly good ; the general expression sad and reflective, with a strong admixture of determination. The chief peculiarity of the race is that the thigh, instead of being longer, is rather shorter than the leg ; and the whole build is admirably adapted for mountain climbing. The Aymara possesses a dogged determination which nothing can shake, and he undoubtedly cherishes the hope of one day crushing his white oppressors. He can march great distances, as much as seventy miles in one day, with a small bag of parched corn as his only food. The foot post from Tacna to La Paz, a distance of 250 miles, was regularly done in five days.

These people, if their hearts are in a cause, make most formidable troops. But as a rule they are indifferent to the miserable treasons and revolutions of the white population. They bide their time.

In 1828 Sucre was driven from Bolivia ; and from 1829 to 1839 the supreme power was, for ten years, in the hands of Andres Santa Cruz, a noble Indian of Huarina, who conceived, and for three years maintained the Peru-Bolivian Confederation. He was succeeded on February 9th, 1839, by General Velasco, who, in 1841, gave place to General José Ballivian ; and in 1847 another revolution gave General Belzu the supreme power in Bolivia until 1855.

In 1854 the Aymara Indians had made arrangements for a general rising against the whites, but the insurrection was indefinitely deferred because the omens were unfavourable. The Aymara Council had taken a brown and a white llama, to represent the two races, and forced them to swim across the river Ilave. The white llama got across while the brown one was carried away by the stream. From this result the Indians drew the conclusion that the white race was still too powerful, and that they must wait.

They, therefore, looked on with indifference at the expulsion of General Belzu in 1855, at the accession of General Cordova, and at the election of Dr. Linares as President of Bolivia in 1858.

The fall of Linares in January, 1861, was the prelude to the accession to power of men of the worst character. General José Maria Acha, from 1861 to 1864, held office during a period of shocking outrages. In October, 1864, a certain General Yanez committed a massacre of important people in La Paz, including the ex-president Cordova. This enraged the Indian population, who assembled in thousands, and put Yanez and his accomplices to death. Acha was succeeded by a soldier of the same stamp, named Melgarejo, who was expelled by the Indians in 1871, and his successor, Morales, was shot in 1872.

During the rule of Melgarejo a Bolivian Navigation Company was formed, in 1868, with a large concession from the Government, with the great object of opening up a route down the rivers Mamoré and Madeira to the Atlantic. The scheme promised to give easy access to half a million square miles of land in Bolivia and Brazil, traversed by great navigable arteries, forming a natural canal system such as is possessed by no other state in the world. Of the people within Bolivian territory two-thirds at least live in the Amazonian basin; yet there is no outlet for their produce. Millions of sheep and alpacas roam over the mountains; vast herds of cattle cover the plains of Moxos; hundreds of tons of the finest coffee in the world rot on the bushes, while only about ten tons a year are sent abroad. The crops of cereals and of sugar-cane are alike without a market. Sixty-five kinds of rare and beautiful cabinet woods stand, untouched by man, in the great virgin forests. The mountains contain veins of silver, copper, and tin. All are useless for lack of means of communication. The failure of the Navigation Company was a great misfortune, yet a country with such boundless resources must have a great future.

The population has increased since the time of Bolivar, yet it is impossible to increase the revenue, for the people have no markets for their produce. There are concessions for roads and public improvements without number, yet nothing but mule tracks between the chief cities. There is a race capable of great progress, a prolific brave and ambitious people with a mighty future before them. All that is needed is a good road to break their isolation.

On the death of Morales, Dr. Frias held the reins of government as President of the Council, until Colonel Adolfo Ballivian, son of the former President, arrived from Europe. Unfortunately this promising statesman died in February, 1874, and was succeeded, after another interval of temporary rule under Dr. Frias, by General Don Hilarion Daza, a military adventurer of the lowest and worst type, in May, 1876. Yet Bolivia has been governed by some men of talent and education. Among these may be mentioned the gallant and upright General Sucre, the able and ambitious Santa Cruz, Dr. Linares and Dr. Frias, who were both statesmen of integrity and patriotic aims ; the accomplished Adolfo Ballivian, and the existing President Campero. It is true, however, that during long intervals Bolivia has suffered under the misrule of military adventurers of a different stamp. Isolation has been the ruin of the country, and when routes are opened, a prosperous future must be in store for it.

CHAPTER VI.

THE REPUBLIC OF CHILE.

ON the declaration of Chilian independence, General O'Higgins was chosen as head of the new State, with the title of Supreme Director. He threw open the ports to foreign trade, invited the settlement of European merchants, and made numerous internal improvements. But he was accused of opposing free institutions, and of striving to retain all power in his own hands. He was therefore called upon to surrender his charge, and he consented, placing the command in the hands of a provisional government in January, 1823. The fallen Director, so ungratefully treated by his own country, retired to Peru, and was generously received in the land of the Yncas. The Government presented him with a fine estate called Montalvan, in the valley of Cañete, where he passed the remainder of his days. O'Higgins died at Lima, in 1842. His colleague, San Martin, died in 1850 at Paris.

On the abdication of O'Higgins, his rival, General Don Ramon Freire, received the important charge— an officer who had fought in all the battles of the war of independence, by the side of his predecessor. Freire convoked a constituent assembly, and this body framed a constitution which was so defective that its working proved to be impracticable. A second assembly was then called together, and Freire resigned his office in 1827. A period of great confusion ensued. There were civil wars, and governments followed each other in quick succession. In 1830, the conservative party, as it was called, got possession of supreme power. The liberals rose in arms under General Freire: in a few months 2000 men were killed and wounded, and finally the liberals were defeated in the battle of Lircay. Freire was taken prisoner and banished.

General Prieto, the victor of Lircay and head of the conservative party or " Pelucones," as they were nicknamed, was elected President on September 17th, 1831, with Don Diego Portales, a very able and ambitious man, as Vice-President. A new constitution was promulgated in 1833, which gave very extensive executive powers to the President. Viewing with continued disgust the success of his opponents, General Freire attempted another insurrectionary movement in 1836. He hired two vessels in Peru, and landed at Chiloe, where he intended to organize his base of operations. But Portales was prepared for him. On putting foot on shore he was arrested, and once more banished from his native land. After some years General Freire was allowed to return, and, living apart from politics, he died in 1851.

Chile was fortunate in becoming the adopted country of two literary men of great ability—a Spaniard named José J. Mora, who was a poet and a scholar; and Don Andres Bello, a native of Venezuela, who resided at Santiago for thirty-six years, as a writer and teacher. Bello was Rector of the University, and his work on the law of nations enjoys a European reputation. The French naturalist, Claude Gaye, was employed to explore the country, and he completed a great work on its natural history in twenty-eight volumes; and Don Andres Gorbea, a Spanish professor, taught mathematics and the exact sciences for nearly thirty years.

The Government of Prieto and Portales conducted the departmental administration with great ability; but their policy was illiberal and retrograde, and they undertook that unjustifiable and aggressive war against the Peru-Bolivian Confederation, which ended in the downfall of Santa Cruz. Portales was assassinated by some mutinous soldiers who had been ordered to embark, in June, 1837; but his policy, which has been discussed in the chapter on Peru, was continued by his successor. In 1840, Mr. William Wheelwright introduced steam navigation into the Pacific, by running two paddle-wheel steamers between Valparaiso and Callao, and afterwards extending the line to Panama.

General Bulnes, the officer who had defeated Santa Cruz at Yungay, succeeded Prieto as President in 1841, with General Cruz as his Minister of War, and Don Manuel Montt in charge of justice and public instruction. This administration was as retrograde and conservative as its predecessor. But literature was encouraged, and the new university of Chile, with Bello as its first rector, was inaugurated by Montt in 1843. Its members especially devoted themselves to the preparation of a national history. Don Andres Bello was entrusted with the work of preparing a civil code, and several schools were established for teaching agriculture, navigation, art, and music. The new consolidated debt was found to amount to 1,700,000*l.*, and the interest has since been regularly paid. The unpaid interest of the public debt was capitalized.

In 1851 Don Manuel Montt was elected President of the Republic, the opposition liberal candidate being General Cruz, a hero of Chacabuco and Yungay. The party of Cruz broke out in rebellion, and Bulnes commanded the constitutional army. On December 8th the sanguinary battle of Longamilla was fought; and the revolt was not suppressed until 4000 men had fallen victims. Under the rule of Montt the railway from Valparaiso to Santiago was commenced, the coal mines of Lota were opened, gas was introduced in the principal towns, many German colonists settled near Valdivia in the extreme south of the republic, and Port Montt was founded. Schools and public libraries multiplied rapidly, and an astronomical observatory was formed on the hill of Santa Lucia, in Santiago. Professor Philippi arrived to teach natural history at the university, while Pissis made a topographical and geological survey, and completed a map of the republic. At the same time all attempts to introduce more progressive institutions were violently suppressed, and many liberal statesmen were banished.

At last insurrections broke out in several places in 1859, and during four months a civil war raged, causing the death of 5000 men. The liberal chief, Pedro Leon Gallo, held possession of Copiapo, and having defeated the Government troops in the battle of Los Loros on March 14th, he entered Coquimbo. But in the next month he was beaten by General Vidaurre at Cerro Grande, and his forces dispersed. In the following September Vidaurre himself was killed in an outbreak at Valparaiso ; and the insurrection was suppressed with difficulty. The most influential Liberals, such as Gallo, Vicuña Mackenna, and Santa Maria, were banished. The streets of Lima were full of Chilian exiles.

Don José Joaquin Perez succeeded Montt as President in 1861. He had been a diplomatist in Europe, was not committed to strong views, and was thus able to rally round him the statesmen of both parties. In September, 1863, he opened the railway from Valparaiso to Santiago.

Perez found a strong liberal party which desired political and constitutional reform, and was opposed to the government of Montt, the conservatives called *Pelucones*, who were opposed to reform, and the nationalists who had served under Montt. There was a coalition between the moderate liberals and conservatives to which Perez entrusted power, while the advanced liberals under Gallo and the brothers Matta formed a fourth party of radicals. The war with Spain, from 1864 to 1866, was an episode which led to no ulterior consequences, except an offensive and defensive alliance between Peru and Chile.

In 1871 Don Federico Errazuriz was elected President in succession to Perez, and he formed a conservative ministry. But at the same time a great reform was introduced, by the abolition of all ecclesiastical tribunals. Henceforward the clergy were to be tried, without special privileges, by the civil and criminal courts of the republic; while the new penal code imposed penalties on preachers who incited to disobedience of the laws. These reforms separated President Errazuriz and the moderate liberals from the conservative party, and the coalition came to an end. Public works were pushed forward with great energy. The national debt was largely increased, and there were recurring deficits. In this unsatisfactory financial condition Errazuriz resigned his post. He was succeeded in 1876 by Don Anibal Pinto, a brother-in-law of General Bulnes, and son-in-law of General Cruz.

In 1877 the population of Chile was reported to be 2,136,724 souls, having doubled since 1835, when it was 1,013,332. The capital contains 180,000, and the principal port of Valparaiso 100,926 souls. There were 806 public elementary schools, with 62,224 scholars of both sexes, besides half as many private schools. Higher education is provided for by the university, which confers degrees, and seventeen colleges in the different provinces. The public expenditure on education amounted to 233,414*l.* The budget of 1876 for ordinary expenditure was 3,366,080*l.*

In time of peace there is a small but thoroughly efficient army of 4000 officers and men, and a national guard 25,000 strong. The navy had been increased since the Spanish war, gradually and systematically, until it was by far the most powerful in the Pacific.

There is also an admirably organized hydrographic service.

The ordinary revenue amounted in 1874 to 3,080,164, and in 1875 to 3,330,741. It is raised from customs and excise duties, a tobacco monopoly, a tax on revenues derived from land, on transfers and licences. The foreign debt amounted in 1879 to 7,895,200*l*., and the internal debt to 2,185,920*l*. ; the charge for interest being 939,403*l*. In 1878 the value of the exports was about 8,500,000*l*. (4,381,466*l*. mineral, and 2,168,390*l*. agricultural produce), and of imports 7,000,000*l*.

Chile has, owing to special circumstances and her advantageous position, made more steady and greater advances in civilization than the other Spanish republics. While Bolivia labours under the difficulties of her isolation, and the progress of Peru has been retarded by a similar disadvantage as regards several important provinces, Chile consists of a long and narrow strip of country, easily accessible at all points by short routes from the sea, and with railroads connecting the principal towns. While the population of Peru and Bolivia consists of a noble but long-oppressed race of Indians, with a small governing class of Spanish descent, in Chile (except in the extreme south) the amalgamation of races has been completed, and the population consists of one people speaking one language. The upper classes are Basques or Spaniards, the rest descendants of half-castes.

The Chilian Republic owed her prosperity and her position among other American republics to the faithful fulfilment of her engagements, to the honourable

character of her upper classes, and to the laborious
endurance and capacity for toil of her population.
All who know the brave little nation which nestles under
the shadow of the mighty Andes must wish it well.
But with greater advantages the Chilians ought not
to have forgotten that they have greater responsi-
bilities.   Their duty was to have discarded a policy of
encroachment and conquest, and to have striven to
influence their neighbours, who are also their kindred,
by a policy of friendliness, forbearance, and good-
will.

Part II.

THE WAR.

CHAPTER I.

CAUSE OF THE WAR.

In the extreme south of Peru the arid strip of land
along the Pacific coast, between the Andes and the
sea, forms the province of Tarapaca. Further south
stretches the desert of Atacama, which was included
in Alto Peru, the modern Bolivia. When the Republic
of Bolivia was created, it was agreed that its limits
should be conterminous with those of Alto Peru, so
far as the Atacama region was concerned. Both
Tarapaca and Atacama appeared to be forbidding
wildernesses. The silver-mines of Guantajaya and
Santa Rosa, near Iquique in Tarapaca, were known.
Otherwise the deserts were believed to be of no value.

But in course of time it was discovered that these
deserts abounded in mineral wealth, that both in
Tarapaca and Atacama there were inexhaustible beds
of nitrate of soda and borax, that in Atacama there
were some of the richest silver-mines in the world,
and that guano deposits had accumulated on the
rocky promontories of the coast.

If this wealth had not been brought to light, the

rights of Peru and Bolivia to their respective territories would never have been disputed. Chilian
capital was embarked in some of the enterprises for
utilizing the desert products, labourers from Chile
immigrated in considerable numbers; and a neighbour, who was both powerful and astute, began to
covet this Naboth's vineyard. The usual question of
a disputed boundary was soon raised.

The rights of the case are as follows. When the
South American republics became independent their
limits were, by general agreement, fixed according to
the *uti possidetis* of the year 1810, that is to say that
the boundaries of Spanish provinces, as recognized at
that time, were adopted as the boundaries of the
republics. On this principle the boundaries of the
Bolivian province of Atacama, on the Pacific coast,
extend to the southern limit of Peru on one side and
to the northern limit of Chile on the other. Both
had been clearly defined before the year 1810. The
Peruvian limit, which is that of the province of
Tarapaca, commences on the coast near Tocapilla in
22° 33′ S., and passes up the ravine of Duende to the
river Loa. It was carefully delineated in 1628, and
the boundary-marks are recorded in a document
which is still extant. The northern limit of Chile was
fixed at a place called El Paposo, in 25° 2′ S.[1]

In 1776, when the viceroyalty of Buenos Ayres

[1] The map of La Rochette (1807) places Paposo in 25° 46′ S.
Colonel Ondaza's map (1859) in 25° 33′ S. The Admiralty chart in
25° 2′ S.; with which the " Geografia Nautica de la Republica de
Chile," by Vidal Gormaz (p. 108) agrees. Vidal Gormaz notices that
in the old maps Paposo is placed forty miles too far south.

was created, orders were given that the province of Charcas should be included in it. The limits of Charcas (modern Bolivia) were then said to be well known, and to have been defined in the ninth law for the Indies (Titulo 15, Book ii.). The coast province of Atacama was there declared to extend to the first Chilian inhabited place at Paposo. The same boundary is given in the official descriptions by Dr. Cosme Bueno.[2] It is shown on De la Rochette's valuable map of South America, published in 1807, which was based on original Spanish authorities, including Malespina and the " Mapa de las fronteras del Reyno del Peru, 1787." Moreover this boundary was tacitly accepted by the Chilians. In their official map, accompanying the work of Claudio Gaye, Chile ends at Paposo. After Fitz Roy's survey, when the sailing directions were being prepared, inquiries were made of the Chilian authorities as to the position of the boundary, and it was placed to the south of 25° S.[3] On Colonel Ondaza's official map of Bolivia (1859) the boundary is placed correctly at Paposo. The topographical map of Chile by Pissis only extends to Copiapo, 27° 20′ S. It will thus be seen that the boundary between Chile and Bolivia, according to the *uti possidetis* of 1810, was south of 25° S.; and that this was acknowledged by implication, even on the part of the Chilians themselves.

---

[2] See Diccionario Historico-Biografico del Peru, por Manuel de Mendiburu, iv. p. 198.

[3] " South American Pilot." Part II. Sixth edition, 1865, p. 327. " Between the bight of Hueso Parado and Punta San Pedro :" that is in 25° 30′ S.

It was only when the great value of Atacama was discovered that any question was raised. Then Chile laid claim to the 23rd parallel. It has been shown that her boundary was south of 25° S. This was, therefore, an unjustifiable claim, and as such all subsequent arrangements that were based upon it, were vitiated. The Bolivian Government must have been ignorant of the rights of the case, for they appear to have looked upon the consent of Chile to accept the 24th parallel as a concession. Chile had no more right to 24° S. as a boundary than she had to 23° S. But General Melgarejo, the President of Bolivia, agreed to a treaty with Chile, in that sense, bearing date the 10th of August, 1866. It, however, was never ratified by the Bolivian Congress. Chile consented to withdraw her more exaggerated claim, and to adopt 24° S. as her boundary.[4] In return for this pretended concession it was further stipulated that Chile should receive half the value of customs dues from minerals exported between the 23rd and 24th parallels, while Bolivia was to have the same privilege as regards the coast-line between the 25th and 24th parallels. As the whole territory in question belonged by right to Bolivia this was a tolerably cool arrangement on the part of Chile, especially as the rich deposits are situated to the north of 24° S.

The object was gained. The thin edge of the wedge had been driven in. Chile acquired recognized rights within Bolivian territory, which were pretty sure to

---

[4] The Chilians then erected a boundary pyramid on the coast, fifty feet above the level of the sea, in 23° 58′ 11″ S. (intended as 24° S.) to mark their new temporary boundary. Vidal Gormaz (*ubi sup.*), p. 115.

be infringed in some way or other. As this result was almost certain, it may fairly be assumed that it was intended. For it enabled Chile to continue a dispute which could only lead to some opening for active interference, the forerunner of annexation. The Chilian share of the dues was not paid, the Bolivian officials did not keep their accounts properly: in short, there was no difficulty about finding new grievances. In 1870 the rich silver-mines of Caracoles were discovered north of 24° S., and Antofagasta is the nearest port. The Bolivian Government, in consideration of receiving a sum of $10,000, granted a concession to a company which was to work the nitrate deposits, construct a mole at Antofagasta, and open a road to Caracoles, with depôts of water. The company made a railroad instead of a road, and large works were undertaken for the extraction of nitrate. This Antofagasta Company, worked with English and Chilian capital, was under English management, and largely employed Chilian labour.

In this state of affairs the year 1873 opened, when Colonel Adolfo Ballivian was elected President of Bolivia during his absence in Europe. He was an accomplished and enlightened statesman, and was thoroughly alarmed at the complicated relations between his country and Chile, foreseeing their obvious tendency. He had an opportunity of discussing the subject with Don Manuel Pardo, the President of Peru, on his way to Bolivia, and the result was that a treaty was signed between the two republics, with the object of guaranteeing the integrity of their respective territories. The treaty bears date

February 6th, 1873. It was approved by the National Assemblies of Peru and Bolivia in the following summer.

The preamble of this treaty declared its object to be the mutual guarantee of the independence, sovereignty, and territorial integrity of the two countries, and defence against exterior aggression. Each contracting party reserved the right of deciding whether the danger threatening the other came within the intention of the treaty. But when a *casus fœderis* was once declared, the treaty obligations were to come into force. It was next provided that all conciliatory means possible were to be employed to avoid a rupture ; and especially that a settlement through the arbitration of a third power was to be sought. It was agreed that, as opportunity offered, the adhesion of other American States to the defensive alliance should be invited. An additional article provided that the treaty should be kept secret, so long as the two contracting parties did not consider its publication to be necessary.

It has since been alleged that the additional article was successfully maintained in force, and that the existence of the treaty was unknown to the Chilian Government when war against Bolivia was commenced. This, however, was not the case. The Argentine Republic was officially invited to become a party to the treaty, and the question was discussed in 1877 in the Senate at Buenos Ayres, the Chilian Minister there being informed of the existence of the treaty.[5]

---

[5] "Cueston Chileno-argentina," por M. Bilbao (Buenos Ayres, 1878), p. 27.

The Chilian Minister at La Paz knew of the treaty in 1874, he hurried forward negotiations in consequence of his knowledge, and he referred to the treaty in a work which he published at Santiago in 1876.[6] If Chile herself had magnanimously become another party to the defensive alliance, although she would not have extended her limits by violence and conquest, she would, on the other hand, have maintained her former reputation as a peace-loving and civilizing power, to which she can no longer lay claim. Her objections to the treaty could only arise from intentions which were neither peaceful nor civilizing.

Colonel Ballivian died in February, 1874, and soon afterwards the Chilian Envoy, Don Carlos Walker Martinez, who was acquainted with the contents of the Secret Treaty of 1873, began to press the acceptance of another arrangement upon the Bolivian Government, which was then represented by Dr. Frias, the Minister of Foreign Affairs being Don Mariano Baptista. This new negotiation resulted in another treaty, dated the 6th of August, 1874, by which the Chilian claim to half the proceeds of export duties in Bolivian ports was withdrawn. But by Article IV., all Chilian industries established on the Bolivian coast were to be free of duty for a space of twenty-five years, and this was to be granted "in consideration of concessions on several important points agreed to by Chile."[7] That is to say that Bolivia

6 "Pájinas de un viaje al través de la America de Sur," por Carlos Walker Martinez (Santiago, 1876), p. 217.

7 "En virtud de concesiones otorgadas en diversos puntos de importancia por Chile."

was to give up her right to levy duties at her own
ports, because Chile consented to waive a claim to
Bolivian territory which was baseless and unjust.
The Bolivian Congress declined to ratify this treaty,
which consequently never had any binding force.
Bolivia, in her isolated position, naturally and justly
looked to her mineral wealth for some addition to
her revenue. The National Assembly decreed, on
February 14th, 1878, that the concessions made .by
the executive to the Antofagasta Company were approved on condition that an export duty of ten
centavos the cwt. was paid on the nitrate. This was
acknowledged to be a very moderate impost, and the
Chilians have actually enforced a higher duty since
their occupation.

In December, 1878, the English manager of the
Antofagasta Company, Mr. George Hicks, was called
upon by the Prefect of the province to pay the duty
which had become due since the promulgation of the
law. Mr. Hicks refused payment, and the Prefect
ordered the sale of so much of the company's property by auction, as would cover the amount due.
It was fairly open to argument whether Mr. Hicks
and the Antofagasta Company were Chilian subjects,
whether the injustice of the original claim to Bolivian
territory did not invalidate any subsequent agreement
arising from it, and whether the refusal of the Bolivian
Congress to ratify the Treaty of 1874 did not destroy
its binding force. There certainly never was a dispute more obviously suited for arbitration, if a friendly
settlement was desired. But it was not desired. Without declaring war the Chilian Government commenced

hostile operations as soon as the news from Antofagasta arrived, and seized upon the Bolivian ports of Antofagasta, Cobija, and Tocapilla; the invading troops at the same time marching into the interior, and beginning the war by bloodshed at Calama.

Peru offered her good offices as a mediator. No pretext had as yet been alleged for making war upon her, but there was a grievance which was eventually used in order to establish a case. This grievance arose in the following way.

Don Manuel Pardo, the President of Peru, in his efforts to alleviate the financial difficulties of his country, and as almost a last hope, resolved to make the nitrate deposits of Tarapaca a Government monopoly. The law to this effect was promulgated on January 18, 1873, and was to come into force two months afterwards. The State was to pay a fixed price to producers, and was to be the sole exporter. But this measure was financially a failure; and another law of May 28, 1875, authorized the State to buy up all the nitrate works. The legislation relating to Tarapaca may have been unwise, and it may have been disadvantageous to the English, Chilian, and other speculators who had embarked their capital in the nitrate works; but it cannot be pretended that Peru was not within her right in adopting these measures. They could not form a just pretext for war,[8] but they have been made use of as a grievance

---

[8] "Necesario es confesar que para adoptar aquella u otra medida de igual índole, hallábase el Presidente Pardo bajo el amparo del derecho estricto de las naciones, porque era dueño de lejislar sobre cosa propia domestica como mejor viera convenir a los intereses de su patria."—Vicuña Mackenna.

in the long diplomatic notes which have from time to
time been put forward by Chile in justification of her
aggressive policy.

Stripped of rhetoric and of suggestions of motives,
the manifesto of the Chilian Minister of Foreign
Affairs in defence of the war, published after the war
was virtually over (December 21st, 1881), contains
this grievance against Peru, and nothing more. Peru,
he complains, had established a nitrate monopoly in
her own dominions, which would injure the prospects
of Chilian capitalists and labourers. Now it could
not be pretended that Peru had not the right to make
any such arrangement within her own territory ; and
yet the verbose and rhetorical manifesto gives no
other explanation and raises no other point. It is
clear, therefore, that the policy adopted by Peru as
regards her own internal affairs was the only real
cause of offence, and that it was not a just pretext
for war. The conclusion is inevitable that Chile
made war on her neighbour without just cause. At
last this has been confessed. "The *salitre* territory
of Tarapaca," admits the Chilian Minister, "was the
real and direct cause of the war." Consequently, we
may fairly add, the war was unjust.

The offered mediation was, however, accepted at
the time, and Don José Antonio Lavalle was received
at Santiago as special envoy. It would appear that
the Peruvian diplomatist was ignorant of the Treaty
of 1873, and even denied its existence when the
Chilian Minister referred to it, though afterwards he
was supplied with a copy. But the more astute
Chilians had had full cognizance of it since 1876

certainly, if not since 1874, and they have endeavoured to make capital out of Lavalle's ignorance.
The Peruvian envoy's efforts were properly devoted
to mediation. Chile had already invaded Bolivian
territory, and with this serious fact before him, Señor
Lavalle made the following proposals—first, that
Chile should evacuate the Bolivian port of Antofagasta while an arbitrator should decide the question
in dispute ; second, that there should be a neutral
administration in the port and territory so evacuated,
under the guarantee of the three Republics ; third,
that the customs and other revenues of the territory
should first be applied to the local administration,
the surplus being divided equally between Chile and
Bolivia.

If Chile had desired peace, this Peruvian proposal
was a fair basis for negotiation. But Chile had no 
such desire. On the contrary, she intended to extend
the war by fixing a quarrel on Peru. The defensive
treaty only obliged Peru to make common cause with
Bolivia, in the event of arbitration and all other
means of obtaining a peaceful solution having failed.
Chile took care that they should not be tried. The
proposals of Señor Lavalle were declined. Demands
that could not honourably be complied with were
made. All defensive preparations on the part of
Peru must cease ; the Treaty of 1873 must be abro-
gated ; neutrality must be declared at once. All
things being ready, the Chilian Government dismissed Señor Lavalle, and declared war upon Peru
on the 5th of April, 1879.

The official notes and declarations on both sides

are very contradictory and very diffuse; but facts speak for themselves. The pretexts for making war were unjust and baseless. The intentions of Chile were conquest and annexation; those of Peru and Bolivia were the defence of their own territory.

CHAPTER II.

THE contest between Peru and Chile was one, the result of which depended entirely upon the possession of the sea. All the Peruvian railways were at right angles with the coast, and there were no means of conveying troops except by sea. The distances are enormous, and the marches are over vast desert tracts, without shade or water, the fertile valleys occurring at long intervals. Consequently an invader in possession of the sea can select his point of attack at pleasure, and, so far as the region between the Andes and the sea is concerned, its conquest is then only a question of time.

Chile had been quietly but busily increasing and strengthening her navy for the last six years, and when she declared war upon her neighbours it was very formidable. It consisted, in the first place, of two powerful ironclads of the newest construction, which were designed by Reed, and built at Hull in 1874-75. These are the sister ships *Almirante Cochrane* and *Blanco Encalada*, of 3560 tons, and 2920 horse-power. They carry six 9-inch M. L. Armstrong guns of 12 tons, some light guns, and two Nordenfelt machine guns. The armour is nine inches thick at the water-line, and six to eight inches round the battery. During the war they only had lower masts and fore-yards, with iron shields round the tops. They are both fitted with twin screws.

Chile also had two sister corvettes, the *Chacabuco* and *O'Higgins*, of 1670 tons and 800 horse-power, armed with three 150-pounder, 7-ton Armstrong guns, and four 40-pounders; the *Magallanes*, armed with one 150-pounder and two small guns; the *Abtao*, an old corvette with three 150-pounders; the *Covadonga*, a wooden screw gun-boat (captured from Spain in 1866) of 600 tons, and armed with two 70-pounders and three small guns; the *Esmeralda*, a wooden corvette, built in 1854, of 850 tons, carrying twelve 40-pounders on the upper deck; and ten steam transports.

While Chile had been arming, Peru, in order to mitigate her financial difficulties, had been retrenching. In 1878 we find her turret-ship conveying a commission of scientific naval officers to Payta, consisting of Captain Camilo Carrillo, the Director of the Naval School,[1] and Professor of Astronomy and Spherical Trigonometry at the Lima University, two commanders, two lieutenants, and two students of the Naval School, to observe the passage of Mercury over the sun's disc on the 6th of May. The Peruvian navy was particularly interested in this observation,

---

[1] The Peruvian naval school was established in 1870. The number of students was thirty; and there were four exhibitions of $16 a month enjoyed by four of the students. A preparatory school on board the steamer *Meteoro*, of which Captain Carrillo was also director, was opened in 1874: and there were 140 students.

because it was the same by which the illustrious Humboldt decided the longitude of Lima in 1802. Training schools were being established at Callao ; young officers, such as Juan Salaverry and others, were turning their attention to the survey of navigable affluents of the Amazon. The thoughts of the service were rather of peaceful scientific work than of war. No new men-of-war had been obtained within the last ten years. The existing vessels were of old type, and none could successfully cope with the new ironclads of Chile.

The Peruvian turret-ship *Huascar* was built at Birkenhead by Messrs. Laird in 1866. She is 200 feet long, 1130 tons, and 300 horse-power. The armour round her revolving turret is only five and a-half inches in thickness, and there is a belt of four and a-half inches. Such armour was worse than useless against the fire of the Chilian ironclads, for the shells penetrated and burst inside. She was armed with two 10-inch Dahlgren 300-pounders and two 40-pounder Whitworths. Peru also had a broadside ironclad of the old type, built in London in 1865, under instructions from Captain Garcia y Garcia. This was the *Independencia*, 215 feet long, 2004 tons, and 550 horse-power, with only four and a-half inch armour. She was armed with twelve 70-pounders on the main deck, and two 150-pounders, four 32-pounders, and four 9-pounders on the upper deck. There were also two wooden corvettes. Of these, the *Union*, was 242 feet long, 1150 tons, 400 horse-power, armed with twelve 70-pounders and one 9-pounder. She was capable of going thirteen knots.

The *Pilcomayo* is properly the *Putumayo*, an Amazonian affluent, after which she was to have been named. It was a mistake of the painter. She is 171 feet long, 600 tons, 180 horse-power, and was armed with ten guns—two 70-pounders, four 40 pounders, and four 12-pounders.

These four vessels composed the Peruvian navy, for the antiquated monitors *Atahualpa* and *Manco Capac* must not be included in the list of sea-going ships. They were sister ships, built in the United States, and purchased at an extravagant price in 1869. They were 253 feet long and 2100 tons, with ten inches of iron armour on the turrets. The turrets were armed with two 15-inch smooth-bore Rodman guns. These structures were nothing more than floating forts. The *Atahualpa* was permanently stationed at Callao, and the *Manco Capac* at Arica.

The two Chilian ironclads, if well manned and properly handled, were much more than a match for the navy of Peru. The Chilians had double the number of vessels, twice the aggregate tonnage, and more than double the weight of metal. The Chilian fleet had some officers who had served for a few years in the English navy. Several were of English extraction, and the number of English names that occur in the Chilian official war despatches is surprising ; such as Condell, Cox, Christie, Edwards, Leighton, Lynch, Macpherson, Pratt, Rogers, Simpson, Smith, Souper, Stephens, Thomson, Walker, Warner, Williams, Wilson, and Wood.

The Chilian army, though on a peace footing, had been very carefully trained for active service, and supplied with the latest inventions and improvements. The Chilian lower orders are descendants of half-castes; all speak Spanish, and they have lost all tradition of their Indian ancestry. They make good fighting machines, and were in a fairly respectable state of discipline. But they are without pity or scruple when excited by drink and success. Their cruelty was only too surely proved by the extraordinary proportion the dead bore to the wounded on the fields of battle. They were well clothed and fed, their uniform being a tunic, trousers, and cap, made of a sort of *karker* or brown holland, and a pair of untanned, brown leather boots, well adapted for the kind of country over which they had to march. They were armed with the Gras or Comblain rifles, both good weapons.

The Chilian cavalry are fine stalwart fellows, admirably mounted, and armed with sabres and Winchester repeating rifles. They are much brutalized by harassing warfare with the Araucanian Indians, and seldom give quarter. The artillery are especially effective, with well-found accoutrements and mules in fine condition. Their field-guns, of European manufacture, are principally Krupps and Armstrongs, and they also have Gatling and Nordenfeldt machine guns. Their 12-pounder Krupp guns have a range of 4000 yards, so that they can commence an action by heavy artillery fire which cannot be returned. These enormous advantages over the Peruvian troops are sufficient to account for the success of the Chilian operations. When on a peace footing the army of Chile consisted of 2500 infantry,

800 artillery, and 700 cavalry; besides a large force of 25,000 national guards or militia, which was raised to 55,000 on the declaration of war. The Atacama and Copiapo militia regiments were mainly composed of miners; the Navales were boatmen from Valparaiso, whilst the Valparaiso regiment was recruited from mechanics of that town.

When the war broke out the Peruvian army had, on the other hand, been very considerably reduced. In 1860 the army consisted of 9500 men and 3940 gendarmerie; and in 1870 of 12,000 men. Don Manuel Pardo, on succeeding to office in 1872, made great reductions, retaining only a small effective force. So that in 1879, although there had since been an increase, the nominal numbers were only 4500; five battalions of infantry of 500 officers and men each, three regiments of artillery (1000 officers and men), two brigades of cavalry (780 officers and men), besides 5400 gendarmerie. The force cannot be homogeneous as the infantry is mainly composed of pure Ynca Indians speaking Quichua, the cavalry and artillery of negroes or half-castes. The dress of the infantry is white-cotton cloth, and they were armed with the Martini-Peabody rifle. The very small force of cavalry was wretchedly mounted, but the negro horsemen are often muscular fellows, accustomed to the management of horses and mules. They were armed with Winchester repeating rifles. The artillery was almost useless against the Krupp guns of Chile. It mainly consisted of field-guns of Lima manufacture, and of a very inferior kind. The rations of the Peruvian soldiers were ample, being

1½ lb. of beef daily, besides a pound of bread and vegetables.

(The army is recruited by force, so that a more lawless tyranny than the Spanish *mita* has been introduced by the emancipated colonists. Villages are surrounded, and all the men that can be caught are driven away to serve in the ranks. The system is as objectionable as anything that existed in Spanish times, because it is put in force in defiance of the law. So strong is the feeling of the Peruvian people generally against this oppression that, in the reformed constitution, promulgated on November 25th, 1860, forced recruiting was declared to be a crime.[2] Yet military dictators and presidents have hitherto been able to set the laws enacted by civilians at defiance.

The Ynca Indians were an imperial and conquering race. They are sober, obedient, brave, and capable of enduring hunger and thirst and fatigue with more courageous endurance than any troops in the world. They are unequalled in their power of making long marches over desert and mountainous tracts without food. No torture can force from them a confession or a secret. When they are dragged from their homes to defend the quarrels of Spanish creoles in which they take no interest, they will seldom fight, and they often seek the first opportunity of returning home. But when they once believe in a commander, as they did in Castilla, they become undaunted soldiers. If love and home associations are combined with that confidence, they are not easily conquered. These considerations explain the

---

[2] " El reclutamiento es un crimen." Titulo xvi. 123.

strange contrasts in the conduct of Ynca soldiers on different occasions.

The wives of Peruvian soldiers, called *rabonas*, are allowed to follow the regiments in which their husbands are serving. They receive no rations, but subsist on a share of what is served out to their husbands. These faithful and enduring creatures follow the army during long, weary marches, carrying the knapsacks and cooking utensils, besides being occasionally burdened by having an infant strapped on their backs. Directly a halt is called, the *rabona* busies herself in preparing food for her husband, and generally has something ready for him the moment he is dismissed from the ranks. In battle she is to be found tending the wounded, administering to their wants, and alleviating suffering caused by intense thirst. Water is very scarce and precious in the sandy deserts of Peru, but the *rabona* generally has the means of moistening the parched lips of a wounded man. Again, she may be seen seeking the prostrate form of some loved one, and imprinting on his lips the last kiss, heedless of the bullets that whistle round her. Callous to the dangers to which she is exposed, and indifferent to the issue of the fight, her thought is to find and succour those she loves. Many of these poor women are killed in battle.

The Bolivian army consisted of Colla (so called Aymara) Indians, who are more thick-set than the Yncas, and with a build even better adapted to mountain climbing. Without shoes, without food or shelter, these Aymara soldiers can endure fatigues under which any European or Chilian would sink, with only a few grains of toasted maize and a pellet of coca. But Bolivia was taken as much by surprise as Peru. The Government only possessed 1500 Remington rifles; the rest of the army had the old flint-lock muskets.

Shortly after the declaration of war a presidential decree raised the nominal strength of the Peruvian army to 40,000; and this was followed by a subsequent order, dated December 26th, 1879, by which all the male population of Peru, between the ages of eighteen and thirty, was called upon to join the regular army; while all between thirty and sixty were to be embodied in the reserve.

CHAPTER III.

THE Chilian conquests began on the 14th of February, 1879, when Colonel Sotomayor, with 500 men, suddenly seized upon the Bolivian port of Antofagasta. He then marched into the interior, and occupied the station of the rich silver-mines of Caracoles on the 16th. The Bolivians were entirely unprepared for this attack, which was made without any declaration of war. Their coast province is for the most part a sandy desert, broken by rocky and barren ranges, thinly inhabited, and without defence of any kind.

General Daza, the President of Bolivia, on receiving the news, declared war upon Chile on the 1st of March.

The Prefect, Dr. Zapata, and the other Bolivian authorities, fled to Calama, a small village on the banks of the river Loa, about eighty miles from the sea, and nearly due north of Caracoles. It is on the road into the interior from the port of Cobija to

Potosi, and is inhabited chiefly by muleteers and their families. Here the Prefect was joined by Dr. Cabrera (sub-prefect), and a few officers who fled from Caracoles on the approach of the Chilians ; and at last 135 brave but badly-armed countrymen, including the officials and officers from the coast, were assembled at Calama. Taken by surprise, separated by vast deserts and chains of mountains from all help, this little band of patriots stood at bay, to strike at least one blow before the province was lost.

Colonel Sotomayor began his march from Caracoles to Calama, with a force of 600 men, including infantry, cavalry, and artillery, on the 21st of March. The distance is about fifty miles, and the troops were followed by twenty carts laden with provisions, forage, and timber for making a bridge over the river Loa. The colonel travelled in a comfortable carriage drawn by four strong mules ; while the soldiers took turns on the carts. On the night of the 22nd they reached the head of the ravine leading down to the valley of the Loa, almost in front of Calama, which is on the northern side of the river. The ford of Topater leads to the village. The bridge had been destroyed. Further up the stream there is another ford called Huaita.

Early in the morning the cavalry was divided into two bodies ; one under Ensign Quesada, advancing to the ford of Huaita, the other towards Topater, led by Captain Vargas and Lieutenant Parra. The infantry followed, also in two columns. The artillery was stationed on the hill facing the Topater ford. The object was for the cavalry to drive the enemy from the shelter of walls, houses, and heaps of forage, before the infantry advanced.

Dr. Cabrera, who directed the movements of the Bolivians, posted his men on the road leading up the valley, at a height which enabled them to command the approaches from the fords. When he saw the invaders advancing to the ford of Topater, at six a.m., he ordered a gallant youth, named Eduardo Avaroa, a native of Calama, to descend to the river and open fire upon them from behind the huts. Poor young Avaroa was just married, and had a happy home among the clover fields of Calama. He crossed the river with twelve men, and prepared to defend the pass. He saw the overwhelming force approaching, but he had no thought of forsaking the post that had been entrusted to him. There he fell fighting, and when he had fallen his body was run through by the sword of an advancing Chilian. The cavalry under Vargas then crossed the ford, and was received with a well-directed volley from twenty-four men posted on the other side, which emptied seven of the Chilian saddles. The rest dismounted and were driven back towards the village. At that moment the main force of infantry, led by Colonel Ramirez, marched over the prostrate body of the young hero Avaroa, and crossed the river ; while the artillery opened fire. For three hours the little band of patriots sustained the unequal fight, and then retreated up the road over the Andes to Potosi, leaving twenty dead on the field. Calama is one out of the only two villages in which the nearly extinct Atacama language is spoken.

This was the first encounter in the war; and it redounded to the credit of the handful of men who strove to defend their country against such tremendous odds.

After the action Colonel Sotomayor, with an escort, rode down the valley of the Loa to Tocapilla, where he found that both that port and Cobija had been taken possession of by the fleet under Rear-Admiral Williams. On the 29th Sotomayor returned to Antofagasta, Ramirez having remained in command at Calama.

The delay in declaring war on Peru, while the Chilian president and his minister were playing at diplomacy with Señor Lavalle, gave time for the aggressors to occupy all the Bolivian ports and to prepare their fleet. So that when the mask was thrown aside on April 5th, a fleet under Admiral Williams at once established a blockade at Iquique, the principal port of the Peruvian province of Tarapaca, and began to harry the coast. The Chilian ships suddenly appeared off the different ports, destroyed the lighters and launches, broke the machinery for loading vessels with guano, and demolished piers and moles. If there was any show of resistance, as at Mollendo on the 17th of April, they opened fire on the houses.

On the morning of the 18th of April the ironclad *Blanco Encalada*, accompanied by the *O'Higgins*, proceeded to the bombardment of a defenceless town. Pisagua, on the coast of Tarapaca, was at that time a place containing about 4000 inhabitants, a large proportion of whom were foreigners engaged in the shipment of nitrate of soda. The Chilians, without communicating with the authorities on shore, despatched their boats with the object of destroying the numerous launches used for the shipment of nitrate, which were moored off the custom-house, at the south end of the town. Most of the launches were owned by foreigners, and were therefore neutral property. When the owners became aware of the intentions of the Chilians, they opened fire with their rifles, and this was of course returned. A few Peruvian soldiers—the garrison of the town—who had remained in the custom-house until this moment, made their way to the shelter of some rocks, and also began to fire at the enemy. The men-of-war replied with their heavy guns, a shell from which set the town on fire.

An attempt was then made by the Chilians to land, which was frustrated by the Peruvian soldiers. Still the bombardment continued. Neutral flags, which were displayed from some houses, were disregarded, and shot and shell fell indiscriminately about the town. In the drawing-room of the British Vice-Consul's house one poor woman received her death wound from a shell which, at the same time, wounded a poor little child who was lying on her breast. Another entered the bedroom where the Vice-Consul's wife was engaged in collecting a few necessaries before leaving the house. It passed within a few inches of her head, while others crashed through the house, dealing death and destruction around. By noon the greater part of the town was in flames, when the Chilians, apparently satisfied with their work, steamed out of the bay. On the following day the remains of three women were found amid the ashes of the British vice-consulate, which was completely destroyed.

The excuses made for the bombardment of defence-less towns, like Pisagua and Mollendo, were that there was some show of resistance to the destruction of property.

CHAPTER IV.

DESTRUCTION OF A CHILIAN CORVETTE BY THE "HUASCAR"—LOSS OF THE "INDEPENDENCIA."

ON May 16th, 1879, the President of Peru, General Prado, left Callao to take command of the army in the field, then assembling at Tacna in the south. His squadron consisted of the *Huascar*, commanded by that heroic seaman Miguel Grau, the *Independencia*, Captain Moore, and three transports.

By a curious coincidence the Chilian Admiral Williams, whose flag was hoisted on board the ironclad *Blanco Encalada*, had determined to make a reconnaissance to the northward as far as Callao, and he left Iquique on the same day that the Peruvian squadron set out for the south. The blockade of Iquique was entrusted to two small vessels, the *Esmeralda* and the *Covadonga*. As the Chilians kept well out to sea that their movements might not be observed from the shore, and as the Peruvians hugged the coast on their way southward, the rival squadrons never sighted each other.

After landing the President at Arica, Captain Grau, who had obtained intelligence of the departure of the Chilian Admiral, determined to proceed at once to Iquique, with the *Huascar* and *Independencia*, and attack the small wooden corvette and gunboat which had been left to continue the blockade. Early in the morning of the 21st of May the Peruvian ironclads appeared off the port of Iquique, and at daylight they sighted the Chilian corvette *Esmeralda*, commanded by Captain Arthur Pratt, and the *Covadonga* gunboat, under Captain Condell. Grau singled out the *Esmeralda* for attack, leaving the *Independencia* to chase the gunboat. At about eight a.m. Captain Pratt saw his danger, hoisted the signal to prepare for action, and endeavoured to entice his larger enemy into shoal water by steaming in towards the land. But, at this critical moment, one of his boilers burst, which reduced his speed from about six to less than three knots.

It is impossible to help being struck with admiration at the gallantry displayed by the commanders of these two small Chilian vessels, who, regardless of the superior strength of the attacking force, summoned the crews to their guns, and prepared their vessels for action, resolved at any rate to strike a blow in honour of their flag, before they yielded to overpowering odds. The size and armaments of the four vessels will be found in detail at pages 94 and 95. The *Esmeralda* began the action by firing a broadside at the *Huascar*, while the *Covadonga* rounded the island of Iquique, keeping as near as safety would admit to the breakers, closely pursued by the *Independencia*. For two hours a cannonade was kept up between the *Huascar* and *Esmeralda*, at distances ranging from 800 to 1000 yards, the *Huascar* being unable to come to closer quarters owing to the shallow water. Fire from some field-guns on shore at last obliged the *Esmeralda* to come out, when a shell from the turret ship struck her just above the water-line, killing several men and setting the ship on fire. The fire was quickly put out, and on the whole very little harm was done by the long artillery duel, owing, no doubt, to want of training among the crews of both ships.

At last it became necessary for Captain Grau to bring matters to a conclusion by the use of his ram. The *Esmeralda* was struck by her antagonist on the port side, abreast of the mizen mast, but apparently sustained little injury from the shock.

As the two vessels came into contact, Captain Pratt, with sword in one hand and revolver in the other, jumped on board the *Huascar*, calling upon his officers and men to follow. But the two vessels disengaged so quickly that a serjeant was the only man who had time to obey the orders of his commander. Pratt rushed along the deck of the *Huascar*, and Captain Grau, anxious to save him, cried out, "Surrender, captain! we desire to save the life of a hero!" But he would not listen, shot the only person on deck—a signal-officer named Velarde—and at last had to be shot down himself to prevent further mischief. The command of the *Esmeralda* then devolved on Lieutenant Luis Uribe.

Captain Grau made a second attempt to ram, and he was again successful, striking the *Esmeralda* on the starboard bow at an angle of about 45°. This time the effect was palpable, for the water rushed in through a gaping aperture, the engine-room was filled, the fires were extinguished, and the powder magazine was flooded, the men who were serving it being drowned before they could make their escape. Before the *Huascar* could extricate herself, Pratt's action in boarding was repeated by Second Lieutenant Serrano, accompanied by a few men, who jumped on board the ironclad ; but they were immediately shot down by men stationed in the turret and pilot tower.

By this time only about half the men were left un-injured on board the *Esmeralda*. She was perfectly helpless, a battered wreck upon the water, the guns and engines useless, and the ship gradually settling down. As she would not surrender, Grau had no alternative but to ram a third time, striking her full on the starboard side abreast the main chains, and discharging his guns into her at the same time. A couple of minutes afterwards the *Esmeralda* went down. Out of the crew of 200 officers and men, fifty were saved, and these owed their lives to hammocks and wreckage floating about in the water, which supported them until they were picked up by the boats from the *Huascar*. Lieutenant Uribe was rescued half an hour after the ship sank, floating about with a hammock under each arm, in a very exhausted state. The combat lasted four hours ; but after the first show of resistance had been made, the obstinate and useless continuance of the fight involved an unnecessary sacrifice of life. For this, however, Captain Pratt was not responsible, as he fell in the early part of the action.

Captain Grau addressed a letter to the widow of his brave adversary on the 2nd of June. " Captain Pratt had died," he said, " a victim to his excessive intrepidity, in the defence and for the glory of the flag of his country." Grau had carefully collected everything that was likely to be valued on the person of Captain Pratt, and he continues, " I sincerely deplore this mournful event, and in expressing my sympathy I take the opportunity of forwarding the precious relics that he carried on his person when he fell, believing that they may afford some slight consolation in the midst of your great sorrow." It is pleasant, in the course of these deeds of horror and destruction, to meet with such traits of thoughtful tenderness in the character of the great Peruvian hero. He was soon, only too soon, to meet his own death, fighting against greater odds.

Although the *Huascar* was frequently struck by shot and shell, she was practically uninjured. The fire of the *Esmeralda* was ineffective, for the sides of the *Huascar* could not be penetrated by her adversary's missiles. When the *Esmeralda* was rammed for the third and last time, the shock was so great as to cause some slight damage to the bows of the *Huascar*, so that the foremost water-tight compartment was filled. The failures to destroy the *Esmeralda* when she was rammed on the two first occasions are attributed to the *Huascar* having been stopped too quickly, and to her engines having been reversed some time before the collisions took place, the force of the blows being thus materially diminished.

While the *Huascar* was engaging the *Esmeralda* the gunboat was hotly pursued by the *Independencia*, a desultory fire being kept up from both ships. The commander of the *Covadonga*, named Charles Condell, is the son of a Scotch merchant captain. His mother was a Peruvian of the Piura family of La Haza, and his maternal uncles and cousins were in the Peruvian navy. Cunningly tempting the Peruvian ship to follow, Captain Condell steered in for the land near Punta Gruesa, about ten miles south of Iquique, taking the little gunboat over a patch of foul and rocky ground which projects off that point. The stratagem answered only too well. Captain Moore, excited by the chase, followed heedlessly, and drawing much more water than the *Covadonga*, his precious, indeed priceless charge ran upon the rocks.

Condell then turned his gunboat round, and placed her in such a position that the guns of the stranded ironclad could not bear upon her, while she was able to maintain a deliberate and unreturned fire at short range upon the wreck, from her two guns. This galling fire was kept up until the approach of the *Huascar* warned Captain Condell that it was time to sheer off and seek safety in flight. He escaped because the *Huascar* was obliged to devote all her energies to the rescue of the survivors from the ill-fated *Independencia*, which became a total wreck.

This fatal accident was a death blow to the cause of Peru. The strength of the Chilian fleet, before unequal, was now overwhelming. Complete preponderance was only delayed for a time by the brilliant exploits of Captain Grau. He exchanged a few shots with the *Blanco Encalada* on the 3rd of June, but easily out-manœuvred her, and on the 7th arrived safely in Callao Bay.

Captain Moore, the unfortunate captain of the *Inde-*

I

pendencia, was overwhelmed with grief and shame. He strove manfully to make up for one fatal moment of heedlessness, by devoting his life to the service of his adopted country, and, soon afterwards, he secured for himself the death of a hero at Arica.

CHAPTER V.

(THE *Huascar* now became the sole hope of Peru. While her gallant commander out-manœuvred the immensely superior forces of the enemy, and kept his ship on the seas under the Peruvian flag, the Chilians did not dare to undertake any important expedition. The coasts were safe from serious attack. For more than four months this feat was achieved, and Peru was safe-guarded by her heroic son.

During the month of July the *Huascar* was engaged in harassing the enemy, and keeping him in a constant state of alarm and preparation. Most of the ships of the Chilian fleet were employed in blockading Iquique ; and Captain Grau had received instructions from the President of Peru not on any consideration to risk an action with the Chilian ironclads if it could possibly be avoided. Owing to his superiority in speed he was long able to comply with these orders, though on one occasion, in spite of his precautions, the necessity for fighting an action became almost unavoidable. At midnight, on the 9th of July, knowing that the blockading squadron always stood out to sea for the night, he crept cautiously out of the harbour of Iquique, all lights being extinguished, and

I 2

perfect silence maintained. Suddenly he found himself close alongside a steamer, which he had no difficulty in recognizing as the Chilian transport *Matias Cousiño*. He fired a gun to enforce his demand of surrender, but the transport, by skilful handling, contrived to elude her powerful adversary. At last, seeing escape impossible, the Chilian crew lowered their boats with the intention of abandoning the vessel and escaping to some of the blockading ships, which they knew could not be at any very great distance.

At this critical moment, probably attracted by the report of the *Huascar's* gun, the Chilian sloop *Magallanes*, commanded by Captain Latorre, unexpectedly made her appearance. Grau was at first rather perplexed in the darkness, believing that the new arrival was one of the ironclads. But soon discovering his mistake he endeavoured to ram her, and a desultory fight was carried on for some time, until the moon, rising above the summits of the hills, revealed to the Peruvian commander the unwelcome sight of the *Cochrane* approaching at full speed. With a parting salute to his assailant he steamed away, and escaped into Arica.

Shortly after this night action Captain Grau, in company with the *Union*, made a successful cruise along the Chilian coast, which was to some extent retaliatory. The launches moored in the bays of Chañaral, Carrizal, Huasco, and Pan de Azucar were destroyed, and a merchant ship was captured at Chañaral. During the cruise the enterprising commander obtained information that two vessels laden with warlike stores for the Chilian Government were expected from Europe. He, therefore, despatched the *Union* to the Strait of Magellan to intercept them. On the 18th of August she appeared under French colours at Punta Arenas, and succeeded in obtaining coals and provisions. This is a Chilian colony, but the governor, who was fully aware of the character of his visitor, caused the supplies to be sent on board, in hopes of getting rid of her quickly, knowing that one of the expected vessels was actually off Cape Virgins, the eastern entrance of the Strait.

He also caused intelligence to be circulated regarding the two vessels, leading the Peruvians to believe that they had already passed to the westward. Acting upon this false information the *Union* started off in hot pursuit, narrowly escaping an action with two Chilian men-of-war which had been sent down to convoy the expected vessels from the Strait.

The cruise of the *Union* was not, however, barren of results, for whilst returning to the north, having previously joined company with the *Huascar*, the two vessels sighted the fine Chilian transport *Rimac* off Antofagasta, at daybreak on the 23rd of July. This was an important capture, for, besides being a fine, powerful steamer, the *Rimac* had on board a regiment of cavalry, consisting of about 300 men, with a like number of horses. The officers and men were landed at Arica, whence they were subsequently sent to Callao as prisoners of war. The horses were utilized in the Peruvian army, and the *Rimac* was armed and commissioned as a Peruvian cruiser.

Hitherto no act of aggression had been committed

on the town of Iquique by the blockading squadron ; but on the 16th of July, at seven o'clock in the evening, without any previous warning, the Chilians suddenly opened fire, and kept up a bombardment for two hours. The excuse made by the Chilian admiral for this outrage was that he intended it as a reprisal for an alleged unsuccessful attempt to destroy one of his vessels with a torpedo. He said that his men had orders to fire high, and in the direction of a body of troops stationed on the hills. This statement was corroborated to some extent by the people on shore, who reported that most of the shot went over the town. Little injury was inflicted, the casualties amounting to two men and three children killed, and seven or eight persons wounded.

On the 27th of August the *Huascar* paid a visit to the port of Antofagasta, where she found the Chilian men-of-war *Magallanes* and *Abtao* at anchor in the bay, the latter with her machinery in a disabled condition. Captain Grau immediately opened fire upon these vessels, but they were moored under shore batteries in which some heavy guns were mounted, so that he was unable to capture them. The *Huascar* received a 300 lb. shot through her funnel which, bursting, killed one of her officers. If Captain Grau, instead of engaging the ships and forts, had thrown some shot and shell at the condensers on shore, which supplied the town with water, and had destroyed them, he would have compelled a force of 7000 Chilian troops, encamped ready to invade his country, either to surrender or to perish miserably for want of water. Escape by land was quite impracticable, and there were no ships to convey them to any other port. His conduct in sparing the condensers at Antofagasta was most noble and humane.

It was on this occasion that the first torpedo was used during the war. A Ley torpedo was launched by the *Huascar* and directed towards the *Abtao*, but through some derangement in the machinery it had no sooner been shot into the water than it turned round and came straight back towards the *Huascar*. If it had struck her the fate of the turret ship would have been sealed ; but one of her officers, Lieutenant Diez Canseco, seeing the imminent danger, sprang overboard and succeeded in deflecting it from its course. This gallant conduct saved the ship.

During the time of anxiety and watchfulness, when Grau was striving ceaselessly to protect his country from invasion, there were several places whence he kept a careful look-out, which will always have a melancholy historical interest attaching to them. To the south of Antofagasta, in 23° 52′ S., rises the Morro Jara, with a scarped cliff bare and desolate. On its northern side is the anchorage of Bolfin, a desolate place called also by the fishermen "the nest." Here the *Huascar* often anchored at night watching for some transport laden with soldiers for the invading army.

There was much discontent in Chile at this time, owing to the inactivity of the fleet ; and the feeling became so strong that a new Minister of War was appointed, in the person of Don Rafael Sotomayor. His first act was to raise the blockade of Iquique, and to order the two ironclads singly to Valparaiso, to undergo a thorough overhaul of their machinery and hulls.   It had been proved that in their present condition they were no match in speed for the redoubtable *Huascar*.   The wooden ships were also taken in hand, their bottoms cleaned, and machinery repaired.   In short, the navy was thoroughly re-organized.   A number of fast merchant steamers were hired as transports to convey troops along the coast, and a few were purchased to be commissioned as men-of-war.

Admiral Williams resigned on account of ill-health, and partly, no doubt, in consequence of the failure of his naval operations.   He was succeeded by Rear-Admiral Galvarino Riveros, who hoisted his flag on board the *Blanco Encalada*.   This officer, the son of an old hero of the war of independence, by the daughter of Colonel Cardenas of the old royal army, is a native of Valdivia.   His parents died when he was a boy, and he was brought up by Colonel Aldunate, his father's old companion in arms, who sent him to the military academy at Santiago in 1843.   In 1848 he entered the navy, serving under Simpson and Muñoz, and became a full captain in 1876.   Riveros was the first scientific explorer of the river Tolten in 1860, and he was sent to Europe to bring out the steamer *Maria Isabel*.   Since 1863 he served a good deal on the Atacama coast in the *Esmeralda* and *Abtao*, and in 1872 he was Marine-Governor of Valparaiso.   The command of the *Cochrane* at the same time devolved on Captain Latorre, who had displayed great energy while he was employed in the little *Magallanes*.

The capture of the *Huascar* was now the great object of the Chilian Government, for she effectually prevented the prosecution of those schemes of devastation and conquest upon which the once peaceful and civilizing republic had unfortunately entered.

CHAPTER VI.

THE career of the *Huascar*, after the loss of her consort, when, single-handed, she long eluded the chase of the two Chilian ironclads, each more powerful than herself, and kept the enemy in a state of constant alarm, is the most interesting episode of the naval war in the Pacific—a war of which Miguel Grau is the true hero.

This brave patriot was the son of a Colombian officer, whose father was a merchant at Cartagena. The name clearly points to Catalonian ancestry. In the veins of Peru's champion flowed the same blood as gave life and vigour to the fleets of Aragon. A descendant of that race of sturdy seamen which long lorded it in the Mediterranean, was now to win undying fame in the Pacific. The father, Juan Miguel Grau, came to Peru with General Bolivar, and was a captain at the battle of Ayacucho. His comrades returned to Colombia in 1828 ; but the attractions of a fair Peruvian induced the elder Grau to settle at Piura, and there young Miguel was born, in June, 1834. The child was named after the patron saint of his native town. His father held some post in the

Payta custom-house, but he does not appear to have been in good circumstances, for his son was shipped on board a merchant vessel at Payta, at the early age of ten years. He knocked about the world as a sailor-boy, learning his profession thoroughly by hard work before the mast for the next seven years, and it was not until he was eighteen that young Grau obtained an appointment as midshipman in the then very humble navy of Peru. He was on board the *Apurimac* when Lieutenant Montero mutinied in the roadstead of Arica against the government of Castilla, and declared for his rival Vivanco. The friendless midshipman probably had no choice but to obey orders, and follow the fortunes of the insurgents until the downfall of their leader; besides, Montero was a fellow-townsman, being also a native of Piura. As soon as the rebellion was suppressed, in 1858, Grau once more returned to the merchant service, and traded to China and India for about two years.

Miguel Grau was now one of the best practical seamen in Peru, well known for his ability, readiness of resource, and courage, as well as for his genial and kindly disposition. When, therefore, he rejoined the navy in 1860, he at once received command of the steamer *Lersundi*, and soon afterwards he was sent to Nantes with the responsible duty of bringing out two new corvettes, the *Union* and *America*.

He attained the rank of full captain in 1868, and commanded the *Union* for nearly three years, and afterwards the *Huascar*, the turret-ship on board which he won his deathless fame. In 1875 he was a deputy of Congress for his native town, and was an ardent supporter of the Government of Don Manuel Pardo. He paid a visit to Chile in 1877, was at Santiago, and for a short time at the baths of Cauquenes. The object of this visit was to bring the body of his father, who had died at Valparaiso, to Piura, to be buried by the side of that of his mother. When the war broke out he had completed twenty-nine years of service in the Peruvian navy, and was Member of Congress for Payta. Admiral Grau was married to a Peruvian lady of good family, Doña Dolores Cavero, who, while mourning her irreparable loss, found some consolation in the way the services of her gallant husband were appreciated by his country.

The last great sacrifice for that country, now in her utmost need, was about to be made. On the 1st of October a squadron, consisting of two ironclads and several other vessels, all carefully and thoroughly re-fitted, was despatched from Valparaiso for the purpose of forcing the *Huascar* to fight, single-handed, against hopeless odds. This fleet first visited Arica, and there it was ascertained, on the 4th of October, that the *Huascar*, in company with the *Union*, was cruising to the southward. The speed of the Chilian ironclads, after their cleaning, was now superior to that of the *Huascar*. It would be the pursuer's own fault if he failed to bring matters to a decisive issue the first time he succeeded in meeting his gallant adversary.

The Chilian admiral ordered his fastest ships—the *Cochrane*, under Captain Latorre, with the *O'Higgins* and *Loa*—to cruise from twenty to thirty miles off the land, between Mexillones Bay and Cobija, whilst he himself, in the *Blanco*, with the *Covadonga* and *Matias Cousiño*, vessels of inferior speed, patrolled the coast between Mexillones and Antofagasta. The fleet was thus posted in such a manner as to intercept all vessels proceeding to the northward, unless they had previously been made acquainted with the disposition of the Chilian ships.

The Peruvian Government had recognized the energy and gallantry of Don Miguel Grau since he had commanded the *Huascar*, by advancing him to the rank of Rear-Admiral; while the ladies of the town of Truxillo, in the northern part of Peru, as a further reward for his great services, had presented him with a handsomely embroidered ensign, the work of their own fair hands, with a request that it might be the flag under which he would fight, when an opportunity of engaging the enemy occurred.

The end of the Peruvian sailor's glorious career, and with it of all hope for his country, was now close at hand. The *Huascar* and *Union* were cruising together in the vicinity of Antofagasta, watching the Chilian vessels in that port, and doing their utmost to impede the military preparations for the invasion of Peru. Early in the morning of the 8th of October, in total ignorance of the proximity of his enemies, Grau steamed quietly to the northward, closely followed by the *Union*. The weather was thick and foggy, as is not unusual on the coast at that time of the year, when close to the land. As the dawn gradually broke, the fog lifted slightly, and they were able to make out three distinct jets of smoke appearing on the horizon immediately to the north-east, and close under the land, near Point Angamos. This is the western extreme of Mexillones Bay. Admiral Grau at once suspected that these jets of smoke could proceed from no other funnels than those of the hostile vessels which were in pursuit of him. He signalled the presence of the enemy to his consort, steered to the westward for a short distance, trusting to what he believed to be the superior speed of his two ships for the means of escape, and then hauled up to the north-west. Soon the light enabled him to recognize the Chilian ironclad *Blanco*, the sloop *Covadonga*, and the transport *Matias Cousiño*. All was going well for the Peruvian ships, which appeared to be gradually but surely increasing the distance from their pursuers, when, at 7.30 a.m., three more jets of smoke came in sight, in the very direction in which they were steering. It was soon discovered that they were issuing from the funnels of the ironclad *Cochrane*, the *O'Higgins*, and the *Loa*.

Grau's situation now became critical in the extreme. Escape was barred in every direction ; and soon it became evident that the advancing Chilian ironclad would intercept the *Huascar* before she could cover the distance between her position and safety.

Grau fully realized his danger. Seeing that escape was impossible, he resolved to make a bold dash at his enemies, and fight his way through or perish in the attempt. He prepared his ship for action, keeping close into the land, in order that the coast might form a background, and make the aim of the enemy more uncertain. The *Union* was ordered to part company, and exert her utmost efforts to escape, as, with the *Huascar* gone, she would be the only effective vessel left to Peru. This, in consequence of her great speed, she had no difficulty in accomplishing. The *Union* was commanded by Captain Garcia y Garcia, an accomplished officer, who had been entrusted with important diplomatic missions by President Pardo, and had negotiated the Treaty with China. He is the author of a volume of sailing-directions along the coast of Peru, and other works. Painful as the necessity for parting company with the *Huascar* must have been, it was obviously the best course for the public service.

At twenty-five minutes past nine the first shot in the first and only action that has ever taken place between sea-going ironclads, was fired at the *Cochrane* from the *Huascar's* turret, at a distance of about 3000 yards. It fell short. The second and third shots were fired with the same results. The fourth also falling short, ricochetted and pierced the armour plating of the Chilian ironclad, passing through the galley. Up to this moment the *Cochrane's* guns had been silent. She now opened fire, and the battle was kept up with spirit on both sides until the end. The fourth shot from the *Cochrane* struck the turret of the Peruvian monitor, and temporarily disabled its revolving apparatus. The *Huascar's* turret was worked by hand, and not by steam, as are the turrets on board similar vessels in our service.

Almost at the same moment a shot from the *Huascar* struck the side of the Chilian, loosening and slightly indenting one of the iron plates. The ships had now closed considerably, and Admiral Grau made an attempt to ram his antagonist. This manœuvre was frustrated by the quickness of the *Cochrane's* movements, for, being fitted with twin screws, she was able to turn in half the space that was required by the *Huascar*, and Captain Latorre handled his ship with great skill and judgment. Several subsequent attempts to ram also proved unsuccessful. The ships were now engaging at about 300 yards, although, in the course of their manœuvres, this distance was frequently decreased to about 100 or even fifty yards, when an incessant mitrailleuse and rifle fire was kept up on both sides. At five minutes to ten, just half an hour after the first shot had been fired, a shell from the *Cochrane* struck the pilot tower of the *Huascar*, in which were Admiral Grau and one of his lieutenants. It exploded inside, destroying the tower, and killing its occupants. So deadly was the explosion that only a portion of a leg of the brave admiral was afterwards found. The body had been blown to pieces. He fought and died off Point Angamos. His deeds of patriotic heroism will never be forgotten, and Grau will be known in history as the Hero of Angamos.

Up to the moment of the bursting of the fatal shell the *Huascar* had been manœuvred with skill and daring; yet the firing on both sides was indifferent, a very small percentage of the shots taking effect.

Shortly after ten a.m. the *Blanco*, which had been pounding up astern ever since daylight to close with the enemy, reached the scene of action, and on arriving within 600 yards, fired her first shot at the doomed *Huascar*.

On the death of the admiral, Captain Don Elias Aguirre, the senior surviving officer, assumed command. But his head was taken completely off by a shell from the *Blanco* a few minutes after he had succeeded to the post of honour. Captain Don Manuel Carbajal, the next in seniority, was severely wounded by the explosion of the same shell which killed Aguirre. No sooner had Lieutenant Rodriguez, by virtue of his rank, succeeded to Carbajal, than he also was added to the long list of slain. He was killed by a shot which, striking the turret at a tangent, glanced by the port out of which the unfortunate officer was leaning while directing the gun's crews inside. He was succeeded by Lieutenant Don Enrique Palacios, who, before the end of the action, was in his turn severely wounded by a fragment from a shell. The command then devolved on Lieutenant Don Pedro Garezon.

By this time the *Huascar* was quite disabled. Her steam steering gear had been rendered useless by the same shot which killed the admiral, and from that time the ship had to be steered by relieving tackles hooked below. As there was no voice-tube leading from the upper deck to the place where the men were steering, the words of command had to be passed down by messengers, which produced great confusion. A shot had also entered the turret, injuring one of the guns to such an extent as to render it useless, besides killing and wounding several men. The turret was also disabled. Still the unequal contest was maintained.

K

There was a momentary cessation of hostilities, caused by the flag of the *Huascar* being down, owing to the halliards having been shot away. But the colours were quickly rehoisted, and the Chilian iron-clads again opened fire. Several attempts were now made, on both sides, to bring the matter to an issue by means of the ram, but all failed. At the short ranges the effect of the machine gun fire was very deadly, the Gatling gun in the *Huascar's* top being silenced by the more effective fire of the Nordenfeldts, with which the Chilian ironclads were armed.

At eleven o'clock, one hour and a half after the commencement of the action, the *Huascar's* flag was at length hauled down. Through some inadvertence the engines were not stopped at the same time, and the Chilians continued to fire upon her, although several men were observed on the deck, waving white handkerchiefs as an indication of surrender. At length a boat from the *Cochrane* was lowered and sent to take possession of the hard-won prize. Lieutenants Simpson and Rogers, and an engineer, with half a dozen men and four soldiers went in her. There were at least three feet of water in the hold of the *Huascar*, and the lining of the pilot tower, in which the admiral was killed, had caught fire. When Lieutenant Simpson came on deck, he was received by Lieutenant Garezon, one of the junior officers when the action commenced, but now in command.

The scene on board was a terrible one. Dead and mutilated bodies were lying about in all directions, whilst the captain's cabin was blocked up by a heap of mangled corpses. Both upper and lower decks presented a shocking spectacle, being literally strewn with fragments of human remains. Out of a complement of 193 officers and men, with which the *Huascar* began the action, sixty-four, or nearly one-third, were killed and wounded. The survivors were ordered to assist in extinguishing the fire, and were kept at work by the captors until the water-tight doors were reported closed, the valves shut, the engines in working order, and the magazine safe. They were then treated as prisoners of war. Out of the crew of 170 there were thirty Englishmen, twelve other foreigners, and the rest, forming the great majority, were Peruvians.

This was entirely an artillery combat, the ramming tactics, though adopted by both sides, having entirely failed, whilst torpedoes were not used. The number of rounds fired by the *Cochrane* was about forty-six, while the *Blanco* fired thirty-one. Out of these seventy-seven shots, only twenty-four took effect on board the *Huascar*, or a little less than one-third. Only Palliser shells were used by the Chilians. They burst after penetration, showing that the weak armour of the *Huascar* was worse than useless. The *Huascar* fired about forty rounds, her guns being served with great rapidity, but there was a want of precision in the aim, owing to insufficient practice. Those shots which struck the *Cochrane* at a distance of about 600 yards, at an angle of 30°, penetrated about three inches, starting the bolts and inner lining, and breaking an iron beam. The projectiles were broken into small fragments by the impact.

On the same afternoon the Chilian ships, with their

prize, anchored in Mexillones Bay, where the remains of the Peruvian naval hero, together with twenty-five of his gallant companions in arms, were interred.

This action showed the importance of artillery fire, and the necessity for paying close attention to the exercise and efficiency of captains of guns. It also exemplified the great difficulty of successfully carrying out ramming tactics. Another lesson it has taught us is the error of not having the steering arrangements below the water-line, and well protected by armour. For the *Huascar's* helm was disabled three times, first the fighting-wheel being destroyed, and twice afterwards the relieving tackles. The action off Point Angamos was the first hostile encounter between ships of modern construction, and it is, therefore, desirable to study the details very attentively.[1]

The Peruvians now had only two wooden corvettes. The little *Pilcomayo* was chased and captured by one of the Chilian ironclads on the 17th of November; but the *Union* eluded pursuit until the end of the war, and achieved at least one gallant naval feat in spite of all the ironclads of Chile.

---

[1] See a paper on the capture of the *Huascar*, in *Engineering*, of January, 1880. Also a paper by Lieutenant Madan, R.N., in *Journal of United Service Institution*, May, 1881. Vol. xxv. No. cxii.

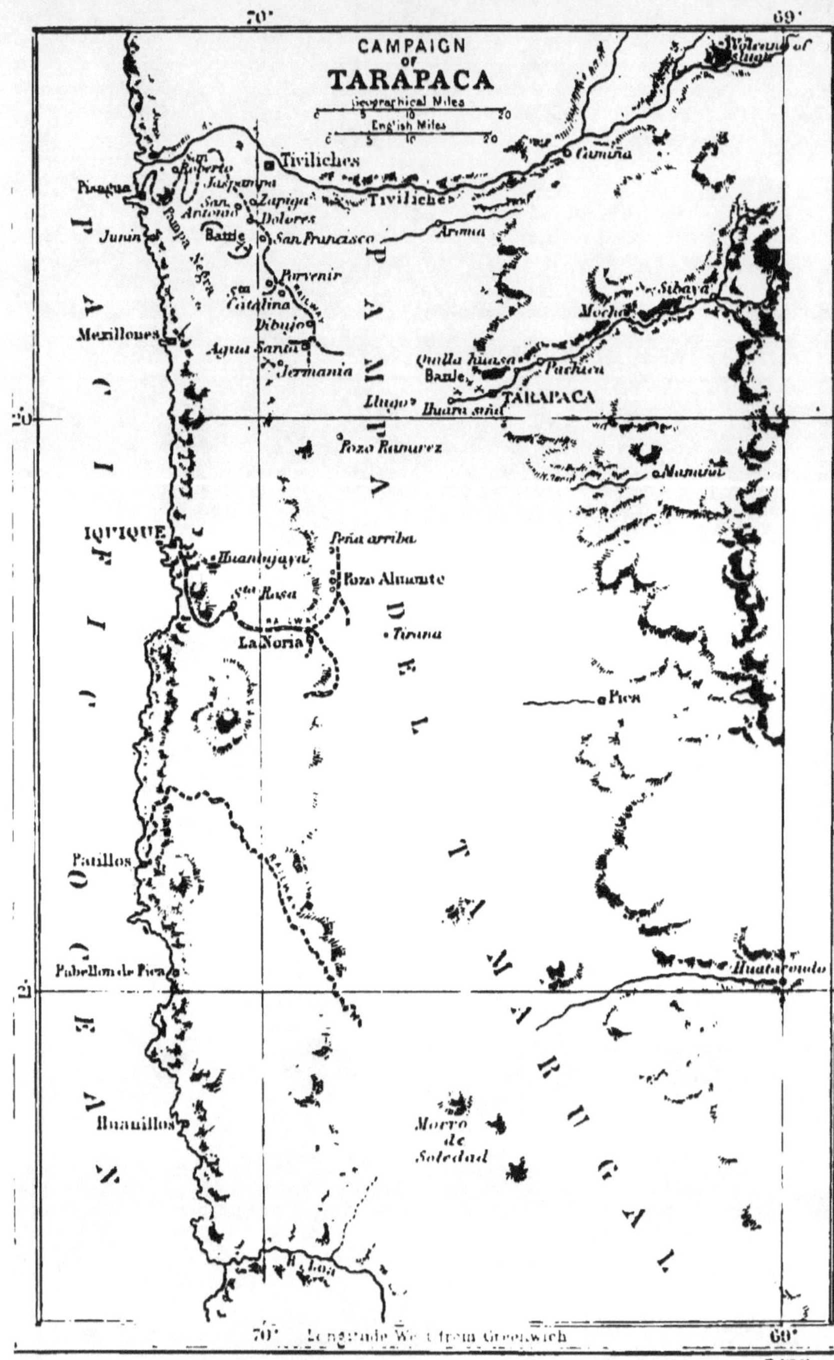

CAMPAIGN
OF
TARAPACA
Geographical Miles
English Miles
70°
69°
Volcano of Isluga
Camiña
Tiviliches
Pisagua
Puerto Junguya
San Antonio
Zapiga
Tiviliches
Arena
Junin
Dolores
Battle
San Francisco
Sibaya
Pampa Negra
Porvenir
Mocha
Sn Catalina
Mejillones
Dibujo
Agua Santa
Quilla huasa
Pachica
Jermania
Battle
TARAPACA
Llugo
Huara suñi
20°
Pozo Ramirez
Namani
IQUIQUE
Peña arriba
Huantajaya
Pozo Almonte
Sta Rosa
La Noria
Tirana
Pica
PACIFIC OCEAN
PAMPA DEL TAMARUGAL
Patillos
Huataconta
Pabellon de Pica
21°
Huanillos
Morro
de
Soledad
Loa
70° Longitude West from Greenwich 69°
F. Weller.
London Sampson Low, Marston, Searle, & Rivington

CHAPTER VII.

THE difficulty of defending any coast-line 1400 miles in length, with the sea under the absolute control of the enemy, must be very great under any circumstances, but in Peru the peculiar formation of the country makes it an almost impossible task. For the Peruvian coast is a rainless region, and its fertile valleys occur at long intervals between vast tracts of waterless desert. In the southern part of the coast these deserts cover nearly the whole area, and the tiny green oases are separated from each other by great distances. In rear of the coast region are the stupendous cordilleras of the Andes; so that, with the ports blockaded, the movement of troops from one threatened point to another is impossible, within any required time.

It was unknown at what point the invasion would commence. The capital might be attacked, or the Tacna region, or the province containing the nitrate deposits; and it was necessary to make preparations for defence everywhere; but on the whole it was believed to be most probable that the first descent would be made on the most southern province of

Tarapaca.   For here the difficulties of a defending force, great everywhere, are most formidable.

Tarapaca is a strip of desert extending ·from the defile of Camarones, south of Arica, to the river Loa, which separates it from Bolivia.   There is an arid range of hills parallel with the sea-shore, some thirty miles in width, and rising to from 3000 to 6000 feet, covered with sand and saline substances.   Between this coast range and the cordillera of the Andes is the great desert plain called the " Pampa de Tamarugal," from 3000 to 3500 feet above the sea, and about thirty miles wide, which extends the whole length of Tarapaca and Bolivian Atacama.   It contains sufficient nitrate of soda for the consumption of Europe for ages.   Here and there a few thorny *tamarugos* or *algarrobos* (*Prosopis horrida*) are met with, existing on the morning mist, which the sun disperses.   They give their name to the desert.

The streams flowing seaward from the Andes in deep ravines seldom reach the sea.   Most of them have their mouths at the opening of the Pampa de Tamarugal, and the few inhabitable places are along their banks.   To the north, and separating the province from Arica, is the profound ravine of Camarones extending from the Andes to the sea.   A vast desert separates it from the gorge of Tiviliches, which contains two alfalfa farms, and opens upon the sea at Pisagua.   There is no other watercourse which extends across the desert to the ocean, until the banks of the river Loa are reached, on the southern frontier of Peru.

Yet a few streams find their way as far as the

Pampa de Tamarugal, where they are lost. Such is the ravine of Tarapaca itself, just half-way between Camarones and the river Loa, forty leagues from each, where there is a little town surrounded by clover fields, in a deep gorge. Pica, twenty-one leagues further south, is in another such ravine, at the foot of the Andes, and is famous for its vine-covered hill. Another march of twenty leagues to the south brings a weary traveller to Huataconda, and the next green valley is Calama, on the river Loa, in Bolivia. There are also a few watering-places, at great distances, in the desert.

The deposits of nitrate of soda are either on the western side of the Pampa de Tamarugal, or in some of the hollows of the coast range, but not nearer the sea-shore than eighteen or twenty miles. The refining works, called *oficinas*, backed by rocky hills, look at a distance like the old ruined castles of Syria. The raw substance, called *caliche*, occurs in deposits averaging 500 yards across, with a depth of seven to eight feet. Those already examined cover fifty square leagues, and, allowing one hundredweight for each square yard, they contain 63,000,000 tons. The *caliche* is conveyed from the deposits to the *paradas* or boilers, where it used to be broken into small pieces, with iron bars. Now steam power is used. The pieces are boiled in the *paradas*, the fragments and sediment removed, and the water, saturated with nitre, allowed to settle, when crystallization takes place. Since steam machinery has been intro-duced 2500 cwts. can be produced in a day. This industry employed thousands of hands. Railroads connect the various *oficinas* with the sea-ports of Pisagua, Iquique, and Patillos. That from Pisagua, the most northern, zigzags up the coast range to the verge of the Tiliviche ravine and then turns south, to tap the various works in that district. The Iquique railroad goes south and then east to La Noria, finally trending north towards the Pisagua railroad, which it is eventually to join. But there were still twenty miles of desert between the Pisaguan terminus of Agua Santa, and Peña-arriba at the end of the Iquique line. Iquique was the central and principal port of Tarapaca, and the capital of the province. In 1876 the population of the province was 42,000, of whom about half are alleged to have been Chilian immigrants. When the war broke out great efforts were made to concentrate an army in Tarapaca, before communication by sea could be cut off; and the Peruvian troops continued to arrive in March, April, and May. The Bolivian army, 4000 strong, under the President Don Hilarion Daza, reached Tacna in Peru, on the 30th of April. The Peruvian General, Don Juan Buendia, was appointed commander-in-chief of the army of Tarapaca; and on the 20th of May the President of Peru, General Don Mariano Ignacio Prado, arrived at Arica, the port of Tacna, to organize the army in the field. Next day he received the disastrous news of the loss of the *Independencia*. After saluting the President of Bolivia, General Prado proceeded at once to Tarapaca for a tour of inspection, which lasted from the 25th of May to the 3rd of June. He brought with him two battalions of Bolivians under Colonel Villamil, to be stationed at Pisagua, while Peruvian troops garrisoned the other two ports of Iquique and Patillos. General Prado proceeded from Pisagua to Iquique, where he remained a week, returning by land to Pisagua, and thence in a row-boat to Arica. The force in Tarapaca was brought up to 9000 men, but the cavalry were not properly mounted, and the field artillery was antiquated.

Here, among these trackless deserts, the descendants of the Yncas were assembled to strike a blow for the right. Juan Buendia, their general, was a gentleman of good family, descended from the Marquises of Castellon. Born at Lima in 1814, he entered the Peruvian artillery, and became a colonel in 1848. He was no longer young, though still upright and active. He had a well-earned reputation as a good officer and for personal bravery, and he had never betrayed a trust. He was a tall and handsome man. Courteous and well-bred, his eloquence had gained him influence in Congress, while his agreeable manners made him a great favourite in society. Yet he had remained a bachelor. His zeal and energy were shown on his way from Callao to assume command. There being danger from Chilian cruisers he landed at Chala, and rode to Arica in three days, with his personal staff, a distance of sixty leagues. If his age was a drawback to his efficiency, and he was sometimes inert and at others rash, he never failed in personal courage when the time for fighting came.

The chief of the staff, Colonel Don Belisario Suarez, amply made up for any deficiencies in the commander-in-chief. He was the ablest and most enterprising officer in the Peruvian army, and, like his chief, he was a man of staunch loyalty. From the time he became a captain of artillery, in 1866, he had ever been faithful to his trust.

The first division was at first commanded by Don Manuel Velarde, a well-bred and polished gentleman who had been Prefect of Lima under Don Manuel Pardo. He was still young, and had the reputation of being a smart officer and a man of the world. He had won the good will of the Chilians by his treatment of the *Esmeralda* prisoners. But it was Justo Pastor Davila who led the first division at Tarapaca. A native of Moquegua, with Ynca as well as Spanish blood in his veins, Davila is impetuous and valiant in the field, active and enterprising. He was Prefect of Iquique when the war broke out. Colonel Don Victor Fajardo, another divisional chief, was the son of an old soldier of the army of San Martin, a Chilian who settled at Ayacucho and made his home there. He was looked upon as one of the bravest officers in the Peruvian army. Colonel Don Francisco Bolognesi was the son of an Italian settled in Lima, and related to the wife of Dr. Weddell, the learned quinologist. He was in the artillery, and in 1859 was sent to Europe by General Castilla to select field-guns. On his return he became commandant of the artillery at Lima. Don Alejandro Herrera was another officer of good repute. The second division was led by Don Andres Avelino Caceres, a native of Ayacucho, who had previously commanded the battalion *Zepita*, composed of his fellow-townsmen. He is a valiant soldier, seamed with scars, and has lost the use of one eye in action.

The artillery consisted of sixteen old-fashioned bronze guns, afterwards abandoned. Their commander, Don Emilio Castañon, preferred to arm his men with Winchester repeating-rifles. Castañon was a native of Tacna, his father having been prefect. He was a man of education who had studied in Europe, and he introduced into the Peruvian army a chassepot rifle reformed on his own plan, which was known as the " Rifle Peruano."

There were also several younger officers of great promise in command of battalions in that army of Tarapaca. The name of one of the bravest takes the memory back to a heart-rending scene on one of the steep slopes of the Andes, some thirty-seven years ago. Among the distinguished families of Cuzco, was that of Zubiaga, of Basque descent, but long established in the capital of the Yncas. Doña Francisca de Zubiaga, the heroine of many a strange adventure, married the President Gamarra ; and her brother, a brave officer and a true gentleman, was General Juan Bautista Zubiaga, who became Prefect of Ayacucho in 1840, when Gamarra attained to supreme power in Peru. The family of Tello y Cabrera resided in a large corner house facing the plaza of Ayacucho, and soon there was a marriage between Doña Micaela de Tello, the youngest of four sisters, and the prefect. A year had scarcely elapsed before General Zubiaga had to take the field against insurgents in the cause of constitutional right, and a few days after he had torn himself from the last embrace of his young bride their child was born. Doña Micaela was counting the days to the time when she might present her husband with this pledge of their love, when—one dark night —an Indian messenger ran breathlessly into the courtyard. A battle had taken place in a wild and remote part of the mountains called Ynca-huasi, and the general was believed to be mortally wounded. It was a pitiless night, rain was coming down in torrents and a thunder-storm was bursting over the town. Micaela had not reached her seventeenth year. She resolved to start at once, with her child in her arms, to soothe the last moments of her beloved. No persuasion could stop her, and she must have her brother's roan, for it was said that a horse of that colour never tired. At midnight the young bride, with the child before her, and the faithful Indian Quispi at her side, galloped out into the storm on the good roan horse. Sixteen hours brought her to Ynca-huasi. Her husband was still alive. He lived to clasp his child to his heart, to hear the words of love, and he died in his wife's arms.

Micaela was for many months between life and death. Little Agustin at last reconciled her to life. Her whole soul was wrapped up in the longing hope that the son should be as good, as loyal, and as brave as his father. For this she lived. Her home was in a large family house, shared with brother and sisters and their children. But Micaela and her boy were always looked upon as, in some sense, apart and sacred. Agustin returned his mother's love. He strove to please her in all things, and when he came home, his first thought was to run to his mother's room. There was another lad who was very dear to the young widow, a nephew and godson of the general

with the same name, Juan Bautista Zubiaga. He
was tall and strong, quick-witted, and fond of adventure, generous and ever ready to interfere to prevent
wrong or tyranny. So he grew up, and after a careful education he entered the Peruvian army. When
ruin threatened his country Lieutenant-Colonel Juan
Bautista Zubiaga was a mature man, brave and loyal,
the counterpart of his uncle. He was stationed in the
capital of the Yncas, second in command, under
Colonel Caceres, of a battalion of the men of Cuzco,
who were devoted to him, called the *Zepita* battalion.
Zubiaga and his men marched from Cuzco over the
wildest pass in the Andes, arriving in Tarapaca during
the month of April.

At the same time another battalion, named 2° *de
Mayo* in memory of the day when the Spanish fleet
was repulsed from Callao in 1866, was ordered to the
front. It was composed of the men of Ayacucho,
and commanded by an officer of the same stamp as
Zubiaga. Manuel Suarez was a native of Cuzco, and
nephew of that good and just Vice-President, Dr.
José Manuel del Mar, whose influence obtained full
justice for the illustrious General Miller in 1860.
Manuel Suarez led his men from Ayacucho across
flooded rivers, over inundated plains and snow-covered
passes, to the coast. The *Zepita* and 2° *de Mayo*
battalions formed the division of Colonel Caceres.
The Puno battalion was commanded by Don Rafael
Ramirez de Avellano, who was soon afterwards taken
prisoner.

The Bolivian contingent at Pisagua was under Don
Pedro Villamil, a native of Sorata, whose father had

made money at the gold washings of Tipuani.   Don
Pedro had been educated in France, and served in
Algiers under Bugeaud and Lamoricière.   He was an
accomplished officer, but now old and rather infirm.
Colonel Villegas was an Indian of the province of
Chichas, in the far south of Bolivia, and a man who
had made a considerable fortune by persevering
industry.   He commanded the other Bolivian division
in Tarapaca.

The colleague of Colonel Villamil, at Pisagua,
was Colonel Don Isaac Recabárren of Arequipa, who
was appointed military governor of the port by General Buendia.   He was a talented and trustworthy
officer, but at this moment he was bowed down with
grief by the news of his young wife's death, which
arrived a short time before the enemy's fleet.

General Buendia, in his difficult position, at first
had some hope that help might come from the side of
Bolivia, but, although efforts were made to support
him, the enormous distances and absence of all
resources made success impossible.   General Campero,
the ablest and most experienced officer in Bolivia,
succeeded in bringing together three battalions of
troops in the extreme south of the Republic, and
in arming them with Remington rifles obtained
from Buenos Ayres.   His own countrymen from
Tarija, to the number of 500, formed one valiant
corps, called *Chorolque*, which was led by Colonel
Ayaroa of La Paz, and there were some other recruits
from Porco and Potosi.   Campero first established
his headquarters at Santiago de Cotagoitia, in Chichas,
and in August his vanguard marched as far as Lipez,

but it was found impossible to get sufficient supplies and transport together so as to advance to the coast deserts; and eventually the attempt was abandoned and the leader fell back to Oruro. He was soon wanted for more important duties.

Meanwhile the Chilian cavalry in the Bolivian coast province made numerous raids to cut off supplies coming to Tarapaca from the south. Major Soto, in command at Calama, established an outpost at Quilla-gua, lower down on the river Loa, whence incursions were made. On one occasion fifty head of Salta cattle were seized, on another 189 mules, while stores of firewood and forage were burnt. The muleteers from Salta, in the Argentine Republic, brought much-needed supplies to Tarapaca, and these Chilian depredations increased the difficulties of the Peruvian army.

Colonel Suarez, ever on the alert, made a recon-naissance to Huatacondo, and on October 10th he attacked a strong Chilian picket at Quillagua on the Loa, capturing some mules. Eventually he selected a hill in the desert, on which there is a clump of *tamarugo* thorns, called Soledad, whence he could watch the Chilian outposts, and keep their depredations in check.

After the loss of the *Huascar* it was evident that a large invading force would soon be landed, with all the advantages of cavalry, modern artillery, and ships full of supplies of all kinds as a base of operations. The odds against the little Peruvian army were over-whelming. All chance of succour from General Cam-pero in the south being gone, but one hope remained.

A Bolivian force, under President Daza, might advance from Arica and take the invaders in the rear while engaged with Buendia's army.

Such an arrangement was actually made, but Daza was incapable. He began his march from Tacna with 3000 men, and loitered three days at Arica. At last, on the 11th of November, he started, being accompanied for a league on his road by General Prado, the President of Peru. On the 12th he marched over five leagues of sandy desert, and reached the oasis of Vitor. He advanced one more march to the defile of Camarones, and on November 16th he abandoned the work he had undertaken, and returned to Tacna, his own soldiers threatening to shoot him as a coward.

The army of Tarapaca was thus left to its fate. It was indeed a forlorn hope, and nobly did the Yncas and Aymaras enter upon the struggle. It was as hopeless and not less glorious than that which their ancestors as bravely faced, when the Pizarros seized the sacred capital of their sovereigns. The worst of the older conquerors sought for gold, their Chilian imitators wanted to appropriate manure. The Yncas, at both periods, upheld the noblest cause for which men can fight and die—the defence of their fatherland.

CHAPTER VIII.

THE DEFENCE OF PISAGUA—SLAUGHTER AT JER-MANIA—BATTLE OF SAN FRANCISCO.

IN November, 1879, that destructive invasion, which had been successfully prevented by the gallantry of the Peruvian navy for nearly a year, began to spread havoc and desolation over the coast region. The loss of the *Huascar* destroyed the last barrier of defence.

The invading host was gathered at Antofagasta, and transports were collected ; the secret of the exact point of attack being successfully kept. The two most likely places were believed to be Patillos or Pisagua ; but it was necessary to retain garrisons at all the landing-places, so that the defending forces were unavoidably scattered.

The Chilian army, consisting of 10,000 men, including 850 admirably mounted cavalry, and thirty-two long-range field-guns, was embarked at Antofagasta on board four men-of-war and fifteen transports, on the 28th of October, the destination being Pisagua, a distance of 274 miles. The embarkation was badly managed, the ambulances and medical stores being left behind, and the concerted arrangements being defective. General Escala was the

L

Chilian commander-in chief, and he was accompanied by Señor Sotomayor as Minister of War "in campaign."

The coast at Pisagua consists of cliffs over 1000 feet high, rising at very steep angles, and only leaving room on the beach for a thin line of houses forming the town. The distance between the mouth of the Tiviliche ravine to the north, and the southern point, called Pichalo or Huayna Pisagua, is three miles. At each extremity there was a fort armed with one gun. Between the two points there is a small hill rising from the beach, with a stretch of sand on its northern side, called "Playa Blanca." The town of Pisagua was a little to the south. At the beach north of the town were the railway-station, offices, and some heaps of coal and mineral. The railroad winds up the cliff in long zigzags, and the station at the summit is called "El Hospicio." Six miles to the south is the small anchorage of Junin.

General Buendia arrived at Pisagua in the evening of the 1st of November. His small force consisted of about 600 Indians of La Paz, commanded by Colonel Villamil, and some 300 boatmen and volunteers of Pisagua, led by an able Peruvian artillery officer, Don Isaac Recabárren. At dawn, on the 2nd of November, Buendia, Villamil, and Recabárren received the report that steamers were in sight, and soon there were nineteen hostile vessels in the Pisagua anchorage. The general posted the Bolivians along the four zigzag lines of the railway between the sea-shore and the "Hospicio" on the summit, and also behind the buildings and coal heaps. Recabárren had some of his men among the ruins of the town, and others at the station. It will be remembered that Pisagua had already suffered from a bombardment early in the year.

The first hostile act was the bombardment of the two little one-gun forts by the men-of-war. The fire of the *Cochrane* and *O'Higgins* disabled the gun in the southern work, and the men abandoned the northern one. This caused a long delay, and it was 9.30 a.m. before the first batch of boats shoved off and pulled towards the *Playa Blanca*. While the Chilians were landing, a tremendous fire from the men-of-war opened on the defenders who occupied the line of railway. The Bolivians kept up a brisk rifle fire as the boats touched the shore, and gallantly disputed every inch of ground. The men-of-war sent as many as 610 shells among them, and 4380 rifle shots were poured into their ranks. Colonel Villamil directed operations half-way down the cliff, while General Buendia was on the summit. Colonel Recabárren had been badly wounded. The enemy's troops kept on landing until their numbers were overwhelming, some being put on shore to make flank attacks, and General Escala himself landed at Junin. The beach is described, at this time, as looking at a distance as if it was covered with flocks of white gulls—the bodies of Bolivian dead in their white uniforms of coarse Cochabamba cloth.

Buendia had sent for reinforcements to be hurried up, but the time was too short, the gallant defenders were decimated and in danger of being outflanked, and at eleven a.m., after a struggle against enormous odds, which had lasted for five hours, the order was given to retreat. The allies had fought with great bravery. The Chilian loss amounted to 235 killed and wounded, most of the wounded dying of neglect. That of the defenders was probably much heavier, owing to the tremendous fire from the ships, to which they were exposed. A few Bolivian wounded were taken prisoners. Among them was a young lad of seventeen, a sub-lieutenant named Emilio Calderon, native of Corocoro. He wept at being called upon to die so young, but not on his own account, his grief was for his unhappy mother in her far-distant home.

General Buendia assembled the remnant of his brave little force, which had retired in good order, at the station of San Roberto, ten miles from Pisagua, and on the next day he was at Agua Santa, the terminus of the railway, whence he marched southward to form a junction with the rest of his army. A troop of wretchedly mounted cavalry, consisting of ninety-four men, under Captain Sepulveda, formed a feeble sort of rear-guard.

Pisagua became the scene of most disgraceful excesses during the night of the 2nd. The town had been set on fire by the shells of the Chilian ironclads, and afterwards the men were allowed to indulge in drunken orgies, and to rob, burn, and destroy in all directions. The invading soldiery gained for themselves an unenviable notoriety for every kind of cruelty and excess whenever a battle was gained or a town captured. General Escala hastened to get possession of the line of railway as far as the Agua Santa terminus, a distance of fifty miles; and on the

4th, a body of 175 cavalry, under Colonel José Francisco Vergara, the general's secretary, was despatched in advance to make a reconnaissance. He came in sight of the small mounted rearguard of the Peruvians, at Jermania near Agua Santa, on the 6th ; and feigned a retreat to draw the poor victims out on the plain. The commander of this doomed little band was José Ventura Sepulveda, a gallant young fellow, whose father was a Chilian colonel settled at Lima: his companions were Lieutenants Arnao, Mazo, and Loza, with the Bolivian Chocano. The men were only armed with carbines and miserably mounted. No sooner were they clear of the hills, than the vastly superior force of splendidly mounted Chilian cavalry, 175 strong, wheeled and charged them. Sepulveda was sabred and received three mortal wounds when on the ground. All the other officers were cut down. The rest was a massacre. No quarter was given, and nearly all were killed ; seventy dead bodies being scattered over the plain, out of an original troop of ninety-four men. The Chilians did not lose a man—it was a sickening butchery.

Meanwhile the Chilian army had easily occupied the whole line of the railway. After ascending the cliff at Pisagua by zigzags, the line forms a wide curve, eventually turning due south. Here is the station of Jaspampa, at the head of the ravine of Zapiga, and 3700 feet above the sea ; a strategic position of importance, commanding the direct road from Iquique to Arica, and the valley of Tiviliche. Four miles to the south of Jaspampa is the *oficina* of San Antonio, and six miles further on is that of Dolores, a still more important position because here there is a good supply of water. Then come, in consecutive order, the *oficinas* and stations of Porvenir, Santa Catalina, Dibujo, Agua Santa, Jermania. The two first are close to Dolores, but Santa Catalina is nine miles from Dibujo, and Dibujo three and a half from the terminus at Agua Santa.

With a line of railroad, inexhaustible supplies of water at Dolores, and strong positions, the powerful Chilian army had no difficulties. Large tanks of water were sent along the line in trains, between Dolores and Pisagua.

Meanwhile reinforcements of infantry and cavalry arrived. There was an army of over 10,000 men of all arms between Pisagua and Dolores. Near the *asiento* of Dolores there is a hill rising 800 feet above the plain, with a plateau on the summit, about 250 yards wide, and three miles in length, running east and west, the hill of San Francisco being its most eastern front. In its centre there is a slight ravine which gave it the name, in former times, of "Cerro de la Encañada." On this hill of San Francisco an army of 10,000 men could be formed in a position of great strength. In front is a broken plain called the "Pampa Negra," and at its eastern extreme—two and a half miles away—is the *oficina* of Porvenir. The mass of the Chilian army, under Colonels Sotomayor and Amunátegui, was established on the hill of San Francisco and the adjoining heights ; while smaller detachments were at Pisagua with General Escala, and along the line of railway. By the 19th of November over 6000 men, with thirty-two pieces of artillery of long range, were assembled on the hills, and reinforcements were close at hand.

The Peruvian general was now in extreme difficulties. His command was literally and in truth a forlorn hope. With a few thousand men, practically no cavalry, and a dozen antiquated field-guns, with but a few days' provisions, supplies of ammunition fast running short, and surrounded by a trackless, waterless desert, he had to face the invading army. That army was 10,000 strong, with thirty-two field-guns of long range, and a large force of cavalry splendidly mounted. It was posted in an almost impregnable position, with abundant supplies of water brought hither and thither by train, and connected with its base, whence succour of all kinds could be received by a railroad.

Never were more hopeless odds combined against brave men. Their enemies have not the generosity to admit that the Peruvians fought a good fight against these odds, but the facts which they cannot conceal abundantly prove it. When General Buendia arrived at Iquique, he called a council of war, and, by the advice of Colonel Suarez, it was resolved to concentrate all available troops at Pozo Almonte. This station has a supply of water, and is near the terminus of the Iquique railroad. An interval of more than twenty miles separates it from Agua Santa. The divisions of Velarde, of Caceres, and of Bolognesi assembled under the command of Suarez at Pozo Almonte, on November 8th. The Bolivian division of Villegas was scattered in detachments at ports along the coast, another company was at Soledad in the far south. There were long marches, with extreme suffering from thirst and heat, all patiently borne. The force amounted to 10,000 men on paper, but from this the heavy losses at Pisagua, the garrison at Iquique, and the difference between nominal rolls and actual numbers must be deducted. In reality there were barely 6000 fighting-men assembled at Pozo Almonte. Up to the last moment there was the hope of succour from General Daza, but this failed them utterly.

Want of provisions and ammunition necessitated immediate action. There was no choice except between instant retreat, or the assault of an almost impregnable position defended by a superior force. It is a glorious reflection for the vilified and down-trodden people of Peru that their gallant sons chose to strike a blow for their country even in the face of such odds, preferring duty to safety. Yet the troops were on the verge of starvation.

In the afternoon of the 16th of November this forlorn hope commenced its march against the enemy in three parallel columns. The Bolivians were in the vanguard, with a small Peruvian detachment, under the personal command of General Buendia. Suarez led the divisions of Velarde and Villamil, with a few antiquated field-guns under Colonel Castanon. The reserve was composed of the flower of the army, the divisions of Caceres and Bolognesi. Small detachments from the Cuzco and Ayacucho battalions formed a light division in advance of the whole force. On the 18th the terminus of the Pisagua railroad at Agua Santa was reached, and the men were horrified at the sight of the dead bodies of those who had so recently been butchered by the savage Chilian cavalry at Jermania. Sepulveda and his slaughtered comrades were decently interred, and the indefatigable chief of the staff was occupied all night in seeing that his men were fed and supplied with ammunition. Next day there was a march of fourteen miles to the sand-hills of Chinquiquiray, about a league south-west of San Francisco. Between the two heights was the " Pampa Negra." The gallant army of the allies uttering patriotic shouts, with their banners interlaced, then marched over the plain to the *oficina* of Porvenir, where there is a supply of water. Many were about to die for their country.

In front, crowning the hill, were the serried ranks of the invaders, with their cavalry massed round the *oficina* of Dolores to defend the water-tanks, and their terrible rows of thirty-two field-guns ready to open fire. Bravely the allies advanced in perfect military order in three parallel columns. The four light companies, consisting of the flower of the Ynca and Aymara Indians, of men from the sacred city of Cuzco and from the sacred lake of Titicaca, formed the vanguard under Colonel Lavadenz. Buendia established his headquarters at Porvenir ; while Suarez, on his famous white horse, galloped from company to company forming the line of battle and exhorting the soldiers to fight for their fatherland.

The plan appears to have been to occupy the line of railway, cut off the enemy from the water-supply at Dolores, and then force on an action at a disadvantage. The three first divisions for the attack were under General Villegas, Colonel Davila, and Colonel Lavadenz, on the extreme right. In the centre were Velarde and Bolognesi ; and Villamil with the survivors from Pisagua was on the left. Caceres, with part of the two battalions of Cuzco and Ayacucho, formed a reserve. But Zubiaga and Manuel Suarez were in the vanguard with their picked men—brave and true hearts, fit leaders of the Ynca chivalry. The sun was burning fiercely. It was now nine in the morning. At that moment the news of the cowardly desertion by Daza was passed through the ranks. Despairing but undaunted they stood ready to die for the fatherland. They shouted resolutely as the general passed. *Morituri te salutant.* But it was resolved that there should be rest during the forenoon, for the men were dead tired and exhausted from want of food. Meanwhile Colonel Espinar, a man of extraordinary nerve and great courage, closely inspected the enemy's line within pistol-shot. Ladislao Espinar was a native of Cuzco, a man scarcely thirty-eight though prematurely grey. Tall, well-formed, high spirited, he was noted for his impetuous valour. The Grand Marshal Castilla had noticed his prowess, and advanced him to the rank of lieutenant-colonel. He had been some years in retirement ; but when his country was in danger Espinar hurried to Iquique as a volunteer. At first he was made controller of the hospital, very uncongenial employment ; but in the previous May he had been placed at the head of a small intelligence department, and had scoured the country from the Loa to Camarones. He was now to find a hero's death, and to win undying fame as the brave leader of a forlorn hope.

He reported that the enemy's position might be surprised and outflanked by the ravine of San Francisco, crossing the hill ; for that the artillery was too much in advance of the line, and without immediate protection. The light division of Lavadenz, under the guidance of Espinar, made a dash at the ravine, followed by two of Davila's battalions, at about three p.m., while Villegas occupied the *oficina* of San Francisco at the foot of the hill. Bolognesi, Caceres, and the brave Fajardo kept together a strong reserve at Porvenir. So the battle began ; but the light division was met by a tremendous fire of artillery, no less than 400 shells and grenades being hurled amongst them in their first rush. Then died the gallant young Indian officer, Mariano Mamiani, a woodsman from the Chinchona forests. Next fell the horse of the intrepid Espinar, who was leading on the men of Cuzco in the very face of the Chilian guns. Instantly he was on his feet, shouting, "To the cannons ! to the cannons !" and rushing up to the very muzzles, was followed by the Ynca chivalry. The Chilian artillerymen were falling back. At that supreme moment a ball pierced the forehead of Espinar. A cry of grief and horror ran through the foremost ranks of his townsmen. The hero of Cuzco had fallen, with his feet under the invader's gun. Then a close and overpowering mass of Chilian infantry dashed down with their bayonets at the charge. The men of Cuzco long stood firm, so firm that two of them were transfixed at the same instant that they transfixed their antagonists. Overpowered by numbers they fell back, while the division of Villegas, issuing from the *oficina* of San Francisco, boldly began to ascend the ravine from the east. Received by a deluge of iron hail from the field-guns, while they were attacked in flank by more Chilian infantry, they too gave way, having received 112 shots from each man of the regiment that assailed them, and eighty shells from the artillery. General Villegas fell wounded in the front rank.

Disputing every foot of ground, the Peruvians retreated down the hill, and made their way in good order to Porvenir. They were not followed. It was now five in the evening. It was a heroic struggle; but alas ! the battle, so gallantly contested, was lost.

The Chilians lost 208 in killed and wounded, including their leader, Colonel Sotomayor. As at Pisagua most of the wounded died from neglect. The Peruvian dead numbered 220, the wounded 76—a suggestive proportion ! But to the Peruvian army defeat was ruin. It was without cavalry, without food, without stores or resources of any kind, without a base. There was but one thing left. The survivors must be rescued from the pitiless deserts to fight for their country elsewhere. The Bolivians retreated by way of Tarapaca to the highlands. Colonel Suarez called together the reserve and the surviving heroes of the assault, and began his retreat from Porvenir at midnight. The guns were taken a short distance, but it was lost labour to drag them over the deserts when they were useless against the Chilian Krupp guns on the field of battle. Colonel Castanon decided upon abandoning them, and arming his men with rifles. Proudly but sadly the remains of the army retreated to the village of Tarapaca.

The Chilians did not follow them. The cavalry, so brave among the poor fugitives at Jermania, were now satisfied with the capture of a few wounded at Porvenir and of the abandoned guns. The Yncas who had been over the crest of San Francisco hill, and beyond the muzzles of the Chilian guns, were left to retire unmolested. Driven back but unconquered, they were even now marching to victory.

Iquique was no longer tenable, and the town was given up to the blockading squadron. The prefect-general, Don Lopez Lavalle, went on board the English man-of-war *Shannon*, on the 20th of November, while Colonel Rios, in command of the garrison, retreated with about 600 men to join the Peruvian army at Tarapaca, bringing with him a much needed supply of ammunition.

The indefatigable Suarez had galloped to the ravine of Tarapaca in advance, to collect food for his famished troops, leaving Bolognesi in command. That veteran brought the men safely to the green oasis on the 22nd, and at length they got food and rest. Few soldiers in the world could have endured the extremities of thirst, hunger, heat, and fatigue as these poor Indians had done. Colonel Rios arrived soon afterwards with the Iquique garrison, consisting of 400 soldiers, and 200 boatmen under two gallant brothers of Piura, José Maria and Sisto Melendez. They marched no less than fifty leagues in three days, reaching Tarapaca on the 26th. These troops were all volunteers, animated by patriotic feelings, and ready to die in defence of their native province. The Loa battalion consisted entirely of coast Bolivians from the conquered province to the south, men in whom the ethnologist would take the deepest interest, for their villages of Calama and San Pedro are the only places where the nearly extinct Atacama language is still spoken. The other two battalions of Tarapaca and Pica were made up of patient and laborious coast Indians, who dreaded the forced recruiting, but were ready to fight as volunteers against a foreign invader. Colonel Rios, who commanded them, was a valiant and honourable chief, possessing the full confidence of his men.

CHAPTER IX

THE PERUVIAN VICTORY AT TARAPACA.

THE Peruvian army had made a gallant fight in defence of the invaded province, but the odds were too heavy ; and the general now prepared to evacuate a position which, without supplies and without chance of succour, was untenable. Before starting on the long march across the deserts between Tarapaca and Arica, it was decided that the sorely-tried soldiers should have a short rest in the ravine where they had at last halted.

The gorge of Tarapaca has its source in the cordillera of Lirima, with the frowning volcano of Isluga, 17,000 feet above the sea, on its north flank, and the mighty peak of Lirima to the south. A stream flows down the ravine, which is lost as soon as it reaches the Tamarugal desert, and when there are thunderstorms in the mountains, great floods, called *avenidas*, carry destruction down the valley. There are green alfalfa fields on each side of the stream, and a few villages of fifteen to twenty huts along its course. High up, near the source, is Sibaya, where sheep and llamas are raised. Lower down is Mocha in a milder climate, and here a little wheat and maize are cultivated ; but the gorge is still so narrow as scarcely to admit of a small field and a few willow-trees on either bank. At Mocha dwelt the family of Quispi Socso, descendants of the Yncas, who were exempted from tribute by reason of their lineage. At Pachica, four leagues from the mouth of the ravine where the desert begins, the valley widens to 400 yards, and there is an expanse of verdure. Two leagues lower down is the watering-place of Quilla-huasa, then the village of Tarapaca itself, and near the opening on to the desert is the last watering-place of Huara-siña, and a few huts. Tarapaca is a group of mudhouses, with a small square, and an old church which was shaken down by the earthquake of May 9th, 1877. There are fig-trees and willows round it, and a few lucerne fields, but the valley is here only 600 yards wide. Quilla-huasa is a long mile above the village, and Huara-siña the same distance below it. The steep sides of the ravine rise up very abruptly, with a perfectly flat crest, so that, in approaching across the desert laterally, the gorge is not perceived until the traveller is close upon it. The road to Tarapaca from Iquique and the coast leads across the Pampa de Tamarugal, and up the ravine by Huara-siña. From the north-west it is approached over a hill between two ravines, called the Cuesta de la Visagra ; and a side ravine leads down into that of Tarapaca by a hut, where there is water, called San Lorenzo. Tarapaca is 3800 feet above the sea.

The ravine, grateful as its appearance must have been to the weary men who had marched for fifty hours over the waterless desert, could furnish but limited supplies. It was necessary to separate the little force, the vanguard and first division being sent up to Pachica. There remained with General Buendia, at Tarapaca, the division of Caceres, comprising the two battalions of Cuzco and Ayacucho (called 2° *Mayo* and *Zepita*) originally numbering 1036 men on paper before the battle of San Francisco; but since terribly thinned down by losses : the division of Bolognesi numbering 880 men on paper, before the battle ; the division of *Exploradores*, now a mere skeleton ; 600 men from Iquique ; and the artillerymen, once numbering 150. The whole number of effective fighting men, at the outside, was a little over 2000, without cavalry or artillery. But they were all staunch and true, the pick of the imperial Ynca tribe and men of the coast fighting for their homes.

The Chilian general, after hesitating for several days, at last resolved to despatch a carefully-selected force against the retreating enemy, with the intention of intercepting and dispersing the remnant. The command was given to Colonel Don Luis Arteaga, and he was accompanied by Colonel Vergara, the general's secretary, who committed the slaughter at Jermania. The force placed under his orders consisted of 2000 infantry, all picked men, 150 cavalry, and 150 artillery with ten field-guns of long range. The infantry was composed of the second regiment of the line under Colonel Ramirez, with Major Vivar as his second ; the " Zapadores," under Don Ricardo Santa Cruz ; and the regiment of Chacabuco.

The plan of attack was intended to effect the complete destruction of the Peruvian army at Tarapaca. For this purpose the force was divided into three

M

divisions. The right, consisting of the 2nd regiment under Ramirez, with two guns and fifty cavalry, was to march up the ravine to the village by Huara-siña. The left, under Santa Cruz, with a chosen body of infantry, cavalry, and four Krupp guns, was to march along the crest of the ravine, go down to the watering-place at Quilla-huasa, and so cut off the retreat of the Peruvians up the ravine. Then the centre, led by Colonel Arteaga himself and consisting of 900 men and four guns, was to descend upon Tarapaca and destroy the remains of the Peruvian army, whose retreat was to have been cut off at both ends by the other two divisions. A spy, named Laiseca, who had been a miner, actually went into Tarapaca and returned with a full report of the state of affairs. The destroying force started from the railway station of Dibujo, where the men were able to fill their *caramayolas* or water-bottles, on November 26th. That night Arteaga encamped at Lluga, in the middle of the Pampa de Tamarugal. Early on the morning of the 27th the march to Tarapaca was continued in three divisions. There was one of the thick desert mists, called *camanchaca*, which impeded the march, but at 6.30 a.m. the fog dispersed, and there was a blazing sun for the rest of the day. The three divisions then proceeded in the preconcerted directions.

On that eventful morning the unsuspecting Peruvian troops were resting under the willow-trees, with arms piled. Colonel Suarez was sitting under a verandah, giving orders about serving out a few pounds of llama flesh to the Iquique boatmen, who had arrived the night before. Facing him, and nearly over his head, was the clear-cut line of the crest of the ravine touching the blue sky, and as yet unbroken. Suddenly a muleteer galloped breathlessly up to the steps, and reported that the enemy was in force upon the heights. In quick succession came another and another messenger, with the news that the enemy was advancing up the ravine to Tarapaca. At the same time the two lieut.-colonels, Manuel Suarez and Juan Bautista Zubiaga, were talking to the officer of the guard, Don Pedro Ferrer. A sub-lieutenant, a mere lad named Daniel Osorio (killed that day), ran up in great excitement, and said that the enemy was surrounding them. Zubiaga smiled and patted him on the back. In another minute the skyline was broken by moving columns of armed men, and there was a call to arms.

Buendia and Suarez made their dispositions on the instant. They seemed to be surrounded. The division of Caceres was to climb the ravine side, and attack the enemy actually in sight—of course the division of Santa Cruz on its way to Quilla-huasa. The division of Bolognesi, with Castañon's artillerymen, was to protect the other side; while General Buendia, with the remainder of the force, was to resist the advance of the enemy up the ravine and defend Tarapaca itself. A messenger was sent to Pachica for the vanguard and first division.

Colonel Suarez, on his now famous white horse, led the troops up the steep hill, by a precipitous winding footpath. It was ten a.m. Off the path it was like scaling a wall; and on the crest, formed on level ground, with rifles at the ready, and four Krupp guns, stood the Chilian foe. Calmly, and with undaunted mien, the Yncas climbed the precipitous ascent. Zubiaga led on the men of Cuzco on the right. His second, Benito Pardo de Figueroa, of noble lineage in Lima, and related to the Chilian General Blanco Encalada, was on his left. In the centre were the men of Ayacucho under Manuel Suarez. Caceres, too, was in the front line. The ascent occupied a long half-hour. There was a shout of triumph as the Yncas reached the crest. Santa Cruz threw his men into skirmishing order, advanced rapidly, and formed a semicircle, with the two extremes on the edge of the ravine, and the artillery on the left. He opened a withering fire, expecting to hurl the Peruvians back and down the precipice.

For five minutes the Chilians seemed to gain ground, when the boatmen of Iquique reached the crest, and there was a pause. Then the Yncas charged, led on by Zubiaga. One ringing cheer and he was dead. A bullet had pierced his brain. He fell under the muzzle of a Chilian gun, as Espinar of Cuzco had fallen at San Francisco. Yet another hero falls. Manuel Suarez is dead, with a ball through his forehead. They died in the moment of victory— that victory which their deaths made certain.

The Yncas of the ancient city saw their leaders fall. They set their teeth and charged, not wildly, but steadily and with a purpose. The men of the imperial tribe were in earnest now, and on equal terms, for the Krupp guns were captured ; and the Chilian half-castes had found their match. In vain

Santa Cruz fell back, and formed another line at right angles with the ravine ; in vain the whole centre division, led by Arteaga himself, came to his help. They continued, though fighting bravely for a long hour, to give way. Isaac Recabárren, recovered of his wound received at Pisagua, had taken the place of the dead heroes, and gallantly led the charges. But alas! the best blood of Peru was being poured forth along this path of victory. Pardo de Figueroa, and his brother Francisco, had fallen. Carlos Odiaga, lying dangerously ill in Tarapaca, sprang from his bed, by a last effort climbed the height, and was killed in the thickest of the fight. Poor young Daniel Osorio, who brought the news in hot excitement that morning, was dead ; and Meneses and Torico, and the young brother of the gallant Caceres, all dead. By 11.15 a.m. each of the Chilians had fired 150 rounds. Seeing the advance of Arteaga, Colonel Rios, with the patriots of the coast, rushed up to the rescue. He fell mortally wounded ; and both the brothers Melendez, who came to avenge the death of Grau, the hero of Angamos, were killed, fighting by the side of Rios. The Krupp guns of Arteaga's division kept up a deadly fire on the Peruvians climbing up the hill-side.

But it was all of no avail. The Yncas were in earnest now ; for once they were on equal terms, and the mixed race must find its level. At noon the other Krupp guns were captured, and the Chilians were beaten all along the line. Fire was opened upon them by Captain Manuel Carrera from their own field-guns. The victory of the Peruvians on the " Cuesta de la Visagra" was secured. The Chilians fled towards a sandy hill called the "Cerro de la Minta," about a mile to the westward, in front of Huara-siña. Their retreat was only prevented from being converted into a rout by the cavalry under Villagran, which had watered the horses at Quilla-huasa, and now protected the fugitives. Colonel Caceres received the felicitations of the chief of the staff on the field of battle.

Meanwhile General Buendia was engaged in the ravine, with the division under Ramirez. That officer, guided by the spy Laiseca, advanced from Huara-siña with the second regiment of the line and two Krupp guns, intending to occupy Tarapaca. Hearing the fire of Santa Cruz on the heights, he led his men on. Bolognesi came out to meet him along the eastern slopes, while the Bolivians of the Loa division were at the bottom. The general directed the movements in person. There was a desperate struggle in the outskirts of the village. Here stood the humble dwelling in which the Grand Marshal, Ramon Castilla—the man who gave twenty years of peace to his country—was born. On that spot the enemies of his country were defeated, but at how great a cost! The first to fall was Francisco Perla, the second in command of the Loa division. The young lad Enrique Varela, fragile as a reed but steady as a rock, was wounded ; and the half-English Pezet, grandson of a former President of Peru, and Felipe Flores of Cuzco, fell dead The little band, though falling fast, defended the place with desperate tenacity. There were 107 dead bodies on one spot.

The Chilians in the ravine began to fall back at the same time as their comrades on the heights. In their flight they left their colonel behind, mortally wounded. The standard of the regiment was captured by Mariano Santos, a native of Acomayo. They never stopped until they reached Huara-siña, several taking refuge in roadside huts. At the watering-place they encountered Arteaga, Vergara, Santa Cruz, and the fugitives from the heights.

Fortunately for the Chilians they had an effective body of cavalry, while the Peruvians had none. There was also a detachment under Major Echanez, which had been sent to attack Bolognesi on the hill-slopes, but had failed to do so. These men had not been engaged, and had refreshed themselves at the watering-place of Huara-siña. They formed a rally-ing pivot. The leaders had apparently lost their heads; but there was a little old man in the artillery who had risen from the ranks, named Benavides. Mounted on a mule, he gathered the unwounded men together, cheered them up with dry, comic speeches, and got them to face the advancing enemy, supported by charges of cavalry. The division of Caceres had been fighting for several hours, and the men were exhausted. Benavides not only rallied the Chilians, but gained several hundred yards of ground. While Arteaga and the other chiefs sat down to breakfast, the men got water, and the wounded were attended to and collected by the brave Dr. Kidd, a native of York. At 3.15 p.m. Colonel Arteaga began his meal. Ten minutes afterwards he was effectually disturbed.

The message to the vanguard at Pachica, which was sent off by General Buendia in the forenoon, never arrived until two p.m. The troops, about 1000 strong, at once set out. Colonel Davila, with the men of Puno under Manuel Chamorro, ascended the heights; while Herrera, with the hunters of Cuzco under Fajardo, marched down the ravine. This succour completed the victory. The Peruvians advanced shoulder to shoulder, firing as they came. The Chilians did not even stop to receive them. Colonel Arteaga gave the order for the whole force to retreat. A troop of mules had just brought him supplies of food and water, and with this consolation, and two out of ten guns, he accepted his defeat, and marched away over the Pampa de Tamarugal. If the Peruvians had had any cavalry, or if their ammunition had not been so nearly exhausted, the Chilian defeat would have been converted into a total rout.

But the victory of the Peruvians was complete. They had driven the Chilians back at all points, they retained the whole battle-field, they captured eight guns and one standard, and they quietly continued those preparations for their march, which had been interrupted. It was three days after the Peruvians had gone, that General Baquedano at last sent a column from Dibujo, under Colonel Urriola, to collect the wounded and bury the dead. The Chilian loss amounted to 687 killed and wounded. The Peruvians had 19 officers killed and 16 wounded, 236 men killed and 262 wounded; a total loss on both sides of 1220 men!

The valiant little army, terribly thinned in its

efforts to save the province of Tarapaca, began its sad and weary march to Arica on the following day, with fifty-two Chilian prisoners. That night a full moon rose over the volcano of Isluga, and lighted them on their way. Their route was by what is called the "altos," along the skirts of the cordillera. The first rest was in the gorge of Aroma ; the next at Camiña, 6000 feet above the sea, where there are green clover-fields, vines and olives, and *huacas*, or burial-places of the Ynca ancestry. At Camiña there was a halt of a day, for before them was the long desert march to Camarones. At length Arica was reached on the 18th of December. The success of the retreat was mainly due to the exertions of Sub-Prefect Felipe Rosas, in collecting provisions.

General Buendia and Colonel Suarez on their arrival were very unfairly put under arrest, and ordered to be tried for the loss of the province. They ought to have been received in a very different way. But they were soon released by superior authority, fully reinstated, and entrusted with important commands.

When all the difficulties of the position are fairly considered—the absence of food and supplies of all kinds, the destruction of all means of communication with any base, the impossibility of receiving succour—it must be allowed that General Buendia adopted the proper course when he decided upon leaving the province after the failure of his brilliant assault on the hill of San Francisco. He thus saved the flower of his army, and did the best possible service to his country under the circumstances. Even to do this he had not only to fight a battle, but to gain a victory.

It is terrible to think of the cost of that victory, of all the precious lives that were lost, of the grief and anguish that was caused. Chile has won, and she has got the manure she coveted. Peru has lost, not the province only, but the flower of her youth— her noblest and best. Sorrow and mourning spread over the valleys of the Andes. Yet there was consolation. Her lost ones were not conquering invaders ; they fell in a just and holy cause—the defence of their native land.

CHAPTER X.

NICOLAS DE PIEROLA AS SUPREME CHIEF OF PERU —GENERAL CAMPERO, PRESIDENT OF BOLIVIA.

THE loss of Tarapaca led to revolutionary changes in the Governments both of Peru and Bolivia. General Prado seems to have despaired of success, with the means at his disposal. He has shown that he is personally brave by his conduct in 1866, when the Spanish fleet attacked Callao. He has qualities which attached many warm and faithful friends to him, and in quiet times he might have filled his post with credit. But he was incapable of facing a great emergency.

The President handed over the command of the Peruvian troops at Arica and Tacna to Admiral Don Lizardo Montero, and embarked on board an English mail steamer on the 26th of November. Returning to Lima, he resumed office as President, relieving the Vice-President, General La Puerta, of the duties which he had temporarily performed. Three days afterwards, on December 2nd, a letter was published, in which the President announced his return. He declared his determination to repair the disasters which the arms of Peru had sustained, and that he would utilize the abundant resources of the country with this object, until the hour arrived for fulfilling his duties as a soldier.

After the publication of this letter, the people of Lima were naturally amazed to hear that the President had suddenly, and without warning, abandoned his country in its direst necessity. He embarked on board the mail steamer bound for Panama, and the following decree was published in the morning after his departure :—

" Mariano Ignacio Prado, Constitutional President of the Republic. Inasmuch as I am authorized to leave the country by a legislative resolution of May 2nd, 1878, and very urgent and important matters demanding my presence abroad, and it being my duty and desire to do all I can in favour of the country, I decree, solely, that the first Vice-President take charge of the Presidency of the Republic, in conformity with Articles 90 and 93 of the Constitution.

" Given in the Government House, &c., &c.,
" The 18th day of December, 1879."

A second document was addressed to the nation and the army, briefly stating that his motives for leaving the country were very great and very powerful, and promising to return in due time. It bears the same date.

General Prado saw the inevitable disasters that were approaching, and he hoped to avert them by obtaining some help, either in money or *matériel*, or intervention, from Europe or the United States. There is no reason to suppose that he was actuated by any other less worthy motive. Yet nothing can excuse this sudden desertion of his post.

General Prado is, nevertheless, the hero of the 2nd of May, 1866, the day on which the Spanish fleet was repulsed from Callao. The most popular writer in Chile has declared Prado to be one of the loyal and honoured friends of that country, and the most generous subscriber to the works of the Paseo de Santa Lucia at Santiago. "It seemed right that such noble disinterestedness should be recognized by the erection of a monument which, while it was a memorial to General Prado, should also serve as a national tribute, on the part of Chile, to one of the most noble deeds in the annals of America. Such was the defence of Callao against the Spanish fleet by General Prado."[1] Thus it was resolved to erect a monument in memory of the action of May 2nd, on the height of Santa Lucia, in the capital of Chile. Until the magnanimous feeling which suggested this act returns to the Chilian people they will continue to be losers by reason of their "glorious" war.

Once more the aged and infirm Vice-President, General La Puerta, assumed office. The Minister of War was General Don Manuel Gonzalez de La Cotera, an educated officer who has travelled in Europe. He is an incorrigible intriguer, mistrusted by his superiors, but a favourite with the men. He is a native of Piura, of good family, and began his military career as a cadet in 1868. La Cotera was resolved to maintain the constitutional government in power if

[1] "El Pasco de Santa Lucia. Lo que es i lo que debera ser." "Segunda Memoria." (Santiago, 1873.)

possible, but Lima was in a state of excitement and scarcely suppressed anger.   All through the day after the president's flight great crowds assembled in the streets.   Next day, in the afternoon, Colonel Arguedas, in the barracks of the Inquisition Square, refused to obey orders to send a detachment to the palace.   His battalion broke out into mutiny.   La Cotera marched against the insurgent troops, and a heavy fire was opened upon his followers from the house-tops.   He retreated to the palace, and soon afterwards Don Nicolas de Pierola, at the head of another insurgent battalion, appeared in the great square, and there was more firing.   Altogether sixty men were killed and about 200 wounded.   The armed populace now declared openly for revolution, and Pierola placed himself at the head of the movement.

Assembling all the troops that adhered to him, he marched to Callao, and got possession of the port early on the 22nd.   The Archbishop of Lima, who sympathized with Pierola, now intervened and succeeded at last in persuading the Vice-President to resign his charge.   In the morning of December the 23rd Don Nicolas de Pierola made his solemn entry into the capital, and was proclaimed Supreme Chief of the Republic.

Nicolas de Pierola comes of an old Catalonian stock.   The home of his ancestors was in the little village of Pierola, in the mountains twenty miles from Barcelona, famous for its vineyards and for the boar and wolf hunts in the vicinity.   The American branch of the Pierolas settled at Camaná, on the coast of Peru, near Arequipa.   Here young Nicolas was born

on the 5th of January, 1839, the son of the learned
naturalist, whose honourable career has already been
noticed.[2] His father, though Finance Minister under
Castilla, was strictly honest, and died poor. He
brought up his son in the same habits of purity and
thrift. But he died when the lad was barely seventeen, and the young Nicolas became a second father
to his little brothers and sisters. His protector and
tutor was Dr. Huerta, now Bishop of Arequipa, who
was then rector of the seminary of Santo Toribio at
Lima. Of his brothers Emilio was a naturalist like his
father, and died in 1879. Exequiel is in the artillery,
and Carlos distinguished himself by his gallantry in
the defence of Lima. Don Nicolas is married to a
granddaughter of Agustin Iturbide, the ill-starred
Emperor of Mexico, and their son, aged about
eighteen, was by his father's side at the battle of
Chorrillos.

Pierola was educated at Santo Toribio, but he
decided upon a legal career, and, becoming an advocate in 1860, he founded a review called *El Pro-
greso Catolico*. In 1864 he became editor of *El
Tiempo*, in which periodical he defended the administration of President Pezet, so that he fell with his
patron when Prado's insurrection was successful.
He travelled for some time in Europe. President
Balta appointed Pierola to the ministry of finance on
January 5th, 1869; and he shares with his chief the
credit of the great public works that were executed
or projected, and the discredit of the ruinous loans
During the subsequent administrations of Pardo and

[2] See page 46.

Prado, from 1872 to 1878, he was always conspiring, and when the war broke out he was residing in Chile. He offered his services to his country, and was allowed to return to Lima in 1879.

The Supreme Chief is vivacious in conversation, has an agreeable address, and speaks French fluently. His countenance is bright and pleasing, and his smile almost captivating. He has a clear intellect, great decision of character, self-confidence, and extraordinary tenacity of purpose inherited from his Catalan ancestors.

The secret of his success appears to have been the confidence felt by the people in his audacity, and in his ability to stem the tide of invasion. Pierola grasped the situation in which the country was placed. He felt that the constitutional government, deprived of its head, would be incapable of meeting the emergency. He, therefore, stepped forward and boldly seized the helm in the hour of extreme peril. His ability was tacitly acknowledged by the various leaders of parties. These men, instead of harassing their distracted country by adding the evils of civil contention to its difficulties, patriotically accepted the leadership of Pierola, and maintained unwavering loyalty towards him during the war. Pierola showed himself to be a great war minister, and for his services in her sore need he has deserved well of his country.

The new ministry, appointed by the Supreme Chief, included men of position and ability. The Minister for Foreign Affairs was Don Pedro José Calderon, a native of Lima and an old schoolfellow of Pierola, who was envoy in Germany during the Balta administration.   Don Nemesio Orbegoso, the Minister of the Interior, is a son of the former President, and had been Prefect of his native town of Truxillo.   Colonel Miguel Iglesias, who took charge of the war department, is a wealthy landed proprietor at Caxamarca, with a character for probity and for stoutness of heart.   He afterwards brilliantly maintained his reputation for valour in the moment of his country's extremity, on the Morro Solar.[3]

The change in the government of Bolivia took place under different circumstances.   Ever since his desertion of the army of Tarapaca, and his retreat from Camarones, his own troops had felt ashamed of their leader.   This man is one of the worst public characters that has been churned up to the surface in the caldron of Bolivian revolution.   Hilarion Daza was of low origin, born at Sucre or Chuquisaca.   His father's name, which for some reason of his own he dropped, was Grossoli.   Young Daza was brought up to an idle life, and so he continued until the revolution of Linares, when he took service under some military chief, and in 1862 was made a sub-lieutenant.   Another change got him his captaincy, and returning to Sucre, he led the life of a conspirator.   In 1864 Daza obtained the rank of major by joining Melgarejo in his successful revolution.   General Nicanor Flores and the poet Nestor Galindo, author of a volume of sonnets entitled " Lagrimas," rose against the tyranny of Melgarejo in 1865, but they were defeated.   A dark suspicion hangs over the name of Daza in con-

---

[1] See page 243.

N

nexion with the death of young Galindo. When another revolt broke out against Melgarejo at Sucre, Daza carried the news to La Paz by galloping at the rate of fifty leagues a day, without rest, for 500 miles. For this service he was made a colonel, with command of the first regiment of Bolivia, called "Colorados." But in 1870 he betrayed Melgarejo, and was a turbulent supporter of Morales. In 1872 he married a lady, named Benita Gutierrez, of Sorata. Daza was proclaimed President of Bolivia on May 4th, 1876. His predecessor, Melgarejo, was one of the worst characters that profligate revolutions have thrown to the surface in South America, but he was at least brave. Daza has not displayed that quality, and he has shown himself to be as ignorant as he is incapable.

Daza was encamped with the Bolivian army at Tacna. On the 27th of December he went to Arica, by invitation from Admiral Montero, to discuss the plan of the campaign. At four p.m. he proceeded to the railway station at Arica, to return to Tacna. He had got into the train, when a telegram was handed to him. He read it, and jumped out as if some one had struck him. The telegram announced that, during his absence, the Bolivian army had risen at the call of some of the superior officers, that he had been deposed, and that Colonel Don Eleodoro Camacho was elected to command the army in his place. Daza remained at Arica. If he had gone on in the train, he would have been taken out by his own men and shot. They searched the train for him at the first station. Montero condoled with him, but declined to interfere. On the 4th of January, 1880, he began a journey on horseback to Mollendo, and went thence by train to Arequipa. There he heard of the revolution which had broken out at La Paz on the 28th of December, and he consequently took the steamer for Panama and went to Paris.

General Don Narciso Campero was proclaimed at La Paz, and his nomination was cordially accepted by the army at Tacna. He was elected constitutional President of Bolivia on the 5th of June, 1880, but previously he was called upon to perform anxious service in the field.

If Daza is the worst, Campero is one of the best examples of a South American military statesman. Born in the province of Tarija, in the extreme south of Bolivia, he received an exceptionally good education, and, surrounded by an atmosphere of treachery and intrigue, he has ever maintained a well-earned reputation for honesty and candour. Naturally gifted with ability and powers of application, he improved himself by a residence in Europe, and afterwards was Minister for Bolivia in England and France, where, during the years 1872-73, he took great interest in the project for making the river Madeira navigable. In the success of this enterprise, now indefinitely postponed, General Campero looks forward to the future prosperity of his country. As an organizer the new President was unsuccessful in his efforts to succour the Peruvians in their gallant attempt to defend Tarapaca. His failure was not, however, due to any want of energy or foresight on his part, but to the insurmountable natural difficulties.

N 2

As a conductor of the war the Bolivians had selected the best man their country contained, in Narciso Campero; while Nicolas de Pierola was endowed with ability, untiring energy, and courage, and, in her death struggle, he served Peru well and faithfully.

CHAPTER XI.

BLOCKADE OF ARICA AND CALLAO.

THE year 1880 was the saddest that had dawned upon the land of the Yncas since, 348 years before, Pizarro entered upon his career of conquest at Tumbez.

Already, before that year of desolation began, the Chilian fleet had commenced the blockade of Arica. Three men-of-war made their appearance a few days after General Prado had sailed for Callao. Chile now had three powerful ironclads, besides several corvettes, and she had increased her navy by the purchase of a steamer called the *Angamos*, with a most formidable armament, though only consisting of one gun. It was an 8-inch breech-loading Armstrong of eleven and a half tons, and eighteen feet four inches long, mounted on a central pivoted slide. The range of this gun was 8000 yards, far out of reach of any guns at Arica. The port of Arica is an open roadstead, protected to the south by a lofty cape called the Morro, and the rocky island of Alacran. The town stretches along the beach from the Morro, and the surrounding country is desert and sandy, though there is a fertile valley up the watercourse of the Azapa, which reaches the sea to the north of Arica. The railroad to Tacna passes along the beach for a short distance, and then runs a little east of north. The defences consisted of twenty rifled guns, ten planted on the Morro, and the rest in forts on the beach north of the town, called *2° de Mayo*, *Santa Rosa*, and *San José*. The accomplished Captain Camilo Carrillo, of the Peruvian navy, was commandant of the batteries. The harbour defence monitor, *Manco Capac*, commanded by Captain Don José Sanchez Lagomarsino, was moored under the protection of the forts. There was also a small torpedo brigade on the island of Alacran, commanded by Lorencio Prado, a son of the President.

The Chilian blockading squadron had not been many days in Arica roadstead before the defenders made an attempt to destroy the corvettes *O'Higgins* and *Chacabuco* by means of a steam launch, armed with a spar torpedo. It failed, however, and the launch ran on shore, and was broken up by the heavy surf which rolls in along the coast.

The next offensive operation showed how completely the possession of the sea placed the Peruvian coast at the mercy of the invaders. They could land where they pleased, and the unfortunate people and their possessions were at the mercy of the enemy. At dawn, on the 31st of December, the Chilian squadron landed 500 soldiers under an engineer officer named Aristides Martinez, at the little port of Ylo, north of Arica. Ylo is connected by a railroad with the town of Moquegua, the centre of rich vine-growing valleys. The invaders reached Moquegua by train, exacted a contribution of provisions, and returned to Ylo. They then dismounted the railway locomotives, and embarked again on the 2nd of January. The object appears to have been to strike terror, and to show how suddenly and unexpectedly a Chilian force could make its appearance.

On the 27th of February, 1880, the Chilian commander sent the ironclad *Huascar* closer in towards Arica, for the purpose of reconnoitring the forts and batteries. On getting within range, fire was opened upon her by the guns on the Morro, and by the *Manco Capac*, and a desultory action ensued, which lasted for about an hour, when the *Huascar* retired out of range. Soon afterwards the Chilians observed a train full of soldiers about to start for Tacna. So the blockading squadron again steamed in to shell the train, which brought about a second engagement. This time the *Huascar* was struck by a shell which killed seven and wounded nine officers and men, including two lieutenants. The *Manco Capac* then got under weigh, and the *Huascar* once more steamed in towards her adversary. On nearing the harbour-defence monitor, the captain of the *Huascar* observed that she had a torpedo-boat alongside, so he renounced his first intention of attempting to ram, and ordered the helm to be put hard over, so as to increase his distance. At that moment a shell from the *Manco Capac* struck the mizen-mast of the *Huascar*, exploded, and blew the captain, named Thomson, literally to pieces. The first lieutenant continued the action, assisted by the *Magallanes*, for an hour longer, when the *Manco Capac* returned to her anchorage. During these engagements the *Huascar* discharged 116 projectiles, 35 from the eight-inch guns in her turret, and 81 from her 40-pounders, besides firing 600 rounds from the Hotchkiss and Gatling guns. The *Magallanes* was struck three times in her hull, and the *Huascar* received a shot in her hull which caused her to leak badly. Two days afterwards the *Angamos* bombarded the town of Arica with her solitary 8-inch Armstrong, at the amazing distance of 8000 yards, the *Huascar* joining her later in the day. This was continued for five days, the *Angamos* hurling 100 projectiles from her huge gun. Much terror was caused to the inhabitants, but as the houses are built of large sun-dried bricks, called *adobes*, the injuries they sustained were comparatively unimportant.

So February passed away, and during the month of March the little Peruvian navy, consisting of one wooden corvette, added another daring feat to its achievements. Arica, the headquarters of the allied army, being closely blockaded, Captain Villavicencio, in command of the *Union*, determined to land supplies in spite of the whole ironclad fleet of Chile. Having embarked a cargo at Callao, consisting of six Gatling guns, several thousand rifles with ammunition, and clothing for the troops, besides a torpedo-boat named the *Alianza*, the gallant little *Union* set out on her daring expedition at daylight, on the 17th of March.

Suddenly appearing off Arica, Captain Villavicencio succeeded in eluding the blockading squadron anchored in the roads, and safely landed his valuable cargo. On discovering that they had been outwitted, the Chilians sent in an overwhelming force, consisting of the *Cochrane* and *Huascar* ironclads and the *Amazonas* to attempt the destruction of the *Union*. But this powerful fleet would not venture within range of the guns on the Morro. The ships kept at the very respectful distance of 7000 yards, at which range their firing was not very effective. Afterwards the two ironclads closed to 3500 yards, when some better practice was made. A shell from the *Cochrane* burst over the *Union*, wounding twenty and killing two men. At three p.m. the Chilians ceased firing, and stood to the northward in company, thinking that the *Union* would attempt to escape in that direction. Captain Villavicencio closely observed their very unintelligent movements, adroitly slipped out of the anchorage, and steamed full speed to the south, obtaining a clear lead of four miles. He was immediately pursued, but with such a start he could laugh at his enemies, who were soon out of sight. So the *Union* returned safely to Callao.

On the 6th of April a Chilian squadron, consisting of the *Blanco Encalada*, bearing the flag of Rear-Admiral Riveros, the *Huascar*, the *Angamos*, the *Pilcomayo*, and the *Matias Cousiño*, proceeded north-wards towards Callao. Remaining out of sight, a torpedo-boat was sent in at 4.30 a.m., of the 10th, to attempt the destruction of the *Union*, as she lay along-side the mole or *darsena*. The attempt failed in con-sequence of booms and other obstructions which had been placed round the ship ; and another attempt next day was equally futile. In the forenoon of the 10th the hostile fleet arrived in the bay, and officially notified the blockade to the Peruvian authorities and to foreign representatives. From that date Callao was closely blockaded by the enemy for nine months.

Neutral merchant ships were warned to leave the roads within eight days, after which time the Chilian admiral declared that he would feel himself at liberty to bombard the town.

Callao is built along a spit of land and on the shore of a large bay facing north, two lines of railroad connecting it with Lima, a distance of eight miles over a plain which rises slightly to the foot of the maritime cordilleras. The spit is separated from the high and barren island of San Lorenzo by a channel called the " Boqueron." Callao is the headquarters of the English Pacific Steam Navigation Company, and the Company has works consisting of steam cranes for loading and unloading, iron and brass foundries, artificers' shops with steam power, and store-houses covering an area of 60,000 square yards. Callao has a floating dock capable of lifting 5000 tons, and a new work, including docks and piers, was commenced in 1870, called the *Muelle y darsena*. The total length of the sea-wall comprised in this work is 4520 feet, enclosing a space of fifty-two acres, with berthing accommodation for large ships. There are also eighteen steam cranes, a triple line of rails, lighthouse, and supplies of fresh water for shipping at eight points. The defences consisted, in the first place, of the two old historical round towers of Callao Castle, now called " Independencia" and " Manco Capac," the former mounted with two 500-pounder Blakeley guns, and the latter with four 300-pounder Vavasseurs. On the spit there were two 1000-pounder smooth-bore Rodman guns. On the beach were the two revolving armoured turrets called " Junin" and " Mercedes," one north of the town, the other on the spit to the south, each with two 500-pounder Armstrongs. Between them were forts "Ayacucho" and "Santa Rosa," with two 500-pounder Blakeley guns on each. Besides the heavy guns there were six smaller batteries called "Maypu," "Provisional," "Zepita," "Abtao," "Pichincha," and "Independencia," with two, five, eight, six, four, and six 32-pounders respectively. These small guns were of very little use.

The *Atahualpa* (harbour defence monitor) and the *Union*, with three school ships and some transports, were moored inside the *darsena*; and the Peruvians had a Herreschoff torpedo-boat and several steam launches. But a fatal mistake was made in not having fortified the island of San Lorenzo, which became the headquarters of the blockading squadron.

Thus the desolating work continued, and now the Chilians had arrived to extend havoc and destruction over this thriving and important commercial sea-port. On the 22nd and 23rd of April they bombarded Callao at ranges varying from 5000 to 7000 yards, firing 127 shot and shell; the Peruvian guns returning the fire with 170. But the long range rendered this attack comparatively harmless.

Don Nicolas de Pierola, as the Peruvian ironclads were lost to the country, turned his attention to the careful organization of a torpedo brigade. He caused to be launched several floating mechanical torpedoes on McEvoy's plan of a vibrating weight releasing a trigger. Some were placed in the Boqueron passage, in the hope that the current would carry them down to the Chilian guard-ship. Two of these torpedoes were found by the Chilian steamer *Amazonas*, floating just below the surface. One was sunk by firing at it with rifles, but the other was secured, and towed to San Lorenzo, where it exploded directly it touched the ground, with such force that the brass lid belonging to it was sent flying into the air to a height of over 150 feet. The violence of the explosion led to the supposition that it was charged with about 100 lbs. of dynamite. It was of a cylindrical shape, the outer shell being of copper. A wheel was fixed at one end, so arranged as to revolve on coming in contact with any heavy body.

In revenge for these attempts Admiral Riveros again bombarded Callao during the afternoon of the 10th of May. The squadron fired 400 projectiles which were replied to by the forts and batteries on shore. The principal object of the Chilians was the destruction of the vessels that were sheltered behind the walls of the *darsena;* and a school ship, besides several boats and barges, was sunk. On the other hand the hull of the *Huascar* was struck three times, her steering gear being injured by one shot, which for a time made her useless. Another shot hit her at the water-line, filling one of the wing compartments.

The Chilians increased the effectiveness of the Callao blockade during the month of May by the addition of several swift torpedo-boats. Of these the *Fresia* and *Janequeo* were built at Yarrow, and sent out from England to Valparaiso in sections on board an English merchant-ship, a breach of neutrality which ought to have been prevented. It is sad to reflect how very, little harm these misguided countries could have done to each other if it had not been for the means of destruction supplied to them by England, Germany, and the United States. The *Fresia* and *Janequeo* were of steel, with five watertight compartments, seventy feet long, and with a speed of eighteen knots. The *Janequeo* was fitted with three McEvoy patent duplex outrigger torpedoes, one on a boom rigged out on the stern, the others on side-swinging booms. These two boats also carried a Hotchkiss machine gun each. The *Guacoldo* was another of these boats, built in America for the Peruvian Government, and sent out by the Isthmus of Panama. She was captured by the Chilian transport *Amazonas* on her voyage to Callao. Two more, the *Colo-colo* and *Tucapel*, were of a smaller class, built on the Thames by Thorneycroft, and armed with outrigger torpedoes and machine guns. These boats, in consequence of their great speed, were used to keep watch over the Peruvian ships at night, and were regarded as the eyes of the blockading squadron during the dark hours. They were in charge of energetic and intelligent officers, whose vigilance during the long blockade was unceasing.

The *Janequeo* was commanded by Lieutenant Senorét, and the *Guacoldo* by Lieutenant Goñi. These two boats were cruising in company and reconnoitring the entrance to the docks early in the morning of the 25th of May in pitch darkness, when they suddenly found themselves close to a Peruvian steam launch, the *Independencia*, commanded by Lieutenant Galvez, and manned by a few soldiers with a mitrailleuse. The launch turned to re-enter the *darsena*

closely pursued by the *Janequeo*. On nearing his
adversary Lieutenant Senoret tried to destroy the
launch with his stern torpedo, but failing to place
it in contact, he attempted, as the two boats sheered
outwards from each other, to bring his port swinging
torpedo into action. The boats at this time were
so close that there was no room for the spar to
swing out. Imagining, however, that it was in contact
with his opponent's hull, and sufficiently far from
his own, Lieutenant Senoret pressed the firing key
of the battery and exploded the torpedo. At the
same time Lieutenant Galvez threw a 100 lb. case
of powder on the sloping deck of the *Janequeo*, and
exploded it by firing his revolver. This caused the
immediate destruction of the torpedo-boat. She filled
and sank, the officer and men escaping in a small
boat. The *Independencia* sank soon afterwards, eight
of her men having been killed by the explosion.
The gallant Lieutenant Galvez and seven men were
picked up by the *Guacoldo*. Doubt has been cast
upon the daring act of the Peruvian lieutenant, but
Lieutenant Senoret gave distinct evidence that there
were two explosions.

After this affair the blockade of Callao, and the
adjacent ports of Ancon and Chancay, was maintained with redoubled vigilance.

71°
7
17
Tumila
Estrella de los Angeles
Alto de la villa
MOQUEGUA
Ticapampa R.
Ilo R.
RAILWAY
Hospicio
Mirabe
ILO
Sama
Locumba R.
Buena vista
Sama R.
ITE
Morro de Sama
PACIFIC OCEAN
8
18
TACNA
N
RAILWAY
CAMPAIGN
OF
TACNA
Geographical Miles
10   20
English Miles
10   20
ARICA
Morro
71 Longitude West from Greenwich

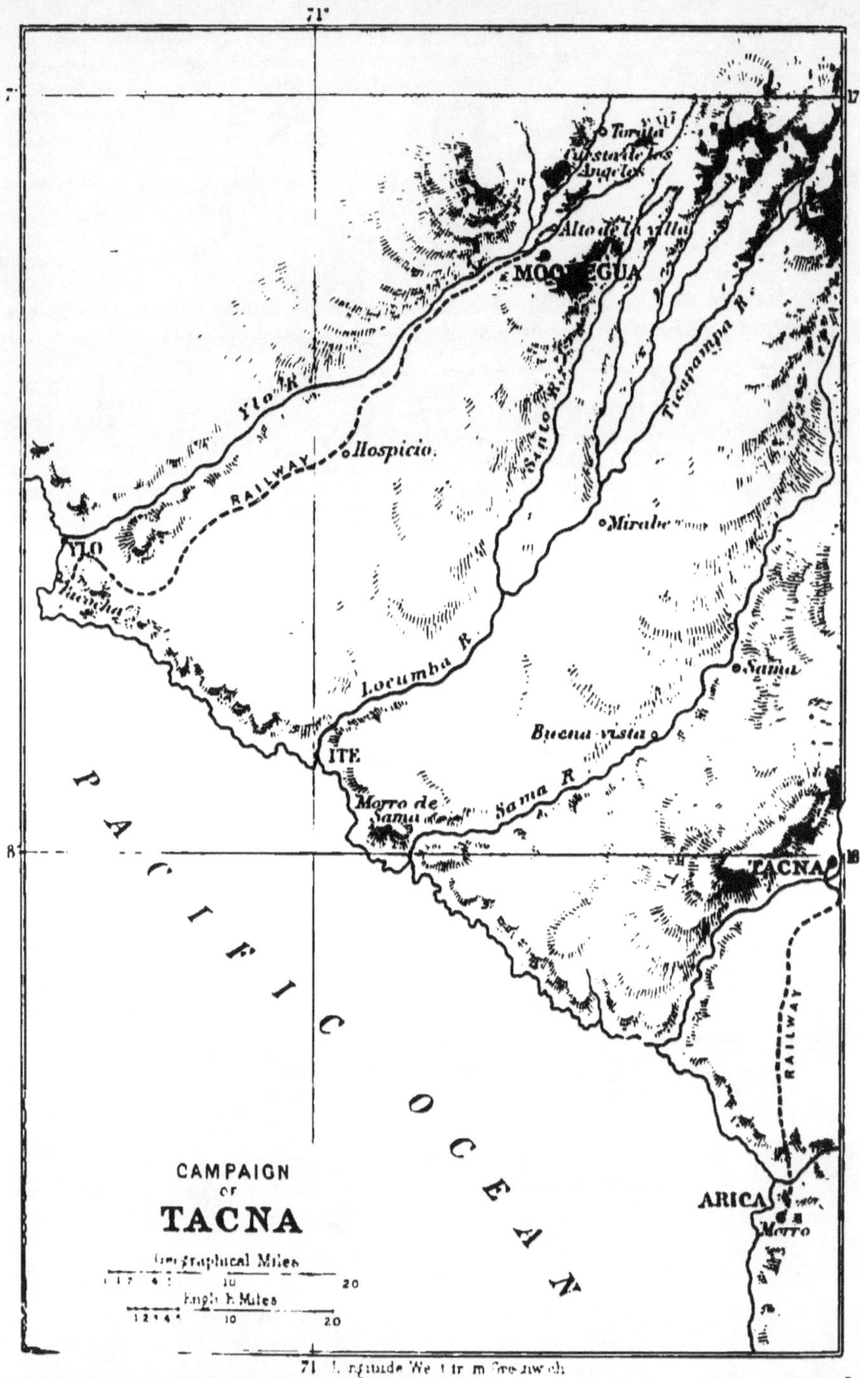

F. Weller, sc.

CHAPTER XII.

THE TACNA CAMPAIGN.

THE Chilians had now conquered and occupied the coveted nitrate provinces, the annexation of which was the real object of the war, and they had destroyed the Peruvian fleet. All reasonable pretext for further operations, involving bloodshed and destruction, had ceased to exist. The continuation of such work was unnecessary for the invader's avowed objects. But a nation that once enters upon a career of glory and ambition will not readily desist. Success is apt to blunt and often to destroy the moral sense. So it was with Chile. The conquerors of the Tarapaca province determined to extend their desolating inroads over the more northern Peruvian departments of Tacna and Moquegua; and to destroy the allied army assembled at Tacna.

The plan was for the invading forces to effect a landing to the northward, so as to cut off the allies from all communications, and then fall upon them in their isolated position. With complete command of the sea, and superiority in every military point of view, there was little difficulty. A fleet of sixteen transports and men-of-war was assembled at Pisagua, and 10,000 men were embarked on the 24th of

February, 1880. They were put on shore at Ylo and Pacocha two days afterwards, and on the 28th an additional force of 4000 men was landed. On the 8th of March 2000 men, led by Colonel Orozimbo Barbosa, were disembarked at the port of Islay further north. They marched thence to Mollendo, the port of Arequipa, and committed the most useless and deplorable acts of destruction. Telegraph works, rolling stock, railroad, and the fine new mole were all demolished. The marauders returned to Ylo on March 14th.

General Don Manuel Baquedano was now appointed to the command of the Chilian invading army, to succeed General Escala. Ylo is connected with the town of Moquegua by a railroad, and at that time there was a small Peruvian force, commanded by Colonel Don Andres Gamarra, in a strong position beyond Moquegua, on the road to the little town of Torata, on the spurs of the Andes. Between Moquegua and Torata there is a very rugged and difficult range of mountains which only offers one tolerable line for a road, which is by the " Cuesta de los Angeles." Up this ascent there is a zigzag path, with scarped defiles on either side. Here Gamarra had entrenched himself.

The position of Los Angeles is historical. It was here that the Spanish General Valdez repulsed the attacks of the patriots led by Alvarado on January 19th, 1823 ; and it is an interesting fact that Espartero, then a young colonel of thirty, but afterwards Duke of Victory and Regent of Spain, commanded the left wing of the army of Valdez on that occasion. The same position was occupied by Pierola, in his insurrection against the government of President Pardo, in 1874. But General Buendia, who was the adviser of Señor Pardo, knew that the failure of Alvarado, in 1823, was due to his having confined his movements to an attack in front. He, therefore, sent Montero, the present admiral, by a long round to make a simultaneous assault in the rear. These tactics were successful, and Pierola was entirely defeated.

The Chilian general, in his attack on Colonel Gamarra, faithfully copied the plan of President Pardo's adviser. On the 20th of March his troops occupied Moquegua ; and he ordered the volunteer regiment of Copiapo to scale the heights on the right of the Peruvian position ; while a thousand men under Colonel Muñoz, made a long round to fall upon the Peruvian left rear. Baquedano then got his artillery into position, to open fire on the zigzag road in front of Gamarra's entrenchment. At dawn, on the 22nd of March, the Peruvians found themselves fiercely assaulted by the Copiapo men, on their right flank ; while their reserve was as unexpectedly attacked in rear by Muñoz. At the same moment a storm of shell was showered upon the defenders from the Chilian field-guns. For more than an hour the Peruvian soldiers, though overmatched and surrounded, steadily held their ground. At length they fell back, leaving twenty-eight killed and many wounded on the field. Torata was occupied by the Chilians on the same day, but subsequently abandoned. The immediate object of Baquedano was to close the roads by which the army at Tacna could communicate with the rest of Peru, and receive supplies or reinforcements.

Preparations were then made for the advance against the allied army at Tacna. From Ylo the distance of eighty miles is occupied by a desert intersected by two narrow but fertile valleys, called Locumba and Sama. Carts were landed for carrying stores, provisions, forage, and supplies of water in casks. While these preparations were being made, Colonel Vergara, the hero of the butchery at Jermania, got a second opportunity of distinguishing himself by swooping down upon another body of wretchedly mounted Peruvians under Colonel Albarracain. On the 17th of April, his cavalry once more annihilated the poor wretches who fled before them, killing about 150, and leaving the dead bodies with ghastly sabre-cuts, scattered over a distance of several leagues.

General Baquedano, accompanied by Don Rafael Sotomayor, the Minister of War "in campaign," set out from his camp of Hospicio, on the railroad between Ylo and Moquegua, on the 27th of April. His troops marched in separate divisions, with cavalry and powerful batteries of Krupp field-guns of long range. On the 20th of May, the Chilians encamped at a place called Yarao, near the village of Buenavista in the Sama valley. Here the War Minister, Sotomayor, the man to whom the conception of this deplorable campaign was due, died very suddenly of apoplexy.

Meanwhile the allied army, cut off from communication by the blockade and by the vast distances over desolate wildernesses, was in a most difficult position. Tacna is a town situated on the Pacific side of the Andes, in a fertile plain running north and south between two ranges of hills. The high road to Bolivia passes through it and winds along over the mountains. Tacna, with its seaport of Arica, is the outlet for Bolivian commerce, and, previous to the desolating Chilian invasion, they were both very thriving places. Tacna had a population of 14,000 souls.

When President Prado deserted his post, he left the Peruvian army in command of Admiral Montero. The career of this ambitious officer had been one of intrigue and adventure. Lizardo Montero is a native of Piura, a fellow-townsman of Miguel Grau, and like Grau he adopted the sea as a profession. He is first heard of when General Vivanco began a revolt against the government of Castilla, in 1856. At that time the *Apurimac* frigate was the largest vessel in the Peruvian navy, and she was lying at anchor off Arica. While her captain, a rough old Chilian seaman named Salcedo, was on shore, the crew led by young Montero mutinied, declared for Vivanco, and steamed away, leaving Salcedo storming on the beach. Montero at once went to Islay, then the port of Arequipa, and took possession. In the following year, Castilla besieged Vivanco in Arequipa, but the daring Montero, after a hard street-fight, took Arica, so that the President was cut off from his communications both at Islay and Arica. When Vivanco was beaten, Montero surrendered the *Apurimac* and succeeded in making his peace. Since then he has always been prominent. Don Manuel Pardo rewarded him for his excellent services in putting down the rebellion of Pierola in 1874, by placing him at the head of the navy. In 1876 he was the candidate for the presidentship against Prado, and when the war broke out he was Senator for his native town of Piura. In his fidelity to the best interests of Peru in her great need, and in his zealous efforts to organize an efficient force at Tacna, Montero has atoned for the turbulence of his earlier career. He is married to Doña Rosa Elias, a daughter of the wealthy family of vine-growers at Pisco and Yca. The admiral's army consisted of the remnant of the heroes of Tarapaca, and such recruits as had since been collected. Pierola sent a friend of his own as Prefect of Tacna, with political powers at which a factious man might have taken offence. This was Don Pedro del Solar, a lawyer and editor of the *Patria* newspaper. Montero, however, received him in a proper spirit, allowing no personal feelings to interrupt the harmony of official work at such a crisis. "It seems to me," he said to Dr. Solar, "that between you and I, we have to save our country."[1]

Since the fall of Daza the Bolivian army at Tacna had been commanded by Colonel Don Eleodoro Camacho, a native of Cochabamba, and a lawyer as well as a soldier. His original command had been the third column of the vanguard, consisting entirely of young mounted volunteers of his native town, all law students. This vanguard or " Legion Boliviana "

---

[1] " Se me figura que entre vm. i yo habremos de salvar a nuestra patria.'

was composed of three volunteer regiments of young patriots from the towns of Chuquisaca, La Paz, and Cochabamba ; commanded respectively by Colonels Saravia, Pinto, and Camacho. The rest of the army was in four divisions ; but a large proportion had already suffered severely in the Tarapaca campaign.

General Campero placed complete and deserved confidence in Colonel Camacho ; and on the 19th of April, the President arrived from Bolivia to assume the command in chief. Admiral Montero, with the Peruvians, then became second in command ; while Camacho was second in the Bolivian army. Campero held a review of the allied army on the 22nd, and was well satisfied with its appearance, but he deplored the total absence of all means of transport. This necessitated exclusively defensive tactics. The artillery also was very defective ; and there were no arrangements for obtaining information. The army only numbered 10,000 men on paper, and of these 2000 formed the garrison of Arica. A battalion of Indians from the President's native province of Tarija, called " Chorolque," numbering about 1000 men, arrived early in May. But the total of actual fighting-men did not exceed 9000, against 14,000 Chilians.

Considering the great superiority of the Chilian army in numbers, in cavalry, and above all in artillery, General Campero resolved to select a good defensive position and await an assault. Tacna is bounded on the north-west by a number of arid hills of heavy sand, which makes the ascent difficult. Here he hoped he might be able to select a position where the enemy's cavalry would be useless, and which

would offer advantages in resisting an attack.   After
a long and careful examination of the ground, he
moved the encampment to a small plateau which
dominated the adjacent plain.   The flanks of this
position were defended by deep ravines, there was a
steep glacis in front, and the approach to Tacna was
commanded.   Some rough field-defences were thrown
up, and each soldier was supplied with a sack to fill
with sand, so that he could quickly form a shelter
against rifle firing.   In these dispositions of his small
force Campero showed himself to be an able strate-
gist.   But he only assumed the command when it
was too late.   In disposing his army in line of battle,
the general entrusted the centre to Colonel Castro
Pinto, who commanded a volunteer regiment composed of the enthusiastic youth of Chuquisaca.   The
left wing was directed by Colonel Camacho.   Admiral
Montero, with the Peruvians, was on the right, Colonel
Velarde acting as his chief of the staff.   Here, too,
was Colonel Belisario Suarez, who had been the soul
of the Tarapaca campaign.   Caceres, Davila, Fajardo,
three surviving warriors of that ravine of victory, were
once more in command of divisions ; with Colonels
Cesar Canevaro and Miguel Iglesias of Caxamarca,
soon to do good service again before Lima.   Colonel
Panizo had charge of the artillery.   Don Pedro del
Solar, the Prefect of Tacna, had collected a reserve of
a few hundred volunteers and police. General Perez, a
Bolivian, acted as chief of the staff for the whole army.

The Chilian army was, meanwhile, encamped on
the banks of the Sama river, about sixteen miles
to the westward.   The superiority of Baquedano in

cavalry enabled him to make a reconnaissance in force
to within gunshot of Campero's position, while the
allied general was unable to advance beyond the line
of his outposts. On the 25th of May the Chilians
encamped within six miles of Tacna.

On the 26th Baquedano advanced his army, with rifle
skirmishers on each flank, to a position well outside
the range of his enemy's artillery. Here he stationed
a reserve under Colonel Muñoz. At ten a.m. he
opened a tremendous fire from his long 12-pounder
Krupp guns, which have a range of 4000 yards.
They did their fell work with deadly precision, cutting
up and demoralizing the defenders of the position
long before their few short-range guns could return
the fire. For a long hour this artillery fire had to be
endured,—a severe trial to the men. The Chilian
infantry was then formed in four divisions, each
composed of 2400 men. The first, under Colonel
Amengual, was the first to become engaged, attacking
the extreme left of the allied position. The two next,
led by Amunategui and Barcelo, assaulted the allied
centre; while the fourth, under Barbosa, the marauder
of Islay and Mollendo, attacked Montero on the right.

The weakest point of the allied position was on the
left, where Camacho led; and it was to this point that
Baquedano directed the largest assaulting column.
At noon the battle had become general all along the
line; the Chilian artillery continuing a plunging fire
over the heads of the infantry, and especially con-
centrating it on the allied left. The brave Aymara
Indians and the gallant young volunteers held their
own unmoved, undaunted either by the long and

trying bombardment or by the constantly renewed charges of the Chilian infantry. At length, decimated by the terrible fire, and with the poor boys of Cochabamba, the " Libres del Sur," as they called themselves, almost annihilated, the left wing gave ground. Campero immediately sent up the reserves to reinforce it, and the combat was continued with renewed ardour. For a moment there was a bright flash of hope.[2] The Chilian column now wavered, and was hurled down the hill to the point where the assault commenced. But the advantage could not be secured, owing to a protecting charge of cavalry, and to a renewed fire of artillery. The infantry re-formed, and again dashed up the hill. For two long hours the heroic Aymaras, against all these fearful odds, had maintained their ground. Still they faced the foe for some time longer, constantly with ranks ever thinning from the fire of the Krupp guns. It was not until two p.m. that the survivors finally gave way. Camacho himself was severely wounded.

The right wing, under Admiral Montero, also made a gallant resistance. The Yncas, survivors of the victory of Tarapaca, resolutely withstood the withering fire of the artillery and the repeated charges, emulating the glorious defence of their Aymara brethren. Caceres had two horses shot under him, and his " right hand," young Carlos Llosa, fell by his side. It was not until the invaders had lost 2128 killed and wounded, that the defenders of their native land were overwhelmed. At this moment the Bolivian General

[2] " There were moments when the victory seemed to hang in the scales."—*General Campero's Report.*

Perez fell mortally wounded. The slaughter among the brave Indians was most grievous.

General Campero fell back to Tacna, hoping to organize a second resistance. But this was soon found to be impossible, and he continued his retreat, with the remnant of his army in good order. This is proved by their having brought away two field-guns, though the rest were lost. On the 29th Campero rested his men at Corocoro, where he received the gratifying news of his election as Constitutional President of Bolivia, and next day he continued the march to La Paz. Montero, with the Peruvians, retired by way of Torata. Sorrowfully the victors of Tarapaca now retreated with their numbers still more thinned. Brave Fajardo had been slain at the battle of Tacna. There were many other losses, for 147 officers had fallen, and, in their deaths, they refuted the calumny that Peruvians will not fight.. Sad and heart-broken, the gallant knot of survivors strove to encourage their long-suffering companions in arms. Their anguish could not be repressed altogether. Some expression of it was wrung from them. " I confess," wrote Colonel Caceres, in his report, " that I have had the weakness to weep over so terrible a disaster. Better for me to have shown my patriotism and devotion to duty by the sacrifice of my life." Brave heart ! How far more noble are the sorrowing words torn from the very heartstrings of a patriot, struggling against hope in a losing cause, than the vulgar boasting of a conqueror![3] The despondency was but for a

---

[3] "In a false quarrel there is no true valour."—*Much Ado about Nothing*, Act v. Sc. I.

moment. Soon the survivors were again rallying to strike another blow in defence of their fatherland.

The allied army had fought a good fight.[1] Their inferiority in numbers, in drill and experience—and, above all, in artillery and cavalry—told fatally against them. If there had been anything like equality in these respects, the heights of Tarapaca tell clearly how different would have been the result. The defeat of Tacna was a great calamity. A victory of the imperial races—of the Quichuas and Aymaras—would have prevented unspeakable bloodshed and misery in the near future. But it was not to be.

Great efforts had been made to send succour to the allied army at Tacna before it was too late ; but the trackless deserts intervened. The command of the sea gave the Chilians an advantage against which no exertions, no energy could make head. Yet, in spite of the blockade, the Peruvian transport *Oroya* landed troops, arms, and clothing at Camaná, one of the ports of Arequipa, on the 30th of April, under the command of Colonel Isaac Recabárren, the defender of Pisagua. During May a force of 2000 men was assembled at Arequipa under the veteran Colonel Leyva. On the 22nd of May an advance was made to the southward, but the Chilians had too long a start. The crushing news from Tacna reached Leyva a march or two beyond Moquegua, and he was forced to fall back on Arequipa.

To complete the military occupation of the neigh-

---

[1] " Batieronse los ejercitos aliados con indisputable intrepidez, y hubo cuerpos que se cubrieron de legitima gloria, como el Zepita, el Ayacucho y otros."—*Vicuña Mackenna.*

bourhood of Tacna, a division of the Chilian army, under the command of the marauder Barbosa, was sent to attack and occupy the town of Torata early in July. This involved a march of about forty miles to the northward. The object of the expedition was to disperse any small bodies of the allied army that might have assembled, and to deprive them of a rendezvous. The place was defended by a few Peruvian soldiers led by Colonel Prado, a nephew of the President, who were dispersed by the Chilians with a loss of twenty-nine killed and three wounded. This extraordinary proportion of killed to wounded, which was generally the case after one of these encounters, shows the savage way in which the Chilians conducted the war.

A few days after the Chilians had occupied Tacna, General Baquedano began his operations for the assault and capture of the seaport of Arica. On the 2nd of June 4000 Chilians, under Colonel Lagos, preceded by four squadrons of cavalry, started for Chacalluta, a small village within easy reach of Arica, whence it had been arranged that the attack should be made. The arrival of these troops naturally caused great excitement and consternation among the inhabitants of Arica. Many took refuge in the Azapa valley, and a number of women and children sought protection on board the neutral men-of-war in the roadstead. There they remained, helpless and horrified spectators of the closing act in the bloody Chilian drama.

At the commencement of the war, Arica, which was much more populous before the great earthquakes of 1868 and 1877, numbered about 3000 inhabitants. To the south the Morro is 700 feet high, with a perpendicular sea-face. It is the western termination of a ridge which forms the southern boundary of the Azapa valley. Two sand-bag forts, each with four small guns, were constructed on the ridge; and on the Morro itself there was a fort containing nine heavy guns, the largest being a 150-pounder Armstrong. A few Gatling guns had also been placed in position on the summit. North of the town were the three batteries, close to the sea-shore, called Santa Rosa, 2° de Mayo, and San José. In the two latter there was one heavy gun, and in San José were two 150-pounders. Shelter trenches extended from the beach towards the valley of Azapa, with earthworks and sand-bag defences. Under the forts was the monitor *Manco Capac*.

The defence of Arica was entrusted to the brave Colonel Don Francisco Bolognesi, one of the heroes of Tarapaca. The batteries on the Morro were under the command of Captain Moore, the unfortunate captain of the *Independencia*, who was resolved to obtain forgiveness for his fatal error on that 21st of May, by his resolute defence of the fortress. With him were 250 of the *Independencia's* ship's company. He wore the dress of a civilian and a Panama hat, refusing to put on uniform again until his good services had atoned for the loss of his ship. By his side was the gallant young Alfonso Ugarte, a wealthy native of Tarapaca, who had been educated at Valparaiso. When the war broke out he was on the point of starting for Europe, on a tour of pleasure. He at once abandoned the design, became a volunteer, and was wounded in the defence of his own province. Colonel Inclan of Tacna, Arias, Varela, and the three Cornejos, also rallied round Colonel Bolognesi. Admiral Montero himself would have been there, if his retreat in the direction of Arica had not been cut off by the Chilians. The garrison consisted of 300 artillery apprentices in the forts, and about 1400 riflemen, mostly volunteers, besides the men of the *Independencia*.

General Baquedano established his headquarters at Chacullata, and posted his powerful artillery in positions suited for covering the assaulting parties. On the 5th of June he sent a flag of truce into the town with a summons for unconditional surrender. This demand was indignantly refused by Colonel Bolognesi, after consultation with his officers; and the Chilian general gave orders for the artillery to open fire, and continue during the rest of the day. On the 6th the fleet, consisting of the *Cochrane* ironclad, *Magellanes*, *Covadonga*, and *Loa*, commenced a bombardment of Arica, which was answered by the *Manco Capac*, and the shore batteries. During this engagement both the *Covadonga* and the *Cochrane* were struck by shell from the guns of the Morro and the *Manco Capac*. The *Covadonga* received two shots between wind and water, and had to be sent to Pisagua for repairs. In the battery of the *Cochrane*, whilst they were loading one of the heavy guns on the starboard side, a shell from the Morro entered the port at which the gun was being worked in a downward direction, and, bursting at the muzzle, not only ignited the charge (fifty pounds of pebble powder) which had just been put into the gun, but also the spare charge which was in the powder-case in rear. So fatal were the consequences of this combination of explosions, that twenty-eight men were seriously injured, seven of whom afterwards died.

The Chilian general entrusted the operations connected with the assault of the forts to Colonel Pedro Lagos. He had 4000 men, besides cavalry and artillery. He told off 1000 men to attack the three little redoubts on the beach to the north, 2000 to attack the Morro and the sand-bags in rear, and 1000 as a reserve. All the works had been erected for mounting guns to be used to seaward, and there were very slight defences on the inshore faces, while the so-called forts below the Morro were merely lines of sand-bags. The Chilians had an overpowering superiority in numbers at all points, much more than two to one of disciplined troops against volunteers.

Still they proceeded with the utmost secrecy and caution. The cavalry kept up the camp-fires to deceive the garrison, while the infantry crept to their assigned positions in the dead of night, ready to assault at dawn of the 7th of June. At the first sign of daylight 2000 men made a rush at the sand-bags below the Morro, cut them open with their knives, and in a few minutes slaughtered the unfortunate volunteers. A dozen or so fled towards the Morro, and were bayoneted as they ran. At the same time 1000 men attacked the three redoubts on the beach, and easily carried them by assault. The defenders at that moment fired some mines by electricity, which only injured their own people. The main force, having cut the sand-bags, rushed up the Morro by the inland or easiest ascent, and were received by a rifle-fire from the fort; but they quickly climbed the low parapet in vastly superior force. The Chilian soldiers behaved like savages, killing ruthlessly, and giving no quarter. When the officers saw that the fort was taken, they raised a white flag on the point of a sword and grouped themselves round a gun, as if to die on the altar-steps of their unhappy country. Here stood Bolognesi, Moore, and Alfonso Ugarte. The Chilians slaughtered them without mercy. Bolognesi was pierced by a rifle-ball, and his brains were then beaten out. Ugarte was killed, and the body hurled over the cliff into the sea. The heart-broken mother offered $1000 for even a scrap of the clothes of her heroic son. But nothing was ever found. The whole affair, from the commencement, was little better than a massacre. Indeed, the Chilian historian himself compares it to the massacre perpetrated by Pizarro at Caxamarca. As many as 600 of the brave defenders of the forts were bayoneted, most of them in cold blood. About 150 ran down the steep sides of the Morro, and reached the town; but they were followed and shot down. As on other occasions the proportion of killed to wounded was monstrous—700 to about 100.[4] After the capture of Arica the usual drunken revelries took place, and the town was fired in several quarters.

As soon as the forts were captured, Captain Lago-

---

[4] "Se lanzaron como lobos enfurecidos sobre arremolinado rebaño y comenzaron a matar y matar sin que valiera llanto, ni edad, ni perdon. Se forman pantanos de sangre."—*Vicuña Mackenna*, III. p. 1142.

marsino, of the *Manco Capac*, to prevent her from falling into the hands of the enemy, ordered the crew into the boats, opened all the valves, and in a few minutes she heeled over and sank. The Chilian admiral so far mitigated the horrors of the work in which his country was engaged, as to grant permission to the Peruvian steamer *Limeña*, under the red-cross flag of the Geneva Convention, to transport the wounded from Arica to Callao. These poor fellows, who had received their injuries at the battles of Tacna and Arica, were left uncared for by the Chilians, and many had perished for want of proper attention. The surgeons of the Chilian army only looked after their own wounded, and would not devote any of their time to the unfortunate Peruvians, who were left to die as they fell, if they escaped the knives of their ferocious victors.[s] It would, therefore, have been an act of wanton barbarity on the part of Admiral Riveros if, under such circumstances, he had not allowed the *Limeña* to proceed to Arica without fear of molestation from the force under his command. She successfully conveyed to the hospitals in Lima and Callao the wounded Peruvians who had survived the sanguinary struggles in which they had been engaged in defence of their country. Many a poor fellow who had given up all hope of seeing his home again, was thus restored to his friends with a renewed lease of life.

---

[s] The Chilian soldiers carried long knives, with which they despatched the wounded.

CHAPTER XIII.

THE blockade of Callao was now the principal enterprise of the invaders, while they made preparations for another and still more devastating descent upon the coast. With her navy destroyed, the Peruvians could no longer defy the enemy's ironclads or outwit them by superior seamanship. Still they could make attempts to destroy the blockading ships, and their efforts are remarkable alike for originality and for the ingenuity displayed by those who undertook them.

Late in the afternoon of the 3rd of July a small coasting vessel was observed by the blockading squadron, apparently endeavouring to work up along the coast to Ancon, a port about sixteen miles from Callao. The armed transport *Loa*, under Captain Peña, was ordered to intercept her. On approaching, Captain Peña sent his lieutenant, Martinez, to examine the vessel. He found her at anchor and abandoned by her crew, although all sail was set. But she was filled with provisions of various kinds, such as poultry, vegetables, and fruit, a rich prize for men who had been so long engaged in the monotonous duties of a blockade, generally on salt provisions. The bait was too tempting to be resisted; besides, there seemed to be no reason to suspect that the prize was anything but what she seemed to be. She was accordingly taken possession of. But the suspicions of Lieutenant Martinez appear to have been aroused to some extent, for thinking it just possible that an infernal machine might have been attached to her anchor, he gave orders for the cable to be cut, instead of weighing. He then, in obedience to instructions from Captain Peña, towed her alongside the *Loa*.

The captain then ordered the fruit and vegetables to be hoisted out, but as the last package, which happened to be a sack of maize, was lifted, there was a terrific explosion. A breach more than fifteen feet long was made in the ship's side at the water-line, through which the water rushed, and in five minutes the sea had closed over the ill-fated *Loa*. Captain Peña, three of his officers, and fifty men perished. The neutral men-of-war, which were lying at a distance of four miles off, sent boats which succeeded in saving the lives of thirty-eight of the crew. The mechanism, the exact arrangement of which was never ascertained, was supposed to have consisted of a case, with 250 pounds of dynamite, stowed in the bottom of the boat under the cargo. In this case it is believed that an apparatus was arranged so ingeniously that, on the removal of a certain pressure from the lid, a spring would be released and cause the explosion. The unpacking of the cargo had the effect of removing the pressure.

On the 13th of September the Peruvians scored another success, by destroying the Chilian sloop of war *Covadonga*. On the previous day she had been detached from the squadron off Callao, and ordered by Admiral Riveros to blockade the port of Chancay, a few miles north of Ancon. She was commanded by an officer named Pablo Ferrari, who had recently been promoted into her, out of the *O'Higgins*. The *Covadonga* was a small vessel of 600 tons burden, carrying two 70-pounder 6-inch Armstrong breech-loading guns, besides three others of smaller calibre. This armament had been put into her after the memorable encounter with the Peruvian ironclad, *Independencia*.

A railroad runs from Lima to Chancay, and Captain Ferrari was sent with orders to destroy the bridge and railway station, lest they should be used for transporting troops. This he failed to do, but whilst in the bay his attention was directed to a launch which, with a rather smart-looking gig, was lying at anchor about 300 yards off the railway mole. As his object was the destruction of the enemy's property, Captain Ferrari opened fire upon these boats. The launch was quickly destroyed, but the gig being uninjured, was ordered to be appropriated for the use of the *Covadonga*. A boat was lowered down and sent, in charge of a midshipman named Gajardo, with orders to examine the gig, and, if he considered her to be in good condition, to tow her alongside.   The caulker of the ship was sent to assist in this survey; and, as all seemed sound, the prize was towed alongside.   She turned out to be a life-boat with air boxes at both ends.   She had been freshly painted and cleaned, was fitted with cushions in the stern sheets, and was fully equipped.   Captain Ferrari was so pleased with her appearance, that he determined to make her his own gig, ordering her to be hoisted up to the starboard waist davits. The moment the tackles were hauled taut, an explosion took place.   The ship filled rapidly, and went down in about three minutes.   Her starboard side was completely crushed in by the tremendous force of the explosion, and all the boats on that side were blown to atoms.   The ship sank in eleven fathoms of water, so that a portion of her mastheads remained above the surface.   Fifteen men succeeded in effecting their escape in one of the boats, and reached the Chilian sloop *Pilcomayo*, which was blockading the neighbouring port of Ancon.   Many of the crew perished, including the captain, but forty-nine, who sought refuge in the rigging, were rescued by the Peruvian boats from the shore.

It is supposed that the air-boxes, or the double bottom usually supplied to such life-boats, must have been charged with dynamite, and that the chain-slings to which the tackles were hooked, passed through a tube into one of these buoyancy chambers.   These however, instead of being clenched to the kelson were, in all probability, attached to one or more safety pins, which, on the tackles being hauled taut, were pulled out, thus releasing a catch or spring, and thereby causing the charge to explode. This is only a supposition, for the details of the mechanical arrangement of this particular machine have never been divulged; but it would appear from telegrams found in the palace at Lima after the Chilian occupation, that a Peruvian naval officer, named Oyague, was the contriver of the scheme.

The loss of the *Covadonga* was felt very deeply by the Chilians, not so much on account of her value as because she had been captured from the Spaniards in 1866, being the only trophy of that war. The mother country cannot be expected to share in this amiable feeling; and Spaniards naturally rejoice that their insurgent colonists have destroyed the poor little *Covadonga* amongst them, in the course of their intestine feuds.

But the Chilians were so angry at the destruction of their cherished prize, that Admiral Riveros was ordered to bombard three defenceless towns, if the Peruvian Government did not deliver up the *Union* and the *Rimac* within twenty-four hours. The reply to the Chilian Admiral, dated September 22nd, was that the two ships in question were in Callao harbour, and that he had better come and take them. "As for the threat of bombarding the ports of Chorrillos, Ancon, and Chancay, it is worthy of the manner in which the Chilians are carrying on the war."

In consequence of the receipt of this reply the Chilian squadron actually bombarded three defenceless towns for several hours. These acts will ever remain a blemish on the Chilian arms. As if ashamed of the orders they had to carry out, it is alleged that

the firing from the ships was by no means as good as
usual, and that most of the shells fell over the houses,
without doing much damage.

During the month of September a Chilian expedition, consisting of 3000 men, was organized, and
placed under the command of a certain Captain
Patrick Lynch of the Chilian navy, but of Irish
extraction. He was then a man of about sixty years
of age, but active and energetic, and in his youth he
had been allowed to serve for eight years in the
British navy, seeing service during the war in China
in 1841-42. His instructions were to proceed to the
different ports along the coast of Peru, for the purpose
of destroying private property, seizing merchandise,
and damaging public works—such as piers, railroads,
and custom-houses. The division under his command
was of such strength as effectually to overcome any
local opposition that might otherwise have been
offered. These instructions were quite contrary to
the usages of civilized warfare, and they prove how
demoralizing an effect the career of conquest and
"glory" had had upon the Chilians. When they
entered upon this business, the Chilian commanders
proclaimed that their troops never made war upon
private property, that they came only to fight the
enemy in the field, that the interests and the honour of
private people were safe under the glorious banner of
Chile, that to all pacific and unarmed inhabitants they
brought protection, that their persons and property
were sacred and inviolable.[1] A short year had scarcely

[1] Here is the declaration of the Chilian Government when the war
began : "Nada de destrucciones insensatos de propriedad que a nadie

passed—a year of carnage and destruction—before a contradiction was given to this proclamation.

Lynch was ordered to ravage the whole coast from Callao to Payta, and he executed his instructions to the letter, destroying government and private property in every direction. The injury he inflicted, not only on the seaport towns of Huacho, Supé, Chimbote, Salaverry, Truxillo, Pacasmayo, Chiclayo, Eten, Lambayeque, and Payta, but on all the adjacent villages, farms, and plantations, was incalculable. The work of destruction was undertaken systematically and ruthlessly. Dynamite was the explosive used for destroying iron piers and all massive buildings. Houses that were set on fire were previously besmeared with petroleum or some other equally inflammable substance.

During the visit of these marauders to the port of Chimbote, Captain Lynch, escorted by 400 men, made an excursion to the sugar plantation of Puente, in the fertile valley of Palo-seco. This was one of the finest and best managed estates in the country, and was the property of Don Dionisio Derteano. There were 6000 acres under cultivation, affording employment to several hundred labourers, and the best English machinery was used. Over twenty-six miles of rail-road were laid down on the estate, connecting different parts with the works and offices. Captain Lynch, on his arrival, demanded black-mail to the amount of 16,500*l.*, declaring that if it was not forthcoming he

aprovechan i que redundarian en daño de nuestros mismos : nada de violencias criminales contra personas indefensas."—*Vicuña Mackenna,* IV. p. 573.

would destroy the place. Señor Derteano's son asked for three days in order that he might telegraph to Lima for the amount. But the Supreme Chief, Pierola, prohibited the payment of any black-mail to the Chilians. Señor Derteano had, therefore, no option but to inform the brigands that he was prohibited from meeting their demand. Then the odious work began. Nothing was left but ruin and desolation. The factories, the dwelling-houses, the store-houses, were all destroyed. On the railroad the line was torn up in several places, and the carriages and locomotives shattered to pieces. Even the gardens in front of the houses, which had been prettily and tastefully laid out with much care and skill, were a scene of wild confusion. Choice flowers and plants were wantonly trampled under foot. Orange, lime, and other fruit-bearing trees were barbarously cut down. Books of great value were burnt. All the furniture was destroyed ; while dastardly cruelty was added to spoliation. Pet dogs were killed, and English race-horses of great value were shot. The sugar-crops were all set fire to, and the once fertile fields were converted into black calcined surfaces. Rice, sugar, and other goods to the value of 8000*l.* (50,000 silver soles) were put on board the Chilian ships, and carried off. Much of the property belonged or was mortgaged to British subjects, and the destruction and appropriations were in spite of protests from H.B.M. Minister.

The Puente estate is close to the great Ynca road which, though constructed centuries ago, is still, in places, in a perfect state of preservation—a silent testimony to the wonderful civilization of the Yncas. It is a pity that the Chilians could not have been brought to reflect on the contrast between the civilizing work of the Yncas and their own barbarous deeds.

After leaving Chimbote, where the railway rolling stock, custom-house, and mole were destroyed, Lynch directed his course northwards, and captured paper notes to the value of 100,000*l.*, and postage stamps worth 5100*l.*, which had been manufactured for the Peruvian Government in the United States, and were being brought to Callao in an English steamer. He then put in to Payta, captured a small Peruvian steamer, destroyed the custom-house, the rolling stock of the railway, and seized all the cotton in the port, besides other merchandise. Having robbed the people along the coast to the utmost, he returned to Arica, where his proceedings received the cordial approbation of his Government. Thus ended this expedition of pillage and lawless plunder ; a lasting disgrace to the perpetrators, as well as to the Government which planned and approved their proceedings. It is condemned by the best of the Chilians themselves.[2]

The advisers of Pierola, wholly unable to protect their countrymen from such attacks, continued to devote much attention to the possibility of destroying the Chilian fleet. The blockading ships, to avoid being surprised at anchor, put to sea every night, cruising

---

[2] " Ibamos a resucitar los dias de los corsarios en nuestro propio suelo, cuando el mundo entero, de comun acuerdo, acababa de abolirlos. La espedicion Lynch ha hecho inmensos y irreparables males."—*Vicuña Mackenna*, IV. p. 556.

off the port until daylight, when they returned to the anchorage off San Lorenzo. Taking advantage of their temporary absence, the Peruvians prepared a large boat which was ballasted to a certain draught, and so fitted with valves that, by working automatically, they could sink the boat to any previously arranged depth below the surface, at a given time. In this boat an iron tank had been placed containing a large quantity of gunpowder. A machine, regulated by clockwork, was attached to the tank, and set to release a spring at any settled time which, striking a detonator, would ignite the contents of the tank.

This ingenious machine was brought out from Callao during the night of the 9th of October, while the Chilian ships were at sea, and moored close to the billet of one of the enemy's ironclads. It was then submerged, but not to the required depth. By some mistake the necessary quantity of ballast had not been put on board, so that, instead of the launch being below water and invisible, she was so close to the surface as to attract attention. On the return of the squadron the half-submerged object was observed, and the senior officer, Captain Latorre, sent a boat to examine it. The inspection confirmed his previous suspicions, and he was making preparations to destroy the launch when it suddenly exploded with a tremendous report at 9.10 a.m. of October 10th, the exact time, it was afterwards ascertained, that the machinery had been set to explode. If the proper quantity of ballast had been put on board, the attempt would probably have succeeded, and one of the ironclads would have been destroyed.

The last action during the course of the blockade took place on the 6th of December. A small Peruvian steamer, named the *Arno*, was observed by the Chilians to be steaming outside the *darsena* with a lighter in company. No sooner were they seen than a rush was made for them by the three torpedo-boats, *Fresia*, *Guacolco*, and *Tucapel*, at full speed. The Peruvian launch was armed with a couple of 40-pounder Armstrong guns, and showed a desire to come to close quarters, which caused the torpedo boats to sheer off on each side; a brisk fire being kept up on both sides. The guns in the batteries on shore then began to take part in the proceedings, and this brought in the blockading squadron, which engaged the forts at a range of about 6000 yards. The action thus became general; and it was necessary for the neutral men-of-war to move out of the way. The firing continued for an hour and a half, the Chilians sustaining the temporary loss of the *Fresia*, the finest of their torpedo-boats. She was struck by a shell from one of the shore batteries, at a distance of about 2000 yards, and she went down in fifteen fathoms off San Lorenzo. The Chilians set to work to raise her, and succeeded perfectly; so that in a fortnight she had resumed her duties as one of the blockading squadron.

The *Angamos* then opened fire on the *Union* at the enormous range of 8000 yards, and out of eleven rounds one actually struck her, penetrating the upper deck, and passing through her side. The batteries did not remain silent, but the Peruvian shells fell short by 1500 yards of the place where the Chilian ship was engaging them.   So that after a time they ceased firing, as it was only a waste of ammunition.

The *Angamos* has shown the immense advantage of using very long range guns.   She was originally an Irish pig-boat named the *Belle of Cork ;* and it is very noteworthy that such a vessel should be able to attack strongly fortified towns with perfect impunity. She possessed the two great *desiderata* of an efficient man-of-war, namely speed and a long-range piece of ordnance.   Her single gun was a 180-pounder 8-inch B.L. Armstrong.   With this weapon she was a terror to the batteries and forts of Arica and Callao, and if she had met any of the enemy's ships, with her superior speed she could have selected and regulated her own distance.   Thus she would be a formidable antagonist even for an ironclad.   Although the English squadron in the Pacific at that time had vessels carrying twelve and eighteen ton guns, there was none that could compete with the *Angamos* either in speed or length of range ; and therefore nothing that could control her actions if once the open sea was gained.   She would have made it unpleasantly warm either for the *Triumph* or the *Shannon,* and as for an engagement with vessels of the *Thetis* or *Pelican* class, or even with vessels commonly called "gems," such as the *Torquoise,* the chances would be very much in favour of the pig-boat.   The gun of the *Angamos* was not, however, perfect. After doing a large amount of mischief along the coast, it suddenly, in the very act of being discharged, recoiled so violently that it disconnected itself from the carriage and disappeared overboard.   It was on the 11th of December, and the sixth discharge during that day. It had probably been injured not only by the great number of times it had been fired (380 in ten months), but also by the very large charges of powder that were always used. At first it was supposed that the gun burst, and fell overboard in two pieces. But the entire piece may have recoiled through the trunnion coil. Unluckily it sank in very deep water, and the position was uncertain, so that the exact nature of the accident has not been ascertained.

With the exception of the assistance which the Chilian men-of-war rendered to the army at the battle of Miraflores, this was the last action of any importance in which the Chilian navy took part. It is to be observed that in the numerous affairs that took place in the bay of Callao between the Chilian ships and the Peruvian forts, the former took especial care of their vessels, and but rarely permitted them to approach within range of the enemy's guns.

It was well-known to the Chilians that numerous torpedoes were laid down in Callao Bay, and at the anchorage off Chorrillos. No less than 150 of these machines were reported to be moored in a certain line off the port of Callao, and immediately after the occupation of that town by the Chilians, steps were taken to find and remove them. Several were picked up, but they were found to be in a harmless condition, owing to the corrosion caused by their long immersion in the water. These torpedoes were of a conical shape, the outer casing being made of zinc. They were about three feet in length, with a diameter at their base of two feet four inches. They were constructed in two separate compartments, the lower one charged with from thirty to fifty pounds of dynamite, whilst the upper one was a buoyancy chamber, and was hermetically sealed. A rope fastened to the apex of the cone moored it at a regulated depth below the surface. These machines were fitted to explode by a fuze kept in a safety position by a large horizontal iron wheel, three and a half feet in diameter, secured to the top of the torpedo by brass spiral springs. The centre was fitted with a small pricker, which, on anything coming into contact with the wheel, would release a hammer, and this, on falling, would strike a percussion cap, and thus explode the dynamite.

The principle of construction was good, but the torpedoes were hurriedly and cheaply manufactured, and being of poor materials, became worthless after a short period of immersion.

During the war the Peruvians used, or had in their possession, the following different kinds of torpedoes :—

1. Ericson's gun torpedo.

2. Harvey's towing torpedo.

3. Ley's torpedo.   These are said to have been sent from New York, by Panama, at heavy cost.

4. Hardley's torpedo (supposed to be an improved Ley).

5. McEvoy's outrigger torpedo.

The Chilians only used the McEvoy outrigger torpedo, but they were also provided with the French towing torpedo.

The war clearly demonstrated the great value of torpedoes and torpedo-boats for defensive purposes, and the moral effect they produce on the enemy forms an important part of their value. If either of the belligerents had possessed the Whitehead torpedo, carried in one of the fast torpedo-boats, there were several opportunities of using it with advantage. The value of fast torpedo-boats in maintaining a blockade cannot be over-estimated. They are not only the "eyes" but the "legs" of a squadron. Not only are they of use in preventing the escape of any of the enemy's ships, but they also afford protection to their own fleet, giving timely notice of approaching danger at night by a prearranged system of flashing lights, and in the daytime by their great speed. The thoroughness of the blockade of Callao was undoubtedly due, in a great measure, to the Chilian torpedo-boats.

CHAPTER XIV.

IN October, 1880, an attempt at mediation was made
by the United States. On the 6th of that month Mr.
Osborn, the American minister at Santiago, addressed
a letter to the Chilian Minister of Foreign Affairs,
proposing that a conference should be held for the
purpose of discussing terms of peace between Peru,
Bolivia, and Chile, at which the United States representatives offered to assist with their good offices as
mediators. He further suggested that the conference
should take place on board one of the American men-
of-war off the port of Arica, in presence of the representatives of the United States accredited to the three
republics.

The governments referred to accepted the offer of
mediation under the form of "good offices," and it
was arranged that the conference should take place
on board the U.S. corvette *Lackawanna* in the port of
Arica.

The plenipotentiaries for Peru were the naval
captain and diplomatist Don Aurelio Garcia y Garcia

and Don Antonio Arenas (formerly commissioner for the constitution of 1860) ; and for Bolivia Don Mariano Baptista and Don Juan Carrillo. Chile was represented by Colonel Vergara—the hero of the cavalry butcheries, and now Minister of War—Don Eulogio Altamirano, and Don Eusebio Lillo. The first meeting took place on the 22nd of October, when Mr. Osborn, the American minister in Chile, took the chair, supported by Mr. Christiancy and Mr. Adams, American ministers respectively for Peru and Bolivia. Mr. Adams opened the proceedings by expressing the feelings of friendship entertained by his country for the three republics, of regret at the existence of the war, and of longing for its termination. But he added that the American representatives did not intend to take any part in the discussions, though they would be glad to help by friendly co-operation. He concluded with these words, " I beg and entreat you, that you will do all in your power to obtain peace, and I hope in the name of my government that your efforts will lead you to this end."

The Chilian representatives then presented copies of a memorandum of the essential conditions which their Government demanded in order to arrive at peace. The first meeting then adjourned. These demands were the cession of the whole province of Tarapaca southwards from the ravine of Camarones, and of the whole Bolivian coast province ; the payment to Chile of the sum of $20,000,000, of which $4,000,000 to be paid in cash (about 2,500,000*l.*) ; the return of all private property of which Chilian citizens had been despoiled ; the return of the transport *Rimac* ;

the abrogation of the defensive treaty of 1873 between
Peru and Bolivia; the retention of the territory of
Moquegua, Tacna, and Arica, occupied by the Chilian
forces until the other conditions are complied with; and
an obligation on the part of Peru never to fortify Arica.
These excessive demands could only have been
made with the intention of breaking off the conference
and continuing the war.   At the second meeting
Señor Arenas said that the conditions had produced
upon him a very painful impression, because they closed
the door upon any reasonable or tranquil discussion.
He said that the doctrines of annexation through conquest were recognized in other times and in distant
regions; but that they had never before been in-
voked in Spanish America from the time of the Independence, having been considered as incompatible
with the bases of republican institutions.   He expressed a belief, therefore, that a peace founded upon
a revival of the obsolete right of conquest would be
an impossible peace.   If this condition is insisted
upon, he concluded, all hope of peace must be abandoned.   The Chilian Altamirano had nothing to
reply beyond the declaration that Chile must be
compensated for her sacrifices, and that the conquered
provinces owe their progress entirely to Chilian labour
and capital.   The latter assertion is both irrelevant
and erroneous.   Those provinces owe their progress
mainly to English capital, and only partly to Chilian
labour.
The Bolivian representative frankly admitted that,
on the ground of her success, Chile might justly claim
an indemnity, and proposed that she should retain the

territory she had occupied until that indemnity had been raised from its revenues, but he could not agree to permanent annexation of territory. It would destroy all chance of peace and progress, leaving to one side the sullen labour of revenge, and to the other the sterile and costly task of preventing it.

Captain Garcia y Garcia then proposed that the questions in dispute should be submitted to the arbitration of the United States; but this again the Chilian representatives peremptorily refused, thus once more showing their determination to make a reasonable settlement impossible. They also declined even to consider the arrangement for a full war indemnity, suggested by Bolivia. The second Bolivian representative concluded the discussion with one more eloquent and well-reasoned, but fruitless appeal to the Chilians. Mr. Adams expressed the profound regret of himself and his colleagues at the failure of their efforts. It is difficult to understand the object of the Chilian Government in consenting to the conference, when they so clearly showed, both by their demands for the annexation of conquered territory and their refusal of arbitration, that their lust after " glorious victories " was not satisfied.

They had resolved still further to extend the horrors of war, by sending an expedition against the capital of Peru. The victors actually possessed all they demanded, and yet the baleful influence of military glory, bought at the price of untold misery, still urged them on in their sanguinary career. An expeditionary force of 30,000 men of all arms was organized, transports were purchased or chartered, and the resources of the country were taxed to the utmost for objects of mischief and destruction.

The expeditionary army was formed into three divisions. The first, consisting of 9000 men under the command of Captain Lynch, was ordered to land at Pisco. The second, under General Sotomayor, numbering 7500 officers and men ; the third 6300 strong under Colonel Lagos ; and the reserve, 1250 strong, were to follow as soon as all the preparations were complete. The artillery, thoroughly equipped and with excellent mules, comprised 103 officers and 1486 men, with 77 mountain and campaign guns, 8 Gatlings, and 2 Nordenfeldts. The force of the army that was actually brought into the field made a total of 1202 officers and 24,956 men,

<pre>
Infantry, 1008 officers and 22,169 men
Cavalry,   91   ,,   1301 ,,
Artillery, 103   ,,   1486 ,,
           ————   ————
           1202   ,,   24,956 ,,
</pre>

exclusive of commissariat, ambulance corps, teamsters, carriers, and camp-followers. These probably swelled the numerical strength of the force to at least 30,000. The Commander-in-Chief was that General Don Manuel Baquedano, who had already spread havoc and desolation over Southern Peru. General Maturana was chief of the staff, Colonel Velasquez commanded the artillery brigade, and Colonel Letelier the cavalry. The men were armed with breech-loading rifles, and wore a serviceable uniform. The cavalry were well mounted, and the guns were of the newest types from Krupp and Armstrong.

On the 19th of November the first division arrived off Pisco, which place was held by a small garrison under Colonel Zamudio, who retreated after a few shots had been fired. The Chilians then landed, and a detachment was sent to occupy the town and valley of Yca, which is connected with the port of Pisco by a railroad. The rest of the expeditionary force was to be disembarked in Curayaco Bay, about three miles north of Chilca, and 107 miles from Pisco. This bay, although exposed to a heavy and dangerous surf, is partially protected from the prevailing southerly winds by a slightly projecting promontory called Point Chilca. It had been selected as the place offering the greatest facilities for the landing of troops and stores, while it is only ten miles from the fertile vale of Lurin, and about twenty-five from Lima itself. The division under Lynch was ordered to march by land from Pisco to Curayaco.

On the arrival of the Chilian army, Admiral Stirling, the Commander-in-Chief of the English Pacific Squadron, signified his intention to the officers commanding the other neutral men-of-war off Callao of applying to the Peruvian and Chilian authorities for permission for an English naval officer to join the headquarters of each of the belligerent armies, to watch and report proceedings. Permission having been obtained, two officers were selected from the English, French, Italian, and American squadrons, eight in all. The English officers chosen for this responsible duty were Commander Dyke Acland and Lieutenant Carey Brenton, both of H.M.S. *Triumph*, the flag-ship in the Pacific. The first-named officer was sent to Pisco, and was attached to the staff of Captain Lynch, with whom he marched from Pisco to Lurin. Mr. Carey Brenton was accredited to the Peruvian army before Lima, and was generally with the division commanded by Colonel Caceres. It would have been difficult to have found two officers possessing qualifications more particularly fitted for the delicate and onerous duties that were required from them.

CHAPTER XV.

THE DEFENCE OF LIMA.

LIMA, the city of the kings, the wealthy and prosperous capital of Peru, was now threatened with all the horrors of war. Her long line of houses and lofty towers are visible from the sea, with rocky mountains rising immediately in rear, until lost in the clouds; and a fertile plain extends in front down to the forts and shipping of Callao, which form the foreground. It is indeed a noble site, worthy of the capital of a far-reaching state, embracing many climes and regions. Here the conqueror founded the new capital on the banks of that river of the ancient oracle, "Rimac," or he who speaks, which, flowing rapidly from the cordillera, seems to talk in never-ceasing murmurs, as it spreads fertility over the great plain. From "Rimac" is derived Lima in a softened form; but Pizarro, on that 18th day of January, 1535 —the day of the founding—named it "Los Reyes," in honour of his sovereigns, Juana and her son Carlos. The arms granted to the city seem also to refer to the three kings of the east. Here the high-born viceroys of the Spanish kings strove vainly to execute the beneficent decrees of their masters; here were planned the voyages of discovery in search of Australia and the Isles of Solomon; here St. Toribio and Santa Rosa lived their saintly lives; while poets and writers added lustre to the gay and pleasure-loving society of the city of the kings. This queenly city of the Pacific in due course became independent of the proud old country; foreign merchants and contractors crowded her streets, her wealth increased, and in spite of a turbulent and restless beginning, her independent life was bearing prosperous and abundant fruit. The old mud walls of the viceroys have given place to shady *alamedas*, the great national exhibition buildings of 1872 are surrounded by pleasant gardens, and all the modern improvements indicate the absence of thoughts other than those of peaceful advancement.

The population of Lima in 1880 was estimated at 100,000 souls; but this is certainly below the truth. There are 15,000 foreigners, including a large colony of Italians. The upper classes were gay and pleasure-seeking, like their predecessors in the days of the viceroys. Many families were ennobled in colonial times; some are of illustrious descent. The majority probably derive their origin from Andalusia or Castile, yet the numerous Basque names show that nearly as many are from the freedom-loving sister provinces of Cantabria. But there was quite as much business as pleasure on the banks of the Rimac. The city was full of foreign merchants' houses, of contractors and speculators, of French and Italian shops, of busy mechanics. It was full, too, of churches and nunneries, as well as of taverns, idlers, and vice. A great and busy city, throbbing with thousands of different aims and desires, with manifold interests—a mighty and complicated machine, not lightly to be broken and mangled without heavy guilt resting on the destroyer.

That destroyer was almost at the city gates. The gay and thoughtless youths, the workmen and the idlers, the students and mechanics, all were suddenly called upon to face death in defence of the capital—all that could bear arms—there could be no exceptions. The national army was destroyed, and the conquerors were landing on the coast. The army could do no more. It had fought well and bravely far away in the south ; it rests now in heaps round the bones of Zubiaga and Manuel Suarez and the gallant boy Osorio, on the Cuesta de La Visagra ; it is scattered in ghastly piles along the deserts of Tarapaca ; it whitens the sand hills of Tacna ; it sleeps with Bolognesi on the Morro of Arica. There are *huacas* full of the bones of heroes ; but there is no longer an army for Peru in her last extremity.

Nicolas de Pierola only saw the danger, to strive heart and soul to avert it. He was full of hope and ardour—mad bragging arrogance his enemies called it. Be it so. He did not despair of his country in her great need, and the survivors of the death-dealing campaigns rallied round him. The venerable Buendia was by his side ; Admiral Montero, escaped from Tacna ; Garcia y Garcia, who had just spoken so nobly at the abortive conference ; all rallied round the man who was ready to make one last effort. There, too, were Suarez of the white horse ; Caceres, who saw the Chilian infantry fly before him down the slopes of Visagra ; Davila, who led the vanguard at Tarapaca ; Silva, Canevaro, and Iglesias—all good men and true. But how few! How many brave ones are lost for ever—the flower of the army. If 2000 of the veterans could gather round the few surviving chiefs, it would be all ; but there were barely as many as that. A decree was issued ordering every male resident in Lima, between the ages of sixteen and sixty, to join the army, of all professions, trades, and callings. Alas! decrees alone cannot make an army. Six months is not sufficient time to create veteran soldiers. Crowds could be sent to the sand hills to fight bravely and to die. They were patriots, but not soldiers.

The artillery was very inferior. There were more than a hundred guns, but they were manufactured in Lima, and had not been sighted, while their range was far shorter than that of the Chilian Krupps and Armstrongs. The engineers were actively employed, under the personal direction of Pierola, in laying down mines and torpedoes fitted with a percussion arrangement, so as to explode on contact. They were placed in front of positions to be occupied by the Peruvians, and were charged with ten pounds of powder. But they were never of any use in checking the advance of the enemy.

On paper it was arranged that each division of the army should be composed of three brigades, and each brigade of three battalions numbering 1500 men, with a battery of artillery. This gave 5000 men as the nominal strength of a division. There were four divisions, commanded by Suarez, Caceres,

Davila, and Iglesias. Pierola assumed the duties of commander-in-chief, and General Don Pedro Silva, as chief of the staff, controlled all the military details.

When the news reached Lima that the enemy had actually landed, business was in a measure suspended. By a decree, all shops, banks, and public offices were closed between the hours of three and six p.m., the time being notified by the tolling of the great bell in the cathedral. This, too, was the signal for all who had been enrolled to assemble for drill. The young idlers, the shop-keepers and apprentices, clerks and artificers, all were called to arms. One corps was commanded by Don Juan de Aliaga, the Count of Luringancho. The lawyers were enrolled under Señor Unanue, and the members of the press had the wealthy Derteano for their leader. Still more useful service was done by Don Luis Milon Duarte, a young doctor and owner of estates at Concepcion. He collected about a thousand sturdy natives of the Xauxa valley, and marched them into Lima on the 6th of July. Numerous foreigners, too, who had made their homes in Lima, could not fail to catch the enthusiasm. A great number of Italians, especially, wished to strike a blow in defence of their adopted country.

It is a very serious thing to draw away the whole party of order from a great city. Lima contained a dangerous class, like London or Paris ; not so numerous, but, in some respects, more formidable. There was a mass of 30,000 idle negroes and half-castes ready for any mischief, numbers of bad characters of all sorts, and a Chinese colony, hated by the more lazy and worthless zambos and mulattos. Such dangers were little thought of with the enemy at the gates; but they existed, and added to the real horrors of the situation.

Yet all looked bright and peaceful. The villages round Lima were embosomed in their fruit orchards; the clover fields bordered with willows, and often with white daturas, looked bright and green; the pleasant villas enlivened the landscape, the busy sugar estates were at work, and all was set in a frame of rocky mountains and bright blue sea. From Lima a railroad runs south, over the plain, to the fashionable bathing-place of Chorrillos, named after the "little springs" which issue from the neighbouring cliffs. There is a station at Miraflores, a place made up of country houses with large gardens, once the favourite residence of San Martin. Here was the villa of Don Felipe Barreda, father-in-law of President Pardo, where the wealthy merchant loved to assemble the learning and fashion of Lima at his pleasant open-air breakfasts, and where he had endowed a well-conducted village school. Of late years many other villas had risen up round the two "miradores," or look-out towers of Miraflores. The most beautiful was that of the banker Schell and his hospitable wife, with its tasteful gardens and aviaries. The next station was Barranco, a smaller place of the same kind, built near the steep banks of a shallow ravine opening to the sea. Further east was the more agricultural village of Surco, and the *haciendas*, or estates of La Palma, Tebes, and San Juan. The river Surco is led from the Rimac above the city, and irrigates this eastern side of the valley. Chorrillos had long been a very fashionable resort for sea-bathing, with numerous handsome villas, hotels, and shops. There was also a large building for the military academy. Above it rises the lofty headland called Morro Solar. To the east the Lima valley is bounded by rocky mountains, and to the south-east a desert separates it from the equally fertile valley of Lurin.

When it became certain that the invading army would land to the south of Lima, the advisers of Pierola decided upon forming a line of defence by the arid sandy hills on the verge of the desert, and extending from the Morro Solar and Chorrillos to the mountains on the east. The time was very short, and it was not possible to do more than dig a few ditches, throw breastworks across the roads, and in front of the main positions, and place the guns. The line was of immense extent, at least six miles long, and was broken by barren hills, about 100 feet high, and gullies. The Morro Solar is 600 feet above the sea, with Chorrillos at its northern base. The fertile estate of Villa is on the south-east, with reedy lagoons between the fields and the sea frequented by wild duck.

The chain of sand hills which formed the line of defence extends from the Morro Solar, by a shoulder between Villa and Chorrillos, to a height called Santa Teresa. Thence it turns sharply to the north, above the fields of the San Juan estate to that of Monterico-chico, overlooking Até and the Rimac. The line is crossed by three roads going from the Lima valley across the desert to Lurin. One leads from Chorrillos, over the shoulder at the foot of the Morro Solar, to the estate of Villa. Another passes by the estates of La Palma and San Juan, entering the desert near the centre of the line. The third goes direct from Lima, by the estate of Tebes, to Pachacamac in the Lurin valley, and is the most inland or eastern route. This outer line of defence was about ten miles from Lima, and the hastily-drilled people of the capital, with many recruits from the interior, but a pitifully small sprinkling of soldiers, were encamped there among the sand hills, under the lead of the indefatigable and undaunted Pierola.

A second line of defences was prepared, which passed just outside Miraflores, only six miles from Lima, and was at least four miles long. So the preparations were completed. There were double lines of defences, miles long; just as if there was effective artillery to be mounted and served, and a disciplined army to hold the positions. There were many unserviceable guns. There were a few brave hearts, a few good men and true, a few thousands of gallant young fellows who were not soldiers, and a great rabble. It was right that a stand should be made. The capital must not fall without a blow struck in its defence. But how piteous to think of those thousands falling in heaps, in a fruitless attempt to bar the way, in a last vain effort to save their country. Yet by the memory of such achievements do nations, rising from the ashes of adversity, learn the lessons which bring prosperity and good fortune.

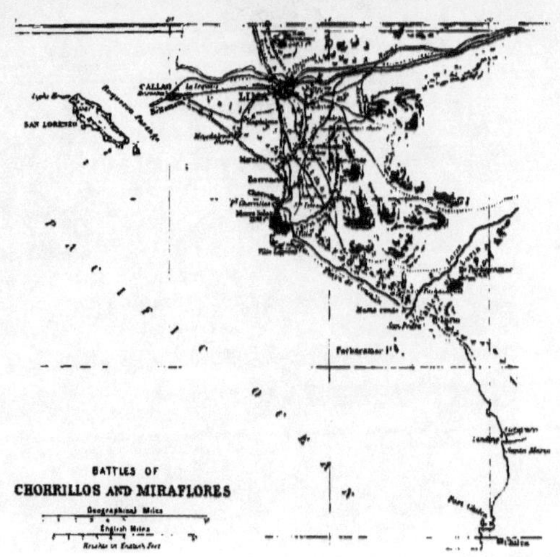

BATTLES OF
CHORRILLOS AND MIRAFLORES
Geographical Miles
English Miles
Heights in English Feet

CHAPTER XVI.

THE BATTLES OF CHORRILLOS AND MIRAFLORES.

THE first division of the Chilian army, which landed at Pisco, marched northwards on the 13th of December to form a junction with the rest of the forces which disembarked at Curayaco, a point nearer Lima. The valley of Pisco is famed for its vineyards. They produce a spirit called "Italia" and excellent wine. There were no serious difficulties in the march from this valley, and a small steamer, the *Gaviota*, kept on a parallel line with the column of troops. The first march was to Tambo de Mora, at the mouth of the river of Chincha, where the *Gaviota* landed fresh bread for the men. A party under the engineer Villarroel went on in advance, opening wells at which the soldiers could fill their *caramayolas* or water-bottles. Chincha is a large and fertile valley where sugar-cane is extensively cultivated ; but an invasion was calculated to disorganize the community, for the labourers consist of two races, Chinese and negroes, which hate each other. The freed negroes had risen only a year or two before, and committed several murders. The Chincha valley is a place of historical interest. Here Almagro was encamped for several months in 1537, when he came down from Cuzco to settle the limits of their governments with Pizarro. Here the marshal began the foundation of a city which was to rival Lima, and to be called Almagro; and here he consented to submit his quarrel with Pizarro to the arbitration of the monk Bobadilla. The estate of Laran, in the vale of Chincha, was supposed to be in the same latitude as the temple of the sun at Cuzco. Really Cuzco is in 13° 30′ S. and Chincha in 13° 29′ S.

Lynch's division marched in a leisurely way, resting a day at Chincha. In crossing the strip of desert between Chincha and Cañete there was an attack on the outposts by some patriot skirmishers under cover of the morning mist; and on the 19th the broad and fertile vale of Cañete was at the mercy of the invaders.

There were reminiscences connected with this valley which might have suggested moderation to a Chilian soldier. General O'Higgins fought and bled for Chile; he was engaged in all the battles in the war against the Spaniards, and he secured independence for his countrymen. In return he was hunted out of his native land by the ungrateful Chilians, and he died in exile. Peru received him as an honoured guest, and granted him an estate. He found a home among hospitable strangers, and lived for many years at Montalvan, in the valley of Cañete. Did not one Chilian think of this while their leader was cattle-lifting and threatening destruction round the old home of the Chilian patriot O'Higgins? In the house at Montalvan still hung the portraits of the general, of his mother the fair Isabel Riquelme, and of several soldiers of the war of independence; as well as large pictures of the battle of Rancagua and of the deposition of O'Higgins. Even these were not held sacred. Lynch pulled down and carried off one of the most valuable pictures. His men, who had charge of it, got drunk and left it on the road. It is now lost. Lynch then stopped at the next estate that came in his way, that of Gomez, belonging to Don José Unanue, a scion of one of the most distinguished families in Peru. The learned Don Hipolito Unanue was the dear and intimate friend of General O'Higgins, whose agreeable society soothed the weary years of the patriot's exile. But what cared Lynch! He demanded a number of horses and bullocks which did not exist, and he declared that he would burn and destroy the house and the valuable buildings and machinery if this requisition was not complied with. Eventually he was satisfied with black-mail to the amount of $20,000. That night his division reached Cerro Azul, a little port at the northern end of the rich valley of Cañete.

On the 21st the Chilians marched across another desert to the hamlet of Asia, where there are wells, and then onwards to the large grazing farm of Bujama, resting there until the 23rd. From this point the Peruvian cavalry of the "Torata" regiment, concealed to a great extent by trees and bushes, annoyed the advancing columns by a desultory fire, two Chilians being killed, and three wounded. In return Lynch ordered all houses on the line of march to be burnt, and caused a prisoner to be shot in cold blood. In this frame of mind he entered San Antonio in the

R

beautiful valley of Mala.   When he arrived there was
a pretty little town, with a handsome church, surrounded by fruit gardens.   When he departed there
was a heap of smouldering ruins.

This charming spot was the place where Pizarro and
Almagro had their last interview on the 13th of
November, 1537.   The conference closed by widening
the breach between the two old friends, and Almagro
departed in haste, fearing treachery.   An honourable
cavalier of the Pizarro faction warned him of danger
by humming two lines of an old ballad under the
window :—

> " Tiempo es el cavallero,
> Tiempo es de andar de aqui."

A more ruthless destroyer than Pizarro was now at
Mala.   Yet the place is suggestive of other feelings
than revenge and hate.   The beautiful valley, with its
rapid river, is a grateful change from the sandy
desert.   Here are groves of oranges and bananas,
vines and maize-fields, and rows of graceful willows,
forming a pleasant contrast to the adjacent wilderness.
Here, too, in the old days, was abounding and cordial
hospitality.   Lynch and his companions regaled
themselves on the luscious fruit, rested under the
delicious shade, then burnt down the church and town,
and marched away, leaving desolation and ruin
behind them.   A march of five short leagues brought
them to Chilca, a small Indian village in a little oasis,
from which all the inhabitants had fled.   After allowing his camp-followers to pillage the poor people's
houses he set out again ; and on the 25th Lynch and

his division arrived at Curayaco, the place where the rest of the army was disembarking. This experienced cattle-lifter brought with him 200 cows and bullocks, several horses, 600 donkeys, and 1000 Chinese labourers from the estates, who were freely allowed to pillage and burn in his rear. He was twelve days marching 114 miles.

Meanwhile the main body of the army, under General Baquedano, landed at Curayaco. Colonel Vergara had been promoted to the post of Minister of War "in campaign," and accompanied the expedition. The landing at Curayaco commenced on the 22nd, and continued during the two following days. The cavalry, under Colonel Letelier, was pushed forward to occupy the valley of Lurin. A Peruvian cavalry detachment was surprised by Colonel Barbosa on the 27th of December, at Manzano, in the upper part of the Lurin valley; and upwards of a hundred men and horses were taken prisoners. The Peruvian Lieut.-Colonel Aróstegui was shot by the Chilian soldiers after he had surrendered. This was the same force which had harassed Lynch's division on his line of march. The disaster was the more serious as all the effective cavalry of the Lima defending army did not number 600 men.

Lurin is a beautiful little valley on the south side of a river flowing to the Pacific. It contained three sugar-cane estates, and the two villages of Lurin and Pachacamac. The house of one estate, called Buenavista, stands on an isolated rock, with a broad arcade in front of the rooms, overlooking a sea of verdure.

Fruit-gardens flourish round the pretty village of Pachacamac, and willows pleasantly cast their shade across the irrigating streams. On the northern side of the river the desert commences abruptly, and extends to the first line of defence in front of the valley of Lima. Here, on the desert river bank, are the ruins of the ancient city of Pachacamac, with its temple rising up in three broad terraces, and overlooking the sea. Near the beach there is a lagoon abounding in fish, and the small farm of Mamaconas. On the land side the great roofless houses and courts, and the silent streets of the city of the dead, stretch away from the foot of the temple. The whole scene is deeply interesting. On one side of the river are the old ruins with all their romantic associations, and the rolling sand hills. On the other the bright and smiling vale of Lurin, so soon to be converted into a scene of mourning and desolation by the invaders.

It was on the 30th of January, 1533, that Hernando Pizarro, after passing over the site of the future city of Lima, reached the famed temple of Pachacamac. Such reports had been received of its wealth that his brother had entrusted him with the conduct of a long and perilous march from Caxamarca to ascertain the truth. Miguel Astete, who accompanied him and wrote the narrative, afterwards settled at Cuzco. His descendants shared the honours of the Tarapaca victory, and fought in defence of Lima. Pizarro and Astete lodged in one of the great courts, with small chambers opening to them, which are still standing in gloomy shade, half filled with sand. The fierce conqueror broke the idol of Pachacamac into pieces before

the people, and taught them the sign of the cross.
The lords of Mala, of Huarca (Cañete), and of Chincha
came to him with presents, and were kindly received ;
but after this visit the sacred coast city ceased to be
inhabited. There it has stood for 350 years of solitude,
with the smiling valley on its flank, and the river
almost washing its walls. Worse invaders than the
Pizarros were now to waken the echoes in its sand-
filled streets. Pizarro showed favour to the chief of Mala.
The " men of Chile " burnt Mala to the ground.

The once merry village of Lurin was completely
gutted by the Chilians. Most of the houses were converted into ruins, whilst all the furniture and house-
hold goods of the poor people were wantonly destroyed.
Even the church was not respected, the interior being
used as a stable for the horses of General Baquedano.
He established his headquarters at the estate of San
Pedro, on christmas day.

Here the Chilian leader, with his army, remained
for three weeks, making preparations for his final
advance on Lima, reconnoitring the Peruvian line of
defence about ten miles to the north, collecting provisions and munitions of war, and maturing his plans.
He had an effective force of 26,000 fighting-men, over
70 field-guns of long range, and a large and well-
mounted body of cavalry. His task was neither
complicated nor difficult. With veteran Quichua and
Aymara soldiers to attack, in the same numbers, the
result might have been different. But the overwhelming numbers of thoroughly disciplined Chilian troops
merely had to carry a line of sand-hills defended by
brave but inexperienced townsmen and recruits.

In the upper part of the valley of Lurin there are
two farms called Manchay and Cieneguilla, where the
groves of *algoroba* and other trees help to supply Lima
with firewood.   Thence a desert road, between arid
ranges of hills, leads to the Rinconada de Até, a
corner of the valley of Lima on the extreme left of
the Peruvian position.   Até is a little village with a
few small lucerne farms round it, watered by an
irrigating channel from the Rimac.   The distance
between the two valleys by this route is fifteen miles.
There was some idea of marching by this " Camino
de los Lomeros," as it is called, with the whole Chilian
army, and thus completely outflanking the defenders
of Lima.   Colonel Barbosa, with a force of 2000 men
of all arms, was sent to reconnoitre in this direction on
the 9th of January, and he reached the point where
the desert road enters upon the clover-fields of Até.
The Peruvians were digging a trench across the ravine.
The Chilian cavalry charged and the workmen fled,
seven being left dead on the field.   Barbosa then
retreated back to the Lurin valley, with a report that
he had killed forty-two of the enemy.   The same
afternoon the Supreme Chief Pierola visited the
spot, and determined to strengthen the extreme left
of his line of defence with a large part of the division
of Davila.

But the Chilian general decided against a flank
march by the " Camino de los Lomeros."   He would
be completely separated from his ships, to which he
looked for co-operation, there is not a drop of water
along the fifteen miles of desert between the Lurin
valley and Até, and the difficulty of debouching into

the plain in the face of a numerous enemy would be formidable. On these grounds he preferred the plan of a direct attack.

The first division, under Lynch, was to form the Chilian left wing, marching along the road by the sea shore, called the "Playa de Conchan," a distance of nine miles, assaulting the line of defence between the Morro Solar and Santa Teresa, and coming down upon Chorrillos. The second division, under General Sotomayor, was in the centre, and had orders to break the line in front of San Juan, and then co-operate with Lynch against Chorrillos. The third, led by Colonel Lagos, was on the extreme right, with the duty of keeping the enemy's left in check or supporting the centre under Sotomayor. The reserve, under Colonel Martinez, was placed in the space between the left and centre, ready to give assistance as circumstances might require.

The defenders of the capital, marshalled to receive the invaders, were ranged along the first line of defence. On the extreme right Miguel Iglesias was under the brow of the Morro Solar with 5000 men. His colonels were Noriega, Valle Riestra, Arguedas, Cano of Caxamarca, Borgoño of Truxillo, Panizo, who commanded the artillery at Tacna, Rosa Gil at the head of the Callao volunteers, and Carlos de Pierola with the guards of Lima.

In the centre was Caceres defending the hills of Santa Teresa and San Juan ; with the battalions of Marino, of Ayarza, and of Canevaro. The latter was transferred to the division of Davila, on the left, just before the battle. Here were Manuel Velarde,

Mariano Bustamante, the Sub-Prefect of Lima, and the gallant young Reinaldo Vivanco.

The division of Suarez formed a reserve, with Isaac Recabárren, who fought under the shadow of a great sorrow, and Buenaventura Aguirre, who was wounded at the first battle, and slain at the second.

The Supreme Chief had his headquarters at Chorrillos, in the villa of Don Manuel A. Fuentes, the learned statistician. Round him were the veteran generals of the republic, the aged Vargas Machuca, who remembered the days of the viceroys, Pedro and Francisco Canseco, the brothers-in-law of President Castilla, Echenique the former President, and Andres Segura. Buendia, Montero, and Leyva, worn and battered from the fateful southern campaigns, were his honorary aides-de-camp. General Silva was his chief of the staff, Captain Garcia y Garcia his Secretary, and his young son, just eighteen, was also by his side. All that remained of the military order, from extreme old age to boyhood, had come out to face death, and, if need be, to die for their country in her great need.

Commencing the march from Lurin in the evening of the 12th of January, 1881, the Chilian plan was to attack the defences at dawn on the 13th, taking the Peruvians by surprise.

The first division marched half-way across the desert, with its left resting on the sea-shore, halting at midnight in front of the Peruvian positions of Villa and Santa Teresa, and about two miles from them. Sotomayor led his division across the Lurin river, up the ravine of Atocongo to the table-land of La Tablada, where he also halted at midnight. The third division reached the same plateau. At dawn they all began to advance, but as the first division had much the shortest distance to march over, the action began first on the Chilian left, with a smart fire from the Peruvian lines at five a.m. Here the heavy odds against the defenders were increased by a cannonade from the men-of-war. Yet their resistance was steady and tenacious. They had scarcely lost any ground when Baquedano ordered the reserves to advance between Santa Teresa and San Juan, and attack on the flank. Then the gallant Peruvian right wing was driven back, but not broken. It retreated steadily up the Morro Solar. An hour after this attack began, at six a.m., the second Chilian division charged the defences in front of San Juan, nearly the centre of the position, and carried the hill at the point of the bayonet; while there was a frightful slaughter of the unfortunate people under Canevaro, who faced the third division. They were attempting to retreat when Baquedano, at 7.30 a.m., let loose his cavalry along the road to Tebes, who cut down the fugitives in all directions, and covered the plain with dead bodies as far as Tebes and La Palma. The defenders of San Juan, under Caceres, retreated in better order towards Chorrillos.

Among the dead was young Juan Castilla, the only son of that President who gave long years of peace to Peru. He was serving as brigade-major to Colonel Canevaro, and fell, sword in hand, pierced by the bullets of the advancing Chilians, while in the act of gallantly rallying his brigade. An English friend thus speaks of this brave Peruvian :—" He was a noble young man, a dashing soldier, a true and enthusiastic patriot, a sincere and hospitable friend. Educated in England, he excelled in all field-sports. His manly form and cheery voice will be sadly missed for many a long day in future amicable contests, either in the *mêlée* while struggling to score for his side the first 'touch-down' or 'goal,' or while running between the wickets for a fiver." Like Tirado, Echenique, and other Peruvians, poor young Castilla was an excellent cricketer and football player. Another youth who died for his country was Reinaldo Vivanco, eager and zealous, and brave to audacity. He fell gloriously, sabred by the Chilian cavalry. He atoned, in his death, for any injury that the restless ambition of his father General Vivanco may have done to his country. The name will not in future recall the seditious revolts of the accomplished though turbulent father, but the heroic death of the gallant son, killed fighting in the noblest cause for which a man can draw his sword.

The interest now centres on the little knot of valiant warriors fighting for their country on the Morro Solar. Colonel Miguel Iglesias, himself a rich landed proprietor of Caxamarca, had with him a body of his countrymen, descendants of the victims who were massacred by Pizarro and his ruthless followers in the square of Caxamarca. They formed a dauntless front, to sell their lives more dearly in opposing invaders who were closely imitating the work of those first Spanish conquerors. Supporting them were a few Indians of Ayacucho, brethren of those who followed Caceres at Tarapaca and at Tacna.

Lastly there were some Lima volunteers under Don Carlos de Pierola, a younger brother of the Supreme Chief.

Baquedano now re-arranged his line. The first division was to assault the Morro, while the reserve attacked it on the opposite side. The second was to advance on Chorrillos by the road from San Juan, and the rest of the troops were to be assembled near the houses of San Juan. The firing was kept up steadily on both sides for several hours, the Peruvians under Iglesias making a steady defence. Lynch was now fighting desperate men who were defending their country at its last gasp. He sent urgent appeals for succour and reinforcements. The general ordered up brigade after brigade to help him, and the patriots were slowly driven by overpowering numbers from post to post, making a brave resistance at each step. Finally they were driven out to the point of Chorrillos, where a heavy fire from long range field-guns was opened upon them. At length, to save the gallant remnant, Iglesias surrendered ; with Colonel Noriega, a veteran of the school of Castilla ; Colonel Cano, of Caxamarca ; Colonel Pablo Arguedas ; and Don Carlos de Pierola. Noriega, Arguedas, and Pierola were wounded.

The reserve under Suarez ought to have reinforced Iglesias. But, alas ! he who had been the life and soul of the Tarapaca defence was fated to lose his prestige on this disastrous day. He said his orders were contradictory. At all events he did not advance. But others took his place. Isaac Recabárren, the defender of Pisagua and victor at Tarapaca, got 1000

men together, and hurried forward to defend Chorrillos.   Caceres, too, rallied 2000 men, and supported
him.   They were furiously attacked by the second
Chilian division.   Long the desperate struggle was
maintained in front of Chorrillos.   Recabárren fell
severely wounded ; and this last remnant of defenders was overpowered.   The Chilians as usual
gave no quarter, and bayoneted not only all the
wounded, but defenceless civilians.   Here the aged
Dr. Maclean, a respected English physician long
resident in Lima, was foully murdered.   The Chilian
rioters soon set the houses on fire, and the town was
burnt amidst the most hideous scenes of slaughter
and rapine.   Dreadful as were the atrocities committed by the Chilians during the day, they were
as nothing in comparison with the horrors enacted
after dark.   There were no more Peruvians of
either sex to kill, so the drunken savages turned upon
each other.   No less than 400 were killed in this way,
fighting with senseless fury, or being burnt by the
flames which they had themselves kindled.   The thirst
for blood was unsated, and shots were heard in all
directions through the night.   The foreign flags, flying over the houses of neutrals, were torn down, and
lighted torches applied to the most inflammable parts
of the buildings, amidst ribald jests and bursts of
drunken laughter.   The British Minister's house was
levelled to the ground, as well as the church.   The
town was utterly destroyed.   Vergara reported that
over 2000 Chilians were killed and wounded ; while
4000 bodies of the young students and mechanics
of Lima—the poor citizens thus making a human

wall between the invaders and their beloved capital
—4000 dead bodies were scattered over the first
line of defence. At two p.m. the slaughter was
finished for the day, having lasted continuously since
dawn. The first Chilian division encamped at the
foot of the Morro Solar, near Chorrillos. The rest of
the army was distributed in the meadows between the
ruined town and San Juan. The large military school
at Chorrillos, the only building left standing, was used
as a hospital.

The Supreme Chief had remained at the front en-
couraging his countrymen until the day was lost. He
then rode from Chorrillos along the beach, managing
to get his horse up some part of the cliff, and so reached
Miraflores, where he laboured to place the second line
in a posture of defence.

In the early morning of the 15th the Diplomatic
Corps at Lima intervened in the hope of preventing
more bloodshed, and averting the horrors of a
battle just outside the capital. This was done
at the request of the Supreme Chief, who desired
to know what would be the bases of peace. The
Ministers of England, France, and Salvador asked
General Baquedano for a suspension of hostilities
with the object of allowing Pierola time to deliberate.
The Chilian commander agreed that the armistice
should last until midnight of the 15th. But he
insisted on carrying out a movement of troops
which had been commenced. The Ministers agreed
to that, with the express condition (accepted by the
Chilian general) that the movement should not extend
beyond the "Gran Guardia" of the army, and that

the line should remain as it was at the moment of the agreement.) There was to be no advance.

(The Foreign Ministers and Admirals, with the Supreme Chief of Peru and some of his officers, then assembled in the beautiful villa of Mr. Schell at Miraflores. Here Pierola entertained his distinguished guests at breakfast, in perfect confidence that faith would be kept, and all hoped that some arrangement would be made with the Chilians before the armistice came to an end.) A golden oriole had perched on a twig close to the windows, and Pierola was explaining the habits of the bird to his foreign guests. At that instant a furious cannonade was heard, and shells began to fly in all directions. There was a cry of treachery. There was no time to get out horses ; admirals and diplomatists had to escape on foot as best they could, and were exposed to great danger. Two days afterwards the golden oriole was found dead in one of the redoubts.

General Baquedano had inadvertently broken the armistice. He had advanced to reconnoitre beyond the line agreed upon.[1] Seeing that an advance was thus made, contrary to agreement, some of the Peruvian gunners mistook it for an attack and opened fire. The action immediately became general.

[1] The terms of the armistice are given in a document dated April 27th, 1881, and signed by Señor Pinto, Minister of Salvador, M. de Vorges, of France, and Sir Spencer St. John, of Great Britain. The same high authorities say that " in the report of General Baquedano the facts are not stated as they took place on the morning of the 15th of January during our interview." This erroneous statement of Baquedano probably accounts for his breach of the armistice. The Chilian historian bears witness that there was no treachery on the side of the Peruvians. "No; tras los parapetos de Miraflores no hubo traicion."—*Vicuña Mackenna*, iv. p. 1182.

On that afternoon the last stand was made behind the last line of defences. The railroad from Lima to Chorrillos passed through it, near Miraflores. East of the railroad the irrigating watercourse of Surco, flowing from the Rimac, passes south-south-west to Surco and Barranco, one branch forming a shallow dry ravine, extending to the sea. This was used as a sort of trench in front of the defences. Near the Rimac, and between Lima and the river Surco, rise the isolated hills of Vasquez with the peak of San Bartolomé. Across the Rimac, and in rear of Lima, is the peak of San Cristoval. These two heights were planted with heavy cannon. The line passed from the hills of Vasquez, along the course of the Surco, by the estates of Piño, Mendoza, San Borja, La Palma, and the Huaca Juliana to Miraflores. There were five redoubts on this line, mounted with artillery, and entrenchments between them. Here Colonel Davila commanded. In one redoubt was Deputy Sanchez. In the next was Ribeiro with the students and gentlemen of the press. Then came the merchants under Manuel Lecco. The *adobe* walls, forming the boundaries of the numerous fields, were pierced for rifles in two rows, for men kneeling and standing. Miraflores may be considered the central point of the position, and hither trains, mounted with guns, could be sent out of Lima with reinforcements. Between Miraflores and the sea the line was continued to a semicircular redoubt on the Peruvian extreme right. Two of the heavy Rodman guns from Callao were placed in it. This work, called the Alfonso Ugarte fort, in honour of the young hero who fell on the Morro of Arica,[2] consisted of sand-bags on a bed of pebbles, with a ditch in front. It was defended by Caceres. It is quite uncertain how many Peruvians lined the defensive works, as they came and went, perhaps 12,000 at the outside, at one time. The Supreme Chief stationed himself in a redoubt on the left. There were 13,000 Chilians actually engaged in assaulting the lines, by their own account.

The battle began at 2.25 p.m. Artillery was brought to bear on the Ugarte fort, and opened fire at 2.35 p.m., while the ironclads *Huascar* and *Blanco*, and the *O'Higgins*, *Pilcomayo*, and *Toro* enfiladed from the sea and disabled the two Rodman guns. The work was very gallantly defended by Colonel Caceres, and the fire was steadily returned. After a long bombardment the Chilian third division advanced in skirmishing order, protected by the artillery, and made a furious charge under Colonel Lagos. Yet it was not until the ammunition of the defenders was exhausted that they at length got possession of the place after a sharp struggle. Caceres had whispered to those around him, "No tenemos ya municiones. Estamos perdidos." This was at 4.30 p.m. The defenders fell back, to reinforce the centre. At the same time a still more severe contest was raging on the Peruvian left. The students and merchants made an attack upon the Chilian first division, supported by the reserves, while the guns of San Bartolomé and San Cristoval kept up a sullen roar in the rear. For a time the vigorous assault of the citizens afforded a gleam of hope,

---

[2] See page 204.

the enemy wavered, their ammunition was failing. But reinforcements came up, and a battery of artillery opened fire from the ridge of " Huaca Juliana." The defenders were forced back, and at last the redoubts were carried at the point of the bayonet. They were filled with dead, poor young lads from the desk and the counter, and many well-dressed men of fashion, and students. One had been whiling away the hours before the battle by reading a story of lives of brave endurance. There was a volume of letters from the Martyr Jesuits in Japan amidst the dead. In one place there was a heap of a dozen Italian youths, volunteers who would not see their Peruvian friends go forth to fight without helping them. They were lads of the " Garibaldi Legion," as was testified by the legend on their caps. Most pathetic was the wall of youthful dead, which the invading soldiery must trample over before the doomed city could be reached.

There were old men as well as young among the heroic dead. Dr. Pino, a learned judge of the Superior Court at Puno, aged sixty ; Señor Ugariza, secretary of the Lima Chamber of Commerce ; Señor Los Heros, the chief clerk of the Foreign Office ; the diplomatist Marquez, brother of the poet ; two editors, members of Congress, magistrates, wealthy landed proprietors, were all lying dead, after fighting in defence of their country's capital. Ricardo Palma, the charming writer of historical anecdotes, was fighting, though fortunately he escaped with life. But his house, with a priceless library of American works, was burnt to the ground.

At 4.45 p.m. the defending fire was slackening. Resistance was now concentrated at the central part of the line near Miraflores. At 5.35 p.m. the centre redoubt was carried at the point of the bayonet, and by six the fell work was done. For nearly four hours the defence had been bravely maintained.

Surely the slander that Peruvians will not fight bravely for their country and die for it ought to be silenced before these facts. At least one enemy has the generosity and the wisdom to do them justice.[2]

The very night before the battle saw the arrival of an important reinforcement. The redoubtable Morochuco Indians, having at length received arms, came down by forced marches just in time to share in the honours of the day. Their chief, named Miola, was among the slain, a fact which the Chilians will have cause to remember, if their predatory incursions ever bring them into the neighbourhood of the wild Andes of Cangallo. The aged General Vargas Machuca, a hero of the battle of Pichincha, now past eighty, was wounded. Generals Silva and Segura, and Colonel Canevaro were also wounded, the latter severely. Caceres received five honourable scars; and the young son of the brave Iglesias was killed.

The Supreme Chief Pierola rode off the field when all was lost, and retired to the little town of Canta in the mountains, accompanied or followed by General

---

[2] "Los Peruanos desplegaron un valor digno de menos desdichada suerte que la que allí les cupo."—*Vicuña Mackenna*, IV. p. 1172.

"Entre los jefes superiores del ejercito Peruano las perdidas fueron numerosas y sensibles, prueba de la honrosa tenacidad con que se batieron."—*Ibid*, iv. p. 1175.

Buendia, Colonel Suarez, and the Secretary, Captain Garcia y Garcia. Pierola appointed Admiral Montero to the direction of affairs in the northern departments, who made his way along the coast, by Huacho to Truxillo, and thence to Caxamarca. Colonel Echenique received charge of the central departments, while Dr. Solar took command at Arequipa. Don Rufino Torico was left in charge at Lima.

Another tale of 2000 dead swelled the number of mourners in Lima. At 6.45 p.m. Miraflores was in flames. The savage victors sacked and burnt all the pleasant country houses, and destroyed the lovely gardens. This once charming retreat shared the fate of Chorrillos and Barranco. It has become a wilderness of ruin and desolation.

Lima, the great city, would have shared the fate of Chorrillos and Miraflores if the Chilians had had their way. (Its rescue from destruction is due to the firm stand made by the British Minister, Sir Spencer St. John, backed by the material power and calm resolve of the English and French Admirals. On the 16th, Don Rufino Torico, the Municipal Alcalde of Lima, made a formal agreement with the Chilian general to surrender the unfortunate city.

During the night the dangerous classes ran riot, the Chinese quarter was gutted, and if the foreigners had not formed an efficient volunteer corps, the whole place might have been sacked. On the 17th the Chilian troops took possession of Lima. General Baquedano, with his headquarter staff, made his entrance on the following day, and established himself in the palace.

In the two battles the Chilian losses were reported to be 5443, of whom 1299 were killed, and 4144 wounded. The Peruvians lost far more heavily, the proportion between killed and wounded telling, as usual, a tale of savage butchery. There were said to be 6000 killed and 3000 wounded.

At Callao, as soon as the fatal news arrived, it was determined to destroy all the remaining ships and as many guns as possible, rather than that they should fall into the hands of the enemy. The *Union* became a wreck. The monitor *Atahualpa* was sunk. The school-ships *Apurimac*, *Meteoro*, and *Marañon*, and the steam transports *Rimac*, *Chalaco*, *Talisman*, and *Limeña* were all destroyed. The *Meteoro* was intended for a preparatory school. The *Marañon* was the naval college ; and the school for apprentices was on board the *Apurimac*, an old frigate of 1853.

After a gallant and well-conducted naval effort, and after three hard-fought campaigns, the coast of Peru was conquered, and the capital was occupied by the enemy. The unfortunate people had to drink the cup of sorrow and humiliation to the dregs. Although the Peruvian and Chilian governing classes are one people, having a common ancestry, often bound together by the ties of kindred, with the same religion, speaking the same language, with the same history until recent years, and the same traditions ; yet the conquerors showed no relenting, no wish to soften the calamity. Not only were they harsh and exacting, but they pushed their power of appropriating and confiscating to unprecedented lengths. Black-mail was extorted from private citizens, with threats that their houses would be destroyed if the demands were not immediately met. 'Public property, unconnected with the war, was seized, The public library of Lima was carried off! Even the picture by Monteros of the obsequies of Atahualpa was stolen! In all this is seen the demoralizing effect of a policy of military glory and conquest. Peru may possibly find a new and better life through adversity. The influence of such prosperity as Chile has sought and won must be altogether evil.

CHAPTER XVII.

VÆ VICTIS.

THE whole coast of Peru, including her capital, has been prostrate under the heel of the conqueror since those days of hideous slaughter in January, 1881. But the coast, though the best known part of Peru, is far from being the most extensive or the most important part. Cuzco, the ancient capital, the city of the Yncas, is beyond the reach of Chilian occupation ; and there are centres of population and local government at the Andean cities of Caxamarca and Huaraz, Tarma and Xauxa, Ayacucho and Andahuaylas, Puno and Lampa. Arequipa, too, has not yet been visited with the horrors of war, although it lies more within reach of the invaders.

The Supreme Chief Pierola retired into the lofty valleys of the Andes, remaining for some time at Xauxa, and eventually establishing his headquarters at Ayacucho. Colonel Caceres was in command of the small remnant of the force which retired from the defensive lines before Lima. The conquerors were embarrassed from the first by the possession of the Peruvian capital. After they have ruined the people of the coast by war contributions and sucked them dry, extorting $1,000,000

a month of black-mail from Lima alone, it is clear
that the occupation will necessarily become a drain
on their own finances. (For the enormous duties on
merchandise must eventually ruin foreign trade.(At
first the Chilian authorities were inclined to open negotiations for a peace with Pierola, who was still at the
head of the only recognized government in Peru.)
(Mr. Christiancy, the United States Minister, ascertained that Pierola was ready and willing to treat,
and the Supreme Chief appointed two commissioners
for the purpose.   But suddenly the Chilians declared
that they would not treat with him, and would no
longer recognize him as representing the government
of Peru.   They based this refusal on a charge that
Pierola's secretary had brought against them of having
broken the armistice at Miraflores)   That the charge
was true, although there was no intentional treachery
on either side, has been shown beyond any doubt,
but this was not calculated to make it any the more
palatable.   Thus there was a complete deadlock.

(Some of the leading citizens of Lima, seeing that
there was no probability of successful negotiations
for peace with the Pierola Government, dreading the
exactions of the invaders, and longing to be rid of
them, started a movement for the establishment of
a provisional government.)   The Chilians had been
inconsiderate and ungenerous in their dealings with
the unfortunate conquered people, but in nothing
more than in the selection of a military governor at
Lima.   That post was actually given to the man
who carried ruin and destruction along the northern
coast of Peru, who had burnt private houses and

defenceless towns, seized all he could lay his hands
upon, and desolated many a once happy and prosperous
home. (Captain Patrick Lynch was made Governor
of Lima ; and with him the people would have to
make their account. His employers seemed willing
to come to some arrangement, and he was instructed
to allow the organization of a provisional government.)

At a meeting consisting of about a hundred citizens,
an eminent lawyer was induced to undertake the
thankless task. (Francisco Garcia Calderon was born
at Arequipa in 1832, where he practised as an advocate
until 1859, when he came to reside at Lima. His
"Dictionary of the Jurisprudence of Peru" (1859-62)
is a work of marvellous erudition and research. At
Lima he was legal adviser to several large mercantile
houses, and he made a considerable fortune, without
losing his justly-earned reputation for integrity and
uprightness. He still has great influence in his native
city of Arequipa. The Chilian Governor permitted
the occupation of the little village of Magdalena as
the territory of the new administration, and here Dr.
Garcia Calderon was installed on the 12th of March,
1881. He rallied some influential men around him.
His Minister of the Interior was Don Juan Ignacio
Elguera, a native of Lima, who had charge of the
finances in the time of President Pardo. Captain
Camilo Carrillo had done good service at Arica and
Tacna, and had previously been the moving spirit in
promoting higher education in the navy. He had
also presided over the Chamber of Deputies with tact
and ability, during Pardo's administration. Don
Mariano Felipe Paz Soldan is an eminent geographer

and statistician, and Honorary Member of the Royal
Geographical Society of London. The Mayor, Rufino
Torico, was the second son of the general and received
his education in Europe: a handsome well-bred man
with cultivated manners, and a devoted adherent of
Pierola. Señor Galvez, Colonel Velarde, and General
Canseco—the brother-in-law of President Castilla—are
also persons of distinction. These gave countenance
and strength to the Garcia Calderon Government,
while Admiral Montero, though declining to be
decoyed within the Chilian lines, accepted the office
of Vice-President, and remained in the north.

But the fact that this administration was organized
with the permission and under the auspices of Chile
was fatal to its influence and popularity. Calderon
called together the old Congress which existed before
the war; but only a few representatives answered to
his summons. The Chilians gave permission for the
use of the military college at Chorrillos as a place of
meeting, and there what in England would be called
the "Rump" Congress assembled in sadness and
humiliation. The conquerors believed that Calderon
and his advisers would agree to any conditions that
might be imposed upon them. But the Congress
refused to authorize Calderon to consent to any permanent cession of Peruvian territory, and on the 23rd of
August, 1881, it was dissolved. Meanwhile Calderon
was buoyed up with hopes of intervention from the
United States, hopes which had been strengthened by
the recognition of his government on the part of the
American Minister on the 26th of June. Finding that
these hopes had been raised, and that Dr. Calderon

was too honest and patriotic to be a tool in their hands, the Chilians determined to knock down what they had set up. Calderon's government was abolished, with coarse violence, on the 28th of September, by Governor Lynch, and its head was packed off a prisoner to Chile.

The Supreme Chief Pierola had in the meanwhile summoned a national assembly to meet at Ayacucho, and he resigned his exceptional powers into their hands on the 28th of July. The representatives elected him as Provisional President, but he felt that he had been unsuccessful, and that the most patriotic course would be to retire, at least for a time. He resigned office on November 28th, 1881, and, proceeding to Lima as a private citizen, he has since left the country. Generals Buendia and Silva retired into private life at the same time.

Admiral Montero, in the enforced absence of Dr. Garcia Calderon, then became head of the Peruvian Government, as Vice-President in charge. He remained for some months at Huaraz, in the north of Peru; but in August, 1882, he went to Arequipa, where he was enthusiastically received. He proceeded to form a government. Captain Camilo Carrillo became Minister of the Interior, Dr. M. del Valle of Foreign Affairs, Dr. Epifanio Serpe of Justice, Dr. F. F. Oviedo of Finance, and Colonel Manuel Velarde of War.

Colonel Iglesias, the hero of the Morro Solar, holds the military command in the north, with his head-quarters in the department of Caxamarca. He has summoned a representative assembly of the northern departments to express their views regarding terms of peace. The indefatigable Caceres, now promoted to the rank of general, is in command in the central departments, actively engaged in organizing an efficient force. At Arequipa the accomplished Captain Camilo Carrillo assembled a force of 5000 men, with several guns, and received arms and ammunition by way of Bolivia. Since the arrival of Vice-President Montero at Arequipa, and the assumption of ministerial office by Captain Carrillo, the command of the troops in the south has been given to Colonel Belisario Suarez. Colonel Canevaro, who had recovered from the severe wound he received at the battle of Miraflores, had taken command of the National Guard. The Government of Peru has thus been reorganized, after the interval of unavoidable confusion caused by the loss of the capital, and the paralyzing calamity of January, 1881.

(Bolivia has remained loyally true to her ally, and has also been occupied in the reorganization of her army.) In September, 1882, Montero proceeded to La Paz, to have an interview with General Campero ; and the resolution of the allies seems to be to hold out until less hard and more just and reasonable terms of peace can be obtained from Chile.

Covered with wounds, with her long line of coast mercilessly ravaged, and the flower of her youth destroyed, the land of the Yncas still presents a gallant front to the foe. In this hour of extreme peril there is no civil dissension, and Peru's most turbulent spirits have atoned for past sedition by their patriotic devotion to duty in the face of the enemy.

In civilized warfare a conqueror acts as if his enemy might some day be again his friend, and seeks to lessen, rather than unnecessarily to increase the amount of human misery caused by his mischievous operations. (The Chilians have carried on their war in an opposite spirit. They have made their neighbours taste the full bitterness of defeat by every form of insult and violence, and by a system of wholesale plunder, and they have needlessly extended the area of their destructive operations.

At Lima enormous sums of money have been extorted from private persons, and a great number of leading citizens have been seized and imprisoned, or transported to captivity in remote parts of Chile. The educational establishments, including the colleges of San Carlos and San Fernando, the School of Arts, and the National Library, have been converted into barracks, their treasures robbed or destroyed. The Peruvian students now have neither books, instruments, nor instruction.

(Meanwhile predatory raids have been made into the interior from several points on the coast.) Soon after the occupation of Lima Colonel Aristides Martinez, with an adequate force, was landed at Chimbote, and occupied the city of Truxillo. Another smaller force took possession of Pacasmayo. A third party made a dash at the silver-mines of Cerro Pasco, and penetrated as far as Huanuco, where a revolting slaughter of half-armed Indians was committed. In January, 1882, a force of 5000 men occupied the valleys of Tarma and Xauxa, under Colonel del Canto, who placed garrisons in those towns, as well as at the Oroya bridge, in Concepcion, and in Huancayo. Other parties were sent to Cañete, Chincha, Pisco, and Yca, apparently with the sole object of plunder and useless bloodshed.

The Andean valley of Xauxa, between the maritime and eastern cordilleras, was inhabited in the days of the Yncas by a tribe called the Huancas, who early adopted and identified themselves with the civilization of Cuzco. They made a brave stand against the conquerors led by Pizarro ; and the losses and sufferings caused by Spanish cruelty were partially remedied by an enlightened system, which raises the Huancas, as civilized men, far above their European oppressors. An exact account was kept at every village in the Xauxa valley, by means of the *quipus*, of the losses each sustained during the passage of the Spanish conquerors. The sum total was divided by the number of villages, and those which had suffered more than the average received help and relief to that amount from those which had suffered less.[1]

The descendants of the Huancas were now exposed to a still more cruel invasion. They made a brave resistance to the predatory incursions of the Chilian garrisons, armed only with spears and slings, and were mercilessly slaughtered as their ancestors had been by Pizarro, many villages being burnt. But help was at hand. General Caceres was actively engaged at Ayacucho during the first months of the year 1882, in organizing a force for the defence of the

---

[1] Information received by Cieza de Leon from Huacarapura, Chief of the Huancas, a few years afterwards.—*Segunda Parte de la Cronica del Peru* (Madrid, 1880), cap. xii. p. 43.

interior of Peru. In July he was able to take the field. Colonel del Canto, with the bulk of the Chilian force, was at Huancayo, and there was a garrison of seventy-seven men of the Chacabuco regiment in the town of Concepcion. The first encounter was at Marcabaya, a small village two leagues from Huancayo. The Peruvians then advanced to Concepcion, and, after a long defence of the barracks, the Chilian garrison was cut to pieces on the 9th of July, 1882. Del Canto then assembled the other garrisons from Tarma, Xauxa, and Huancayo, and retreated by way of Oroya to the terminus of the railroad at Chicla. He burnt the town of Concepcion to ashes, in revenge for the Chilian reverse.

Meanwhile a small Peruvian force, under Colonel Tafur, had crossed the Oroya and encamped on the heights of Chacapalca. He was surprised by 300 Chilian carbineers under Lieutenant Stuven, and forced to retreat, with a loss of forty-eight prisoners. The Peruvians still remained in threatening force in the neighbourhood; and Stuven, embarrassed by his prisoners, proceeded to commit a cruel act which shows how utterly demoralized the Chilians had become. He ordered the Peruvian prisoners to be formed in a line, and shot them down to a man. The wounded were despatched by the Chilians with their long knives. The retreat was then continued, and the invaders, covered with disgrace by this act of infamy, evacuated the valley of Xauxa. General Caceres then sent some troops, by a flanking march, to a point down the line of railway, to intercept the retreat of Canto.

On the 22nd of July the Chilian garrison, numbering a hundred men, at San Bartolomé—a place on the railway about fifty miles from Lima—was resolutely attacked. But reinforcements arrived from Lima, under General Gana, and the Peruvians retired over the mountains in good order. The Chilians destroyed several villages along the line, and finally retreated to Chosica, twenty-four miles from Lima.

General Caceres cleared this part of Peru of the invaders. He established his headquarters at Tarma in August, 1882, and continued his labour of arming and organizing his forces. Huancas, Yquichanos, Pocras, and Morochucos flocked in thousands to his standard, all eager to defend their beloved valleys from invasion. But the task of arming and drilling them must needs be slow and difficult. Their leader, however, is one who is not easily turned away from his purpose. Ayacucho is the home of Andres Caceres. He is surrounded by his own people. They know him as the man who has fought for his country in almost every action since the invaders landed at Pisagua. He is covered with honourable wounds He has seen the Chilians flying before his brave Ayacucheños at Tarapaca, and that day justifies the hope of further successes in the same righteous cause. He is a veteran leader of proved valour, long military experience, and capacity.

A similar needless extension of the horrors of war was planned by the Chilians in Northern Peru, where Colonel Iglesias conducted the defence. A force of 300 men advanced from the port of Pacasmayo, up the Jequetepeque valley, with the intention of ravaging the department of Caxamarca. Met by Iglesias at San Pablo, twelve miles from Caxamarca, they were defeated, and fled back to Pacasmayo, leaving their field hospital in the hands of the Peruvians. But they received reinforcements, and eventually, like Pizarro before them, entered Caxamarca as conquering invaders. After converting two of the ancient churches into ruins, and burning several villages, they evacuated the historical city, so famous for similar crimes committed there 350 years ago. They then entirely destroyed the town of Chota, and finally retreated to the coast in September, 1882.

The consequence to Chile of this career of conquest has been rapid moral deterioration in the characters of those employed in such work. First public property only was wantonly destroyed. Then defenceless towns were bombarded. Soon private property ceased to be respected; and Lynch was sent to rob and destroy over an extensive area. Next followed the robbery of pictures and public libraries. Hitherto this was all done, professedly at least, on public grounds. But at last we hear of wholesale robbery and extortion for private enrichment, and the cases have become so gross that Captain Lynch has brought Colonel Letelier and other officers before courts-martial. Thus rapid is the descent down the path of an immoral and selfish policy.

The gains and losses on both sides may now be summed up. Chile has become half-delirious over her "glorious victories," has seized vast quantities of warlike stores, and plundered private persons of large sums of money. She has conquered all the coast of

Bolivia, and the province of Tarapaca, and the rest of the Peruvian coast is at her mercy. Her neighbour's capital is in her hands, the inhabitants crushed under her heel. She has spread ruin, desolation, and death over a neighbouring country; thousands of wives and mothers have been plunged into mourning and despair to satisfy her desire for glory, thousands of homes have been made desolate, of families ruined. These, it will be said, are the inevitable consequences of war, and Chile, in her present mood, will doubtless laugh at such considerations. But what is her real net gain? She has got some manure that belongs to her neighbours. That is all! And against this gain must be set the loss of her character for justice, for humanity, for love of peace. That is the loss now. Hereafter, unless there is a change, she may suffer still more from the predominance of the military element, and of ideas engendered by conquest.

The only hope for Chile is that better counsels may at last prevail. On September 18th, 1881, a new President, Don Domingo Santa Maria, succeeded to the leadership in Chile. Born in 1825, and a graduate of the University at Santiago, Señor Santa Maria has had a long training in official life. He has also known adversity. A member of the liberal party, and joining in its attempted revolutions, he has twice been banished. As an exile he found a home at Lima in 1852, and made a long sojourn in Europe in 1858. In 1863 he was Minister of Finance; and in 1866 he signed an offensive and defensive treaty with Peru against Spain. As Minister of Foreign Affairs he

T

conducted the negotiations with Señor Lavalle before the outbreak of the war. (There is a hope that Señor Santa Maria, who, during his own exile, found a home in Peru, and who has had much friendly intercourse with Peruvians, may have the courage to resist the sanguinary instincts of the Chilian people, and use his influence to obtain magnanimous or at least considerate treatment for his neighbours.) The opposite policy will be even a greater loss, in the end, to Chile than to Peru. Chilian statesmen will do well to remember the old proverb, " La codicia rompe el saco."

The land of the Yncas, hated by bondholders, has been harshly judged. Putting the views of " financiers " and speculators on one side, let us conclude by considering the losses and gains of Peru. Her losses are the " glorious victories," the " Homeric combats," the " Titanic struggles," touching which Chile blows her own trumpet so loudly; and those losses are heavy indeed. The manure may be left quite out of the account in comparison. Peru has lost her bravest sons, her army and navy, the flower of her youth. Before such losses as these the desert province, the manure and like matters are as nothing. And the gains! There are consolations, bright examples, honourable memories which may turn out to be gains for the unhappy people. The life and death of the hero of Angamos will perhaps, in the time to come, be a gain to his country. The way brave Espinar died close to the Chilian gun is a gain. The Ynca chivalry falling thick upon the Cuesta de la Visagra, but victorious, is not wholly a loss. Peru lost her sons, yet gained the examples and the memory.

These deeds, and many more like them, are the deeds of patriots. They could not have been the same, if they had been performed in a civil feud or in an unjust cause. They are reasons for just and honourable pride. So the mourning people may count them as a gain. Their rulers, too, should have learnt patriotism and a truer sense of duty through adversity.[2]

(All, however, now seems dark and confused. Peru waits in broken-hearted suspense, but with undaunted front, for reasonable terms of peace. The province of Tarapaca to Camarones must be ceded. The nitrate and the guano must go with it, and also the claims on the revenue derived from nitrate and guano. These false riches have never been other than a curse to their possessors. They brought the "financiers" in their train. They are the spoils of war now. Other exactions must probably be endured.) Chile has not hitherto shown herself to be either generous or considerate. But when the conqueror is brought to reason, Peru may still be richer and wiser in the time to come.)

The land of the Yncas was a country of vast natural resources before the nitrate was heard of, and will be so when the nitrate is gone. Peru will begin her new life without the foreign debt, for that departs with the manure of which it forms a part. She may yet have a bright and prosperous future before her.

---

[2] The Chilian historian has the following noble passage in speaking of the calamities of Peru :—" Ni en muchos siglos olvidará el Peru tan cruel hecatombe ; pero su propia sangre asi generosamente vertida por el deber habrá talvez de servirle de estimulo y de regeneracion.— *Vicuña Mackenna,* iv. p. 1176.

While Pierola was in power, Don Melchor Terrazas, as plenipotentiary from Bolivia, came to Lima to negotiate a union between the two countries. The discussion of details was satisfactory, and the union of Peru and Bolivia, as the Peru-Bolivian Confederation, was once more proclaimed on the 16th of June, 1880. Subsequent disasters prevented any further progress as regards this measure, and Chile, jealous of any scheme for the prosperity of her neighbours, again objects to it. But Chile is *ultra vires* on this question. If the two republics come to the conclusion that the union will be an advantage to them it will be accomplished. If not they should continue to be friendly neighbours, with the memory of glorious struggles side by side at Pisagua, at San Francisco, and at Tacna. There is hope for both countries, in spite of a disastrous invasion, worse than the conquest of Pizarro, which has filled their houses with mourning. There are still the elements of peaceful advancement and prosperity in the land of the sacred city, and in the land of the sacred lake.

INDEX.

Azapa, valley of, near Arica, 181, 203.

BAIDES, Marquis of, Captain-General of Chile, pacification of Araucanians by, 17.

Ballivian, General José, President of Bolivia, 69.

Ballivian, Colonel Adolfo, President of Bolivia, 71 ; arranged the defensive treaty with Peru, 85 ; death, 71. 87.

Balta, Colonel Don José, President of Peru, 40 ; administration, 43 ; Death, 43 ; Pierola, Finance Minister to, 175.

Baptista, Don Mariano, Bolivian Minister, 87 ; Plenipotentiary at the Peace Conference, 225.

Baquedano, Don Manuel, Chilian General, sends a burying-party to Tarapaca, 168 ; succeeds General Escala, 192 ; at battle of Los Angeles, 193 ; at battle of Tacna, 199 ; attack on Arica, 203 ; commander-in-chief of the army to attack Lima, . 228 ; lands at Curayaco, 243 ; at Lurin, 245 ; orders at battle of Chorrillos, 249 ; agrees to an armistice, 253 ; breaks it, 254 ; enters Lima, 259.

Barbosa, Colonel Don Orozimbo, Chilian, destructive raid on Islay and Mollendo, 192 ; commands a division at battle of Tacna, 199 ; at Torata, 203 ; his reconnaissance to the Rinconada de Até, 246.

Barcelo, Chilian Colonel, in command of a division at Tacna, 199.

Barnuevo (*see* Peralta).

Barranco, near Chorrillos, 236, 255 ; destroyed by Chilians, 259.

Barreda, Don Felipe, his house and hospitality at Miraflores, 236.

Basque settlers in Peru and Chile, 14, 17, 18, 39 ; families of Basque

descent, 50 *n*, 51, 139 ; Lima families descended from, 232.

Battles, Calama, 103, 104 ; between the *Huascar* and the Chilian fleet, 125—132 ; Pisagua, 146—148 ; Jermania, 149 ; San Francisco 154 156 ; Tarapaca, 163—168 ; Cuesta de los Angeles, 192, 193 ; Tacna, 200 ; Arica, 204 ; Chorrillos, 249—252 ; Miraflores, 255, 257.

Belgrano, Patriot General in Upper Peru, 21.

Bello, Don Andres, a learned Venezuelan settled in Chile, 74 ; work of, 75 ; prepared the Chilian Civil Code, 76.

Belzu, General, President of Bolivia, 69.

Benavides, Chilian artillery officer, rallies the troops at Tarapaca, 167.

Bennet (*see* Astete).

Blakeley guns on batteries in Callao Castle, 186, 187.

Blanco Encalada, General, invades Peru, and capitulates, 33 ; Peruvian officer slain at Tarapaca related to, 164.

Blanco Encalada, Chilian ironclad, her armament, 93 ; bombards Pisagua, 105 ; leaves Iquique for the north, 108 ; flag of Admiral Riveros, 120 ; watching for the *Huascar*, 125 ; in action with the *Huascar*, 128, 131 ; begins blockade of Callao, 185 ; bombards line of Miraflores, 256.

Blockade of Iquique, 105, 118, 119, 157 ; of Arica commenced, 181 ; broken by the *Union*, 184 ; of Callao commenced, 185 ; continued, 209—223 ; of Ancon, 190, 212 : of Chancay, 190, 211.

Boatmen, of Iquique (*see* Iquique), of Valparaiso in Chilian army, called "Navales," 98.

Bobadilla, Friar, chosen to arbitrate between Pizarro and Almegro, 240.

Salaverry, General, fatal mistake of Santa Cruz in shooting, 31.

Salaverry, Lieutenant Juan, Peruvian navy, on survey of Amazonian tributaries, 95.

Salaverry port, 41 ; mischief done by Lynch at, 215.

Salta, 143.

Sama, valley of, 194 ; Chilian army encamped in, 198.

San Antonio, nitrate station in Tarapaca, 149.

San Antonio, in valley of Mala (*see* Mala).

San Bartolomé, battery on hill of, 255, 256.

San Bartolomé, station on Oroya railway. Chilians attacked at, 270.

San Borja, estate of, near Lima, 255.

San Borja, College of, for noble Indians, at Cuzco, 12 ; Tupac Amaru educated at, 20.

San Carlos, College of, at Lima, used as a barrack by Chilians, 268.

Santa Catalina, nitrate station in Tarapaca, 150.

Sanchez, Deputy, commands in a redoubt at battle of Miraflores, 255.

San Cristobal, battery on the peak of, which overlooks Lima, 255, 256.

Santa Cruz, General Don Andres, 69, 71 ; at battle of Pichincha, 25 ; President of Bolivia, 31 ; Protector of Peru-Bolivian Confederation, 31 ; good government of, 31 ; efforts to preserve peace with Chile, 31, 32, 33, 34 ; defeated at Yungay, 34, 75

Santa Cruz, Don Ricardo, Chilian officer, in command of a wing at battle of Tarapaca, 161, 163 ; defeated, 164, 165 ; his flight to Huara-siña, 167.

San Fernando College at Lima, used as a barrack by Chilians, 268.

San Francisco hill, Chilian army

massed on, 150, 153 ; allied plan, 153 ; battle of, 154, 155, 276 ; oficina of, occupied by Villegas, 155.

Sangarara, Tupac Amaru defeats Spaniards at, 20.

San José fort at Arica, 182, 204.

San Juan estate, on the first line of the Lima defences, 236, 237 ; position, 238 ; assaulted and carried by the Chilians, 247, 249, 251.

Santalices, Don Ventura, Governor of La Paz, efforts to protect the Indians, 11.

Santiago de Chile founded, 16 ; edifices built, 18 ; Paseo de Santa Lucia at, 173 ; university, 18, 75, 76, 273.

San Lorenzo, near Tarapaca, 160.

San Lorenzo, island of, near Callao, 186 ; mistake of the Peruvians in not fortifying, 187 ; explosion of a torpedo at, 188 ; of another near, 218.

Santa Lucia observatory, 76 ; Paseo de, at Santiago, 173.

San Marcos University, at Lima, 12.

Santa Maria, Don Domingo, President of Chile, notice of. 273 ; hopes of moderate policy from, 274.

San Martin, General, 23 ; his camp at Mendoza, and invasion of Chile, 24 ; embarks for Peru, 24 ; secures Peruvian independence, 25 ; retirement, 25 ; death, 73, 236.

San Pablo, defeat of Chilians at, 271.

San Pedro, in Lurin valley, Chilian headquarters, 245.

San Roberto, station on Pisagua railway, 148.

San Roman, General Don Miguel, President of Peru. 38 ; death, 39 ; government of his Vice-President restored, 40.

Santa Rosa, her saintly life, 232.

Santa Rosa silver-mine, in Tarapaca, 81.

ERRATA.

p. 33, l. 21, *for* 1837 *read* 1838.

p. 52, l. 13, *for* Moyobamba *read* Mozobamba.

p. 83, note, *for* Mendiburn *read* Mendiburu.

THE END.

LONDON:
PRINTED BY GILBERT AND RIVINGTON, LIMITED,
ST. JOHN'S SQUARE.

𝔄 𝔖election from the 𝔏ist of 𝔅ooks

PUBLISHED BY

SAMPSON LOW, MARSTON, SEARLE, & RIVINGTON.

ALPHABETICAL LIST.

A CLASSIFIED Educational Catalogue of Works published in Great Britain. Demy 8vo, cloth extra. Second Edition, revised and corrected, 5s.

About Some Fellows. By an ETON BOY, Author of "A Day of my Life." Cloth limp, square 16mo, 2s. 6d.

Adams (C. K.) Manual of Historical Literature. Crown 8vo, 12s. 6d.

Adventures of a Young Naturalist. By LUCIEN BIART, with 117 beautiful Illustrations on Wood. Edited and adapted by PARKER GILLMORE. Post 8vo, cloth extra, gilt edges, New Edition, 7s. 6d.

Alcott (Louisa M.) Jimmy's Cruise in the "Pinafore." With 9 Illustrations. Second Edition. Small post 8vo, cloth gilt, 3s. 6d.

—— *Aunt Jo's Scrap-Bag.* Square 16mo, 2s. 6d. (Rose Library, 1s.)

—— *Little Men: Life at Plumfield with Jo's Boys.* Small post 8vo, cloth, gilt edges, 3s. 6d. (Rose Library, Double vol. 2s.)

—— *Little Women.* 1 vol., cloth, gilt edges, 3s. 6d. (Rose Library, 2 vols., 1s. each.)

—— *Old-Fashioned Girl.* Best Edition, small post 8vo, cloth extra, gilt edges, 3s. 6d. (Rose Library, 2s.)

—— *Work, and Beginning Again.* A Story of Experience. (Rose Library, 2 vols., 1s. each.)

—— *Shawl Straps.* Small post 8vo, cloth extra, gilt, 3s. 6d.

—— *Eight Cousins; or, the Aunt Hill.* Small post 8vo, with Illustrations, 3s. 6d.

—— *The Rose in Bloom.* Small post 8vo, 3s. 6d.

—— *Under the Lilacs.* Small post 8vo, cloth extra, 5s.

Alcott (Louisa M.) An Old-Fashioned Thanksgiving Day. Small post 8vo, 3s. 6d.

———— *Proverbs.* Small post 8vo, 3s. 6d.

———— *Jack and Jill.* Small post 8vo, cloth extra, 5s.
"Miss Alcott's stories are thoroughly healthy, full of racy fun and humour . . . exceedingly entertaining . . . . We can recommend the 'Eight Cousins.'"— *Athenæum.*

Aldrich (T. B.) Friar Jerome's Beautiful Book, &c. Very choicely printed on hand-made paper, parchment cover, 3s. 6d.

———— *Poetical Works. Edition de Luxe.* Very handsomely bound and illustrated, 21s.

Alford (Lady Marian) See "Embroidery."

Allen (E. A.) Rock me to Sleep, Mother. 18 full-page Illustrations, elegantly bound, fcap. 4to, 5s.

American Men of Letters. Lives of Thoreau, Irving, Webster. Small post 8vo, cloth, 2s. 6d. each.

Ancient Greek Female Costume. By J. MOYR SMITH. Crown 8vo, 112 full-page Plates and other Illustrations, 7s. 6d.

Andersen (Hans Christian) Fairy Tales. With 10 full-page Illustrations in Colours by E. V. B. Cheap Edition, 5s.

Andres (E.) Fabrication of Volatile and Fat Varnishes, Lacquers, Siccatives, and Sealing Waxes. 8vo, 12s. 6d.

Angling Literature in England; and Descriptions of Fishing by the Ancients. By O. LAMBERT. With a Notice of some Books on other Piscatorial Subjects. Fcap. 8vo, vellum, top gilt, 3s. 6d.

Archer (William) English Dramatists of To-day. Crown 8vo, 8s. 6d.

Arnold (G. M.) Robert Pocock, the Gravesend Historian. Crown 8vo, cloth.   [*In the Press.*

Art and Archæology (Dictionary). See "Illustrated."

Art Education. See "Illustrated Text Books," "Illustrated Dictionary," "Biographies of Great Artists."

Art Workmanship in Gold and Silver. Large 8vo, 2s. 6d.

Art Workmanship in Porcelain. Large 8vo, 2s. 6d.

Artists, Great. See "Biographies."

Audsley (G. A.) Ornamental Arts of Japan. 90 Plates, 74 in Colours and Gold, with General and Descriptive Text. 2 vols., folio, £16 16s.

Audsley (W. and G. A.) Outlines of Ornament. Small folio, very numerous Illustrations, 31s. 6d.

Auerbach (B.) Spinoza. 2 vols., 18mo, 4s.

Autumnal Leaves. By F. G. HEATH. Illustrated by 12 Plates, exquisitely coloured after Nature; 4 Page and 14 Vignette Drawings. Cloth, imperial 16mo, gilt edges, 14*s.*

BANCROFT (G.) History of the Constitution of the United States of America. 2 vols., 8vo, 24*s.*

Barrett. English Church Composers. Crown 8vo, 3*s.*

THE BAYARD SERIES.

Edited by the late J. HAIN FRISWELL.

Comprising Pleasure Books of Literature produced in the Choicest Style as Companionable Volumes at Home and Abroad.

"We can hardly imagine better books for boys to read or for men to ponder over."—*Times.*

Price 2s. 6d. each Volume, complete in itself, flexible cloth extra, gilt edges, with silk Headbands and Registers.

The Story of the Chevalier Bayard. By M. De Berville.

De Joinville's St. Louis, King of France.

The Essays of Abraham Cowley, including all his Prose Works.

Abdallah; or, The Four Leaves. By Edouard Laboullaye.

Table-Talk and Opinions of Napoleon Buonaparte.

Vathek: An Oriental Romance. By William Beckford.

The King and the Commons. A Selection of Cavalier and Puritan Songs. Edited by Professor Morley.

Words of Wellington: Maxims and Opinions of the Great Duke.

Dr. Johnson's Rasselas, Prince of Abyssinia. With Notes.

Hazlitt's Round Table. With Biographical Introduction.

The Religio Medici, Hydriotaphia, and the Letter to a Friend. By Sir Thomas Browne, Knt.

Ballad Poetry of the Affections. By Robert Buchanan.

Coleridge's Christabel, and other Imaginative Poems. With Preface by Algernon C. Swinburne.

Lord Chesterfield's Letters, Sentences, and Maxims. With Introduction by the Editor, and Essay on Chesterfield by M. de Ste.-Beuve, of the French Academy.

Essays in Mosaic. By Thos. Ballantyne.

My Uncle Toby; his Story and his Friends. Edited by P. Fitzgerald.

Reflections; or, Moral Sentences and Maxims of the Duke de la Rochefoucauld.

Socrates: Memoirs for English Readers from Xenophon's Memorabilia. By Edw. Levien.

Prince Albert's Golden Precepts.

A Case containing 12 Volumes, price 31s. 6d.; or the Case separately, price 3s. 6d.

Beaconsfield (Life of Lord). See "Hitchman."

Begum's Fortune (The): A New Story. By JULES VERNE. Translated by W. H. G. KINGSTON. Numerous Illustrations. Crown 8vo, cloth, gilt edges, 7*s.* 6*d.*; plainer binding, plain edges, 5*s.*

Ben Hur: A Tale of the Christ. By L. WALLACE. Crown
Svo, 6s.

Beumers' German Copybooks. In six gradations at 4d. each.

Bickersteth's Hymnal Companion to Book of Common Prayer
may be had in various styles and bindings from 1l. to 21s. *Price
List and Prospectus will be forwarded on application.*

Bickersteth (Rev. E. H., M.A.) The Clergyman in his Home.
Small post Svo, 1s.

—————— *The Master's Home-Call; or, Brief Memorials of Alice*
Frances Bickersteth. 20th Thousand. 32mo, cloth gilt, 1s.

————— *The Master's Will.* A Funeral Sermon preached
on the Death of Mrs. S. Gurney Buxton. Sewn, 6d.; cloth gilt, 1s.

————— *The Shadow of the Rock.* A Selection of Religious
Poetry. 18mo, cloth extra, 2s. 6d.

————— *The Shadowed Home and the Light Beyond.* 7th
Edition, crown Svo, cloth extra, 5s.

Biographies of the Great Artists (Illustrated). Crown Svo,
emblematical binding, 3s. 6d. per volume, except where the price is
given.

Claude Lorrain. *	Mantegna and Francia.
Correggio, by M. E. Heaton, 2s. 6d.	Meissonier, by J. W. Mollett, 2s. 6d.
Della Robbia and Cellini, 2s. 6d. *	Michelangelo Buonarotti, by Clément.
Albrecht Dürer, by R. F. Heath.	Murillo, by Ellen E. Minor, 2s. 6d.
Figure Painters of Holland.	Overbeck, by J. B. Atkinson.
Fra Angelico, Masaccio, and Botticelli.	Raphael, by N. D'Anvers.
Fra Bartolommeo, Albertinelli, and Andrea del Sarto.	Rembrandt, by J. W. Mollett.
Gainsborough and Constable.	Reynolds, by F. S. Pulling.
Ghiberti and Donatello, 2s. 6d.	Rubens, by C. W. Kett.
Giotto, by Harry Quilter.	Tintoretto, by W. R. Osler.
Hans Holbein, by Joseph Cundall.	Titian, by R. F. Heath.
Hogarth, by Austin Dobson.	Turner, by Cosmo Monkhouse.
Landseer, by F. G. Stevens.	Vandyck and Hals, by P. R. Head.
Lawrence and Romney, by Lord Ronald Gower, 2s. 6d.	Velasquez, by E. Stowe.
Leonardo da Vinci.	Vernet and Delaroche, by J. R. Rees.
Little Masters of Germany, by W. B. Scott.	Watteau, by J. W. Mollett, 2s. 6d. *
	Wilkie, by J. W. Mollett.

* *Not yet published.*

Bird (H. E.) Chess Practice. 8vo, 2s. 6d.

Birthday Book. Extracts from the Writings of R. W.
Emerson. Square 16mo, cloth extra, numerous Illustrations, very
choice binding, 3s. 6d.

————— *Extracts from the Poems of Whittier.* Square 16mo,
with numerous Illustrations and handsome binding, 3s. 6d.

Birthday Book. Extracts from the Writings of Thomas à Kempis. Large 16mo, red lines, 3*s.* 6*d.*

Black (Wm.) Three Feathers. Small post 8vo, cloth extra, 6*s.*

—— *Lady Silverdale's Sweetheart, and other Stories.* 1 vol., small post 8vo, 6*s.*

—— *Kilmeny: a Novel.* Small post 8vo, cloth, 6*s.*

—— *In Silk Attire.* 3rd Edition, small post 8vo, 6*s.*

—— *A Daughter of Heth.* 11th Edition, small post 8vo, 6*s.*

—— *Sunrise.* Small post 8vo, 6*s.*

Blackmore (R. D.) Lorna Doone. Small post 8vo, 6*s.*

—— *Edition de luxe.* Crown 4to, very numerous Illustrations, cloth, gilt edges, 31*s.* 6*d.*; parchment, uncut, top gilt, 35*s.*

—— *Alice Lorraine.* Small post 8vo, 6*s.*

—— *Clara Vaughan.* 6*s.*

—— *Cradock Nowell.* New Edition, 6*s.*

—— *Cripps the Carrier.* 3rd Edition, small post 8vo, 6*s.*

—— *Mary Anerley.* New Edition, small post 8vo, 6*s.*

—— *Erema; or, My Father's Sin.* Small post 8vo, 6*s.*

—— *Christowell.* Small post 8vo, 6*s.*

Blossoms from the King's Garden: Sermons for Children. By the Rev. C. BOSANQUET. 2nd Edition, small post 8vo, cloth extra, 6*s.*

Bock (Carl). The Head Hunters of Borneo: Up the Mahakkam, and Down the Barita; also Journeyings in Sumatra. 1 vol., super-royal 8vo, 32 Coloured Plates, cloth extra, 36*s.*

Bonwick (James) First Twenty Years of Australia. Crown 8vo, 5*s.*

—— *Port Philip Settlement.* 8vo, numerous Illustrations, 21*s.*

Book of the Play. By DUTTON COOK. New and Revised Edition. 1 vol., cloth extra, 3*s.* 6*d.*

Bower (G. S.) Law relating to Electric Lighting. Crown 8vo, 5*s.*

Boy's Froissart (The). Selected from the Chronicles of England, France, and Spain. Illustrated, square crown 8vo, 7*s.* 6*d.* See "Froissart."

Boy's King Arthur (The). With very fine Illustrations. Square crown 8vo, cloth extra, gilt edges, 7*s.* 6*d.* Edited by SIDNEY LANIER, Editor of "The Boy's Froissart."

Boy's Mabinogion (The): being the Original Welsh Legends of King Arthur. Edited by SIDNEY LANIER. With numerous very graphic Illustrations. Crown 8vo, cloth, gilt edges, 7*s.* 6*d.*

Brassey (Lady) Tahiti. With Photos. by Colonel Stuart-Wortley. Fcap. 4to, 21*s.*

Breton Folk: An Artistic Tour in Brittany. By HENRY BLACKBURN, Author of "Artists and Arabs," "Normandy Picturesque," &c. With 171 Illustrations by RANDOLPH CALDECOTT. Imperial 8vo, cloth extra, gilt edges, 21s.; plainer binding, 10s. 6d.

Bryant (W. C.) and Gay (S. H.) History of the United States. 4 vols., royal 8vo, profusely Illustrated, 60s.

Bryce (Prof.) Manitoba. Crown 8vo, 7s. 6d.

Burnaby (Capt.). See "On Horseback."

Burnham Beeches (Heath, F. G.). With numerous Illustrations and a Map. Crown 8vo, cloth, gilt edges, 3s. 6d. Second Edition.

Butler (W. F.) The Great Lone Land; an Account of the Red River Expedition, 1869-70. With Illustrations and Map. Fifth and Cheaper Edition, crown 8vo, cloth extra, 7s. 6d.

—————— *Invasion of England, told twenty years after, by an Old* Soldier. Crown 8vo, 2s. 6d.

—————— *The Wild North Land; the Story of a Winter Journey* with Dogs across Northern North America. Demy 8vo, cloth, with numerous Woodcuts and a Map, 4th Edition, 18s. Cr. 8vo, 7s. 6d.

—————— *Red Cloud; or, the Solitary Sioux.* Imperial 16mo, numerous illustrations, gilt edges, 7s. 6d.

Buxton (H. J. W.) Painting, English and American. Crown 8vo, 5s.

*C*ADOGAN *(Lady A.) Illustrated Games of Patience.* Twenty-four Diagrams in Colours, with Descriptive Text. Foolscap 4to, cloth extra, gilt edges, 3rd Edition, 12s. 6d.

California. Illustrated, 12s. 6d. See "Nordhoff."

Cambridge Trifles; or, Splutterings from an Undergraduate Pen. By the Author of "A Day of my Life at Eton," &c. 16mo, cloth extra, 2s. 6d.

Capello (H.) and Ivens (R.) From Benguella to the Territory of Yacca. Translated by ALFRED ELWES. With Maps and over 130 full-page and text Engravings. 2 vols., 8vo, 42s.

Carlyle (T.) Reminiscences of my Irish Journey in 1849. Crown 8vo, 7s. 6d.

Challamel (M. A.) History of Fashion in France. With 21 Plates, specially coloured by hand, satin-wood binding, imperial 8vo, 28s.

Changed Cross (The), and other Religious Poems. 16mo, 2s. 6d.

Child of the Cavern (The); or, Strange Doings Underground. By JULES VERNE. Translated by W. H. G. KINGSTON. Numerous Illustrations. Sq. cr. 8vo, gilt edges, 7s. 6d.; cl., plain edges, 3s. 6d.

Choice Editions of Choice Books. 2s. 6d. each. Illustrated by
C. W. COPE, R.A., T. CRESWICK, R.A., E. DUNCAN, BIRKET
FOSTER, J. C. HORSLEY, A.R.A., G. HICKS, R. REDGRAVE, R.A.,
C. STONEHOUSE, F. TAYLER, G. THOMAS, H. J. TOWNSHEND,
E. H. WEHNERT, HARRISON WEIR, &c.

Bloomfield's Farmer's Boy.	Milton's L'Allegro.
Campbell's Pleasures of Hope.	Poetry of Nature. Harrison Weir.
Coleridge's Ancient Mariner.	Rogers' (Sam.) Pleasures of Memory.
Goldsmith's Deserted Village.	Shakespeare's Songs and Sonnets.
Goldsmith's Vicar of Wakefield.	Tennyson's May Queen.
Gray's Elegy in a Churchyard.	Elizabethan Poets.
Keat's Eve of St. Agnes.	Wordsworth's Pastoral Poems.

" Such works are a glorious beatification for a poet."—*Athenæum.*

Christ in Song. By Dr. PHILIP SCHAFF. A New Edition,
revised, cloth, gilt edges, 6s.

Confessions of a Frivolous Girl (The): A Novel of Fashionable
Life. Edited by ROBERT GRANT. Crown 8vo, 6s. Paper boards, 1s.

Coote (W.) Wanderings South by East. Illustrated, 8vo, 21s.

Cornet of Horse (The) : A Story for Boys. By G. A. HENTY.
Crown 8vo, cloth extra, gilt edges, numerous graphic Illustrations, 5s.

Cripps the Carrier. 3rd Edition, 6s. *See* BLACKMORE.

Cruise of H.M.S. " Challenger" (The). By W. J. J. SPRY, R.N.
With Route Map and many Illustrations. 6th Edition, demy 8vo, cloth,
18s. Cheap Edition, crown 8vo, some of the Illustrations, 7s. 6d.

Cruise of the Walnut Shell (The). An instructive and amusing
Story, told in Rhyme, for Children. With 32 Coloured Plates.
Square fancy boards, 5s.

D'ANVERS (N.) An Elementary History of Art. Crown
8vo, 10s. 6d.

—— *Elementary History of Music.* Crown 8vo, 2s. 6d.

Daughter (A) of Heth. By W. BLACK. Crown 8vo, 6s.

Day of My Life (A) ; or, Every-Day Experiences at Eton.
By an ETON BOY, Author of " About Some Fellows." 16mo, cloth
extra, 2s. 6d. 6th Thousand.

Decoration. Vol. II., folio, 6s. Vol. III, New Series, folio,
7s. 6d.

De Leon (E.) Egypt under its Khedives. With Map and
Illustrations. Crown 8vo, 4s.

Dick Cheveley : his Fortunes and Misfortunes. By W. H. G.
KINGSTON. 350 pp., square 16mo, and 22 full-page Illustrations.
Cloth, gilt edges, 7s. 6d.; plainer binding, plain edges, 5s.

Dick Sands, the Boy Captain. By JULES VERNE. With nearly 100 Illustrations, cloth, gilt, 10s. 6d.; plain binding and plain edges, 5s.

Don Quixote, Wit and Wisdom of. By EMMA THOMPSON. Square fcap. 8vo, 3s. 6d.

Donnelly (F.) Atlantis in the Antediluvian World. Crown 8vo, 12s. 6d.

Dos Passos (J. R.) Law of Stockbrokers and Stock Exchanges. 8vo, 35s.

EGYPT. See "Senior," "De Leon," "Foreign Countries."

Eight Cousins. See ALCOTT.

Electric Lighting. A Comprehensive Treatise. By J. E. H. GORDON. 8vo, fully Illustrated. [*In preparation.*

Elementary History (An) of Art. Comprising Architecture, Sculpture, Painting, and the Applied Arts. By N. D'ANVERS. With a Preface by Professor ROGER SMITH. New Edition, illustrated with upwards of 200 Wood Engravings. Crown 8vo, strongly bound in cloth, price 10s. 6d.

Elementary History (An) of Music. Edited by OWEN J. DULLEA. Illustrated with Portraits of the most eminent Composers, and Engravings of the Musical Instruments of many Nations. Crown 8vo, cloth, 2s. 6d.

Elinor Dryden. By Mrs. MACQUOID. Crown 8vo, 6s.

Embroidery (Handbook of). Edited by LADY MARIAN ALFORD, and published by authority of the Royal School of Art Needlework. With 22 Coloured Plates, Designs, &c. Crown 8vo, 5s.

Emerson (R. W.) Life and Writings. Crown 8vo, 8s. 6d.

English Catalogue of Books. Vol. III., 1872—1880. Royal 8vo, half-morocco, 42s.

—— *Dramatists of To-day.* By W. ARCHER, M.A. Crown 8vo, 8s. 6d.

English Philosophers. Edited by E. B. IVAN MÜLLER, M.A.

A series intended to give a concise view of the works and lives of English thinkers. Crown 8vo volumes of 180 or 200 pp., price 3s. 6d. each.

Francis Bacon, by Thomas Fowler. | *John Stuart Mill, by Miss Helen Taylor.
Hamilton, by W. H. S. Monck. |
Hartley and James Mill, by G. S. Bower | Shaftesbury and Hutcheson, by Professor Fowler.
| Adam Smith, by J. A. Farrer.

* *Not yet published.*

Episodes in the Life of an Indian Chaplain. Crown 8vo, cloth extra, 12s. 6d.

Episodes of French History. Edited, with Notes, Maps, and Illustrations, by GUSTAVE MASSON, B.A. Small 8vo, 2*s.* 6*d.* each.
1. Charlemagne and the Carlovingians.
2. Louis XI. and the Crusades.
3. Part I. Francis I. and Charles V.
  ,, II. Francis I. and the Renaissance.
4. Henry IV. and the End of the Wars of Religion.

Erema; or, My Father's Sin. 6*s.* *See* BLACKMORE.

Etcher (The). Containing 36 Examples of the Original Etched-work of Celebrated Artists, amongst others: BIRKET FOSTER, J. E. HODGSON, R.A., COLIN HUNTER, J. P. HESELTINE, ROBERT W. MACBETH, R. S. CHATTOCK, &c. Vols. for 1881 and 1882, imperial 4to, cloth extra, gilt edges, 2*l.* 12*s.* 6*d.* each.

Eton. *See* "Day of my Life," "Out of School," "About Some Fellows."

*F*ARM *Ballads.* By WILL CARLETON. Boards, 1*s.*; cloth, gilt edges, 1*s.* 6*d.*

Farm Festivals. By the same Author. Uniform with above.

Farm Legends. By the same Author. See above.

Fashion (History of). See "Challamel."

Fechner (G. T.) On Life after Death. 12mo, vellum, 2*s.* 6*d.*

Felkin (R. W.) and Wilson (Rev. C. T.) Uganda and the Egyptian Soudan. An Account of Travel in Eastern and Equatorial Africa; including a Residence of Two Years at the Court of King Mtesa, and a Description of the Slave Districts of Bahr-el-Ghazel and Darfour. With a New Map of 1200 miles in these Provinces; numerous Illustrations, and Notes. By R. W. FELKIN, F.R.G.S., &c., &c.; and the Rev. C. T. WILSON, M.A. Oxon., F.R.G.S. 2 vols., crown 8vo, cloth, 28*s.*

Fern Paradise (The): A Plea for the Culture of Ferns. By F. G. HEATH. New Edition, fully Illustrated, large post 8vo, cloth, gilt edges, 12*s.* 6*d.* Sixth Edition.

Fern World (The). By F. G. HEATH. Illustrated by Twelve Coloured Plates, giving complete Figures (Sixty-four in all) of every Species of British Fern, printed from Nature; by several full-page and other Engravings. Cloth, gilt edges, 6th Edition, 12*s.* 6*d.*

Few Hints on Proving Wills (A). Enlarged Edition, 1*s.*

Fields (J. T.) Yesterdays with Authors. New Ed., 8vo, 16*s.*

First Steps in Conversational French Grammar. By F. JULIEN. Being an Introduction to "Petites Leçons de Conversation et de Grammaire," by the same Author. Fcap. 8vo, 128 pp., 1s.

Florence. See "Yriarte."

Flowers of Shakespeare. 32 beautifully Coloured Plates. 5s.

Four Lectures on Electric Induction. Delivered at the Royal Institution, 1878-9. By J. E. H. GORDON, B.A. Cantab. With numerous Illustrations. Cloth limp, square 16mo, 3s.

Foreign Countries and British Colonies. A series of Descriptive Handbooks. Each volume will be the work of a writer who has special acquaintance with the subject. Crown 8vo, 3s. 6d. each.

Australia, by J. F. Vesey Fitzgerald.	Peru, by Clements R. Markham, C.B.
Austria, by D. Kay, F.R.G.S.	
*Canada, by W. Fraser Rae.	Russia, by W. R. Morfill, M.A.
Denmark and Iceland, by E. C. Otté.	Spain, by Rev. Wentworth Webster.
Egypt, by S. Lane Poole, B.A.	Sweden and Norway, by F. H. Woods.
France, by Miss M. Roberts.	*Switzerland, by W. A. P. Coolidg M.A.
Greece, by L. Sergeant, B.A.	
*Holland, by R. L. Poole.	*Turkey-in-Asia, by J. C. McCoan, M.P.
Japan, by S. Mossman.	
*New Zealand.	West Indies, by C. H. Eden, F.R.G.S.
*Persia, by Major-Gen. Sir F. Goldsmid.	

* *Not ready yet.*

Franc (Maud Jeanne). The following form one Series, small post 8vo, in uniform cloth bindings, with gilt edges:—

Emily's Choice. 5s.	Vermont Vale. 5s.
Hall's Vineyard. 4s.	Minnie's Mission. 4s.
John's Wife: A Story of Life in South Australia. 4s.	Little Mercy. 5s.
	Beatrice Melton's Discipline. 4s.
Marian; or, The Light of Some One's Home. 5s.	No Longer a Child. 4s.
	Golden Gifts. 5s.
Silken Cords and Iron Fetters. 4s.	Two Sides to Every Question. 5s.

Francis (F.) War, Waves, and Wanderings, including a Cruise in the "Lancashire Witch." 2 vols., crown 8vo, cloth extra, 24s.

Froissart (The Boy's). Selected from the Chronicles of England, France, Spain, &c. By SIDNEY LANIER. The Volume is fully Illustrated, and uniform with "The Boy's King Arthur." Crown 8vo, cloth, 7s. 6d.

From Newfoundland to Manitoba; a Guide through Canada's Maritime, Mining, and Prairie Provinces. By W. FRASER RAE. Crown 8vo, with several Maps, 6s.

GAMES of Patience. See CADOGAN.

Gentle Life (Queen Edition).   2 vols. in 1, small 4to, 6s.

THE GENTLE LIFE SERIES.

Price 6s. each ; or in calf extra, price 10s. 6d. ; Smaller Edition, cloth extra, 2s. 6d.

The Gentle Life.   Essays in aid of the Formation of Character of Gentlemen and Gentlewomen.

About in the World.   Essays by Author of "The Gentle Life."

Like unto Christ.   A New Translation of Thomas à Kempis' "De Imitatione Christi."

Familiar Words.   An Index Verborum, or Quotation Handbook.   6s.

Essays by Montaigne.   Edited and Annotated by the Author of "The Gentle Life."

The Gentle Life.   2nd Series.

The Silent Hour: Essays, Original and Selected.   By the Author of "The Gentle Life."

Half-Length Portraits.   Short Studies of Notable Persons. By J. HAIN FRISWELL.

Essays on English Writers, for the Self-improvement of Students in English Literature.

Other People's Windows.   By J. HAIN FRISWELL.

A Man's Thoughts.   By J. HAIN FRISWELL.

Gilder (W. H.) Schwatka's Search.   Sledging in quest of the Franklin Records.   Illustrated, 8vo, 12s. 6d.

Gilpin's Forest Scenery.   Edited by F. G. HEATH.   Large post 8vo, with numerous Illustrations.   Uniform with "The Fern World," re-issued, 7s. 6d.

Gordon (J. E. H.).   See "Four Lectures on Electric Induction," "Physical Treatise on Electricity," "Electric Lighting."

Gouffé.   The Royal Cookery Book.   By JULES GOUFFÉ; translated and adapted for English use by ALPHONSE GOUFFÉ, Head Pastrycook to her Majesty the Queen.   Illustrated with large plates printed in colours.   161 Woodcuts, 8vo, cloth extra, gilt edges, 2l. 2s.

—— Domestic Edition, half-bound, 10s. 6d.

"By far the ablest and most complete work on cookery that has ever been submitted to the gastronomical world."—*Pall Mall Gazette.*

Great Artists.   See " Biographies."

Great Historic Galleries of England (The).   Edited by LORD
RONALD GOWER, F.S.A., Trustee of the National Portrait Gallery.
Illustrated by 24 large and carefully executed *permanent* Photographs
of some of the most celebrated Pictures by the Great Masters.   Vol. I.,
imperial 4to, cloth extra, gilt edges, 36s.   Vol. II., with 36 large
permanent photographs, 2l. 12s. 6d.

Great Musicians.   Edited by F. HUEFFER.   A Series of
Biographies, crown 8vo, 3s. each :—

Bach.	*Handel.	Schubert.
*Beethoven.	*Mendelssohn.	*Schumann.
*Berlioz.	*Mozart.	Richard Wagner.
English Church Com-	Purcell.	Weber.
posers.	Rossini.	

* *In preparation.*

Green (N.) A Thousand Years Hence.   Crown 8vo, 6s.

Grohmann (W. A. B.) Camps in the Rockies.   8vo, 12s. 6d.

Guizot's History of France.   Translated by ROBERT BLACK.
Super-royal 8vo, very numerous Full-page and other Illustrations.   In
8 vols., cloth extra, gilt, each 24s.   This work is re-issued in cheaper
binding, 8 vols., at 10s. 6d. each.
   " It supplies a want which has long been felt, and ought to be in the hands of all
students of history."—*Times.*

—————— ——————— ——— *Masson's School Edition.*   The
History of France from the Earliest Times to the Outbreak of the
Revolution ; abridged from the Translation by Robert Black, M.A.,
with Chronological Index, Historical and Genealogical Tables, &c.
By Professor GUSTAVE MASSON, B.A., Assistant Master at Harrow
School.   With 24 full-page Portraits, and many other Illustrations.
1 vol., demy 8vo, 600 pp., cloth extra, 10s. 6d.

Guizot's History of England.   In 3 vols. of about 500 pp. each,
containing 60 to 70 Full-page and other Illustrations, cloth extra, gilt,
24s. each ; re-issue in cheaper binding, 10s. 6d. each.
   " For luxury of typography, plainness of print, and beauty of illustration, these
volumes, of which but one has as yet appeared in English, will hold their own
against any production of an age so luxurious as our own in everything, typography
not excepted."—*Times.*

Guyon (Mde.) Life.   By UPHAM.   6th Edition, crown 8vo, 6s.

HANDBOOK to the Charities of London.   See Low's.

Hall (W. W.) How to Live Long ; or, 1408 Health Maxims,
Physical, Mental, and Moral.   By W. W. HALL, A.M., M.D.
Small post 8vo, cloth, 2s.   2nd Edition.

Harper's Monthly Magazine. Published Monthly. 160 pages, fully Illustrated. 1s.

  Vol. I. December, 1880, to May, 1881.
   ,, II. May, 1881, to November, 1881.
   ,, III. June to November, 1882.
Super-royal 8vo, 8s. 6d. each.

 "'Harper's Magazine' is so thickly sown with excellent illustrations that to count them would be a work of time ; not that it is a picture magazine, for the engravings illustrate the text after the manner seen in some of our choicest *éditions de luxe.*"--*St. James's Gazette.*

 "It is so pretty, so big, and so cheap. . . . An extraordinary shillingsworth—160 large octavo pages, with over a score of articles, and more than three times as many illustrations." - *Edinburgh Daily Review.*

 "An amazing shillingsworth . . . combining choice literature of both nations."—*Nonconformist.*

*Hatton (Joseph) Journalistic London : Portraits and En-*gravings, with letterpress, of Distinguished Writers of the Day. Fcap. 4to, 12s. 6d.

——— *Three Recruits, and the Girls they left behind them.* Small post, 8vo, 6s.

 " It hurries us along in unflagging excitement."--*Times.*

Heart of Africa. Three Years' Travels and Adventures in the Unexplored Regions of Central Africa, from 1868 to 1871. By Dr. GEORG SCHWEINFURTH. Numerous Illustrations, and large Map. 2 vols., crown 8vo, cloth, 15s.

Heath (Francis George). See "Autumnal Leaves," "Burnham Beeches," "Fern Paradise," "Fern World," "Gilpin's Forest Scenery," "Our Woodland Trees," "Peasant Life," "Sylvan Spring," "Trees and Ferns," "Where to Find Ferns."

Heber's (Bishop) Illustrated Edition of Hymns. With upwards of 100 beautiful Engravings. Small 4to, handsomely bound, 7s. 6d. Morocco, 18s. 6d. and 21s. New and Cheaper Edition, cloth, 3s. 6d.

Heir of Kilfinnan (The). By W. H. G. KINGSTON. With Illustrations. Cloth, gilt edges, 7s. 6d. ; plainer binding, plain edges, 5s.

Heldmann (Bernard) Mutiny on Board the Ship " Leander." Small post 8vo, gilt edges, numerous Illustrations, 7s. 6d.

Henty (G. A.) Winning his Spurs. Numerous Illustrations. Crown 8vo, 5s.

——— *Cornet of Horse ;* which see.

Herrick (Robert) Poetry. Preface by AUSTIN DOBSON. With numerous Illustrations, by E. A. ABBEY. 4to, gilt edges, 42s.

History of a Crime (The) ; Deposition of an Eye-witness. The Story of the Coup d'État. By VICTOR HUGO. Crown 8vo, 6s.

History of Ancient Art. Translated from the German of JOHN WINCKELMANN, by JOHN LODGE, M.D. With very numerous Plates and Illustrations. 2 vols., 8vo, 36s.

—————— *England.* *See* GUIZOT.

—————— *English Literature.* *See* SCHERR.

—————— *Fashion.* Coloured Plates. 28s. *See* CHALLAMEL.

—————— *France.* *See* GUIZOT.

—————— *Russia.* *See* RAMBAUD.

——————— *Merchant Shipping.* *See* LINDSAY.

—————— *United States.* *See* BRYANT.

History and Principles of Weaving by Hand and by Power. With several hundred Illustrations. By ALFRED BARLOW. Royal 8vo, cloth extra, 1*l.* 5*s.* Second Edition.

Hitchman (Francis) Public Life of the Right Hon. Benjamin Disraeli, Earl of Beaconsfield. New Edition, with Portrait. Crown 8vo, 3*s.* 6*d.*

Holmes (O. W.) The Poetical Works of Oliver Wendell Holmes. In 2 vols., 18mo, exquisitely printed, and chastely bound in limp cloth, gilt tops, 10*s.* 6*d.*

Hoppus (J. D.) Riverside Papers. 2 vols., 12*s.*

Hovgaard (A.) See "Nordenskiöld's Voyage." 8vo, 21*s.*

How I Crossed Africa : from the Atlantic to the Indian Ocean, Through Unknown Countries ; Discovery of the Great Zambesi Affluents, &c.—Vol. I., The King's Rifle. Vol. II., The Coillard Family. By Major SERPA PINTO. With 24 full-page and 118 half-page and smaller Illustrations, 13 small Maps, and 1 large one. 2 vols., demy 8vo, cloth extra, 42*s.*

How to get Strong and how to Stay so. By WILLIAM BLAIKIE. A Manual of Rational, Physical, Gymnastic, and other Exercises. With Illustrations, small post 8vo, 5*s.*

Hugo (Victor) "Ninety-Three." Illustrated. Crown 8vo, 6*s.*

—————— *Toilers of the Sea.* Crown 8vo. Illustrated, 6*s.* ; fancy boards, 2*s.* ; cloth, 2*s.* 6*d.* ; on large paper with all the original Illustrations, 10*s.* 6*d.*

—————— *and his Times.* Translated from the French of A. BARBOU by ELLEN E. FREWER. 120 Illustrations, many of them from designs by Victor Hugo himself. Super-royal 8vo, cloth extra, 24*s.*

—————— *See* "History of a Crime."

Hundred Greatest Men (The). 8 portfolios, 21*s.* each, or 4 vols., half-morocco, gilt edges, 12 guineas, containing 15 to 20 Portraits each. See below.

> "Messrs. SAMPSON LOW & Co. are about to issue an important 'International' work, entitled, 'THE HUNDRED GREATEST MEN;' being the Lives and Portraits of the 100 Greatest Men of History, divided into Eight Classes, each Class to form a Monthly Quarto Volume. The Introductions to the volumes are to be written by recognized authorities on the different subjects, the English contributors being DEAN STANLEY, Mr. MATTHEW ARNOLD, Mr. FROUDE, and Professor MAX MÜLLER: in Germany, Professor HELMHOLTZ; in France, MM. TAINE and RENAN; and in America, Mr. EMERSON. The Portraits are to be Reproductions from fine and rare Steel Engravings."—*Academy.*

Hygiene and Public Health (A Treatise on). Edited by A. H. BUCK, M.D. Illustrated by numerous Wood Engravings. In 2 royal 8vo vols., cloth, One guinea each.

Hymnal Companion to Book of Common Prayer. See BICKERSTETH.

ILLUSTRATED Text-Books of Art-Education. Edited by EDWARD J. POYNTER, R.A. Each Volume contains numerous Illustrations, and is strongly bound for the use of Students, price 5*s.* The Volumes now ready are:—

PAINTING.

Classic and Italian. By PERCY R. HEAD.
German, Flemish, and Dutch.
French and Spanish.
English and American.

ARCHITECTURE.

Classic and Early Christian.
Gothic and Renaissance. By T. ROGER SMITH.

SCULPTURE.

Antique: Egyptian and Greek. | **Renaissance and Modern.**
Italian Sculptors of the 14th and 15th Centuries.

ORNAMENT.

Decoration in Colour. | **Architectural Ornament.**

Illustrated Dictionary (An) of Words used in Art and Archæology. Explaining Terms frequently used in Works on Architecture, Arms, Bronzes, Christian Art, Colour, Costume, Decoration, Devices, Emblems, Heraldry, Lace, Personal Ornaments, Pottery, Painting, Sculpture, &c., with their Derivations. By J. W. MOLLETT, B.A., Officier de l'Instruction Publique (France); Author of "Life of Rembrandt," &c. Illustrated with 600 Wood Engravings. Small 4to, strongly bound in cloth, 15*s.*

In my Indian Garden. By PHIL ROBINSON, Author of "Under the Punkah." With a Preface by EDWIN ARNOLD, M.A., C.S.I., &c. Crown 8vo, limp cloth, 4th Edition, 3*s.* 6*d.*

Irving (Washington). Complete Library Edition of his Works in 27 Vols., Copyright, Unabridged, and with the Author's Latest Revisions, called the "Geoffrey Crayon" Edition, handsomely printed in large square 8vo, on superfine laid paper, and each volume, of about 500 pages, will be fully Illustrated. 12s. 6d. per vol. *See also* "Little Britain."

———————————— ("American Men of Letters.") 2s. 6d.

JAMES (C.) Curiosities of Law and Lawyers. 8vo, 7s. 6d.

Johnson (O.) William Lloyd Garrison and his Times. Crown 8vo, 12s. 6d.

Jones (Major) The Emigrants' Friend. A Complete Guide to the United States. New Edition. 2s. 6d.

KEMPIS (Thomas à) Daily Text-Book. Square 16mo, 2s. 6d.; interleaved as a Birthday Book, 3s. 6d.

Kingston (W. H. G.). See "Snow-Shoes," "Child of the Cavern," "Two Supercargoes," "With Axe and Rifle," "Begum's Fortune," "Heir of Kilfinnan," "Dick Cheveley." Each vol., with very numerous Illustrations, square crown 16mo, gilt edges, 7s. 6d.; plainer binding, plain edges, 5s.

LADY Silverdale's Sweetheart. 6s. *See* BLACK.

Lanier. See "Boy's Froissart," "King Arthur," &c.

Lansdell (H.) Through Siberia. 2 vols., demy 8vo, 30s; New Edition, very numerous illustrations, 8vo, 15s.

Larden (W.) School Course on Heat. Illustrated, crown 8vo, 5s.

Lathrop (G. P.) In the Distance. 2 vols., crown 8vo, 21s.

Lectures on Architecture. By E. VIOLLET-LE-DUC. Translated by BENJAMIN BUCKNALL, Architect. With 33 Steel Plates and 200 Wood Engravings. Super-royal 8vo, leather back, gilt top, with complete Index, 2 vols., 3l. 3s.

Leyland (R. W.) A Holiday in South Africa. Crown 8vo 12s. 6d.

Library of Religious Poetry. A Collection of the Best Poems of all Ages and Tongues. Edited by PHILIP SCHAFF, D.D., LL.D., and ARTHUR GILMAN, M.A. Royal 8vo, 1036 pp., cloth extra, g'lt edges, 21*s.*; re-issue in cheaper binding, 10*s.* 6*d.*

Lindsay (W. S.) History of Merchant Shipping and Ancient Commerce. Over 150 Illustrations, Maps, and Charts. In 4 vols., demy 8vo, cloth extra. Vols. 1 and 2, 11*s.*; vols. 3 and 4, 14*s.* each. 4 vols. complete for 50*s.*

Little Britain; together with *The Spectre Bridegroom,* and *A* Legend of Sleepy Hollow. By WASHINGTON IRVING. An entirely New *Edition de luxe,* specially suitable for Presentation. Illustrated by 120 very fine Engravings on Wood, by Mr. J. D. COOPER. Designed by Mr. CHARLES O. MURRAY. Re-issue, square crown 8vo, cloth, 6*s.*

Long (Mrs. W. H. C.) Peace and War in the Transvaal. 12mo, 3*s.* 6*d.*

Lorna Doone. 6*s.*, 31*s.* 6*d.*, 35*s.* See " Blackmore."

Low's Select Novelets. Small post 8vo, cloth extra, 3*s.* 6*d.* each.

> **Friends: a Duet.** By E. S. PHELPS, Author of "The Gates Ajar."
>
> **Baby Rue: Her Adventures and Misadventures, her Friends** and her Enemies. By CHARLES M. CLAY.
>
> **The Story of Helen Troy.**
> " A pleasant book."—*Truth.*
>
> **The Clients of Dr. Bernagius.** From the French of LUCIEN BIART, by Mrs. CASHEL HOEY.
>
> **The Undiscovered Country.** By W. D. HOWELLS.
>
> **A Gentleman of Leisure.** By EDGAR FAWCETT.

Low's Standard Library of Travel and Adventure. Crown 8vo, bound uniformly in cloth extra, price 7*s.* 6*d.*, except where price is given.

> 1. **The Great Lone Land.** By Major W. F. BUTLER, C.B.
> 2. **The Wild North Land.** By Major W. F. BUTLER, C.B.
> 3. **How I found Livingstone.** By H. M. STANLEY.
> 4. **Through the Dark Continent.** By H. M. STANLEY. 12*s.* 6*d.*
> 5. **The Threshold of the Unknown Region.** By C. R. MARKHAM. (4th Edition, with Additional Chapters, 10*s.* 6*d.*)
> 6. **Cruise of the Challenger.** By W. J. J. SPRY, R.N.
> 7. **Burnaby's On Horseback through Asia Minor.** 10*s.* 6*d.*
> 8. **Schweinfurth's Heart of Africa.** 2 vols., 15*s.*
> 9. **Marshall's Through America.**

Low's Standard Novels.   Crown 8vo, 6s. each, cloth extra.

Work.   A Story of Experience.   By LOUISA M. ALCOTT.
A Daughter of Heth.   By W. BLACK.
In Silk Attire.   By W. BLACK.
Kilmeny.   A Novel.   By W. BLACK.
Lady Silverdale's Sweetheart.   By W. BLACK.
Sunrise.   By W. BLACK.
Three Feathers.   By WILLIAM BLACK.
Alice Lorraine.   By R. D. BLACKMORE.
Christowell, a Dartmoor Tale.   By R. D. BLACKMORE.
Clara Vaughan.   By R. D. BLACKMORE.
Cradock Nowell.   By R. D. BLACKMORE.
Cripps the Carrier.   By R. D. BLACKMORE.
Erema; or, My Father's Sin.   By R. D. BLACKMORE.
Lorna Doone.   By R. D. BLACKMORE.
Mary Anerley.   By R. D. BLACKMORE.
An English Squire.   By Miss COLERIDGE.
Mistress Judith.   A Cambridgeshire Story.   By C. C. FRASER-
    TYTLER.
A Story of the Dragonnades; or, Asylum Christi.   By the Rev.
    E. GILLIAT, M.A.
A Laodicean.   By THOMAS HARDY.
Far from the Madding Crowd.   By THOMAS HARDY.
The Hand of Ethelberta.   By THOMAS HARDY.
The Trumpet Major.   By THOMAS HARDY.
Three Recruits.   By JOSEPH HATTON.
A Golden Sorrow.   By Mrs. CASHEL HOEY.   New Edition.
Out of Court.   By Mrs. CASHEL HOEY.
History of a Crime: The Story of the Coup d'État.   VICTOR HUGO
Ninety-Three.   By VICTOR HUGO.   Illustrated.
Adela Cathcart.   By GEORGE MAC DONALD.
Guild Court.   By GEORGE MAC DONALD.
Mary Marston.   By GEORGE MAC DONALD.
Stephen Archer.   New Edition of "Gifts."   By GEORGE MAC
    DONALD.
The Vicar's Daughter.   By GEORGE MAC DONALD.
Weighed and Wanting.   By GEORGE MAC DONALD.
                                                    [*In the Press.*

Diane.   By Mrs. MACQUOID.
Elinor Dryden.   By Mrs. MACQUOID.
My Lady Greensleeves.   By HELEN MATHERS.

Low's Standard Novels (continued) :—

> **John Holdsworth.** By W. CLARK RUSSELL.
> **A Sailor's Sweetheart.** By W. CLARK RUSSELL.
> **Wreck of the Grosvenor.** By W. CLARK RUSSELL.
> **The Afghan Knife.** By R. A. STERNDALE.
> **My Wife and I.** By Mrs. BEECHER STOWE.
> **Poganuc People, Their Loves and Lives.** By Mrs. B. STOWE.
> **Ben Hur: a Tale of the Christ.** By LEW. WALLACE.

Low's Handbook to the Charities of London (Annual). Edited and revised to date by C. MACKESON, F.S.S., Editor of "A Guide to the Churches of London and its Suburbs," &c. Paper, 1s. ; cloth, 1s. 6d.

MAC DONALD (G.) *Orts.* Small post 8vo, 6s.

—— See also " Low's Standard Novels."

Macgregor (John) "Rob Roy" on the Baltic. 3rd Edition, small post 8vo, 2s. 6d. ; cloth, gilt edges, 3s. 6d.

—— *A Thousand Miles in the "Rob Roy" Canoe.* 11th Edition, small post 8vo, 2s. 6d. ; cloth, gilt edges, 3s. 6d.

—— *Description of the " Rob Roy" Canoe,* with Plans, &c., 1s.

—— *The Voyage Alone in the Yawl " Rob Roy."* New Edition, thoroughly revised, with additions, small post 8vo, 5s. ; boards, 2s. 6d.

Macquoid (Mrs.). See Low's STANDARD NOVELS.

Magazine. See HARPER, UNION JACK, THE ETCHER, MEN OF MARK.

Magyarland. A Narrative of Travels through the Snowy Carpathians, and Great Alföld of the Magyar. By a Fellow of the Carpathian Society (Diploma of 1881), and Author of " The Indian Alps." 2 vols., 8vo, cloth extra, with about 120 Woodcuts from the Author's own sketches and drawings, 38s.

Manitoba : its History, Growth, and Present Position. By the Rev. Professor BRYCE, Principal of Manitoba College, Winnipeg. Crown 8vo, with Illustrations and Maps, 7s. 6d.

Markham (C. R.) The Threshold of the Unknown Region. Crown 8vo, with Four Maps, 4th Edition. Cloth extra, 10s. 6d.

Markham (C. R.) War between Peru and Chili, 1879-1881. Crown 8vo, with four Maps, &c. [*In preparation.*

Marshall (W. G.) Through America. New Edition, crown 8vo, with about 100 Illustrations, 7s. 6d.

Martin (J. W.) Float Fishing and Spinning in the Nottingham Style. Crown 8vo, 2s. 6d.

Marvin (Charles) The Russian Advance towards India. 8vo, 16s.

Maury (Commander) Physical Geography of the Sea, and its Meteorology. Being a Reconstruction and Enlargement of his former Work, with Charts and Diagrams. New Edition, crown 8vo, 6s.

Memoirs of Madame de Rémusat, 1802—1808. By her Grandson, M. PAUL DE RÉMUSAT, Senator. Translated by Mrs. CASHEL HOEY and Mr. JOHN LILLIE. 4th Edition, cloth extra. This work was written by Madame de Rémusat during the time she was living on the most intimate terms with the Empress Josephine, and is full of revelations respecting the private life of Bonaparte, and of men and politics of the first years of the century. Revelations which have already created a great sensation in Paris. 8vo, 2 vols., 32s.

—— *See also* "Selection."

Ménus (366, one for each day of the year). Each Ménu is given in French and English, with the recipe for making every dish mentioned. Translated from the French of COUNT BRISSE, by Mrs. MATTHEW CLARKE. Crown 8vo, 5s.

Men of Mark: a Gallery of Contemporary Portraits of the most Eminent Men of the Day taken from Life, especially for this publication, price 1s. 6d. monthly. Vols. I. to VII., handsomely bound, cloth, gilt edges, 25s. each.

Mendelssohn Family (The), 1729—1847. From Letters and Journals. Translated from the German of SEBASTIAN HENSEL. 3rd Edition, 2 vols., demy 8vo, 30s.

Michael Strogoff. See VERNE.

Mitford (Miss). See "Our Village."

Modern Etchings of Celebrated Paintings. 4to, 31s. 6d.

Mollett (J. W.) Illustrated Dictionary of Words used in Art and Archæology. Small 4to, 15s.

Morley (H.) English Literature in the Reign of Victoria. The 2000th volume of the Tauchnitz Collection of Authors. 18mo, 2s. 6d.

Music. See "Great Musicians."

NARRATIVES of State Trials in the Nineteenth Century. First Period: From the Union with Ireland to the Death of George IV., 1801—1830. By G. LATHOM BROWNE, of the Middle Temple, Barrister-at-Law. 2nd Edition, 2 vols., crown 8vo, cloth, 26s.

Nature and Functions of Art (The); and more especially of Architecture. By LEOPOLD EIDLITZ. Medium 8vo, cloth, 21s.

Naval Brigade in South Africa (The). By HENRY F. NORBURY, C.B., R.N. Crown 8vo, cloth extra, 10s. 6d.

New Child's Play (A). Sixteen Drawings by E. V. B. Beautifully printed in colours, 4to, cloth extra, 12s. 6d.

Newfoundland. By FRASER RAE. See "From Newfoundland."

New Novels. Crown 8vo, cloth, 10s. 6d. per vol. :—
 The Granvilles. By the Hon. E. TALBOT. 3 vols.
 One of Us. By E. RANDOLPH.
 Weighed and Wanting. By GEORGE MAC DONALD. 3 vols.
 Castle Warlock. By GEORGE MAC DONALD. 3 vols.
 Under the Downs. By E. GILLIAT. 3 vols.
 A Stranger in a Strange Land. By LADY CLAY. 3 vols.
 The Heart of Erin. By Miss OWENS BLACKBURN. 3 vols.
 A Chelsea Householder. 3 vols.
 Two on a Tower. By THOMAS HARDY. 3 vols.
 The Lady Maud. By W. CLARK RUSSELL. 3 vols.

Nice and Her Neighbours. By the Rev. CANON HOLE, Author of "A Book about Roses," "A Little Tour in Ireland," &c. Small 4to, with numerous choice Illustrations, 12s. 6d.

Noah's Ark. A Contribution to the Study of Unnatural History. By PHIL ROBINSON. Small post 8vo, 12s. 6d.

Noble Words and Noble Deeds. From the French of E. MULLER. Containing many Full-page Illustrations by PHILIPPOTEAUX. Square imperial 16mo, cloth extra, 7s. 6d. ; plainer binding, plain edges, 5s.

Nordenskiöld's Voyage around Asia and Europe. A Popular Account of the North-East Passage of the "Vega." By Lieut. A. HOVGAARD, of the Royal Danish Navy, and member of the "Vega" Expedition. 8vo, with about 50 Illustrations and 3 Maps, 21s.

Nordhoff (C.) California, for Health, Pleasure, and Residence. New Edition, 8vo, with Maps and Illustrations, 12s. 6d.

Nothing to Wear; and Two Millions. By W. A. BUTLER. New Edition. Small post 8vo, in stiff coloured wrapper, 1s.

Nursery Playmates (Prince of). 217 Coloured Pictures for Children by eminent Artists. Folio, in coloured boards, 6s.

OFF to the Wilds: A Story for Boys.   By G. MANVILLE
FENN.   Profusely Illustrated.   Crown 8vo, 7s. 6d.

Old-Fashioned Girl.   See ALCOTT.

On Horseback through Asia Minor.   By Capt. FRED BURNABY.
2 vols., 8vo, 38s.   Cheaper Edition, crown 8vo, 10s. 6d.

Our Little Ones in Heaven.   Edited by the Rev. H. ROBBINS.
With Frontispiece after Sir JOSHUA REYNOLDS.   Fcap., cloth extra,
New Edition—the 3rd, with Illustrations, 5s.

Our Village.   By MARY RUSSELL MITFORD.   Illustrated with
Frontispiece Steel Engraving, and 12 full-page and 157 smaller Cuts.
Crown 4to, cloth, gilt edges, 21s.; cheaper binding, 10s. 6d.

Our Woodland Trees.   By F. G. HEATH.   Large post 8vo,
cloth, gilt edges, uniform with " Fern World " and " Fern Paradise,"
by the same Author.   8 Coloured Plates (showing leaves of every
British Tree) and 20 Woodcuts, cloth, gilt edges, 12s. 6d.   New
Edition.   About 600 pages.

Outlines of Ornament in all Styles.   A Work of Reference for
the Architect, Art Manufacturer, Decorative Artist, and Practical
Painter.   By W. and G. A. AUDSLEY, Fellows of the Royal Institute
of British Architects.   Only a limited number have been printed and
the stones destroyed.   Small folio, 60 plates, with introductory text,
cloth gilt, 31s. 6d.

PALLISER (Mrs.) A History of Lace, from the Earliest
Period.   A New and Revised Edition, with additional cuts and text,
upwards of 100 Illustrations and coloured Designs.   1 vol., 8vo, 1l. 1s.

———— *Historic Devices, Badges, and War Cries.*   8vo, 1l. 1s.

———— *The China Collector's Pocket Companion.*   With upwards of 1000 Illustrations of Marks and Monograms.   2nd Edition,
with Additions.   Small post 8vo, limp cloth, 5s.

Pathways of Palestine: a Descriptive Tour through the Holy
Land.   By the Rev. CANON TRISTRAM.   Illustrated with 44 permanent Photographs.   (The Photographs are large, and most perfect
Specimens of the Art.)   Vols. I. and II., folio, gilt edges, 31s. 6d.
each.

Peasant Life in the West of England.   By FRANCIS GEORGE
HEATH, Author of " Sylvan Spring," " The Fern World."   Crown
8vo, 400 pp. (with Facsimile of Autograph Letter from Lord
Beaconsfield to the Author, written December 28, 1880), 10s. 6d.

Petites Leçons de Conversation et de Grammaire: Oral and
Conversational Method ; the most Useful Topics of Conversation.
By F. JULIEN.   Cloth, 3s. 6d.

Photography (History and Handbook of). See TISSANDIER.

Physical Treatise on Electricity and Magnetism. By J. E. H.
GORDON, B.A. With about 200 coloured, full-page, and other
Illustrations. 2 vols., 8vo. New Edition. [*In preparation.*

Poems of the Inner Life. Chiefly from Modern Authors.
Small 8vo, 5*s.*

Pogannc People: their Loves and Lives. By Mrs. BEECHER
STOWE. Crown 8vo, cloth, 6*s.*

Polar Expeditions. See KOLDEWEY, MARKHAM, MACGAHAN,
NARES, and NORDENSKIÖLD.

Poynter (Edward J., R.A.). See "Illustrated Text-books."

Prudence : a Story of Æsthetic London. By LUCY E. LILLIE.
Small 8vo, 5*s.*

Publishers' Circular (The), and General Record of British and
Foreign Literature. Published on the 1st and 15th of every Month, 3*d.*

Pyrenees (The). By HENRY BLACKBURN. With 100 Illustrations by GUSTAVE DORÉ, corrected to 1881. Crown 8vo, 7*s. 6d.*

R*AE (F.) Newfoundland.* See "From."

Redford (G.) Ancient Sculpture. Crown 8vo, 5*s.*

Reid (T. W.) Land of the Bey. Post 8vo, 10*s. 6d.*

Rémusat (Madame de). See "Memoirs of," "Selection."

Richter (Jean Paul). The Literary Works of Leonardo da
Vinci. Containing his Writings on Painting, Sculpture, and Archi-
tecture, his Philosophical Maxims, Humorous Writings, and Miscel-
laneous Notes on Personal Events, on his Contemporaries, on Litera-
ture, &c. ; for the first time published from Autograph Manuscripts.
By J. P. RICHTER, Ph.Dr., Hon. Member of the Royal and Imperial
Academy of Rome, &c. 2 vols., imperial 8vo, containing about 200
Drawings in Autotype Reproductions, and numerous other Illustrations.
Price Eight Guineas to Subscribers. After publication the price will
be Twelve Guineas.

—— *Italian Art in the National Gallery.* 4to.
[*Nearly ready.*

Robinson (Phil). See "In my Indian Garden," "Under the
Punkah," "Noah's Ark," "Sinners and Saints."

Rose (F.) Complete Practical Machinist. New Edition, 12mo,
12*s. 6d.*

Rose Library (The). Popular Literature of all Countries. Each volume, 1*s.*; cloth, 2*s.* 6*d.*   Many of the Volumes are Illustrated —

1. **Little Women.** By LOUISA M. ALCOTT.
2. **Little Women Wedded.** Forming a Sequel to "Little Women."
3. **Little Men.** By L. M. ALCOTT. Dble. vol., 2*s.*; cloth gilt, 3*s.* 6*d.*
4. **An Old-Fashioned Girl.** By LOUISA M. ALCOTT. Double vol., 2*s.*; cloth, 3*s.* 6*d.*
5. **Work.** A Story of Experience. By L. M. ALCOTT.
6. **Beginning Again.** Sequel to "Work." By L. M. ALCOTT.
7. **Stowe (Mrs. H. B.) The Pearl of Orr's Island.**
8. ——— **The Minister's Wooing.**
9. ——— **We and our Neighbours.** Double vol., 2*s.*; cloth, 3*s.* 6*d.*
10. ——— **My Wife and I.** Double vol., 2*s.*; cloth, gilt 3*s.* 6*d.* ·
11. **Hans Brinker; or, the Silver Skates.** By Mrs. DODGE.
12. **My Study Windows.** By J. R. LOWELL.
13. **The Guardian Angel.** By OLIVER WENDELL HOLMES.
14. **My Summer in a Garden.** By C. D. WARNER.
15. **Dred.** Mrs. BEECHER STOWE. Dble. vol., 2*s.*; cloth gilt, 3*s.* 6*d.*
16. **Farm Ballads.** By WILL CARLETON.
17. **Farm Festivals.** By WILL CARLETON.
18. **Farm Legends.** By WILL CARLETON.
19, 20. **The Clients of Dr. Bernagius.** 2 parts, 1*s.* each.
21. **The Undiscovered Country.** By W. D. HOWELLS.
22. **Baby Rue.** By C. M. CLAY.

Round the Yule Log: Norwegian Folk and Fairy Tales. Translated from the Norwegian of P. CHR. ASBJÖRNSEN. With 100 Illustrations after drawings by Norwegian Artists, and an Introduction by E. W. Gosse. Imperial 16mo, cloth extra, gilt edges, 7*s.* 6*d.*

Rousselet (Louis) Son of the Constable of France. Small post 8vo, numerous Illustrations, 5*s.*

——— *The Drummer Boy: a Story of the Days of Washington*. Small post 8vo, numerous Illustrations, 5*s.*

Russell (W. Clark) The Lady Maud. 3 vols., crown 8vo, 31*s.* 6*d.*

——— *See also* LOW'S STANDARD NOVELS *and* WRECK.

Russell (W. H., LL.D.) Hesperothen: Notes from the Western World. A Record of a Ramble through part of the United States, Canada, and the Far West, in the Spring and Summer of 1881. By W. H. RUSSELL, LL.D. 2 vols., crown 8vo, cloth, 24*s.*

——— *The Tour of the Prince of Wales in India*. By W. H. RUSSELL, LL.D. Fully Illustrated by SYDNEY P. HALL, M.A. Super-royal 8vo, cloth extra, gilt edges, 52*s.* 6*d.*; Large Paper Edition, 84*s.*

Russian Literature. See "Turner."

SAINTS and their Symbols: A Companion in the Churches and Picture Galleries of Europe. With Illustrations. Royal 16mo, cloth extra, 3*s.* 6*d.*

Scherr (Prof. F.) History of English Literature. Translated from the German. Crown 8vo, 8*s.* 6*d.*

Schuyler (Eugène). The Life of Peter the Great. By EUGÈNE SCHUYLER, Author of "Turkestan." 2 vols., demy 8vo.
[*In preparation.*

Scott (Leader) Renaissance of Art in Italy. 4to, 31*s.* 6*d.*

Selection from the Letters of Madame de Rémusat to her Husband and Son, from 1804 to 1813. From the French, by Mrs. CASHEL HOEY and Mr. JOHN LILLIE. In 1 vol., demy 8vo (uniform with the "Memoirs of Madame de Rémusat," 2 vols.), cloth extra, 16*s.*

Senior (Nassau W.) Conversations and Journals in Egypt and Malta. 2 vols., 8vo, 24*s.*
These volumes contain conversations with SAID PASHA, ACHIM BEY, HEKEKYAN BEY, the Patriarch, M. DE LESSEPS, M. ST. HILAIRE, Sir FREDERICK BRUCE, Sir ADRIAN DINGLI, and many other remarkable people.

Seonee: Sporting in the Satpura Range of Central India, and in the Valley of the Nerbudda. By R. A. STERNDALE, F.R.G.S. 8vo, with numerous Illustrations, 21*s.*

Shadbolt (S.) The Afghan Campaigns of 1878—1880. By SYDNEY SHADBOLT, Joint Author of "The South African Campaign of 1879." 2 vols., royal quarto, cloth extra, 3*l.* 3*s.*

Shooting: its Appliances, Practice, and Purpose. By JAMES DALZIEL DOUGALL, F.S.A., F.Z.A., Author of "Scottish Field Sports," &c. New Edition, revised with additions. Crown 8vo, cloth extra, 7*s.* 6*d.*
"The book is admirable in every way. . . . . We wish it every success "—*Globe.*
"A very complete treatise. . . . . Likely to take high rank as an authority on shooting."—*Daily News.*

Sikes (Wirt). Rambles and Studies in Old South Wales. With numerous Illustrations. Demy 8vo, 18*s.*

Silent Hour (The). See "Gentle Life Series."

Silver Sockets (The); and other Shadows of Redemption. Eighteen Sermons preached in Christ Church, Hampstead, by the Rev. C. H. WALLER. Small post 8vo, cloth, 6*s.*

Sinners and Saints: a Tour across the United States of America, and Round them. By PHIL ROBINSON. [*In the Press.*

Sir Roger de Coverley. Re-imprinted from the "Spectator." With 125 Woodcuts, and steel Frontispiece specially designed and engraved for the Work. Small fcap. 4to, 6*s.*

Smith (G.) Assyrian Explorations and Discoveries. By the late
GEORGE SMITH. Illustrated by Photographs and Woodcuts. Demy
8vo, 6th Edition, 18s.

—————— *The Chaldean Account of Genesis.* By the late G.
SMITH, of the Department of Oriental Antiquities, British Museum.
With many Illustrations. Demy 8vo, cloth extra, 6th Edition, 16s
An entirely New Edition, completely revised and re-written by the
Rev. PROFESSOR SAYCE, Queen's College, Oxford. Demy 8vo, 18s.

Smith (J. Moyr). See "Ancient Greek Female Costume."

Snow-Shoes and Canoes; or, the Adventures of a Fur-Hunter
in the Hudson's Bay Territory. By W. H. G. KINGSTON. 2nd
Edition. With numerous Illustrations. Square crown 8vo, cloth
extra, gilt edges, 7s. 6d. ; plainer binding, 5s.

South African Campaign, 1879 *(The).* Compiled by J. P.
MACKINNON (formerly 72nd Highlanders), and S. H. SHADBOLT ;
and dedicated, by permission, to Field-Marshal H.R.H. The Duke
of Cambridge. Containing a portrait and biography of every officer
killed in the campaign. 4to, handsomely bound in cloth extra, 2l. 10s.

South Kensington Museum. Vol. II., 21s.

Stack (E.) Six Months in Persia. 2 vols., crown 8vo, 24s.

Stanley (H. M.) How I Found Livingstone. Crown 8vo, cloth
extra, 7s. 6d. ; large Paper Edition, 10s. 6d.

—————— *"My Kalulu," Prince, King, and Slave.* A Story
from Central Africa. Crown 8vo, about 430 pp., with numerous graphic
Illustrations, after Original Designs by the Author. Cloth, 7s. 6d.

—————— *Coomassie and Magdala.* A Story of Two British
Campaigns in Africa. Demy 8vo, with Maps and Illustrations, 16s.

—————— *Through the Dark Continent.* Cheaper Edition,
crown 8vo, 12s. 6d.

State Trials. See "Narratives."

Stenhouse (Mrs.) An Englishwoman in Utah. Crown 8vo, 2s. 6d.

Stoker (Bram) Under the Sunset. Crown 8vo, 6s.

Story without an End. From the German of Carové, by the late
Mrs. SARAH T. AUSTIN. Crown 4to, with 15 Exquisite Drawings
by E. V. B., printed in Colours in Fac-simile of the original Water
Colours ; and numerous other Illustrations. New Edition, 7s. 6d.

—————— square 4to, with Illustrations by HARVEY. 2s. 6d.

Stowe (Mrs. Beecher) Dred. Cheap Edition, boards, 2s. Cloth,
gilt edges, 3s. 6d.

Stowe (Mrs Beecher) Footsteps of the Master. With Illustrations and red borders. Small post 8vo, cloth extra, 6s.

—————— *Geography*, with 60 Illustrations. Square cloth, 4s. 6d.

—————— *Little Foxes.* Cheap Edition, 1s.; Library Edition, 4s. 6d.

—————— *Betty's Bright Idea.* 1s.

—————— *My Wife and I; or, Harry Henderson's History.* Small post 8vo, cloth extra, 6s.*

—————— *Minister's Wooing.* 5s.; Copyright Series, 1s. 6d.; cl., 2s.*

—————— *Old Town Folk.* 6s.; Cheap Edition, 2s. 6d.

—————— *Old Town Fireside Stories.* Cloth extra, 3s. 6d.

—————— *Our Folks at Poganuc.* 6s.

—————— *We and our Neighbours.* 1 vol., small post 8vo, 6s. Sequel to "My Wife and I."*

—————— *Pink and White Tyranny.* Small post 8vo, 3s. 6d. Cheap Edition, 1s. 6d. and 2s.

—————— *Queer Little People.* 1s.; cloth, 2s.

—————— *Chimney Corner.* 1s.; cloth, 1s. 6d.

—————— *The Pearl of Orr's Island.* Crown 8vo, 5s.*

—————— *Woman in Sacred History.* Illustrated with 15 Chromo-lithographs and about 200 pages of Letterpress. Demy 4to, cloth extra, gilt edges, 25s.

Student's French Examiner. By F. JULIEN, Author of "Petites Leçons de Conversation et de Grammaire." Square cr. 8vo, cloth, 2s.

Studies in the Theory of Descent. By Dr. AUG. WEISMANN, Professor in the University of Freiburg. Translated and edited by RAPHAEL MELDOLA, F.C.S., Secretary of the Entomological Society of London. Part I.—"On the Seasonal Dimorphism of Butterflies," containing Original Communications by Mr. W. H. EDWARDS, of Coalburgh. With two Coloured Plates. Price of Part. I. (to Subscribers for the whole work only), 8s.; Part II. (6 coloured plates), 16s.; Part III., 6s. Complete, 2 vols., 40s.

Surgeon's Handbook on the Treatment of Wounded in War. By Dr. FRIEDRICH ESMARCH, Surgeon-General to the Prussian Army. Numerous Coloured Plates and Illustrations, 8vo, strongly bound, 1l. 8s.

* *See also* Rose Library.

Sylvan Spring. By FRANCIS GEORGE HEATH. Illustrated by 12 Coloured Plates, drawn by F. E. HULME, F.L.S., Artist and Author of "Familiar Wild Flowers;" by 16 full-page, and more than 100 other Wood Engravings. Large post 8vo, cloth, gilt edges, 12s. 6d.

TAHITI. By Lady BRASSEY, Author of the "Voyage of the Sunbeam." With 31 Autotype Illustrations after Photos. by Colonel STUART-WORTLEY. Fcap. 4to, very tastefully bound, 21s.

Taine (H. A.) "Les Origines de la France Contemporaine." Translated by JOHN DURAND.
  Vol. 1. **The Ancient Regime.** Demy 8vo, cloth, 16s.
  Vol. 2. **The French Revolution.** Vol. 1. do.
  Vol. 3. **Do.** do. Vol. 2. do.

Tauchnitz's English Editions of German Authors. Each volume, cloth flexible, 2s. ; or sewed, 1s. 6d. (Catalogues post free on application.)

————— (B.) *German and English Dictionary.* Cloth, 1s. 6d.; roan, 2s.

————— *French and English Dictionary.* Paper, 1s. 6d.; cloth, 2s. ; roan, 2s. 6d.

————— *Italian and English Dictionary.* Paper, 1s. 6d.; cloth, 2s. ; roan, 2s. 6d.

————— *Spanish and English.* Paper, 1s. 6d.; cloth, 2s. ; roan, 2s. 6d.

Taylor (W. M.) Paul the Missionary. Crown 8vo, 7s. 6d.

Thausing (Prof.) Preparation of Malt and the Fabrication of Beer. 8vo, 45s.

Thomas à Kempis. See "Birthday Book."

Thompson (Emma) Wit and Wisdom of Don Quixote. Fcap. 8vo, 3s. 6d.

Thoreau. By SANBORN. (American Men of Letters.) Crown 8vo, 2s. 6d.

Through America ; or, Nine Months in the United States. By W. G. MARSHALL, M.A. With nearly 100 Woodcuts of Views of Utah country and the famous Yosemite Valley ; The Giant Trees, New York, Niagara, San Francisco, &c.; containing a full account of Mormon Life, as noted by the Author during his visits to Salt Lake City in 1878 and 1879. Demy 8vo, 21s. ; cheap edition, crown 8vo, 7s. 6d.

Through the Dark Continent : The Sources of the Nile ; Around the Great Lakes, and down the Congo. By H. M. STANLEY. Cheap Edition, crown 8vo, with some of the Illustrations and Maps, 12s. 6d.

Through Siberia. By the Rev. HENRY LANSDELL. Illustrated with about 30 Engravings, 2 Route Maps, and Photograph of the Author, in Fish-skin Costume of the Gilyaks on the Lower Amur. 2 vols., demy 8vo, 30*s.* Cheaper Edition, 1 vol., 15*s.*

Tour of the Prince of Wales in India. *See* RUSSELL.

Trees and Ferns. By F. G. HEATH. Crown 8vo, cloth, gilt edges, with numerous Illustrations, 3*s.* 6*d.*
    "A charming little volume."—*Land and Water.*

Tristram (*Rev. Canon*) *Pathways of Palestine: A Descriptive* Tour through the Holy Land. First Series. Illustrated by 44 Permanent Photographs. 2 vols., folio, cloth extra, gilt edges, 31*s.* 6*d.* each.

Turner (*Edward*) *Studies in Russian Literature.* (The Author is English Tutor in the University of St. Petersburgh.) Crown 8vo, 8*s.* 6*d.*

Two Supercargoes (*The*) ; *or, Adventures in Savage Africa.* By W. H. G. KINGSTON. Numerous Full-page Illustrations. Square imperial 16mo, cloth extra, gilt edges, 7*s.* 6*d.* ; plainer binding, 5*s.*

UNDER the Punkah. By PHIL ROBINSON, Author of "In my Indian Garden." Crown 8vo, limp cloth, 5*s.*

Union Jack (*The*). *Every Boy's Paper.* Edited by G. A. HENTY and BERNARD HELDMANN. One Penny Weekly, Monthly 6*d.* Vol. I., New Series.

The Opening Numbers will contain :—
SERIAL STORIES.

Straight: Jack Archer's Way in the World. By G. A. HENTY.
Spiggott's School Days: A Tale of Dr. Merriman's. By CUTHBERT BEDE.
Sweet Flower; or, Red Skins and Pale Faces. By PERCY B. ST. JOHN.
Under the Meteor Flag. By HARRY COLLINGWOOD.
The White Tiger. By LOUIS BOUSSENARD. Illustrated.
A Couple of Scamps. By BERNARD HELDMANN.
Also a Serial Story by R. MOUNTNEY JEPHSON.

—————— Vols. II. and III., 4to, 7*s.* 6*d.* ; gilt edges, 8*s.*

VINCENT (*F.*) *Norsk, Lapp, and Finn.* By FRANK VINCENT, Jun., Author of "The Land of the White Elephant," "Through and Through the Tropics," &c. 8vo, cloth, with Frontispiece and Map, 12*s.*

Vivian (*A. P.*) *Wanderings in the Western Land.* 3rd Edition, 10*s.* 6*d.*

BOOKS BY JULES VERNE.

LARGE CROWN 8VO. — WORKS.	Containing 350 to 600 pp. and from 50 to 100 full-page illustrations.		Containing the whole of the text with some illustrations.	
	In very handsome cloth binding, gilt edges.	In plainer binding, plain edges.	In cloth binding, gilt edges, smaller type.	Coloured Boards.
	s. d.	s. d.	s. d.	
Twenty Thousand Leagues under the Sea. Part I. Ditto Part II.	10 6	5 0	3 6	2 vols., 1s. each.
Hector Servadac . . .	10 6	5 0	3 6	2 vols., 1s. each.
The Fur Country . . .	10 6	5 0	3 6	2 vols., 1s. each.
From the Earth to the Moon and a Trip round it	10 6	5 0	2 vols., 2s. each.	2 vols., 1s. each.
Michael Strogoff, the Courier of the Czar . .	10 6	5 0	3 6	2 vols., 1s. each.
Dick Sands, the Boy Captain	10 6	5 0	3 6	2 vols., 1s. each.
Five Weeks in a Balloon .	7 6	3 6	2 0	1s. 0d.
Adventures of Three Englishmen and Three Russians	7 6	3 6	2 0	1 0
Around the World in Eighty Days	7 6	3 6	2 0	1 0
A Floating City	7 6	3 6	2 0	1 0
The Blockade Runners .			2 0	1 0
Dr. Ox's Experiment . .			2 0	1 0
Master Zacharius . . .	7 6	3 6		
A Drama in the Air . .			2 0	1 0
A Winter amid the Ice .				
The Survivors of the "Chancellor"	7 6	3 6	2 0	2 vols. 1s. each.
Martin Paz			2 0	1 0
THE MYSTERIOUS ISLAND, 3 vols. :—	22 6	10 6	6 0	3 0
Vol. I. Dropped from the Clouds	7 6	3 6	2 0	1 0
Vol. II. Abandoned . .	7 6	3 6	2 0	1 0
Vol. III. Secret of the Island	7 6	3 6	2 0	1 0
The Child of the Cavern .	7 6	3 6	2 0	1 0
The Begum's Fortune . .	7 6	3 6		
The Tribulations of a Chinaman	7 6	3 6		
THE STEAM HOUSE, 2 vols.:—				
Vol. I. Demon of Cawnpore	7 6			
Vol. II. Tigers and Traitors	7 6			
THE GIANT RAFT, 2 vols.:—				
Vol. I. Eight Hundred Leagues on the Amazon.	7 6			
Vol. II. The Cryptogram	7 6			
Godfrey Morgan	7 6			

CELEBRATED TRAVELS AND TRAVELLERS. 3 vols. Demy 8vo, 600 pp., upwards of 100 full-page illustrations, 12s. 6d.; gilt edges, 1s. each :—
(1) THE EXPLORATION OF THE WORLD.
(2) THE GREAT NAVIGATORS OF THE EIGHTEENTH CENTURY.
(3) THE GREAT EXPLORERS OF THE NINETEENTH CENTURY.

WAITARUNA: A Story of New Zealand Life. By
ALEXANDER BATHGATE, Author of "Colonial Experiences."
Crown 8vo, cloth, 5*s.*

Waller (Rev. C. H.) The Names on the Gates of Pearl,
and other Studies. By the Rev. C. H. WALLER, M.A. New
Edition. Crown 8vo, cloth extra, 3*s.* 6*d.*

—— *A Grammar and Analytical Vocabulary of the Words in*
the Greek Testament. Compiled from Brüder's Concordance. For
the use of Divinity Students and Greek Testament Classes. By the
Rev. C. H. WALLER, M.A. Part I. The Grammar. Small post 8vo,
cloth, 2*s.* 6*d.* Part II. The Vocabulary, 2*s.* 6*d.*

—— *Adoption and the Covenant.* Some Thoughts on
Confirmation. Super-royal 16mo, cloth limp, 2*s.* 6*d.*

—— *See also* "Silver Sockets."

Wanderings South by East: a Descriptive Record of Four Years
of Travel in the less known Countries and Islands of the Southern
and Eastern Hemispheres. By WALTER COOTE. 8vo, with very
numerous Illustrations and a Map, 21*s.*

Warner (C. D.) Back-log Studies. Boards, 1*s.* 6*d.*; cloth, 2*s.*

—— *Mummies and Moslems.* 8vo, cloth, 12*s.*

Washington Irving's Little Britain. Square crown 8vo, 6*s.*

Weaving. See "History and Principles."

Webster. (American Men of Letters.) 18mo, 2*s.* 6*d.*

Weismann (A.) Studies in the Theory of Descent. 2 vols., 8vo,
40*s.*

Where to Find Ferns. By F. G. HEATH, Author of "The
Fern World," &c.; with a Special Chapter on the Ferns round
London; Lists of Fern Stations, and Descriptions of Ferns and Fern
Habitats throughout the British Isles. Crown 8vo, cloth, price 3*s.*

White (Rhoda E.) From Infancy to Womanhood. A Book of
Instruction for Young Mothers. Crown 8vo, cloth, 10*s.* 6*d.*

White (R. G.) England Without and Within. New Edition,
crown 8vo, 10*s.* 6*d.*

Whittier (J. G.) The King's Missive, and later Poems. 18mo,
choice parchment cover, 3*s.* 6*d.* This book contains all the Poems
written by Mr. Whittier since the publication of "Hazel Blossoms."

—— *The Whittier Birthday Book.* Extracts from the
Author's writings, with Portrait and numerous Illustrations. Uniform
with the "Emerson Birthday Book." Square 16mo, very choice
binding. 3*s.* 6*d.*

Wild Flowers of Switzerland.   17 Coloured Plates.   4to.
[*In preparation.*

Williams (H. W.) Diseases of the Eye.   8vo, 21s.

Wills, A Few Hints on Proving, without Professional Assistance.
By a PROBATE COURT OFFICIAL.   5th Edition, revised with Forms
of Wills, Residuary Accounts, &c.   Fcap. 8vo, cloth limp, 1s.

Winks (W. E.) Lives of Illustrious Shoemakers.   With eight
Portraits.   Crown 8vo, 7s. 6d.

With Axe and Rifle on the Western Prairies.   By W. H. G.
KINGSTON.   With numerous Illustrations, square crown 8vo, cloth
extra, gilt edges, 7s. 6d. ; plainer binding, 5s.

Woolsey (C. D., LL.D.) Introduction to the Study of Inter-
national Law ; designed as an Aid in Teaching and in Historical
Studies.   5th Edition, demy 8vo, 18s.

Wreck of the Grosvenor.   By W. CLARK RUSSELL, Author of
"John Holdsworth, Chief Mate," "A Sailor's Sweetheart," &c.   6s.
Third and Cheaper Edition.

Wright (the late Rev. Henry) The Friendship of God.   With
Biographical Preface by the Rev. E. H. BICKERSTETH, Portrait,
&c.   Crown 8vo, 6s.

YRIARTE (Charles) Florence: its History.   Translated by
C. B. PITMAN.   Illustrated with 500 Engravings.   Large imperial
4to, extra binding, gilt edges, 63s.
History ; the Medici ; the Humanists ; letters ; arts ; the Renaissance ;
illustrious Florentines ; Etruscan art ; monuments ; sculpture ; painting.

<hr>

London:

SAMPSON LOW, MARSTON, SEARLE, & RIVINGTON,

CROWN BUILDINGS, 188, FLEET STREET, E.C.